Screeching, the monsters circled her . . .

Mounted on Eriu, Shannivar found herself in the midst of creatures akin to the stone-drakes but four-footed. Jagged spines ran the length of their hunched backs, and the edge of each spike glistened wetly. The nearest pair crouched, forked tails lashing, jaws gaping wide to reveal gullets that glowed like sulfurous mud.

Winged snakes darted overhead. Hissing, the largest one plunged toward her. Shannivar had no space to maneuver and scarcely any time to think.

Eriu, be my wings!

The black horse flexed his back, bringing his rear legs under him. With a powerful thrust, he tucked his front legs. Horse and rider soared. The blasted earth lost its hold on them. For a long moment, they became creatures of air and light.

Eriu cleared the nearest slouching, fork-tailed creature and landed hard but in balance. Shannivar sent Eriu on an oblique path back toward the ice-troll. The monster was staggering on three legs, heaving its body from side to side as if trying to dislodge the arrow in its eye socket.

Shannivar drew even with the troll as she set an arrow to her bowstring. With a shift of her weight, she slowed Eriu's pace. She bent her bow and sighted along her arrow. Up . . .

. . . to where Zevaron clung to his seat atop the wildly swaying troll. He looked down. This time, she saw the flicker of recognition in his eyes. He *knew* her.

Her fingers froze on string and arrow.

THE HEIR OF KHORED

Book Three of
The Seven-Petaled Shield

Deborah J. Ross

DAW BOOKS, INC.

DONALD A. WOLLHEIM, FOUNDER

375 Hudson Street, New York, NY 10014

ELIZABETH R. WOLLHEIM
SHEILA E. GILBERT
PUBLISHERS

www.dawbooks.com

First Printing, June 2014

1 2 3 4 5 6 7 8 9

DAW TRADEMARK REGISTERED
U.S. PAT. AND TM. OFF. AND FOREIGN COUNTRIES
—MARCA REGISTRADA
HECHO EN U.S.A.

PRINTED IN THE U.S.A.

For Dave.

THE SEVEN PETALS
OF THE SHIELD OF KHORED

Eriseth	blue	steadfast, enduring
Benerod	green	healing, compassion
Cassarod	red	courage
Dovereth	yellow	truth
Teharod	pale rose	wisdom
Shebu'od	purple	strength
Khored	gold	unity, purpose

PROLOGUE:

Lycian's Visit

Chapter One

IF there was anything worse than a fool of a husband, Lycian reflected, it was a royal fool. Having stormed away from yet another fruitless attempt to make Jaxar see sense, she found refuge in her private balcony, with its perfumed curtains and satin-cushioned divan. Her white lap-terrier, Precious Snow, licked her ankles and curled up at her feet.

Lycian gazed over the hills of Aidon, searching for a diversion. None of the wonders of the city cheered her. Below an unblemished azure sky, the sun poured over the rooftops of mansions—few as rich as her own, true—and temples to the myriad gods, marketplaces, fountains, and jewel-toned gardens. Farther away, blocks of dingy workshops, piers, and warehouses lined the river. The city teemed with color and riches and music, everything for which she had once yearned. All now lay at her fingertips. All had now turned to ashes.

Where had her life gone wrong? Everything ought to have been perfect. Even as a girl, men had found her beautiful. She had worked hard to keep herself so, applying milk lotion to maintain her flawless complexion, brightening the gold of her hair with chamomile and lemon, and always dressing herself in luxuriant fabrics. At first, her marriage to the brother of the Ar-King, may-his-glory-endure-forever, had seemed a fitting triumph to her conquests. If Jaxar's deformities prevented him from ascending the throne, that mattered little. If she were clever and only a little lucky, her sons would be kings.

But no babe had swelled her belly, not from Jaxar's seed nor from that of the lovers she had taken with suitable discretion. Jaxar was not sterile, she thought bitterly, not with a son from his first wife already grown to young manhood.

How could the fault lie with *her*? With this perfect body? It was not possible! She had visited every temple in the district and quite a few in the coarser parts of Aidon, consulted oracles, and offered sacrifices, all to no avail. Only the priests of the Scorpion god Qr, newly come to fashionable prominence, offered her any hope.

Look to where your husband scatters his seed, thus leaving none for you, they told her.

Tsorreh, that black-eyed witch, that spawn of Meklavar, placed in this very house four years ago by the order of the Ar-King himself, had stolen Jaxar's virility. It could not have been by any natural means, for how could any man prefer such a thin, shriveled thing to Lycian's voluptuous curves? The cause must be sorcery, magic black and forbidden.

Lycian's manicured fingers tightened on the peacock-hued silk of her gown. Sensing her mood, Precious Snow whimpered.

The situation was intolerable, yet she could not openly oppose her husband's wishes. On the other hand, she was not without resources. She had money of her own, access to the household accounts, and the blessings of the priests of Qr, the Scorpion god. They had warned her of the danger. Surely they would know how to rid her of this pestilence and kindle her womb.

In a somewhat calmer state of mind, Lycian went down to the garden atrium, where Jaxar usually took his breakfast. Morning sun slanted into the open space, but dew still dotted the leaves of the flowering plants. The mosaic-topped table had been set with a basket of breads, goblets, and a pitcher. Jaxar was not present, only his son Danar and Zevaron, Tsorreh's infuriatingly arrogant son. Tsorreh didn't look old enough to have a son Danar's age. She must have been little more than a child herself when she'd birthed him.

Zevaron had barged in on them all a short time ago after supposedly rescuing Danar from a bunch of thieves. How he'd found his mother here, four years after the fall of their city, was incomprehensible. But everyone knew the ancient race of Meklavar bred sorcerers. The Ar-King had arrested many of them and—she dwelt upon the thought with a delicious shiver—extracted their confessions under torture.

Lycian's eyes narrowed as she spotted a trickle of blood on Zevaron's chest. The boy was a troublemaker, that much was certain, with his outlandish Denariyan clothing and those watchful, dark-lashed eyes. Yet he was undeniably beautiful and most likely ardent between the sheets . . .

Danar's face paled beneath the tumble of his red-gold hair. "Stepmother—"

"*Mother*," she corrected him.

He did not seem to hear her. "The Ar-King, may-his-wisdom-never-fail, has seen fit to arrest Father and Tsorreh. Only a few moments ago, Lord Mortan and his men took them away."

Tsorreh, taken away? The Meklavaran witch was under arrest? Until now, Jaxar had used his position to protect the hag. But at last Qr had answered Lycian's prayers!

Lycian's flare of triumph quickly turned to consternation. She had not wanted Jaxar himself to be caught in the same net. "They arrested my husband? That cannot be possible! Not the Ar-King's own brother! On what charge?"

Danar lowered himself into one of the chairs around the table. He seemed to be a different person, no longer a gangling boy but a man, slender still, yet with the promise of power in his shoulders. Zevaron remained standing, watchful, like a darker, more intense twin. He reminded Lycian of a panther, sleek and deadly.

"The charge is treason." Danar gestured to a partially unrolled scroll lying amid the crumbs and plates. "Father is accused of plotting to overthrow Cinath."

This must be Tsorreh's doing! Jaxar, that credulous fool, might well forfeit his life as well as his riches. If he were executed, Lycian thought desperately, what then would become of her? Who would befriend a traitor's wife? She would lose everything!

The enormity of the looming catastrophe engulfed Lycian. She struggled to speak, but all that issued from her mouth was a shriek. The harder she tried to control herself, the louder were the sounds that burst from her lungs. Her body contorted with the effort of screaming. The room swayed in her fading sight.

From afar, she heard Danar's voice. "Look to my stepmother!"

Her body went numb, her muscles loose. She found herself on the floor, surrounded by servants. Hands lifted her up. The room blurred—a corridor swept past—then a colonnade–finally she came to rest on her brocaded divan. Gently, her maid bathed her temples and hands with lavender-scented water. A second maidservant fanned her with ostrich plumes.

Lycian felt more like herself once she began to make plans. Jaxar would probably make some ridiculous gesture of loyalty to the witch, but it would not do to cast him aside precipitously. Detaching herself from her husband's misfortune would cost her the many advantages of his rank. He might still be redeemed if only Tsorreh were eliminated. Surely then Jaxar would come to his senses and the Ar-King would embrace his only brother once more. But how to ensure that end? She dared not leave matters to chance. Her enemy was both cunning and resourceful. Now more than ever, she needed powerful allies that even the Ar-King respected.

Relaxing back on the divan, her face cooled by the perfumed breeze, Lycian smiled. Never had the priests of Qr failed her. In fact, it often seemed they were preparing her for a greater destiny, a destiny she so richly deserved.

Zevaron knocked on the door, breaking Lycian's reverie. He explained that Danar had instructed him to escort her wherever she wished to go.

"Very well," she said, resigned to the boy's company. "If Danar has ordered you to accompany me, then I suppose you must. I will be going out shortly." Eyes like onyx regarded her from a face the color of molten amber, but the youth did not withdraw. "Don't stand there gaping! Have my mount made ready immediately."

Energized with new determination, she swept through her inner chambers, Precious Snow yapping at her heels. Her maidservant followed, as humble and attentive as if she had been a slave. Jaxar would not permit slaves in his household, so Lycian had developed her own quite effective methods of managing the staff.

In a satisfyingly short time, Lycian's white onager was carrying her down the hill with Zevaron trotting alongside. The beast had followed this route many times and needed little guidance. As Lycian cradled the lap-terrier in one arm, she reflected that although Danar clearly intended Zevaron to spy upon her, the boy was at least competent. He kept pace with the onager without difficulty, and he looked as if he knew how to use the sword at his belt.

Cinath's palace came into view at the intersection of two broad avenues. Set between silver-white columns, its forecourt statues glinted with gold leaf, lapis, and jade. The sight reminded Lycian of her disappointment when her new husband ignored her wish to live there, insisting on his own residence.

Lycian's onager slowed to an amble. People, most of them on foot, moved through the streets. Some paused to leave offerings of fruit or flowers before the many shrines. From time to time, when one of the pedestrians drew too close, Precious Snow yipped out a warning.

First she was not to live in the palace, she with her beauty and aristocratic breeding, not to mention her royal destiny, and then she was forced to harbor a penniless exile in her own home! Tsorreh—her very name sounded like a curse—claimed to be of the royal house of Meklavar. What nonsense! One look at the woman, with her iron-black hair and work-roughened hands—*and those eyes!*—showed her to be fit only for scrubbing pots. True, the woman could read and write, which was more than Lycian herself could do. And she spoke proper Gelone as well as her own savage tongue and half a dozen others. But what could Jaxar want with such an unfeminine creature? Everyone knew that women were to be treasured for their beauty, not their wits.

Turning away from the direct route to the palace, Lycian

halted in the spacious courtyard leading to the temple of Qr. "Wait here," she told Zevaron, and for the first time she could remember, he nodded in assent. A lesser priest rushed forward to take the reins of the onager. The painted image of a scorpion marked the band tied around the priest's smooth-shaven head.

A second priest bowed to Lycian at the door. Although this particular priest had greeted her many times on former visits, she did not know his name. None of the servants of Qr seemed to have names. Perhaps they surrendered them upon taking their vows.

"How may I serve the noble lady?"

"I must see the head priest at once!"

"But of course, Gracious One. He has been expecting you."

From the walled courtyard and through the massive doors, they passed through a dimly lit hallway. With each step, Lycian felt less oppressed by her situation. She left her cares in the street outside: her fool of a husband, that Meklavaran harlot, the witch's entirely too handsome son, even the nuisance Danar so frequently presented. The stone walls seemed to whisper that all her desires and hopes would soon be fulfilled.

Lycian was safe within the jointed arms of the Scorpion. Indeed, there was no place in Aidon where she would be safer. As she continued down the corridor toward the head priest's chamber, she caught the fleeting impression of an immense, brooding entity, filled with frozen light and flames bright past bearing.

As if echoing across a vast distance, she heard voices:

> *"Come speedily into the world*
> *Across flame, across ice,*
> *Come to us! Come to us!"*

Lycian hid a reflexive shudder. The temperature of the air did not change and yet cold-bumps pocked her skin. She rubbed her upper arms. If Qr would give her what she craved—the royal son and the power that would come to her from him, an end to the witch's miserable existence—

then she must do its bidding. What other choice did she have?

Lycian passed into the torch-lit vestibule that gave rise to corridors leading to the workrooms and other chambers whose purpose she could not guess. At the far end, a gate of copper and silver, the two metals intertwined like frozen flames, guarded the sanctuary. She had rarely been inside that holy place, performing her usual devotions in a small private chapel.

The head priest remained in his chair so that Lycian was forced to stand before him, as awkward as a peasant. In a moment of pique, she thought of sitting in the visitor's chair without his leave. That would show him who was important!

As Lycian met the priest's gaze, however, her eyes went to the scorpion figure on his headband. The many-legged form wavered in her sight. A shadow that was more than mere lack of light passed over the chamber. Surely it was an illusion, an aftereffect of her shock at the news of her husband's arrest.

The priest sat, his gaze steady, his features utterly calm, and *smiled*.

The smile unnerved Lycian more than words could have done. Any hope of seizing control of the situation vanished. She fell to her knees and hung her head. A tear, scalding and unexpected, rolled down one cheek. She had no right to demand anything of such a vast, incomprehensible power. She could only petition. Plead. Beg.

"My child." The priest spoke at last. "I know why you have come."

Lycian dared not look up. "You . . . do?"

"Qr the Inexorable has revealed everything to me."

"Can nothing be done for my husband?" burst from her like the entreaty of a desperate child. "He is enslaved by vile sorcery, obsessed . . ."

"Do not fear, noble lady, for together we will free your husband. We will restore him to favor, and your fortunes as well. You will shine in the eyes of the Ar-King and share in his glory."

Lycian's heart rose. All would indeed be well, she was

certain of it now. A thought coiled through her mind, subtle and intoxicating. Perhaps she would not need her fool
of a husband for long. The Ar-King's wife had died some
years ago and he had not remarried. Or she might raise
her sights even higher. Cinath was failing. Even a blind
person could see that he was not the powerful, decisive
ruler he had been in years past, but a man increasingly
erratic, even paranoid. Look at how he'd turned against his
own brother! Suspicious men were difficult to control. His
son Chion, on the other hand, was ambitious but young,
and receptive to the flattery of women. She'd seen the way
he looked at her.

A voice murmured, "Do you serve Qr and the greater
Power behind Qr?"

She nodded, rapt with visions of glory and power.

"With all your heart and soul? And all your worldly
might?"

Again, a nod.

"And will you do the bidding of Qr without question,
without hesitation, without thought to yourself?"

What a silly question! Was it not the intention of Qr to
place her son upon the Lion Throne?

"Only one person stands between you and all you seek.
Between Qr and the glory to come. She has been your enemy since she was foisted upon you, has she not?"

Tsorreh.

Unbidden, Lycian's lips pulled back from her teeth. She
imagined the witch, with her eyes full of secret magic and
her voice like honey. As long as Tsorreh lived, Jaxar would
never be free. Never!

"She bears a thing that impedes the coming of Qr. Will
you rid Gelon of this menace? Will you serve the Scorpion
God?"

Lycian whispered, "Tell me how."

"Listen carefully . . ."

Lycian stepped into the brightness of the day, the vial the
priest had given her safely hidden in the folds of her gown.

Her heart pounded with excitement, and her cheeks felt flushed. Zevaron, waiting beside her tethered onager, gave her a curious look. She glared at him to forestall any questions. She must let no hint of her intentions show. In due time, perhaps later this very day, she would have her chance.

Chapter Two

WHEN Lycian and Zevaron arrived home, twilight had almost faded to night. The steward greeted her at the door with the news that Danar had been summoned to the royal palace.

"I must go after him," Zevaron said.

"You will do no such thing!" Reminding herself that she must appear to be calm, Lycian controlled her temper. "All will be well. I have prayed to Qr and have received guidance." She strode along the colonnaded walkway leading to the household chambers, then, noting Zevaron's stubborn expression, she added, "You must leave these matters to those who know better. I specifically forbid you to leave this compound or to create trouble where none exists. Make yourself useful in the kitchen."

She expected him to protest, but he did not. Instead, he left with a rapidity that suggested he would rather be anywhere but in her presence. Well, she would not have to endure his insolence for long.

Later that same evening, Lycian heard a commotion downstairs. Her maidservant rushed into her room with the news that Lord Jaxar was home. Pausing at her mirror only long enough to ascertain that her appearance reflected the proper balance between distress and relief, she went down to greet her husband.

Jaxar stood just inside the door, flanked by Danar and the steward. Lycian had never seen Jaxar look so ill, his cheeks bloated and ashen, his breathing labored. The cook emerged from the kitchen, followed by Zevaron.

"Where is she?" Zevaron demanded. "Where is my mother?"

Breathing heavily, Jaxar began, "Zevaron, lad—"

"Cinath still has her? You *left her there?*"

Lycian tensed. The boy was going to make trouble, just as she'd feared.

"Zevaron, that's not fair! Father did what he could," Danar protested.

Jaxar cut him off. "For the time being, I alone have been exonerated. Zevaron, we shall not cease our efforts on your mother's behalf until she is restored to us."

"My husband, you must rest," Lycian interrupted before Jaxar could make any more foolish promises. "After all you have endured, your own health must take priority."

"Go with her, Father, please," Danar said.

Jaxar started to reply, but broke off in a spasm of coughing. Lycian gave orders to convey him to his chamber and summon his physician. With soft words, she settled him in his bed, propped his legs on a pillow, and washed his temples with lavender water.

Lying alone in her own bed that night, Lycian studied the vial the priest had given her. The glass was finely blown, and the cork stopper fitted tightly. When she tilted it, the contents flowed sluggishly, like green-tinted syrup.

"Empty this into water or wine and give it to the witch to drink," the priest had said. *"Then your husband will be forever safe from her influence."*

Lycian folded her fingers around the glass, now warmed by her skin. She imagined Chion, the newly enthroned Ar-King, may-his-seed-be-ever-fertile, bowing before her. Her mind filled with the image of her own womb quickening. Then she saw herself standing on a palace balcony, waving to cheering crowds, one handsome courtier after another kneeling at her feet. The image faded as she slipped into a dreamless sleep.

The next morning, Jaxar was too ill to leave his chamber. His physician prescribed a regimen of rest and baths. The treatment seemed to do Jaxar good. Despite Lycian's objections, he was able to sit up to write his messages. By the early afternoon, he had arranged for Danar to visit Tsorreh, with Zevaron as his bodyguard.

Later that day, Lycian was tired of skulking in her own rooms. At her insistence, Danar joined her for a formal dinner, roast duck with pomegranate sauce, Denariyan red rice, and almond-studded cakes, with an off-sweet wine from their vineyards at Ayford.

"Father's looking better," Danar said. "This whole affair has worn him out, but being home has eased his mind."

"Of course he should be at home," Lycian said, carefully cutting slivers of succulent dark meat. "Where else can he be so well tended? He never should have gotten involved in this dreadful business. But since he did, we must make the best of it. What news do you have regarding—" She could not bring herself to pronounce the name of the witch. "You visited her today, I believe?"

"Yes, in one of the chambers beneath the old temple of Ir-Pilant. It's a nasty hole, not any place you'd want to see someone you cared about. Zevaron was very upset. He hasn't stirred from Father's laboratory since we returned."

"Well," Lycian said brightly, "we must hope she will not be there for long."

She took a sip from her goblet. The pleasant acid tang washed away the lingering greasiness of the duck. Yes, this wine would do very well.

"Since she is permitted visitors, I should bring her some decent provender," she said. "I don't suppose they feed the prisoners properly. Do you think she would like this wine?" Seeing Danar's eyes narrow slightly, she hurried on. "I would not want any man, or any woman for that matter, to suffer as your father has. Perhaps this is an opportunity for me to practice the benevolent charity urged upon us by She Who Blesses Hearth and Home."

"I—I think that is a very noble thought. I would be happy to accompany you tomorrow."

"That will not be necessary. Your father needs you here at home, we cannot both leave him. Do not trouble Zevaron, either. We must consider his feelings as well, poor boy. One of the servants will accompany me."

Danar looked as if he were going to speak again, but Lycian forestalled him, calling for the table to be cleared. Before retiring, she ordered the cook to prepare a basket for tomorrow with bread, a wedge of cheese, apples, a packet of salt-cured olives, and a flask of the Ayford wine.

Lycian and her maidservant had no difficulty gaining entrance to the old temple of Ir-Pilant, although the guard searched the basket and returned it to her without the cheese and all but one of the apples. He would have taken the wine too if he'd thought he could get away with it. Then he guided her along a windowless corridor, gated at both ends. As they descended the rough-cut stairs, the temperature fell. The air turned clammy and stale. Lycian tightened her grip on the basket and tried not to let any part of her clothing brush the walls.

The cell in which Tsorreh was kept was close and dank, not meant to house a prisoner for any length of time. The torch held by the guard revealed stone walls covered with slimy, dark patches, a pile of filthy straw in one corner, and a bucket for waste.

Tsorreh lay with her back against the cleanest part of the wall, her arms folded around her thin body. Her clothes were as filthy as everything else in the cell. She did not look up as the door opened.

Sleeping? Lycian wondered. *Or already dead?*

With a visible effort, Tsorreh pushed herself to a sitting position. "Lady Lycian?"

Lycian felt a pang of unrecognizable emotion at the amazement in Tsorreh's voice at being visited by one who had treated her so harshly.

She has no reason to trust me, Lycian thought. *I wanted her gone and she knew it.*

Grudgingly Lycian admitted to herself that Tsorreh had never behaved in anything but a respectful manner. The gods alone knew how many nights Tsorreh had stayed up, patiently taking notes as Jaxar peered at the stars through his lenses, dusting books, and performing menial tasks no self-respecting Gelonian lady would demean herself with, while she, Lycian, slept in her comfortable bed.

I must tread carefully, lest she ensnare me in her spells as she did my husband. With her resolve strengthened anew, Lycian directed the guard to place the torch in the bracket beside the door and leave them in privacy.

"I may not have welcomed you into my household as was my duty," Lycian said to Tsorreh. "If nothing else, I owed it to my husband to treat any guest of his with consideration. It is too late to remedy that now, except to tell you that Jaxar knows nothing of this visit, nor shall he learn of it. I have come on my own to make amends."

Lycian rushed on, anxious to allay suspicion. "Jaxar is doing everything within his power to obtain your release. I do not think he will rest until you are cleared of all charges."

Tsorreh shook her head. Her braids, freed from their clasp, swung gently with the movement. "No, it is too late for that."

"You must not give up hope! Not when you still have friends. Look, I have brought food and drink to keep up your strength."

Although her gorge rose at the smells arising from the floor, Lycian set the basket down. She broke the loaf in half and held it out. When Tsorreh hesitated, Lycian said, "Jaxar will be vexed if you become ill. You would not want to distress him, would you?"

Tsorreh took the bread in shaking hands. She seemed to have difficulty swallowing.

"The bread is too dry," Lycian said. "Here is an apple"— she laid it on Tsorreh's lap—"and I have brought you some wine. That will warm you, won't it?"

Tsorreh leaned back, eyes closed, as if the effort of even those few small bites had been too much for her. Lycian held the cloth to hide her movements as she emptied the vial into the flask. As the priest had said, the potion was undetectable by smell. The flavor of the wine would surely mask its taste. But Tsorreh was too dazed, or perhaps too sick, to hold the flask. If Lycian left the wine to drink later, who knew what would happen? That greedy guard might steal it.

Overcoming her disgust, Lycian knelt beside the other woman. She would have to burn her gown afterward, but it was a small sacrifice. She would have another made for her, three or four perhaps.

At Lycian's approach, Tsorreh opened her eyes. ". . . such kindness . . ."

The gratitude in Tsorreh's voice brought Lycian a flush of shame.

"For me . . ." Tsorreh went on, "it is over. I have . . . done what I could. Now my son is the next . . . heir . . ."

What was the woman mumbling about? Her mind must have wandered to the past, when she possessed something worth inheriting.

"Come now, drink this." Lycian grasped Tsorreh's shoulder and lifted the flask to her mouth. "The wine will fortify you."

Tsorreh took a sip. Would it be enough?

"It is written," Tsorreh said, her voice steadier, "that a gift . . . rewards the giver even more than the receiver. May . . . your kindness be a blessing . . . all your days . . ."

Lycian urged her to drink again. Tsorreh took more sips along with a few bites of bread, until only a little wine remained in the flask. As soon as Lycian released Tsorreh's shoulder, the younger woman slumped to the floor. Lycian could not tell if the potion had already begun its work or if Tsorreh was exhausted from the effort. It did not matter.

Lycian hid the flask in the basket but left the rest of the food on the neatly folded cloth. The guard, a different one this time, came a few moments after she summoned him.

Under the pretext of performing a private devotion, Lycian left her maidservant on the street and went down to the river, where she filled the flask with water and watched it sink. She washed her hands as well, rubbing them over and over, trying to cleanse them of any taint of having touched the witch. A foul reek clung to her fingers, no matter how many times she rinsed them. In the end, she scooped up handfuls of the coarse river sand and scrubbed her hands until they were raw. When she straightened up, the hem of her gown was sodden and muddy, and her knees were stiff from having crouched there so long.

Only when Lycian arrived at the nearly empty house did she realize fully what she had done. Surely she could not be accused of murder when she had followed the bidding of a god. She had not acted on her own behalf but had taken necessary action to protect her husband. The Inexorable God had commanded it. Qr would protect her, his loyal servant, and reward her with her heart's desire.

At home, Lycian went to convince Jaxar that further involvement with the Meklavaran witch would only damage his position and Danar's as well. She found him in the chamber adjacent to his bedroom. Jaxar sat in his chair, propped up on pillows. His face was the same color as the sun-bleached linen. He had been overexerting himself again.

Danar sat on a cushioned bench along the far wall, his body hunched over, his face buried in his arms. His back shuddered with soundless weeping.

"What is the meaning of this? What has happened?" Lycian asked.

Before Jaxar could answer, Zevaron burst into the room.

"And now the son has come slinking back to us," Lycian sneered, "doubtless to wring your purse, my husband, for as much money as he can. Is there no end to these people imposing on your good will?"

"Lycian, you will *be still!*" Jaxar actually raised his voice at her.

"Lord Jaxar?" Zevaron said.

As Zevaron spoke, Danar looked up. A shiver of understanding passed between them. Zevaron looked as if he had been struck with an axe.

It worked!

Lycian bolted from the room, seeking the staircase leading to her own chambers. Once safely behind her own closed door, she settled herself on the divan and gulped down the perfumed twilight air. Slowly her pulse grew steadier.

It was done. There was no reason for regret. For a time Jaxar would be sad, but that would pass. Then—*ah, then!*—he would turn to her as a husband should. And he must not discover how she had bought his freedom. If she was careful, he would never find out.

She must send Danar away. Zevaron, too, as soon as possible. Surely the witch's spawn would not offer any objections. But in case he did—in case he suspected—

Perhaps a hint to the proper officials that Zevaron was not Denariyan as he pretended, but of the sorcerous Meklavaran race, would do the trick. Tomorrow she would seek counsel at the temple.

Dusk coalesced into night. Although the day had been cloudless, she could make out only a few of the brightest stars. A murky veil had fallen over the city, stretching past the great river to the fertile lands beyond.

In the recesses of her heart, Lycian shivered as the Scorpion God cast its shadow across the Golden Land.

PART ONE:

Tsorreh's Rescue

Chapter Three

THE light was gone, the node of brilliance that had lain beneath her breastbone since she'd fled the ruins of Meklavar. Try as she might, Tsorreh could sense no trace of its comforting warmth.

She had been unprepared to receive it when it came to her during the fall of Meklavar. Widowed only a few days before, she had been desperate to save her adolescent son. After such a bitter siege, there would be no mercy for any of the royal family. Gelonian invaders already rampaged through Meklavaran streets. Her grandfather had promised her escape and safety, not in so many words but in the urgency of his plea.

The old man, however, had been too sick to travel. His heart had given out suddenly. In their last moments together, he had transferred what he carried within his own breast to hers.

She had not understood the gift. How could she, unprepared and untrained? Feverish visions had tormented her through that headlong flight across the Sand Lands. She had seen spirits dancing in the campfires, had stood upon mountains and watched ancient battles, men and monsters who had turned to dust long before she was born. Only gradually had she come to understand what her grandfather had bequeathed to her.

The heart of Khored's Shield.

The *te-alvar* was real, as real as her beating heart. As real as the comet that fell to earth as she and Jaxar watched from his rooftop observatory. As real as her son, separated from her during the battle of Gatacinne and then miraculously restored to her. As real as these prison walls and the knowledge that she would surely die in this place.

As real as the desperate certainty that the *te-alvar* must not perish with her.

Earlier that day, Zevaron had knelt beside her in this filthy, dimly lit cell. Danar had arranged the visit, using his father's rank and influence. Even if she had not already loved Danar as a second son, she would have wept with gratitude at being able to see Zevaron one last time.

"I am here," Zevaron had said once they were alone. *"I will get you out of this terrible place."*

The *te-alvar* had fought her, unwilling to release its hold. But her own life was already lost. The mystical gem must go to another guardian. Then, as if it understood, it had slipped into her hand. Blindly, she had pressed the stone to Zevaron's chest and sensed it penetrate layers of muscle and bone. Pain ripped through her, a burst of white-gold heat.

"Go now," she had said, her voice thick and slow. *"Take my blessings and the hopes of our people with you."*

He had gathered her in his arms. *"I will come back. By all that is holy, I swear I will save you."*

"You have already saved what is most dear to me, my Zevaron."

In his absence, darkness had risen to swallow her up, darkness and pain. She surrendered herself, knowing the pain would last but a brief time.

Perhaps she would see Maharrad again, and her stepson, and her grandfather . . . and her mother, no longer sad but joyous . . . and, after a lifetime, Zevaron. But she would never read her favorite book of poetry or climb to the temple heights and look out over the Sea of Desolation, the *Mher Seshola,* glimmering along the horizon, or hear the songs of the *meklat* marketplace, or sit with Jaxar, watching the heavens.

Some immensity of time later, another voice reached her, one she least expected to hear. She inhaled the cloying sweetness of expensive perfume. Vision returned. Lycian crouched before her, holding a flask to her lips.

Of course the wine was poisoned. Even if Tsorreh had not suspected Lycian's motives, an inner sense scented its *wrongness*.

What did it matter? She would not leave this place alive. Cinath would never release her, for he was too much under the influence of the Qr priests. But the *te-alvar* had now passed safely from her keeping. To Zevaron would come the legacy of Khored, the great king who stood against the incarnation of chaos, called Fire and Ice in the holy texts of her people. Now there was nothing left for Tsorreh to do. Quick or slow, from a poisoned drink or as the last exhalation from an empty husk, as her grandfather had died, her own life would end.

The wine flowed smoothly into Tsorreh's parched mouth and down her throat. A chill ignited in her belly, spreading through her limbs. Shortly afterward, Lycian departed in a rustle of silk.

Tsorreh slumped against the stone wall and let the poison do its work. She could no longer feel her hands or feet. When she tried to move, her muscles would not respond. The end would come quickly now. Jaxar would grieve . . .

And Zevaron . . .

Zevaron would live. He might suffer for a time as she had, being equally unprepared to receive Khored's gem. She had survived and so would he, young and strong and hardened by his years on a Denariyan pirate ship. The *te-alvar* itself would teach him, as it had her.

Tsorreh was almost ready to slip into whatever awaited her, yet some part of her remained untouched by the numbing chill. The poison broke upon it as a storm-driven wave upon a promontory of granite. She sensed a brooding malevolence behind the noxious influence. No ordinary poison this, but one bespelled. One aimed like an arrow, not solely at her flesh but at what she once bore. The magic imprinted upon her spirit flared up.

Sounds wove through the darkness, jumbled bits of memory—the ring of steel, the shouts of men greeting their warrior-king, a ripple of harp and flute, the footfalls of a horse galloping over sand. Now came flashes of light and color, as if she were reliving her life in tiny, disordered pieces—the gates of Meklavar burning in the night, the gleam of sun on the hills of Aidon, a gull wheeling against a perfect azure sky, lines of text dancing across water-stained pages . . .

"Here is the first breath and the last," said her mother's voice. *"Here is love and hatred, folly and wisdom. Here is the story of Khored and how his magic saved the world."*

Beneath her rocked the wooden floor of a ship. She was swaying now, moving through the darkness, letting go, slipping deeper and deeper . . .

The first breath . . . and the last . . .

Water, shockingly cold, flooded over her, filling her nose and mouth. She almost gasped, but some instinct locked her lungs. Thrashing wildly, she met the resistance of a coarse cloth sack. The fabric clung to her face and upper body. A noose bit deep into one ankle, pulling her down, as if attached to a heavy weight. It immobilized her leg with its relentless grip.

Although her eyes jerked open, she could see nothing. In wordless panic, she pushed with her hands—blessedly free—against the sack. She lashed out with her free foot. Her bare toes scrabbled for purchase on the sodden cloth. Her fingers touched a seam in the enveloping sack. Pushing into the narrow gap, she yanked the sides apart as hard as she could. The water was streaming past her; she felt it on her legs. In another moment, she'd run out of breath, and she had no idea which direction was up.

For a terrifying instant, the stitches held. Then they snapped, the seam burst open, and a fresh stream of water swept across her face.

Moving by touch, she pushed away from the last folds of cloth and reached for her ankle. Her fingers found the knotted rope, thick and abrasive. Currents battered her, hurling her this way and that, but the rope pulled her inexorably downward.

If only she could see!

As if in answer to her prayer, streams of brightness appeared above her. She glimpsed a patterning of light, of blue and green and white. *Sun—and air!* But the surface was far, too far . . .

Breathe—she had to breathe!

With a renewed spasm of energy, she clawed at the knot. It was drawn tight around her ankle, held by the tension of the rope. She could not work her fingers beneath it. Tugging on the rope, she tried to dislodge the rock tied to the other end. The next moment, the tension loosened. Water slammed into her, raking her along the stony riverbed. She yanked at the rope, and felt it give and then catch again. Fire laced her lungs. She was almost out of air, out of time.

Motes of liquid light danced before her eyes. They reminded her of the fire-spirits she had glimpsed during that desperate flight across the Sand Lands. Fever had gripped her then, as her body struggled to adapt to the *te-alvar*. Flame-dancers had wavered in and out of her sight. Small and huge, they resembled motes of brilliance, then ribbons of silken fire. She had sensed no danger from them, only a respectful curiosity. The shapes now diving and looping before her eyes were their liquid counterparts.

River-spirits, born of water's magic . . .

With failing strength, she tugged again on the rope. Behind her breastbone, where the *te-alvar* had once rested, an ember flared to life. It pulsed like an echo of her laboring heart. A ripple spread through the water and between the silver-gray eddies.

Her fingers opened, too numb now to grasp the fibrous rope. She no longer felt cold. In a moment, just a moment more, she would surrender to the craving for breath and draw the river into her body.

Tiny spots of warmth pressed into her skin like miniature fingers, droplets of living water summoned by the clear heart of the *te-alvar*. The noose around her ankle loosened. Water churned into flurries of light and froth. She moved through it, lifted as if buoyed up by a thousand bubbles.

Softly, inexorably, the river bore her toward the light. Her head broke the surface. She took one heaving gasp after another. The air tasted strange and wild after the river. Wind ruffled the water and currents pulled at her. The light that had seemed so bright, surely full day, was no more than fading twilight.

A wind-driven wave broke over her head. She choked and sputtered but kept going. Kicking hard, she thrust herself high enough to see where she was. Wharves and their warehouses cast shadows against the falling night. Here and there, a spot of orange light shone. She must be on the outskirts of the city.

Tsorreh tried to propel herself toward the shore, but she was too far out into the river. The current held her fast. Even without the dregs of Lycian's poison in her veins, she could not have fought her way free. The years confined in Jaxar's house had taken their toll on her stamina. She had no choice but to let the river take her where it would.

The river's chill numbed her, and her water-laden gown dragged her down. Her muscles felt thick and unresponsive. Her initial burst of strength was almost spent. Each time she sank below the choppy surface, she battled her way upward more slowly.

As the river carried her along, the last light faded from the western sky. She saw no more orange lights of the dockside lanterns. The waves glimmered under the new-risen moon.

Tsorreh kept on, each stroke of her arms or kick of her legs bringing her just high enough to snatch another breath. She was so numbed with exhaustion and cold that when she slipped beneath the water, she scarcely felt it.

Chapter Four

WATER filled Tsorreh's ears. It rushed through her head like the wind over moon-silvered grasses, like the rustling of a thousand eagles' wings. Something twisted the back of her robe. The next moment, she found herself half-inside a wooden boat. Her belly lurched sickeningly, her body shuddered, and she spewed forth a stream of acid-laced river water.

A man loomed over her, his skin the color of bronze in the light of a lantern suspended from some unseen support. Gray-streaked hair swept back from a high forehead. Eyes glinted beneath shaggy brows. His skin was weathered and his nose long and straight.

Not a Gelonian face, she thought dazedly. *But not Meklavaran, either.*

The stranger pulled her the rest of the way into the boat, rolling her on her side. She retched again. Unable to speak, she tried to reach out to her rescuer. Her body shivered so violently that she flailed about ineffectually. The man rummaged around at the other end of the boat and brought out a blanket. He wrapped it around her as tenderly as if she were a baby.

"Thee is safe now, daughter. That's it, just breathe slowly.

The sickness is because thee has swallowed so much water. It will pass."

She knew this man—she could not place him—she ought to fear him ... and yet, every syllable of his speech conveyed reassurance.

"I mean thee no harm," he hastened to say. "Thee is safe now. *Safe.*" Despite his expression of concern, he kept his gaze averted, avoiding looking directly at her. "Here, let us get thee out of the bilge water. This little boat, steady as she is, is also a bit leaky."

With gentle, strong hands, the stranger helped her to sit. She was shivering too hard to balance on the bench, so he cradled her against his own body, his arms around her. She sensed no threat from him, only fraternal kindness.

Warmth seeped into her from the man's body. She was still sick and disoriented, but after a time she felt strong enough to sit on her own. Her rescuer bent to the oars. Night and river-damp air flowed gently past. Her body swayed with the rocking of the boat. She wavered between elements, water and wind and the dying embers of magic within her.

A time later, she could not be sure how long, the motion of the boat changed. They had come alongside a dock. A grassy hillside rose beyond the rough wood planking. Lights bobbed in the distance, growing closer.

Two men, bearing lanterns, emerged from the shadows. They wore belted robes cut at mid-calf length and tied about the waist with lengths of braided rope. The younger, hardly more than a boy, wore sandals, but his elderly companion hurried forward on bare feet. Neither had been shaved bald like the priests of Qr, and this reassured Tsorreh.

"Is it thee, Brother Benthos?" the younger cried. "Thee was gone so long, we feared something had gone amiss."

Benthos? No, that name was not right.

On seeing Tsorreh, the younger man covered his eyes. The elder looked down at his feet and exclaimed, "What has thee found? A poor soul, rescued from the river! Truly, the Lady gives life to all. We are blessed!"

"Take this woman inside and set her before the hearth,"

Brother Benthos said. "I will come as soon as I have secured the boat."

"I will help thee," said the younger man.

"Mind thy knots, then."

"Come, my child." Still looking away, the old man gestured to Tsorreh. As they went up the path, he handled her
as if she were a precious gift.

A short distance beyond the dock, they began to climb.
The lantern cast a wavering light over the narrow path. To
each side, grasses tangled with vines and an occasional low,
shrubby plant. Within a few paces, Tsorreh faltered. It felt
as if the river still dragged at her. She concentrated on taking just one more step, but each time, it was more difficult
to lift her foot. The dregs of Lycian's poison whispered
through her blood. The darkness shifted, and she felt herself
falling.

"Lady's grace!" Surprisingly agile, the old monk caught
her in his arms and lifted her. She wanted to weep in help-
lessness but no tears came. Her head rested against his
shoulder, her cheek against the rough weave of his robe.

Up and up he climbed. She felt the tautness of his stringy
muscles, the stiffness of his gait, the heaving of his ribs. He
held steadily to his pace until he reached the top of the hill.
Tsorreh made out a crude wall surrounding a compound. A
gate stood partly open. Through it, she glimpsed a stone
building and the edge of a garden.

"Please set me down," she said. "I can walk now. I would
not impose on you any further."

Without comment, he bent so that she slid to her feet.
He slipped one hand beneath her elbow, as much to guide
her as to keep her from falling. She tried to think clearly, to
assess her situation. These monks had treated her with
kindness but they did not know who she was.

Beyond the gate, the smoothed dirt of the path became
a paved courtyard bounded by a low hedge and beyond
them, a dwarfed tree that gave off the fragrance of lemon
laurel. From the shadows, she caught a whiff of lavender.

The fragrances swirled together, filling her head. Her
senses reeled with them. A light bobbed sickeningly as it
approached. Dimly, as if across a great distance, Tsorreh

heard the crackle of flames, smelled burning pitch and wood—*Meklavar, afire!*

No, that was years and miles away... The memory of flames engulfed her. *Not real*, she struggled to form the thought. *Not now. That was long ago.*

Her vision cleared enough for her to make out the quiet, darkened compound. The torch glimmered in its bracket on the building. She felt the gentle pressure of the old monk's hand on her elbow.

"Only a few steps further," he murmured in the soothing tones she herself might have used to encourage a weary child. He guided her to a low building, little more than a hut, on the far side of the garden.

The monk swung the door open and they passed into a narrow room. One end was clearly used as a kitchen and the other was filled with a battered table, cupboards, barrels, and baskets. Strings of onions and bundles of drying herbs hung from the rafters. A small iron cauldron set upon the embers gave off the aroma of rosemary, garlic, and lentils.

Tsorreh sank down onto a bench drawn up before the hearth. The monk wrapped her in a dry blanket and set about stirring the fire to life and preparing a hot drink. She sipped it slowly, tasting chamomile and mint liberally dosed with honey and a medicinal herb she could not identify. Warmth spread through her belly.

Against all expectations, against all odds, and against the plots and machinations of those who wished her ill, she was still alive. Her thoughts were so sluggish, she could not comprehend why. She had been poisoned, she was sure of that much, and yet some force had resisted the insidious soporific, protecting her life.

Some lingering influence of the *te-alvar*? A miscalculation on Lycian's part? If only she could think clearly!

The man who had pulled her from the river entered the kitchen, bringing a cool, damp breeze and an armful of reeds. As he set the reeds down on the stone hearth, the light fell full on his face. Tsorreh drew in her breath. She recognized him now—not *Benthos*, as the old monk had called him, but *Bynthos*, the captain of the *Silver Gull*, who had transported her to Gelon after Gatacinne fell.

Before Tsorreh could speak, the elderly monk stooped over the cookpot, ladled out a bowl, and held it out to her. She stared at it, too dazed to recognize it as food.

"Brother Benthos," the old monk said in hushed tones, "what are we to do with this woman? She will not be strong enough to leave us for some days, I reckon, and she cannot possibly stay in the dormitory."

"No," Bynthos replied, still attending to his work. "For tonight, I will make up a cot for her in my workroom. She will disturb no one there."

"Yes, yes, that would fulfill both our obligation to charity and our vows of chastity. When she has recovered, Father Master will find a suitable sanctuary for her."

Sanctuary . . . No, that was not right. She should not be hiding, she should . . . she could not think what.

Without further discussion, Bynthos went out again. By the time Tsorreh finished the savory soup, he had returned. Silently and with averted gaze, he gestured for her to accompany him.

They proceeded along a smooth-raked path, past gardens where rows of trellised vines and vegetables shone golden in the light of the lantern, and then to a snug shed. Inside, there was a small table, with racks holding various woodworking tools in precise rows and a set of half-completed cabinets. She could detect no menace in the place, only the smells of fresh-cut wood, linseed oil, and soap.

Bynthos put the lantern down on the table and indicated a cot against one wall. It was no more than a lattice of leather straps on a hinged wooden frame, but her muscles melted at the sight. A folded blanket and pile of women's clothing were neatly placed in the middle.

After he withdrew, Tsorreh stripped off her clammy gown and pulled on the ankle-length shift. She examined and then set aside the long-sleeved overdress, hanging loose from pleats gathered into a yoke and ornamented with a few lines of unraveling embroidery. The garments were faded, patched, and too big for her, and there were neither belt nor shoes.

A small set of shelves had been built into the corner and

on them lay two books. Tsorreh picked one up in trembling fingers.

> *"I hear the song of the flute,*
> *The flower blooms, although it is not spring*
> *The sky roars and lightning flashes.*
> *Rain falls.*
> *Waves arise in my heart."*

Across the chasm of a century and more, the dead poet Cilician poured out her longing. Tsorreh had read these very words aloud that first night on the *Silver Gull*, a captive on her way to slavery or death. Bynthos had stood outside the tiny captain's cabin, listening.

"I had no idea this book contained such music," he had said.

She woke, warm as she had not been warm in longer than she could remember. At the limit of her hearing, bees hummed. A bird chirped, to be answered by another. When she shifted, leather straps creaked beneath her weight. The edge of a blanket scratched her chin. Every muscle ached.

Eventually she floated up to full consciousness. A rough towel, a chip of soap, and a basin sat on the table beside a pitcher of water and a plate bearing several slices of bread, freshly baked from the yeasty aroma, and two peaches. She found a privy pot under the cot, washed, pulled on the overdress, and sat on the stool to break her fast. The peaches were delicious. She licked the juice from her fingers.

After a discreet knock, Bynthos entered. As before, he kept his gaze averted, moving with a neat efficiency that reminded her of his shipboard tidiness, as he collected the plate and basin.

"Good morning," she said. "Or is it still morning?"

"Afternoon, lady. Thee had great need of rest."

"*Lady?* Bynthos, my old friend! Do you not know me? Or Brother Benthos—I do not know how to call you now."

For the first time, he met her gaze and looked, really *looked* at her. "Lady Tsorreh! Can it truly be?"

Smiling, she held out her hands. His work-roughened fingers closed around hers.

"But how—Lady of Mercy, what has happened? How did thee come into the river, as one dead but still alive?"

"I am not entirely sure," she said. "The last thing I remember clearly is being in Cinath's prison—"

"Surely, not for these four years!"

"No!" She laughed, despite herself. "Most of those were pleasant enough. For reasons of his own, Cinath gave me into the care of his brother. I could not have had a more benevolent custodian. He became my teacher as well as my friend."

"I have heard of this Lord Jaxar. He is reputed to be an invalid, too weak to pose a threat to the Ar-King, may-the-Lady-see-fit-to-bless-him-with-compassion, but none. has ever accused him of being evil."

"He is a good man," Tsorreh said, "a scholar who wishes only to live in peace. Anyone who says otherwise—even the Ar-King himself—is a fool."

"Lord Jaxar has gained thy loyalty, so he must have some virtue." His expression turned somber. "But how came thee into prison, with so powerful a protector?"

"In recent months, even Jaxar himself fell under suspicion of treason," Tsorreh explained. "I wondered if his association with me was the reason or only an excuse to eliminate him. Even a man without ambition, who wishes only to study the mysteries of the heavens, can have enemies."

And, she reminded herself, *Jaxar's son Danar is heir to the throne after Cinath's own son, Chion.*

"Why seek to eliminate me after all this time?" she wondered aloud, now thinking as much of Jaxar's wife as of Cinath. "Why now?"

"Thee is queen of Meklavar," Benthos reminded her.

He was right. For all her protestations, she was too important to overlook. If the Qr priests had known what she had carried behind her breasts, she would never have left Cinath's presence chamber alive the first time. At least, she need no longer fear for the *te-alvar*'s fate.

Zevaron! O Holy One, protect him! She had seen in his face and heard in his voice how it had almost destroyed him when he believed her dead for the first time. What must he be suffering now? She must send word to him—or would that place him in even more danger than he might be now?—he would not rest until he'd found her—the agents of Qr would suspect!—they might both end up in the river this time—and who knew how many others besides?

Tsorreh reined in her frantic thoughts, telling herself she must not act precipitously. Better to have Zevaron grieve a second time than to risk his life and the *te-alvar*. For the moment, she could not help him. She could not help anyone.

So when Benthos asked, "Would the people of Meklavar rise up and follow their queen?" she answered, "I am no general to lead anyone, especially against such a power as Gelon. What could that accomplish but more death? My people have suffered enough already, without fresh retaliation. When he first had me in his clutches, Cinath did not consider me a threat, or he would never have dismissed me to Jaxar's household."

She had seen Cinath as her enemy because his ambition had driven the conquest of her homeland. Only later, when she was his captive, did she witness the rising influence of Qr throughout Gelon and particularly upon its monarch. The *te-alvar* had shown her visions of an even greater power controlling the cult of the Scorpion god, for Fire and Ice cast its malevolent shadow across many lands. Cinath had once been strong and arrogant, and cruel, but now she pitied him, for he was no longer master of himself or his own destiny.

"Much has changed since I arrived," she commented.

"Aye, that it has. I fear that even the staunchest friendships fare poorly in these treacherous times," Benthos said, shaking his head. "Once, Meklavaran traders were welcomed here, valued for their honesty and industry. Physicians, too, and scribes. Artisans of all sorts. Aidon's gates were open to all. Now Cinath's men search out anyone suspected of sedition, most particularly those of Meklavaran blood."

During the four years of her captivity, Tsorreh had heard of the increasingly precarious position of her countrymen and had regretted that there was little she could do to help them. She might justify herself by saying that as guardian of the *te-alvar*, she dared not risk the loss of the magical gem, and she might argue that she had neither the leadership nor skill at arms to defend her people physically, but in the end, she had failed them.

"Times have indeed changed," Benthos said. "The priesthood of Qr has grown in influence these last few years."

Qr! Tsorreh shuddered the memory of her encounters with the Scorpion priests and what they served. Her thoughts felt sluggish, as if still chilled by the river. She felt exhausted. Hopeless. *Failed, I've failed those I ought to have served.*

"They say Qr will tolerate the worship of no other gods," Benthos went on, seemingly unaware of her reaction. "I think it must be true, for the Ar-King has ordered the closure of many temples. And Cinath, may-mercy-be-admitted-to-the-courts-of-his-heart, has begun a purge of Meklavaran exiles."

"A purge?" His words were like arrows, piercing her heart. She could have—*should have*—found a way to help them. "My poor people! Why do this, when we are already broken and defeated? How can we possibly threaten him?"

"Even a conquered people may exact revenge. My brother monks and I have heard news from thy homeland. They say that a prophet now walks the land, working miracles and preaching sedition. Perhaps Cinath fears the defiance may spread here as well. He could not let thee live, a symbol to rally around."

Yet Cinath *did not deliver the poisoned wine. Perhaps Lycian acted upon his command. She would have been eager to be rid of me.* Lycian prayed to Qr ... and Cinath looked to its priests for counsel. Another thought wound through Tsorreh's mind, one even more disturbing, that the servants of Qr might have arranged the poison ... the motive for killing her was not her own death, but the loss of the *te-alvar*.

"I think ..." Tsorreh said. "It does not matter, for some will seize any opportunity to eliminate those who stand in their way."

Benthos nodded. "The Ar-King uses the rumors from

Meklavar as justification to tighten his control within his own borders. His agents do not care about the guilt or innocence of those they hunt. But enough talk of the schemes of worldly men! Lady, I would hear more of thy story, if thee will tell it."

Tsorreh glanced longingly at the cot as weariness swept through her, but she owed Benthos this much. "I remember being taken to a cell below the old temple of Ir-Pilant and remaining there for a time. Then I . . . I must have fainted and been taken for dead. The next thing I knew, I was in the river. How did you find me?"

"As I take my boat out on the river, looking for wreckage we might use in our holy work, I sometimes find the bodies of unfortunates. Most have died naturally or as the natural result of poverty and overwork. Perhaps they had no families or families unable to bury them properly, or even buy a shroud. I bring them ashore and see to their dignity. Often, I fear, they have been cruelly treated. I have never heard of any put into the river while still alive. Can the world have come to this, execution by drowning? Ir-Pilant was always an honorable sect."

"Perhaps my jailors thought me dead already."

"Perhaps they were all idiots!" Benthos knotted his hands into fists and, with an expression of chagrin, released them.

"Of all things"—she spoke to break the overlong silence that followed—"I never imagined to meet you again, let alone as you are now. Your life must have changed as much as mine since we sailed together on the *Silver Gull*."

"Would thee hear of a miracle?" Bynthos turned to Tsorreh with an angelic smile. "Thee was the beginning of it."

"I was? How?"

"When thee opened to me the wisdom contained in writing, a fire awoke in my belly. A tiger, a hunger. I read the books in my cabin over and over, always searching for more. I do not mean that I found nothing there, only that as much as I consumed led to an even greater desire."

"A passion," she said, remembering her old tutor, Eavonen, whose greatest joy had been the royal library. No one could reach the end of that collection, spanning centuries of careful thought, of soaring poetry, of detailed records of the lives and dreams of an entire people. She did not share that dedication, although she recognized it in others.

"A passion, indeed," he said, "but not a fate, only a step upon the journey. There is nothing that the Lady cannot use to bring us to her."

"We say the same of the Holy One."

"As thee can imagine," Bynthos went on, "there was no man on my ship, or any other, who understood. My crew were good men, with as much honesty as any that ply the waves, but like I once did, they toil for passing pleasures, gold and wine and women. Each day it felt as if they peered at the bright horizon but never truly saw it. The sea, which had once been my freedom, became my prison. Eventually, when fortune turned against me, I sold the *Silver Gull* and made my way to Borrenth Springs, home to many scholars. I thought to study with them."

"To join them?"

"No, not one such as I! I am no learned man, only a sea captain with a little knowledge of my letters. I wished only to read, to listen, to understand what little I could. I took my vows at the temple of the Lady in Borrenth Springs to spend the rest of my days there, in study and service. Then a year ago, the priests of Qr came with orders from the Ar-King. Our small temple and a dozen others were to be given over to the Scorpions."

Bynthos fell silent, leaving Tsorreh to guess about the fate of the books and his brother scholar-monks. Her old friend had good reason for his animosity.

"We do not question the Lady of Mercy," he said in a low voice. "She has never abandoned us, and if we do not serve her with our minds, then our hands and strong backs must be enough. Yet I would not have even this measure of peace without thy initial gift."

She did not know how to answer his gratitude. Indeed, at the time she'd had little idea of any such consequence arising from the book she had read to him. She would not deny even an enemy the treasure to be found in parchment and ink.

Bynthos heaved himself to his feet and began pacing. In

his agitation, he slipped back into common speech. "We must get you out of Aidon to a place of safety."

Going anywhere, except back to sleep, seemed impossible. The small measure of energy that she had felt earlier had disappeared. Her body was still weak from the trials of the night before and her heart from hearing of the renewed sufferings of her people. And Zevaron—*oh, Zevaron!* She was too tired to think what to do for him. She could hardly keep her eyes open. She half-fell, half-lowered herself to the cot.

"Dear lady . . ." She heard Benthos speak, as if across a great distance. "Rest. Thee is safe here."

Chapter Five

TSORREH spent most of the following two days asleep, waking occasionally to the sound of Bynthos reading aloud to her from the *Odes*. Sometimes she thought she heard the plash of water or the gentle soughing of wind, or the cry of a riverbird, but never Lycian's shrill invective. Never the rhythmic tramp of guards. Never the ring of steel or the crash of burning timbers collapsing. Never the jingle of slave chains.

She repeated to herself that she was safe. No one would come looking for her. Lycian believed she was dead and Cinath must also, since his men threw her body into the river. She had a little time to plan where she would go and how she could contact Zevaron without risking detection and arrest for both of them, and Jaxar and Danar as well.

Late afternoon on the second day, while she sipped the broth Bynthos had brought her, another monk came into the workshop. He was lanky and large-boned, almost entirely bald, and his features were so composed, so free from tension, that all the wrinkles seemed to have been smoothed away. She supposed he was the head of the temple, the Father Monk, not by any distinction of dress but by the intense stillness of his manner.

"My daughter," he said, "thee is welcome among us. We

wish we could offer accommodations suitable for a female. It gladdens us to see thee recovering in strength. The Lady has blessed us, that we might express our gratitude to her this way."

Tsorreh gathered that the old monk's use of "we" meant that he spoke for the entire community. "It is I who owe thanks. To Bynthos—Brother Benthos—for rescuing me from the river. To you, for allowing me rest here."

"Brother Benthos has told us of thy kindness to him. Truly, the Lady has worked her mercy through thee. She is the root of all goodness. It is she who puts love into men's hearts, who stays the hand of the wicked. She who nurtures us all as babes at her ever-flowing breast. She feeds us with the milk of her compassion."

Tsorreh had read similar phrases in the holy texts of her own people. "The Lady of Mercy seems very much like the feminine aspect of our own Source of All Blessing. In Meklavar, we do not believe that divinity is either male or female, but transcendent beyond understanding. We human men and women reflect only a small portion of the infinite unity."

"Here in Gelon, we have always worshipped many gods," the Father Monk said sternly. "Each of us in this community leaves behind our past, newborn in the Lady's grace. No man or woman, not even the most wretched sinner, is beyond redemption."

He paused, a deepening of his stillness. "Normally, we do not permit women within our precincts. There can be no doubt that the Lady has sent thee to us for a purpose."

"A . . . purpose?"

"Indeed, she has marked thee for her own, as is clear from thy easy speech on the matter of theology. Tomorrow, Brother Benthos shall convey thee with all seemly haste to our sister convent in Silon. There thee will find sanctuary against the cruelties and violence of the world. Thee will learn the ways of her mercy and take thy place as her true servant."

"I—I don't understand. What is this place?" Tsorreh's mind felt like river silt and her tongue as unresponsive. Protests jumbled together in her thoughts. "Why are you sending me there?"

"It lies halfway between Aidon and Verenzza," the Father Monk said with an encouraging nod. "Not a long or arduous a journey, but one that will hone thy purpose."

Tsorreh did not know how to answer the old monk. She knew only that whatever had preserved her thus far, through fire and ruin, enslavement and attempted murder, had nothing to do with retreating to a cloistered religious community with the clear expectation of her conversion.

With a gentle smile, the only expression to disturb that smooth countenance, the Father Monk departed. Bynthos stood by the door and bowed.

Tsorreh was still trying to gather her thoughts. Clearly, the monks wanted to get rid of her as speedily as possible. "I suppose my presence here must be a disruption to your meditations."

"Some of the brothers have not spoken to a woman for many years."

"My friend," she began, and then paused. "Bynthos, you have more than repaid me. Without you, I would now be as Cinath believes me—food for fishes. So I do not speak from ingratitude now."

His face hardened.

"Your temple is no place for me," she said. "I do not belong to your Lady, but to my own Source of All Blessings."

"The Lady has claimed thee as her own," he said. "She has set her seal upon thee, even as she did upon me."

"Bynthos, no. Listen to me—"

He shook his head, cutting her off. "Thee speaks from ignorance, from darkness. The Lady plucked me from the sea and set before me a great vision. In a similar fashion she took thee for her instrument and in return has given thee the promise of a blessed haven. In Silon, thee will be safe, protected by the Lady's own daughters."

"I do not belong there! Bynthos, if we were ever friends, help me!"

"Where else would thee go? Back to Meklavar?"

Where, indeed? Bynthos had voiced the question that she had not yet answered for herself. Whatever else, she must try to reach Zevaron.

"There is no other fate, not for thee," Bynthos said more gently, "not for any of the Lady's children, except what she decrees. I am sorry the prospect of a life at Silon does not bring thee joy, but I am no longer the captain of my own ship."

There was no use in arguing. Whatever friendship existed years ago between Bynthos and herself, whatever his personal desire, he would not go against the orders of his religious superior. Her only hope was to pretend acquiescence.

Bynthos took her silence for consent. "Rest now, and prepare for the journey. We depart at first light."

Tsorreh pressed herself against the door until the monk's muffled footsteps died away. Her body still craved sleep, but at that moment, she could think of nothing but escaping the monastery while she still could. If she delayed, she might find herself taken under guard to Silon. She forced herself back to the cot and lowered herself onto the thin pallet.

Breathe. Slow, deep breaths. Breathe and plan. She might not have the clear sight once granted to her by the heart of the Shield, nor the burden of safeguarding the living world against Fire and Ice, but she was still *te-ravah* of Meklavar. She could not sit idly by, penned up in a temple while her country bled under Gelonian rule, its people oppressed, its treasures scattered, its heritage forgotten. She did not know what she could do on her own, but in Isarre she might seek counsel with her royal kin.

She was no longer the inexperienced young woman who'd fled Meklavar. In the years since, she'd learned much of Aidon and its inhabitants. She'd gone on errands, mostly for Jaxar, met scholars and tradespeople, and had seen many things. She was no longer ignorant and helpless. Best of all, her enemies now thought her dead. There would be no one searching for her.

Once away from the temple, she would make her way back to the city, although the thought of possibly falling into the clutches of the Qr priests terrified her. Her belly clenched and her heart raced. *Calm, remain calm.*

Tsorreh's gaze lit upon the table, where a wooden bowl held the remains of the meal Bynthos had brought her earlier: bread, olives, and cheese. She ate the olives and a small portion of the bread and cheese. The rest she wrapped in a cloth torn from the hem of her dress.

The best chance to speak privately to Zevaron would be when he left Jaxar's compound, most likely as Danar's bodyguard. Danar could be trusted to keep her secret, of that she was certain. He might even help them get away. They could search out a sympathetic river-captain at the wharves. Bynthos had spoken of a purge of Mcklavaran exiles, so perhaps others of her people were seeking ways out of the city. Failing that, she might make contact with Marvenion, the Meklavaran physician who had prepared medicines for Jaxar at her pleading. Zevaron, who had earned his bread as pirate and bodyguard, might have resources of his own.

Dong! Dong! came the sound of bells calling the monks to prayer. They would be gathering, leaving their workshops and gardens. This would be her best chance to leave the compound unchallenged.

Tsorreh slipped out of the workroom. As she had hoped, the temple compound was deserted. Shadows lay thick and deep between the buildings. The approaching twilight glimmered in the eastern sky but to the west, there was still plenty of light. She made her way between the low hedges, pausing now and again to make sure she had not been spotted. Once, as she held herself immobile, a monk emerged from one of the huts and hurried by, head bowed. He crossed to the far side of the courtyard and placed a bar across a gate there. It was not the gate through which Tsorreh had entered, of that she was sure. There must be a second gate leading inland toward Aidon.

Tsorreh waited while the monk disappeared into the main building. She caught the sound of men's voices singing. Tarrying, she glanced through the shutters of an open window nearby and saw a folded garment lying on a table. It took only a moment to reach in and draw it around her shoulders. It was not, as she had first thought, a typical monk's robe, but a hooded cloak of the same rough fabric. She was so small, it came to her ankles. On close inspection, no one could mistake her for a monk, but at a distance, with the hood covering her face, she might pass unremarked. Beside the door sat a pair of rope sandals. They were too big for her, but better than going barefoot. With rising confidence, she hurried to the gate, unbarred it, and let herself out.

Beyond the gate, a path of beaten earth, wide enough to accommodate a cart, ran between fields of stumpy, heavy-headed grain. She lowered her head and hurried along as quickly as the sandals would allow.

Tsorreh emerged from the night into the outskirts of Aidon and took a moment to assess her surroundings. Rats and small dogs were foraging in piles of refuse. Men in workers' clothing stumbled by, wobbling in the light of their own lanterns. One called out, asking her price for the night, before his friend pulled him on.

The street widened. Both pavement and buildings were in better repair. Tsorreh felt an intimation of chill, as if the darkness had suddenly grown colder. Something hovered, a shadow just beyond the limit of her vision, and then was gone. Shuddering, Tsorreh pulled the hood of her cloak tighter around her face and hurried on. Her pace soon slowed as the burst of strength, fueled by a moment's fear, faded. She plodded on. Her legs ached.

Lights went out. A quarter-moon and stars gave only a paltry light. Tsorreh stumbled through the near-darkness. At last, however, she came into an open space just as the eastern sky began to brighten.

I know this place. I have been here before. But it had not been empty, there had been people and booths, and the smells of spices and flowers. She might be mistaken, and this was not the marketplace where she had first seen the physician Marvenion, but one thing was clear: she could not go on. She'd been walking half the night, and she still had not fully recovered from Lycian's poison and her ordeal in the river. The rope sandals had worn blisters on her feet. She put out one hand to steady herself against the corner of a building, a shop. Abruptly her legs gave way. She managed to lower herself to the pavement and closed her eyes.

Voices woke her. She squinted into brightness. Half the sky was still inky, but already men and carts crowded the square. They talked and laughed as they set up their stalls and loaded them with produce and other goods.

"Ah, there," said a female voice in country-accented Gelone. A woman of middle years, her red hair tied back beneath a white kerchief, bent over Tsorreh. "You're no monkish boy, that's plain, for all you're dressed as one."

The market was coming to life. "Peppers! Fresh sweet peppers! The finest in all Gelon!"

"Spices from Denariya! Ignite the senses! Ward off disease!"

"You can't stay out here. The city guards'll be along shortly." Sturdy fingers grasped Tsorreh under the armpits and hauled her to her feet. "Don't weigh nothing, do you?" The woman lowered her voice. "The Ar-King's Elite Guards, may-they-hope-someday-to-possess-the-common-sense-of-a-gnat, have been asking questions. They're on the hunt for someone."

The woman half-dragged Tsorreh toward the entrance to the shop. By the sign overhead, this shop sold clay idols. Tsorreh eyed the door and the shadowed interior, and felt the strength of the grip on her arm. Ice clenched her belly, so hard and bitter that she bent over.

"Girl, are you sick?"

"No, only tired. If I could—" Tsorreh drew herself upright. "Have you any work for me? In exchange for a meal and perhaps"—she fingered the monk's cloak—"something less noticeable?"

"That I do. Come inside."

The shop was smaller than it had appeared, lined with shelves crowded with statues. Some were glazed in vivid colors, others plain clay, some as long as Tsorreh's forearm, others small enough to fit easily in her palm or into a pocket, or hung around a neck on a chain or leather thong. Tsorreh recognized a veiled female shape as the Lady of Mercy, others as the Guardian of Flocks, the Protector of Soldiers, possibly even the Bounteous Giver of Wine. There were so many Gelonian gods, she could not hope to know them all. To her relief, she saw no scorpions.

The shop woman took Tsorreh into an even smaller back room and cleared a battered stool for her to sit on. From a cupboard, the woman brought out a glass bottle that proved to contain a fermented fruit drink, along with a pile of flat rye cakes, a dish of olives, and a jar containing a paste of garlic and finely chopped herbs.

"Eat all you want, for there's plenty, while I find—where *is* that thing?" The woman began rummaging through a stack of wicker baskets.

Tsorreh used the flat cakes to scoop up the paste. It was strongly flavored and pleasantly oily. The olives were overly salted, but the fruit wine, by contrast, tasted sweet and fresh, and probably not very potent. Suddenly thirsty, she gulped down several cups.

Refreshed by the food and drink, Tsorreh slowly relaxed. By the time the shopwoman returned with a bundle of un-dyed cotton, she was feeling much better. In fact, her situation no longer seemed hopeless. She had survived the river and escaped the monks and their plans for her. People were not so bad, after all—this stranger had offered her unexpected kindness.

Tsorreh managed not to giggle as the shop woman helped her into a long sleeveless coat. It fell in soft folds from the simple yoke to her knees, cut amply so that she could wrap it around herself like a cloak. Tsorreh had noticed such a garment worn by country women. She pivoted, suddenly delighted with her costume. It would explain any lapse or difference in accent. She tried to thank her benefactor, but the shop woman cut her off.

"You sure you're not sick?" The shop woman frowned as she looked at Tsorreh. "You look a bit flushed."

"I'm fine. In fact, I can hardly remember when I felt so well." Tsorreh paused in the doorway. "May the blessings of all the gods of Gelon be upon you."

"That's as it may be. I'm not sure I'm doing the right thing, letting you wander off like this."

"It's market day!" Tsorreh stepped into the paved square, now teeming with farmers and craftsmen at their booths, women with baskets tucked under their arms, fruit-sellers pushing handcarts, and children scampering underfoot. Grinning, she glanced over her shoulder at the shop woman's troubled face. "Don't worry! Everything is wonderful!"

What a day it was! Everything seemed to be gemstone bright, the sun a glowing citrine in a sky of turquoise, the fruits heaped upon the tables like garnets, the green of the vegetables, the brilliance of the eyes of the people passing by. A troupe of street performers plucked their lyres while a dancer in layers of multicolored gauze twirled and stamped, keeping time with finger cymbals. Tsorreh's worries seemed vague and far away as she let herself be swept up into the market.

After a time, the music faded. She found herself at the far corner of the plaza, facing a group of shrines heaped with offerings of wilting flowers and ribbons. Confused, she could not understand how she had gotten here. She'd been at the shop . . . she'd drunk rather a lot of that delicious fruit wine . . .

Beyond the plaza, at the intersection of two broad avenues, women clustered around a fountain that still showed the eroded carved shapes of sea creatures. Laughing and chattering, they dipped their jugs into the water. A boy led a pair of onagers to drink.

A wild idea presented itself to Tsorreh. Once she'd found Zevaron, they'd need a way out of the city. They could travel much farther and faster on one of those beasts than on their own feet. True, she knew little of riding. True also, she had no money, but Jaxar did. If she told the boy she came from Lord Jaxar, that Jaxar would pay him a goodly sum, would he let her take one of the onagers? No, that wasn't at all sensible, that was dangerous to invoke the name of someone so well-known—

"Yip! Yip-yip-yip!"

Barking frantically, a small white bundle of fur burst from the stream of pedestrians. A bedraggled pink ribbon trailed from the topknot over its eyes. Growling and snapping, it headed straight for Tsorreh. She recognized the beast—Lycian's hateful lap-terrier.

Too slow, Tsorreh backed away.

"Precious Snow! Come back here! This instant!" A

woman in gold and ivory silk, mounted on a white onager, emerged from the crowd.

Lycian!

"You there!" she shouted at Tsorreh. "Catch my dog!"

Tsorreh whirled and raced for the far side of the fountain. The women with the water jugs stared at her, openmouthed. No one made any attempt to restrain her, but neither did they move out of her way. She rounded the fountain at a flat-out run. Panting, slipping on the paving stones, she searched for an alley, a door, any way out of public view. The cotton coat tangled in her legs. Her ankles burned where the rope sandals rubbed against the sores from last night.

If she were quick enough—if she could find a hiding place—

If Lycian had seen nothing other than a peasant woman, too stupid to obey orders and too dazed to get out of the way—

Tsorreh stumbled to a halt as Lycian's onager appeared before her. In her confusion, she'd come full circle around the fountain. The onager slid to a halt as Lycian yanked hard on the reins.

"You, woman—I told you—" Lycian's eyes widened as she noticed Tsorreh's face. Recognition swept across Lycian's porcelain features. For a moment, her lips moved soundlessly. The reins slipped through her fingers. Then she opened her mouth and screamed.

"You're dead!" Lycian shrieked, pointing to Tsorreh. *"You're dead!"*

Chapter Six

"GHOST!" Lycian howled. "Evil spirit! Help! Help!"

Lycian's voice, always shrill, sounded more like a vulture's cry than anything made by a human throat. People turned to stare. A couple of child pickpockets bolted, vanishing from sight, and one of the women lost her hold on her water jug and it shattered on the paving stones.

Tsorreh's muscles unlocked. She backed away. Her body responded sluggishly, as if Lycian's terror had snared her as well. She heard a commotion from a nearby street, as if someone were trying to push through the crowd.

"Save me!" Lycian wailed. "O Mighty Qr!"

"Guards!" a man shouted. "Where are the guards!"

Tsorreh glanced around the plaza, searching again for an avenue of escape. On the other side of the fountain, she glimpsed a man in a flowing white robe as he emerged from the crowd. His bald head gleamed in the sun. Across his brow stretched a band bearing the scorpion emblem of Qr. Bile etched Tsorreh's throat. Her stomach lurched.

People were milling around, shouting in confusion. Tsorreh could no longer make out Lycian's words, only the screams that grew even louder. Yipping, the lap-terrier dashed around the fountain. Before the dog could sink its teeth into her ankle, Tsorreh darted straight at Lycian. She

missed the onager's nose by a hand's-breadth and kept going.

The onager, ears pinned against its neck, let out a squeal
of outrage. The poor beast had been pushed beyond the
limit of even the sweetest temper. Tsorreh slowed long
enough to see it rearing, front hooves churning the air, just
as the dog scrambled beneath its belly. Lycian went sliding
over the onager's rump.

Tsorreh did not linger to see what happened next. She
swerved barely in time to avoid a portly man in a rich robe.
Ignoring his astonished cry, she kept going. The uproar—
onager braying, dog barking, Lycian wailing, voices
shouting—was enough to prevent immediate pursuit.

Running as fast as she could in the flopping rope sandals,
Tsorreh headed for the smaller of the two intersecting
streets. A cart laden with barrels moved ponderously toward her. She summoned a burst of added speed. Once past
the cart, she slowed to a walk. A messenger boy might run
about the city without attracting too much attention, but a
woman could not.

Her hopes rose when she spied an alley that left the main
thoroughfare just behind a goldsmith's shop. Within a few
paces, the sounds of the street faded behind her. Heart
pounding, mouth dry, she stumbled to a halt. Shade enveloped her. Her sweat turned cold and her head throbbed. Despite the reek of urine and garbage, she rested her forehead
against the stone wall.

Suddenly her gorge rose and her eyes watered. She
folded over as her stomach emptied itself. By some miracle,
she avoided her clothing. Her mouth tasted vile, but there
was no water to rinse it out.

Realization hit her. *The fruit wine!* Delicious as it had
been, it had been far more potent than she'd thought. It had
tasted so refreshing, and she'd been so thirsty. But she
should have known better. She'd seen how fermented
drinks could rob people of their wits. What a fool she'd been
to imbibe so much.

Straightening up, Tsorreh wiped away her tears with the
back of her hands. Her head was clearer, but she felt weak

and shivery. She must keep going, and find a safe place to rest and recover her strength. She must—

She was not alone in the alley. She spun around, trying desperately to summon the energy for another sprint.

"Lady Tsorreh?" Silhouetted against the brightness of the street, a slender, feminine figure came toward her. Instead of the usual Gelonian gown, the girl wore a long sleeveless vest of blue cotton over full pants, gathered Mcklavaran-style at the ankles. Her hair had been braided with little bells, and her skin was the same honey-gold as Tsorreh's own.

"Lady Tsorreh, it's Rebah. Don't you remember me? We met at my father's house—Marvenion the physician."

Relief swept through Tsorreh. She swayed on her feet. Rebah rushed to her side and caught her before she fell.

"They're h-hunting m-m-me—" Tsorreh stammered.

"They shall not find you if I can prevent it. We must get you to my father's house. This way."

The alley blurred past Tsorreh's sight, then another, this one better smelling. She was aware of stumbling, of leaning into Rebah's wiry strength, of waves of sickness and exhaustion. Of how utterly foolish she'd been. Of a fleeting glimmer of hope.

They left the second alley—or was it the third?—and came to a moderate street of two-story houses with flower pots hanging from balconies. She knew this street, the rows of trees in their planters, the smell of incense from the opened windows, the railings carved like intertwining vines.

Rebah knocked on a gate set in a high stone wall and a servant admitted them. As they hurried across the private garden, Tsorreh wanted to laugh at the propensity of children everywhere to create their own secret adventures. As a child, Zevaron had a similar spirit, and had doubtless gone exploring areas of Meklavar where no prudent person would venture, as had Danar.

They reached the far end of the garden and another gate, smaller and partially hidden by an exuberant growth of Denariyan *yasmin*. The gate led directly into another garden, this one no more than a strip running along the length of the house. Tsorreh almost wept at the scent of the familiar herbs, spearmint, dill, and flowering oregano. She had eaten Gelonian food for so long, she had almost forgotten the taste of Meklavaran cooking.

Moments later, Tsorreh found herself in Marvenion's private chamber. Everywhere she looked in the room—from the soft, garnet-red cushions to the intricately patterned carpet, the round-bellied oil lamp and its sphere of light, the table of carved wood inlaid with mother-of-pearl and silver wire, even the enameled plate of dates rolled in crushed almonds—reminded her of home. Daylight sifted through the window facing the garden. There was no sign of Marvenion's gray tabby, but she had no doubt the cat was around somewhere, keeping the mice at bay.

"Sit," Rebah said with such authority that Tsorreh's legs collapsed under her and she fell onto the low couch. The girl gestured to the dates. "Can you eat?"

Tsorreh shook her head. No matter how good it smelled, the idea of food made her stomach writhe.

"Then I'll bring water. If you feel faint, lie down. Father will be furious if you injure yourself." With that, Rebah left the room.

Tsorreh rested her forehead on her folded arms. Now that she was no longer moving, she realized her head was still whirling. She felt steadier since she had vomited the last of the wine, but she was not at all well. A few moments later, she heard footsteps, then the door latch clicked open and Marvenion himself swept into the room. Rebah followed a step behind.

Marvenion looked very much as when she had first met him, tall but slight of build, with a trimmed, gray-streaked beard, skin like weathered honey, and creases around his eyes. She would have known him anywhere as a countryman, with those arched cheekbones, that nose. He wore the robe and cap of a Meklavaran physician, so she supposed he must have been attending patients.

"I am sorry to interrupt—" she began.

"My daughter tells me you are ill and in peril. *Te-ravah*, how did this come to pass? We heard you were imprisoned, and rumors have it that you are dead."

"Just as well that Cinath believes so." Gratefully, Tsorreh accepted a goblet of chilled, mint-infused tea from Rebah. "But now he will know the truth and will not rest until I am back in his custody. I fear I have brought grave danger to you, my friend."

For a long moment, he did not answer. She wondered if he were looking for a suitably respectful way to withdraw his hospitality.

"I should not have come here," she said.

"Given the state you are in and knowing my daughter as I do, I doubt it was entirely your choice." He sat on the couch beside her. "Now, tell me what has befallen you, so that I may know how best to help you."

As best she could, Tsorreh related her story from the time of her arrest and imprisonment until the moment Rebah found her in the alley. She omitted all reference to the transfer of the *te-alvar*. While she had carried it, she had been unable to even mention its existence. She did not attempt to reveal it now. It must be her secret, and now Zevaron's.

Zevaron would be doubly distraught between the emotional upheaval as he adjusted to the *te-alvar*—without preparation, without warning!—and Tsorreh's death.

At least, he might now hear otherwise. Lycian knew she was alive and had raised the alarm. Jaxar would hear the news, and then so would Zevaron. He would surely search for her and there was no way she could insist that he look to his own safety first. Even if Lycian's outburst were disregarded as a temperamental fit, it would be far too dangerous to try to contact him. Cinath's Elite Guard would have been alerted, even if they were not actively hunting. If a message should be intercepted, if Zevaron should fall into Cinath's hands, it would mean his death as well as hers, and that she dared not risk. No, such a thing was impossible, she saw that now. She must remain hidden and take the gift of whatever life was left to her. The Source of All Blessings had preserved her, for what purpose she did not yet know. She prayed that those she loved were under similar protection.

Marvenion listened silently to Tsorreh's story, although from time to time, his lean features darkened and his eyes grew even more somber. "We must get you out of Aidon without delay."

Just what Bynthos said. "Yes, the city is not safe for me."

"Your timing is auspicious. Reports from Meklavar indicate that our people grow restive under Gelon's harsh rule. This new prophet, Iskarnon, has been rallying the lands around the city, railing against the oppressors, and urging armed revolt."

Tsorreh perceived the direction of Marvenion's argument. She envisioned poorly armed city folk and farmers hurling themselves against disciplined troops. What folly! Even Meklavar's army, led by the best of their generals, had been unable to resist the Gelonian assault.

She shook her head, *No.* No more killing, no more bloodshed. No more wailing in the night. No more widows and orphans, and no more sons crazed with pain and loss.

"As yet," Marvenion persisted, "there have been only scattered incidents, nothing organized. I tell you, Meklavar is like tinder, wanting only a spark. You, my *te-ravah*, will be far more than that spark. Your coming will be as lightning from heaven, a divine wrath that sets all the country ablaze."

Tsorreh could no longer keep silent. "If that is the outcome, then I must never return."

"But you must—it is your duty! If you refuse, we are doomed. Without a cause to rally them—*your* cause—our attempts to free Meklavar will fail."

Tsorreh leaped to her feet. Shaking with fury, she glared down at Marvenion. "I will not be ordered about like a child too young to know my own mind!" She knew her outburst was likely caused by lingering effects of the fruit wine, but her words rang with passion.

"By all that's holy!" she cried. "I have lived through the siege and fall of not one city but two—first Meklavar and then Gatacinne! I have survived the death of my husband, my own flight and exile, and my capture. For four years I have lived as the slave of my enemy in his very stronghold. I am of the lineage of Khored himself!"

Marvenion blanched, clearly taken aback by her transformation from bedraggled fugitive to imperious queen. Rebah watched from her corner, eyes shining.

"I *will not* be commanded," Tsorreh said, "or wheedled, or cozened, or manipulated by guilt. I *will not* be the puppet of you or any man! I am the *te-ravah* of Meklavar, and I will be guided by my own judgment and none other!"

"But—"

Tsorreh cut him off. She was not finished. "You say the people need only a spark to unite them against Gelon. A spark to set them all mad, rushing into more carnage? A spark to ignite a rebellion that cannot possibly succeed?" *And bring my son rushing home to his own death?* "Have we not endured enough death, enough suffering? You ask me now to bring about even more? I say I will not do it!"

She would not waste her people's lives in a hopeless cause. Gelon had Meklavar too tightly chained. But Gelon was not the only country with an effective fighting force. If Isarre threw its power into the liberation of Meklavar, the struggle would be more even. An uprising might stand a chance with Gelonian occupiers forced to fight on two fronts.

When Tsorreh and Zevaron had first fled Meklavar, their destination had been Isarre, the land of her mother's people. They had arrived in the port city of Gatacinne, only to find it under Gelonian assault. Gatacinne had changed hands several times since then and was still far from secure. However, the rest of Isarre, including capital city of Durlnthe, had never been taken. Ulleos of the House of Rynthos, King of Isarre, had stood firm against the worst Cinath could bring to bear.

Meklavar was not going to free itself. To expel the Gelon, it needed allies. As the surviving widow of the last legitimate ruler, *she* needed allies. And as a daughter of the House of Arandel, she had a kinship claim on King Ulleos through his mother's family.

Her original impulse to flee to Isarre had been sound. She had just picked the wrong city at the wrong time. Now she saw Isarre as not only sanctuary but her country's best hope of freedom.

She turned back to Marvenion. "I say that what our people need is hope. *Real* hope. They most certainly do not need a figurehead queen, obedient to the whims of ambitious councilors who hide themselves away while her people face all the danger!"

"But I—"

"Silence! I have not given you permission to speak, any more than I have granted you leave to send me in mindless haste into a vainglorious, ill-conceived, and ultimately doomed insurrection!"

Tsorreh paused for breath. Marvenion slipped from his seat to his knees before her. Tears streaked his cheeks.

"I will return to Meklavar, my friend," she said, "when the time is right."

"Then I do not know what service I can offer you, my *te-ravah*."

Gently she said, "I know our people have been fleeing Gelon. I must leave, as well, and with the utmost secrecy."

Rising, he gathered his dignity about him like an invisible mantle. "The *Te-Ketav* teaches us that even the most tragic circumstances contain the seeds of hope."

"All I ask is that you find me a trustworthy guide."

"I know just such a man."

"Lady Tsorreh!"

Tsorreh jerked awake at the sound of her name, whispered with such urgency. She had rested in Rebah's bed while Marvenion sent word to his contact. About her, the room lay dark and still. The door creaked open, revealing a darkened corridor beyond. Marvenion slipped inside, a shielded lantern in one hand. In the other, he held a cloak of black summer-weight wool, and a sack closed with a drawstring at either end and attached to a strap, meant to cross the chest for easy carrying.

She settled the cloak around her shoulders. On close inspection, no one would mistake her for anything but a woman of Meklavar, but at night, with her face hidden, she might escape casual notice.

Loosening one of the drawstrings, she peeked inside. Several sets of underclothing, not new but clean, were tucked beside a packet of women's cloths. There was also a leather case containing a needle and several lengths of thread, a wooden comb, chalk for cleaning teeth, and a vial of emollient oil. Rebah had provided every comfort.

"Our friend, a man known as Gray, has arranged for transport downriver to Roramenth on the coast," Marvenion said. "He has helped many of us to leave Aidon. If anyone can, he will see you safely out of Gelon." He did not ask her destination.

Marvenion had arranged for the brother of his household steward to escort Tsorreh to an intermediate meeting place. This way, neither he nor her escort could reveal the boat she had taken or the name of its captain.

The steward's brother entered through the side gate, and Marvenion performed a brief introduction. The brother, Parmen, was of middle years and very serious, or else too shy to say much. Tsorreh suspected that Parmen was not his real name; *Parmenion* was more likely, but *Parmen* would allow him to pass here in Aidon.

Outside, the last glimmers of dusk were fading from the western sky. A few stars shone just above the rooftops. Tsorreh paused on the threshold and turned back to Marvenion. The lamp behind him cast his face into shadow. He bowed deeply. She nodded and then followed Parmen into the gathering night.

Chapter Seven

PARMEN led Tsorreh down a series of side streets, angling across the district. After a time, she caught a glimpse of lights in the hills where the noble families dwelled in their walled compounds. She thought of Jaxar and hoped he did not grieve too deeply at the news of her death or do anything rash in response to Lycian's ravings.

Even at this hour, people were still abroad, finishing the work of the day. Several times, Tsorreh saw, or thought she saw, a man making his way through the lessening traffic, following them yet keeping well back. When she turned to look, she saw nothing.

Parmen halted at one of the two-story buildings, a shabby and unremarkable structure. He tapped on the door and was answered by the rasp of a bolt being drawn. When the door cracked open, he bent to speak a few words with the man inside.

"Come in, quickly! Do not stand out here where you can be seen!" Slipping the lantern handle from its peg, the man closed the door behind them and gestured for them to follow. Tsorreh could not guess his origin, for he was certainly not Meklavaran and was too dark-skinned to be Gelon.

The lantern cast shadows over the cramped entryway

and the narrow staircase beyond. The wooden stairs creaked under their weight. The handrail, a rope looped through iron rings set in the walls, had been worn to softness. The stairs led upward to a second landing, which was flanked by two doors. The man led them into the room to the left.

The floor of the chamber was bare, and there was a simple table against one wall, with two chairs. A box-frame bed covered by a threadbare pallet, without blanket or pillow, occupied the corner. The table bore a lantern, unlit, and a chipped ewer of red-glazed clay. Tsorreh doubted anyone regularly lived here; clearly this room was used only for transient meetings.

"You will wait." The man touched a straw to his own lantern, lit the one on the table, and withdrew.

With Parmen standing ill at ease beside the door, Tsorreh settled herself in one of the chairs and laid her sack on the table. The few crumbs of dry bread from a bowl on the table looked dry and coarse. She felt weary and sick, and far too vulnerable.

She was not alone, she argued silently. Marvenion trusted Parmen and the man called Gray. She must rely on the physician's judgment. Try as she might, however, she could not convince herself to relax.

What was taking so long?

"If the doorkeeper does not return soon," she said, "we should leave."

Parmen looked even less happy than before. "Would we be any safer out there than here, where there is only one door to guard?"

"Where we can be trapped," she pointed out.

She heard footsteps on the stairs, soft and muted. The door swung open to reveal a man on the landing, dimly lit by the candle on the table. From her vantage, Tsorreh could only see that he was tall and lean, with dark hair falling to his shoulders. She could not make out his features, beyond the impression of dusky skin. She might have guessed him to be a roughly dressed laborer, except for the grace of his carriage and the watchful calm of his gaze.

Parmen sidled forward, blocking her view, as the stranger stepped into the room.

"Were you seen?" The stranger spoke in clear Gelone. *A singer's voice,* Tsorreh thought.

"No one followed us," Parmen replied.

"No one that you noticed."

"Are you Gray?" Irritation turned Parmen's question into a demand.

"Some call me that. You, however"—Gray's voice was low and smooth—"are not the one I expected."

"I have been entrusted to act for him."

"Ah. Our mutual friend asked my assistance in arranging discreet travel plans for a woman of our people. I take it she sits yonder. But he did not name a destination."

"That is for the lady herself to say. For everyone's safety, it is better that I not know."

Gray moved past Parmen and into the candlelight. Tsorreh's first impression had been right, for he was both graceful and strong. He had arched cheekbones and a wide, generous mouth. Silver glimmered in his hair.

For the slightest instant, a radiance seemed to rise up in him, lighting his features with a hint of rose-hued gold like an intimation of dawn. The effect passed so quickly that Tsorreh must have imagined it.

"Let us depart at once. The longer we tarry, the greater the risk of discovery." Rising, she inclined her head to Parmen. "My thanks to you and to our friend. I will remember you both."

"You may tell him that the lady is now in my care," Gray said, then switched to Meklavaran. "Go now, and may the Shield of Khored protect you."

"May the grace of the Most Holy guide your steps," Parmen replied in the same language. He bowed first to Gray, then, more deeply, to Tsorreh.

As Tsorreh watched the door close behind Parmen, she became aware of Gray's gaze upon her. She drew herself up, conscious of his greater height. "Marvenion did not send word of my destination because I did not tell him."

"When were you planning to reveal that information?" With a fleeting tightness at one corner of his mouth that might have been a smile, he added, "Or must it remain a mystery?"

"I must get to Durinthe as soon as possible. Can you arrange passage to the coast—Verenzza or Roramenth, I don't care—and then find me a ship?"

"Do you think the Ar-King permits sea travel to Isarre?"

"I do not intend to ask his permission. Can it be done or not?"

"It can, if the need is sufficiently great."

"Marvenion would not have asked, otherwise."

Again Gray looked at her with that measuring gaze. Tsorreh felt no sense of threat, only the certainty that this man saw far more than others did. Had he been a Gelon— or a priest of Qr—she would have had good reason to be terrified.

"I do not wonder that you avoided specifying Durinthe," he said. "Any reasonable man would think you were out of your wits."

Of course, she was mad to contemplate such a thing, but what part of her life, since the day Ar-Thessar-Gelon had marched on Meklavar, had been sane?

Except, perhaps, those evenings with Jaxar on the roof of his house as the heat drained from the city sky, charting the stars together. Perhaps the moment when Zevaron had come bursting back into her life. Those times had been havens of joy.

"Durinthe it is." For a moment, Gray looked younger, irrepressibly bold, and she felt safer than she could remember. Then his expression turned serious. "Listen carefully. Even in less dangerous times, traveling with a woman is not easy. Now it is a hundred times more so. It would be difficult enough getting a mouse out of the city, but even worse to attempt to hide here until the hunt dies down."

Hunt? Her stomach went cold. The woman in the shop had mentioned a hunt.

"We must travel fast to reach the coast," he said, "with no allowance for comfort. You have the hands of one who has lived soft. If it comes to a choice between freedom and rest—or food or drink, for that matter—can you manage without complaint?"

"I will do what I must." Tsorreh lifted her chin. "I have survived more than you can imagine."

"I can imagine a great many things." Gray gestured to her sack. "Do you have everything you need?"

"I am as well prepared as I know how to be." Tsorreh paused. "Please tell me what is going on. What hunt?"

"You have not seen the extra patrols? They are combing the city and offering a reward for the capture of Lord Jaxar's traitor son."

"Danar?" Tsorreh said, stunned.

Of course, Cinath would not stop at her own death. He would come next for Danar. Danar, who stood next in succession after Cinath's own son. He was the same age as Zevaron, a capable young man with unexpected depths, who had managed to remain untouched by his stepmother's venom. He'd been like a younger brother to her. Her heart ached for him when she thought of him alone in that great house with Lycian.

Jaxar would have suspected his brother's next move. He would have sent Danar into hiding, out of the city, perhaps out of Gelon. And Zevaron—he would have sent Zevaron with him. For good or ill, Zevaron was now beyond her reach. Just as they had gone their separate ways after being separated at Gatacinne, so must they now. They might never see one another again.

"How soon can we leave?" she said.

"Tonight, under cover of darkness. I know a riverboat captain who can take us as far as Silon. With a little persuasion, perhaps all the way."

Silon, where the Father Monk's temple of the Lady was. But it could not be helped.

Gray went to the bed and pulled aside the pallet. The box frame had been fashioned as a storage place. He took out several bundles, one of which Tsorreh could have sworn contained a short sword, as well as a belt of folded leather, a cloak, and a drawstring sack much like her own. Within moments, he had arranged the sack to cover the long bundle slung diagonally across his back, restored the pallet, and picked up the lantern.

"One thing more," he said, halting her at the doorway with a gesture. "What shall I call you? It will arouse suspicion if you have no name."

"Since you are Gray," she said. "Then I must be Black."

In the light of the lantern, his eyes glinted. "Black?" he echoed. "Nothing so ordinary. I shall call you Lady Amber, you who burn with your own inner fire."

Gray said very little as they slipped along the narrow, barely lit streets and eventually reached the wharves. Lights shone dimly from tavern windows, and a few men went about their business, working on the boats or standing guard over cargo. They looked wary and tough.

They halted in the shadows beside a warehouse. From here, they had a clear view of the market area and the tables where fish were gutted and cleaned. Beyond the market, a riverboat was moored alongside the pier. In a pool of light cast by a lantern hung from one of the tall posts, a single riverman crouched, arranging a pile of ropes and pulleys.

"Remain here while I go ahead," Gray said. "Make no sound and do not let anyone see you."

Then he was gone, striding along the wooden pier. The man on watch got to his feet and the two spoke, heads bent together. Finally the riverman took his lantern and ambled off to the boat. Some minutes later, he emerged and motioned for Gray to come aboard.

Moments dripped by. The boat swayed at its moorings. Tension seeped into Tsorreh as she waited. Surely Gray must have concluded his negotiations by now. What if the captain should refuse, given the increased risk? Would her presence help to persuade him? Would she only make matters worse? Or had Gray walked into a trap?

The night was so still that Tsorreh could hear the creaking of ropes and the splash of water against the hull and the pier posts. She startled at a muted clatter from the direction of the city. A body of men was moving quickly toward the pier, their steps measured and disciplined. Voices reached her, indistinct words, then the sound of scuffling, a bitten-off exclamation, and a thud. Shouting erupted.

"Raid! Raid!" came from the dockside.

"You there!" called out another voice, this one from up the street. "Halt!"

Then the thunderous command: "Open in the name of the All-Glorious Ar!"

Cursing answered the challenge. Tsorreh heard splashing, the ring of metal against metal, feet pounding on the wooden planks underfoot, then war cries chanted in unison.

"Gelon! Gelon! Gelon!"

She inched forward, straining for a clear view. She knew she should stay hidden, that she could do nothing to help. What aid could she offer against armed men, except to be captured or killed? Yet she could not remain safely out of sight, quivering like a rabbit in its burrow.

Summoning her courage, she stepped from her shelter to see the wharf seething with men. Gelon swarmed onto the riverboat. They moved with that disciplined coordination she remembered so well from Meklavar. Their combined weight rocked the craft. Within moments, fighting engulfed the boat.

Suddenly the cabin interior blazed with white-orange light, far too bright to have come from a lantern.

"Fire!" someone shouted.

"Fire on board!"

More men came running, Gelon in armor, rivermen, others that Tsorreh could not make out in the flame-licked confusion. Some were struggling with one another, seemingly unaware of the conflagration. Others rushed this way and that, some perhaps in search of escape, others to block or to pursue. A man in laborer's clothing bent to pick up something, Tsorreh could not make out what. As he straightened up, a Gelon closed with him, sword swinging. Tsorreh thought she heard him scream, but the noise of shouting and the clash of weapons blanketed the cry.

Tsorreh clenched her hands together, as if she could still the uproar of her thoughts. The impulse to rush into the fight was almost overpowering. She shook with the effort of standing still. It was beyond hope that even a man like Gray could fight his way off the boat. Her best chance was to leave while she still could. She had seen enough battles to know how quickly the fighting could shift direction. At any moment, she might find herself in the center of a skirmish.

She wanted to scream in frustration. She had watched, helpless, as her city had burned, as her husband and stepson were cut down, as Gelonian soldiers marched through the streets of Meklavar. *Then* she had been able to do nothing. And *now* she must run away, while a man who had tried to help her met a similar fate.

Fire was already spreading from the riverboat cabin along the deck. More men came running, armed with buckets, pitchforks, and ropes. A few Gelon broke off fighting to help put out the blaze.

A hand, thick and strong, clamped over Tsorrch's mouth from behind. Losing her balance, she fell backward against a man's body. She grabbed the hand over her mouth, digging in her nails, but she was held firm and pulled back into the shadows.

"It's me—Brother Benthos!" a man's voice whispered in her ear. "I'll not harm thee."

Bynthos? How dare he!

Tsorreh forced herself to stand still, to breathe evenly through her nose. Adrenaline rushed through her veins. Her pulse hammered in her throat, but her vision was sharp, her mind clear.

She remembered the man in the shadows during her journey to meet Gray—*Bynthos* had been following her.

He thinks to take me back to the temple. And then to Si-lom!

"Come away, lady. There is no help for thee here, only danger and death—"

Tsorreh sank her teeth into the nearest finger. The skin was tough and tasted of salt, but she held on. Cursing in a most unclerical manner, Bynthos released her mouth. His grasp on her shoulder loosened. She spun around and kicked out as high and hard as she could. Her foot slammed into his thigh near the crease of his groin. Yelping, he folded over. The movement brought his face within her reach. She caught her balance and struck him with all her might, open-handed on the side of his face. The blow was hard enough to spin his head around. Pain lanced up her hand and arm from the impact, but she was too angry to care.

"Don't you *ever* lay hands on me in that manner again!"

"Lady—" he gasped, bending over to knead his injured thigh, then she cut him off.

"I'm not going anywhere with you! In fact—" Panting, she wrenched her thoughts under control. She felt drunk, not on wine but on fury.

Bynthos was wearing the long, coarsely woven shirt and knee-length pants of a common worker. She remembered his strength as he'd rowed the boat on the river, his work-calloused hands. He'd spent most of his life at sea, not poring over books. An active man, a man who loved his ship, a man no stranger to fighting—

She grabbed the loose folds of the shirt, hauled him upright, and shoved him toward the burning boat. "Those men need your help!"

Propelled by her urgency, he took a step toward the conflagration, then hesitated. Perhaps the sight of so many armed Gelon made him hesitate. It did not matter. The fire was rapidly spreading to the pier as well.

She pushed him again. "Never mind the soldiers! You are a ship's captain—look! There's a boat on fire and sailors in need. What greater enemy is there? I cannot help them! You must—*you shall*—do it for me!"

He turned his head toward her, his face reddened by the fires. Nothing of the monk remained. She had called him *captain*, and something within him had answered. But she wasn't through with him.

"My friend is in there—" She jabbed a finger toward the inferno of vessel and pier. He sprinted for the burning boat.

A dozen or more Gelonian swordsmen dominated the pier. Half that number of ordinary men struggled unequally against them, some wielding knives and one, a long-handled trident. Tsorreh watched, heart in throat, as Bynthos swerved to avoid a pair of fighters. A guard rushed at Bynthos, sword glinting red. Without missing a step, Bynthos bent over, grabbed a net, and hurled it. It tangled in the soldier's legs and he went down, flailing. Bynthos raced past him.

The fire flared up. Dark against the brightness, a man burst from the cabin, holding a short sword. He seemed to fly through the flames, as if they could not touch him. A

Gelon moved to intercept him. The short sword cut through the air.

Tsorreh recognized that spiral pattern, for she had seen Zevaron practicing such a move with his swordmaster. But Zevaron had been a boy then, in the untroubled days of Meklavar, with a boy's undeveloped strength, a boy's awkwardness. He had none of the precise, blinding speed of the man before her. Watching the man, outlined against the burning boat and glowing with his own brilliance, something hot and bright and singing rose up behind her throat.

Gray danced between the Gelonian blades as if they were grass, unerringly finding one opening after another. Rose-gold light flashed on his skin, as if he himself were the source of its radiance. Moment by moment, stroke by superbly balanced stroke, he fought his way toward her hiding place. Some of the rivermen, heartened by his fierce energy, renewed their attacks on the Gelon.

One of the Gelon blocked his way, a huge man with a sword to match his size, giving him the longer reach. Gray sank into a fluid stance, circling. His own sword, held low, was almost invisible against the spreading fires. The Gelon bellowed, his words unintelligible in the shouting. The next instant, the two fighters closed. Swords blurred in a storm of strokes. Reflected light flashed like shards of brightness. The Gelon thrust with all his bulk behind the stroke. For a terrible moment, he loomed over Gray's slighter figure. The sound of metal clanging against metal cut through the uproar.

The two men sprang apart. Gray seemed unhurt, still moving with that silken grace. The Gelon stumbled back a step before hurling himself at Gray. Gray retreated before the onslaught, as each blow came heavier and faster than before. Men gave way around them, opening a space. A few stared openly, but a team of roustabouts, hauling water buckets to the burning boat, paid no heed.

In the shifting darkness, Tsorreh caught another figure—a Gelon, moving stealthily toward the fighting pair. He sidled closer, coming up behind Gray, and raised his sword. She stifled a cry of warning. In all likelihood, Gray could not hear her, anyway. Even if he could, she dared not break his concentration.

Gray and his opponent feinted, drew back, and circled one another. The big man moved sluggishly and the tip of his sword lagged. For a moment, he seemed to be staring not at Gray, but at some point behind Gray. Then he stumbled, catching himself. Gray came at him on an angle, stepping low and deep. The second Gelon surged toward Gray.

Gray whirled, but a fraction too late. The second soldier came at him so fast, Gray barely had time to parry the first thrust. He lunged to one side to give himself more room to maneuver beyond the reach of the other man's longer sword. At the same moment, the big Gelon closed in. The two soldiers coordinated their attacks, each forcing Gray toward the other. There was nowhere for Gray to run, almost no room in which he could use his agility and speed. The Gelon were forcing him to divide his defense. One slip, and they would have him.

Wildly, Tsorreh thought of rushing into the fray, but she could not move; she could not breathe. She could not look away.

A man, his shape no more than a shadowy blur, burst from the maelstrom of smoke and flame of the boat. He held a long pole. Clearing the gap to the pier, he raced toward the three fighters. A sudden flare of the fires illuminated his face.

The big Gelon shuffled closer to Gray and pivoted with surprising speed for a man his size, but Bynthos, propelled by the momentum of his charge, was already attacking. His pole whirled and slashed so fast, it blurred in Tsorreh's vision. Turning, the Gelon recoiled, swinging his sword. Bynthos spun out of reach and then stepped in, shifting the pole to ram one end into the Gelon's side. Tsorreh could not follow everything that was happening, it was all too fast.

Gray lost no time in renewing his own fight. Immediately, he bore down on the second Gelon. The Gelon fell back before Gray's rain of blows, lost his footing, and went down. The next moment, Bynthos swung his pole low and caught the larger Gelon on the side of one knee. Tsorreh heard the crack above the uproar of the fighting. The Gelon fell heavily and curled on his side, holding his injured knee.

In the last few moments, the worst of the other fighting had subsided. Most of the rivermen had disappeared, except those still struggling to contain the fires. Many of the Gelon, including the one Bynthos had fought, lay groaning amidst the buckets and crates. The Gelon still standing bolted back the way they had come. Tsorreh had no doubt they had gone for reinforcements.

"Hurry!" Tsorreh called. "Hurry, before they come back!"

Two figures raced toward her. Gray was in the forefront, one cheek smeared with ash and blood. As he passed her, he shouted, "Go!"

She sprinted after him. Bynthos pounded at their heels. From behind them came cries of "Fire! Fire on the pier!" and "'Ware—it spreads!"

They raced on until Tsorreh's muscles burned. Her breath rasped in her lungs. When she stumbled, Bynthos caught her weight and pulled her after Gray into the next alley. She collapsed against the weathered wood wall of a shed.

"We can't stay here." Gray quickly recovered his breath. "I doubt any place within the city is safe for us now. If the guards have discovered Neddas, then they may already be moving to arrest the others."

"This Neddas—your riverman friend—will he tell—?" Tsorreh gasped.

"Neddas will never tell anyone anything," Gray said grimly. "He bought us a chance and we must not waste it."

He turned to Bynthos. "I thank you for your help, friend, but now our brief fellowship ends. The lady and I must be on our way. It would be prudent to not involve yourself with us."

"Hunh!" Bynthos grunted. "It was too late for that when I pulled her from the river. It was for her sake and not thine that I took out that great lumbering oaf of a Gelon. I will not leave her now."

"You know each other?"

"Four years ago, I sailed on this man's ship from Gatacinne." Tsorreh turned to Bynthos. "Make up whatever story you wish, but I will not go back."

"And I have said I will not leave thee. When I came after thee, I thought to save thee from a rash decision. I still believe thee would be safe at Silon, but if thee will not go there, then I will do what I can to protect thee."

"We cannot stand here all night, debating the issue," Gray interrupted. "Be on your way, monk."

"I will not leave her," Bynthos repeated in a tone no less stubborn. "This lady has the most alarming habit of disrupting my life. The first time we met, I could not return to the sea, and now it is she who has plucked me out of the river. I once preached to her about how the Lady of Mercy calls us from our former lives. It seems the Lady has other uses for me besides monkish study."

"Lady Amber," Gray said, "whatever else he may have done, this man fought bravely at my side. Do you trust him?"

In the near-darkness, she felt his gaze on her. Now that the urgency of the moment had passed, she was not sure what she felt. She could not say that Bynthos had rushed into the fray on her command; she could not even be sure that was true. Bynthos could have refused, or fled, or overpowered her and dragged her away. She wondered if any of them truly shaped their own lives or were themselves shaped by something greater.

"Brother Benthos—or Bynthos, I know not how to call him—will not betray us to Cinath." *Or,* she added to herself, *to Qr, which he has every reason to hate.*

A moment passed, pregnant with consideration. "Then let us get ourselves to a place where we can finish our debate in secrecy," Gray said.

Chapter Eight

GRAY lead them through a district of the poorer sort of taverns that still did business at this hour. They approached one from the back, where a scullery boy was emptying pans of vegetable trimmings onto a refuse heap. Gray gave the boy a coin, and the three of them passed through the kitchen and into a back room.

The room contained a single rickety chair and an uneven bed, making the room back at the safe house seem luxurious by comparison. These walls were so thin, they vibrated with the raucous laughter from the common room. The only light came from the gaps around the door.

As soon as Tsorreh stopped moving, her legs began to tremble. She lowered herself to the slat bed, thinking that at least there would be no insect vermin hiding in a mattress.

"Now," Gray said, "both of you—what is this about? Lady Amber, what have you to do with a Gelonian temple? And you, my . . . friend, why have you been following this lady?"

Eyes downcast, Bynthos told the story of the voyage from Gatacinne, his call to the service of the Lady of Mercy, and the river rescue and its aftermath. Tsorreh thought he sounded weary and confused, like a ship after a storm, as if what had once been so clear to him now lay in ruins. When he mentioned how Father Monk had charged him with escorting her to Silon, he seemed to be talking about someone else. She felt herself unexpectedly moved by his plight, by the loss of everything that had given him purpose.

Bynthos sighed. "Peace and contemplation are clearly not my fate. I should have realized when"—he glanced at Tsorreh, who shook her head, warning him not to speak her name—"when the lady reappeared in my life."

"Would it not be safer for him to come with us, than to risk his being captured and questioned?" Tsorreh asked Gray.

"I can fight," Bynthos said, without a trace of false pride. "And handle boats."

"You are indeed a ship's captain?" Gray's voice took on a new tone of interest.

"I was once," Bynthos said. "And perhaps will be again."

Gray shifted in the near-darkness. "The river will be closely watched. We must travel by land, which has its own dangers."

"You will need a second pair of eyes to watch at night," Bynthos pointed out.

"Aye, and a second pair of fighting hands. So be it. Rest here as best you can while I gather what is necessary."

Bynthos curled up on the cleanest patch of floor, while Tsorreh lay down on the bare slats of the bed. To her surprise, she soon managed a fitful slumber.

Gray returned with packs and walking staves for the men, a basket for Tsorreh, and three pairs of worn but stout boots. Tsorreh gratefully accepted hers, for the leather was worn to softness, even though the soles had obviously been repaired many times. With the two pairs of thick socks that Gray handed her, she felt as if she could walk across Gelon.

Bynthos insisted on keeping his sandals. "My feet would not know me in boots."

They set out at first light. Already people were abroad, beginning the day's business: men carrying sackloads of goods or tools slung over their shoulders, women with jars balanced on their heads, carts drawn by donkeys or oxen, boys in slave tunics, and city patrol keeping a watchful eye on everyone. Several times, Tsorreh spotted squads wearing the distinctive colors of the Ar-King.

The southern gates were already open. To one side, a line of clerks sat at a table with their duty charts and coffers. Guards and black-robed officials were questioning everyone entering the city. Only a few of those leaving were stopped, those carrying substantial baggage. Tsorreh and the two men, dressed as common country folk and surrounded by trader caravans, passed through with only a cursory glance.

Dusk found them at a village, a handful of houses with livestock pens, neat stone-fenced gardens, and a single inn and stable. Light streamed from the open windows of the inn, and the breeze carried the sound of laughter and the aroma of bread and onions.

"Wait here," Gray said, ushering them to a grove of knobby-barked trees. A shrine, waist-high and wrought from stone that once must have been fine but now was cracked and weathered, bore a faded garland of flowers.

Tsorreh set down her basket and stretched her aching back. She watched as Gray approached the inn. The door swung closed behind him. She leaned against the nearest trunk, careful to avoid placing her sore back against the hard swirls of bark. She had been tense all day, anxious that her face or accent might give her away.

The door opened and Gray stood silhouetted against a rectangle of orange light. He gestured for them to follow him around to the side, up a flight of stairs, and into a private dining room. Tsorreh heard a burst of laughter from the common room. A lanky, red-faced man wearing an apron, the innkeeper no doubt, brought in a tray laden with food and drink. This he set down on the scrubbed pinewood table and then clasped forearms with Gray. "It is good to see you again, my friend!"

"I do not need to ask if you are well," Gray replied, "for

one look convinces me that the married state agrees with you."

"That it does, and our firstborn shall bear the honor of your father's name."

"May the time come speedily when he can speak it in freedom," Gray said. "Now, these are the friends I told you of. This is Chavan, who has been my ally since my first days in Gelon."

Bynthos nodded, and Tsorreh looked more closely at the innkeeper. *Chavan* sounded Gelonian. With his dark coloring, however, that could not be his real name.

A short, visibly pregnant young woman bustled in, bearing an armful of linens and blankets. "What are you thinking to keep our guests standing around in this manner? And"—to Tsorreh—"you must be exhausted, poor dear! Here, sit down. Drink some of this good ale. It is my husband's brewing and will do you nothing but good."

"Jany will soon have us all in order." Chavan gave his wife an affectionate glance. Remembering the dangers the fruit wine had caused her, Tsorreh declined the ale.

Jany bustled Tsorreh down a short, narrow corridor to a bedroom. "We're nothing fancy, but everything's clean. You'll not be picking up bed-lice in my house. Poor dear, you look as if you've walked halfway across the world."

Tsorreh's body melted into the bed. The ticking was prickly and the linens coarse, but it felt wonderful. The lantern cast a gentle glow.

"Do you need help with those boots? They must come off, you know. It won't do to fall asleep with them on. Your feet need to breathe."

"So my old nurse always said." How long ago that seemed, when she was a girl in Meklavar, when she'd had women about her. Jaxar had been thoughtful and generous, but could not offer the companionship of her own sex. Nor could he protect Tsorreh from his wife's resentment. Tsorreh had been truly alone.

I will not weep in front of this woman, just because she is kind to me. I will not.

Jany lowered herself, somewhat awkwardly because of

her rounded belly, and sat beside Tsorreh. "Have you had a very hard time of it, then? Did you have no husband, no family to protect you? Anyone can see this Bynthos is no kin of yours."

Tsorreh startled, for Jany had addressed her in Meklava-ran. She sat up and took a better look at her hostess, whose features she had been too tired to notice before—the shape of the nose and forehead, the hair worn in Gelonian style but as dark and thick as her own.

"You—you are Meklavaran?" Tsorreh asked in the same language.

Jany's smile crinkled into dimples. "As you are! My real name's Janaya, much easier to pronounce, don't you think? Gray brought me here. It was his idea to change my name to something less, um, noticeable. Gray is one of us, surely you knew that?"

"Yes, I—I did realize."

"He came out of nowhere three, maybe four years ago."

Four years . . . after the city fell . . .

"I was living in Mezzena at the time, with cousins," Jan-aya chattered on. "After my uncle was arrested and his trad-ing business confiscated, Gray found safe places for us. All except my one cousin, that is. He disappeared. We're not sure where he is or if he is still alive."

"I'm sorry to hear that," Tsorreh said.

For a moment, Janaya regarded her. "Yes, I believe you know what it is like to lose everything simply because of who you are. Were you—you have a look about you, such sadness—were you in Meklavar when it fell?"

Tsorreh nodded. "I watched it from the palace walls. The fighting, the burning gates . . . how they brought Maharrad's body into the courtyard . . ." Her throat closed up.

Running with Zevaron for the tunnels through the mountains. Fleeing across the Sand Lands as the te-alvar *woke and spun waking nightmares out of thin air.*

"You must be of noble birth, then, to have known the *te-ravot* well enough to use his name," Janaya said in a small voice.

Tsorreh cursed her moment of unguarded speech. "No,

no, it was a slip of the tongue, born out of fatigue, nothing more."

Janaya bent to slip off Tsorreh's boots. "And here I am, keeping you awake with my idle chatter!" After making Tsorreh comfortable, Janaya bade her good night and left her to rest.

Chapter Nine

THEY departed the next morning, this time with a donkey to carry their packs. Their way wound through gently rolling hills, past fields and orchards, farms and streams. At first, the countryside was lush and fertile. Farm workers waved at them as they passed. The days were filled with sunlight and the air with the honey-sweet smell of ripening grain. They met other travelers along the broader, more well-trodden sections of road, mostly farmers or herdsmen. Once they had to wait while an entire flock of sheep was herded across the road.

Despite the brightness of sky and the fertility of the fields, Tsorreh could not shake the feeling that a shadow lurked just beyond the edge of her vision. The air was warm, yet at odd moments, the back of her neck prickled and cold-bumps roughened her arms.

Twilight was fading when they stopped for the first night in a dell surrounded by tall stones, well away from the road. Bynthos found a tin cookpot in the donkey's packs and proceeded to simmer a mixture of parched wheat, lentils, and dried onions. Tsorreh sat on her cloak, trying to knead sensation back into the muscles of her thighs. Gray set a dish in front of her and handed her the spoon. Tsorreh felt so weary, the smell of the food nauseated her. Although she was sure she could not eat, she hesitated at outright refusal. She felt Gray's eyes upon her. Measuring her. Testing her.

She took a bite, instantly regretting not letting the lentil mixture cool first. Then she was ravenously hungry. She ate until her stomach felt tight. When she was done, Gray offered her a stoppered flask of liniment. Her first reaction was to refuse, but she must be fit to travel the next morning. She dared not risk them all out of foolish pride. In the dark, after Bynthos had extinguished the cooking fire, she bunched up her skirt and rubbed the liquid into her skin. It smelled fresh, with a pleasant pungency. She tumbled into sleep with its odor in her nostrils and its warmth in her thighs.

Over the next few days, Tsorreh found, to her surprise, that she enjoyed handling the donkey and the beast seemed to have a particular affection for her. Often she could coax it into going on when it refused to obey the men.

Gradually the road dwindled into a trail, veering away from the river. Farms here were scarce and poor, often no more than a plot of vegetables and a goat shed. The cottages looked as if they had been cobbled together from the stones that dotted the fields. Gray knew many of these people. Often they were offered a simple meal, tiny reddish beans or barley with bitter greens, and then space in the goat shed. The next morning, they would be on their way, having seen no more of the family than a passing glance.

One night they camped outdoors beside a swift-running stream that cut its way through a ridge of splintered rock. While Tsorreh and Bynthos cleared a sleeping space, Gray went hunting and returned with a couple of rabbits, which he proceeded to skin and roast. After they had finished licking the last juices from their fingers, they gathered near while Gray drew a map in the dirt.

"From here, we must make a choice," he said. "We can either follow this stream east, where it will join the Eel, which flows into the Serpan River at Silon, or we can keep to these hills and make our way to the Serpan further south."

Tsorreh did not want to come within a hundred miles of the Temple of the Lady, but if they were not to spend the next year wandering the back roads of Gelon, they must find a quicker means of travel, and that meant the river.

"The Silon route is shorter," Bynthos said.

Tsorreh wondered if he were scheming a way to convince her to accept Father Monk's plan for her. At Silon, the Lady temple would be all too conveniently at hand. But when he met her eyes, she read no deception there.

"That it is, but more exposed," Gray said. "We'll be among trading folk, going through tax gates here, and then again, here. If anyone's looking for us, that's where they'll be. Yet these hills have their own dangers. They've become a haven for outlaws, close enough to towns to find easy prey, yet rough enough to discourage all but the most determined pursuit."

Bynthos nodded, rubbing his jaw, and said nothing.

"What do you advise?" Tsorreh asked Gray.

"If it were just myself, I would say the hills," he replied without looking at her. "It depends upon our assessment of the risk—brigands who want only our money—"

"Or Qr," she murmured without thinking, "who wants much more." Gray looked sharply at her.

Bynthos picked up his walking staff and balanced it in his hands, as if testing its strength and assessing it as a weapon. "Since we must choose, let it be the wilds. I will put my trust in the Lady's favor and my own strong arms."

As Gray predicted, their progress through the broken hills was slow. They passed a few more villages but did not take shelter there. Instead, they camped out under the sky. Tsorreh could not remember having seen such clear nights, such a radiance spread across the heavens, not since she had left Meklavar. She had not realized how much the lights of Aidon obscured the stars, and wished that Jaxar might be here, watching them with her.

As the land rose, the soil turned rockier and poorer. Wild goats bounded away over boulder-strewn slopes as they approached. They spotted the nests of eagles, and the spoor of foxes, lynx, wild pigs and, once, a bear.

At last they began to descend. The trail became so precipitous that their sure-footed donkey balked. It took all of Tsorreh's persuasion to coax the beast to go on. At intervals, they glimpsed the land below, fields and pastures crossed by good roads. Then the trail turned back on itself, hiding the vista. Gray took the lead, then Bynthos, and finally Tsorreh, murmuring encouragement to the donkey.

The trail narrowed, as if reluctant to speed their passage. To one side, the earth fell away sharply, and splintered rock rose almost vertically on the other. In places, between their feet and the edge there was only a narrow strip of loose soil to which a few withered roots clung.

The terrain below came into view again. Distracted, Tsorreh missed her footing. Her foot dislodged a stone that went clattering downslope. As if in echo, the sound went on, no longer the crack of rock against rock, but the sound of footsteps from below.

"Gray, should we—" Tsorreh began, just as Bynthos called out, "Hoy!"

A band of men rushed toward them around a bend in the trail. There were five or six of them, running single file. The man in the lead was a little ahead, so that Tsorreh noticed him first. He wore stained rags and rope sandals. Exertion reddened his skin. A cut stood out, livid, across one checkbone. Tsorreh had seen that expression before on the faces of the slaves in Aidon. Men like that were dangerous because they had no hope.

Gray reacted first. He grabbed Bynthos by the arm and shoved him back up the trail toward Tsorreh. "Keep her safe!"

Bynthos reached out one arm to Tsorreh. At the same time, Gray spun around and lifted his walking staff in both hands. Facing the oncoming men, he balanced lightly on both feet.

"Let them pass!" Tsorreh cried.

Gray held his ground. Tsorreh dropped the donkey's lead rope and hurled herself at him, thinking to push him out of the way. She stumbled, falling against him as her momentum carried both of them against the rock face. His arms went around her. She felt the heat of his skin and the hairs of his beard against her cheek.

For the merest instant, a fraction of a heartbeat, light flared inside her mind. It was not the blinding, golden brilliance of the *te-alvar*, but a pale, clear rose, like the first intimation of sunrise. It swept through her, cool and exhilarating. The aching emptiness in her breast pulsed. As Gray pulled away, it subsided.

Bynthos wrestled the donkey out of the path as the fleeing men shoved and elbowed their way past. They were clearly bent on escape, not a fight. The stench of their bodies, fear and filth and sweat, washed over Tsorreh. She pressed herself against the vertical rock. The last but one, barefoot and smooth-faced, could have been no more than twelve. Then they were gone, pelting up the trail.

Bynthos rounded on Tsorreh. "If they'd meant us harm—"

"But they did *not* mean us harm!" she retorted. "They wanted only to get past us."

Gray picked up his staff. By some lucky chance, it had not been damaged or gone tumbling downslope. "The real question is *what were they running from?* And is it a danger to us as well?"

"A good question, aye," Bynthos said.

Gray peered at the road below and pointed. "Look there!"

On the slope leading upward from the plain, a small mounted force kicked up a trail of dust. Sun glinted on metal—armor or shields, Tsorreh could not tell. Nor could she could make out their number, only that they were a dozen at least, maybe twenty. A moment later, the pursuers disappeared behind the shoulder of the hill, but the road would soon take them even nearer.

"We must get off the trail," Gray said.

"There's no place to go!" Bynthos protested. "What about the donkey?"

"Leave it!" Gray bounded down the trail, faster than Tsorreh believed possible. There was no time for questions or hesitation. She sprinted after him as fast as she dared. After an instant of hesitation, Bynthos followed.

Gray never missed a step, not even when the pebble-strewn dirt changed abruptly to loose gravel. Bynthos grunted, then slipped and sent down showers of pebbles. Tsorreh landed on a flat stone, only to have it go sliding out from under her. Twisting, she managed to keep her feet as she plunged downward, caught her balance, and went on.

The trail followed the contour of the earth as it descended. It leveled out briefly before dipping once more. Boulders pocked the hill rising to one side. Some stood alone, but others were piled together. Between the massive, splintered rocks, a grove of stunted trees had taken root, their branches springing low from squat, misshapen trunks.

"There!" Gray pointed.

The next moment, he went leaping up the slope. Tsorreh and Bynthos followed as best they could. Tsorreh kept her eyes on the ground, fearful of losing her footing again. When she glanced up, she almost cried aloud, for there was no trace of Gray. He had vanished, as completely as if the hillside had swallowed him up. No, that could not be. Panting and sweating, Tsorreh forced herself to think. Gray must have found a hiding place. He would not have abandoned them, not even to save his own skin. But where was he? In the shadows of the trees? Behind the fractured rocks?

Infused with new energy, she kept going. Within a few paces, the loose stones gave way to dry, twisted grass. The boulders were closer now. She was almost upon them, and still she could not see Gray. She could not draw breath to call out to him. Losing her traction, she went down hard on her knees and hands. Pebbles dug into her palms, hot pinpoints of pain.

Gray burst from between the trees and slid to a halt beside her. He hooked one hand around her elbow, hauled her to her feet, and pulled her up the last stretch. His strength and energy amazed her.

When Gray released her, Tsorreh stumbled to a halt in the copse of trees. Her knees buckled and she collapsed on a drift of dry leaves. The pile was deep with years of debris and unexpectedly soft. Bynthos threw himself down beside her. Gray gestured for them to be still.

Gulping air, Tsorreh strained to catch the sounds of pursuit. Her heart beat so loudly, the oncoming riders must surely hear.

Nothing. Still nothing.

Gray held up one hand, signaling, *Wait here*. With the stealth of a hunting cat, he moved through the trees and up the hill. Tsorreh watched until he disappeared from view behind the boulders. Her skin tingled where they had touched. The place where the *te-alvar* had rested no longer ached with emptiness. Instead, a glimmer of rose-gold light lingered there like a tantalizing echo.

"The fifth alvar . . . Teharod . . . rose for wisdom . . ."

Gray was far more than he appeared, no mere exile and insurgent.

The *te-alvar* Tsorreh once bore had been the heart of the legendary Khored's Shield, one of seven *alvara*, mystically connected crystal petals, thought to be either lost or nothing but myth to begin with. Tsorreh herself had only learned the truth of the *te-alvar* during Meklavar's fall. Now she knew what she had just sensed in Gray.

What was the guardian of an *alvar* doing in Gelon? Where were the others? Scattered and lost? Or carefully protected over the centuries? Tsorreh's head buzzed with questions and regrets.

When the *te-alvar* had come to her, it had shown her how Khored of Blessed Memory had wielded the Shield against Fire and Ice, the embodiment of primordial chaos that threatened to annihilate the living world. Exiled but not destroyed in that terrible battle, Fire and Ice was rousing. Perhaps the scattering of the Shield gems had weakened its prison, or the rise of the Gelonian Scorpion god, Qr, had fed its power, summoned it. It had pulled down a comet from the heavens, smashing the mountains that confined its physical form. Even now, it cast its shadows on every land, and she had no doubt that Qr was a manifestation of its ancient evil.

If the gems could be brought together—Khored's Shield reassembled—the heirs of Khored would have a weapon against the rising power of Fire and Ice.

She had thought her role in safeguarding the world was

done when her death had seemed certain. But if she had not passed the *te-alvar* to Zevaron, she and Gray would now have two of the fabled seven stones.

O Holy One, what have I done?

Her thoughts fractured at a sound from above. "Come up, both of you!" Gray called, making no effort to muffle his words. As she left the shade beneath the trees, she saw Gray standing against the sky.

Bynthos stumbled from their hiding place. "Have you lost your mind? They'll see you!"

"If there were anyone to see, they'd hear you as well, old man."

Tsorreh clambered up the last stretch of hill. She had to use her hands, the ground was so steep. Her palms stung where she had fallen on them. Her skirts clung to her legs and she wished for Meklavaran-style women's pants, gathered at the ankles.

Gray grasped her hand and pulled her to stand beside him. The height gave her a moment's dizziness. The lowest shoulders of hillside sloped down to the plain, and beyond it she saw a river like a silver-white ribbon and a city along its banks. In the distance, she made out boats along the wharves, dark squat warehouses, verdant strips of garden, open plazas, white walls, and red tile roofs.

Silon.

The vista before her wavered. The ghostly suggestion of a many-legged creature hovered over the city. The breath in her lungs turned gelid. Although she was still sweating, she shivered.

"See, down there!" Gray seemed not to have noticed the apparition.

Swallowing hard, Tsorreh scrubbed her eyes, wiping away tears she had not known she'd shed, and followed his gesture. A body of mounted men raced toward the city, almost certainly those they had spotted earlier. The road split into a primary path, continuing to the city gates, and a smaller branch that led to a village of sorts. Here wooden walls enclosed gardens, an orchard, and a handful of buildings. She had seen such a compound recently, had walked its grassy lanes.

"Blessed Lady!" Bynthos cried out.

Smoke billowed upward from the burning roofs of the main buildings. At first glimpse, the plumes were natural gray, but Tsorreh's strangely echoing sight revealed undertones of green and livid yellow, like darkening bruises.

Bynthos fell to his knees, his hands clutched in prayer. His lips moved soundlessly. Unexpectedly moved, Tsorreh reached out to touch his arm. He had already lost one spiritual home, when the Qr cult had taken over the Lady temple in Borrenth Springs.

"I am sorry." She paused, struck by the inadequacy of words. Even if it was not a haven for her, the temple now caught in that monstrous conflagration was—had been—a place of peace, of contemplation and learning.

Bynthos heaved himself to his feet, picked up his staff, and rushed down the hill without another word. Tsorreh took a step after him, but Gray caught her arm. At his touch on her skin, the sickening dizziness lifted. She watched as Bynthos reached the trail and disappeared behind the curve of the hill. The sounds of his passage died away.

She started to speak, but Gray shook his head. "The folk at the temple will need every pair of willing hands. Besides, you and I need to talk."

Chapter Ten

"**Y**OU are no ordinary Meklavaran woman," Gray said as they sat, their backs against the rough stone of the boulder. "Who are you?"

Tsorreh shook her head, wondering how much she dared tell him. How much she *could* tell him. She did not know how to begin. For four years, she had guarded the *te-alvar*, its secret as precious as her own life. Its magic had prevented her from revealing its existence.

"And you are no ordinary man," she said cautiously.

Although his face was shadowed by the rock, his eyes glinted. Did his *alvar* also protect its secret? Hardly understanding what she did, she touched trembling fingers to the gap in the front of his shirt. The skin over his breastbone was fine grained, the hairs curling and crisp.

"Teharod." The name formed on her lips as a whisper, as a prayer.

Light flared rose-gold beneath Gray's skin. Fire stung Tsorreh's fingertips. She jerked away.

Gray took her hand in his. "Are you—"

She hushed him with a look, then guided his hand to her own chest. Through the fabric of her tunic, she felt the warmth of his palm, the light pressure on her breasts. She

met his gaze, inviting him with her eyes to speak. He shook
his head.

Tsorreh tightened her hold on Gray's hand. With their
joined hands, she tapped her chest: "Tsorreh." And then his:
"Gray?"

A smile hovered at the corners of his mouth. "Sandaron."

"Teharod," she said, still with her hand over his chest.
After a pause, Tsorreh pulled their hands back to rest over
her heart. For a long moment, neither spoke. Oceans of
shadow and light surged and fell quiet in Sandaron's rain-
colored eyes.

"Khored," he whispered. He did not mean either the ancient house of her lineage or the fabled king. He meant the
te-alvar. He knew.

Gathering her courage, she wet her lips. "Once, but no
more." The words flowed from her like silk. She had been
released. The long silence lifted from her heart. She had
bent under its weight for so long, she had forgotten how to
breathe.

Sandaron was staring at her intently. Waiting. Her fingers
opened, freeing his.

"How can you speak of"—even now, she could not bring
herself to say the name aloud—"the *alvar*, when you still
carry it?"

"How else could my father have taught me, if I could not
ask? If we could not discuss freely?"

"Your father . . . taught you." Prepared him, as she had
not been prepared. As she in her turn had not prepared
Zevaron.

Sandaron touched the back of her hand and said, "Ordinary human prudence is sufficient for all six lesser *alvara*.
Each of us can sense the presence of the others, but only
when in close proximity. According to the lore, physical
touch is the surest path to recognition. Only the *te-alvar*,
Khored's own stone, protects itself through the silence of its
guardian. Even if I could not feel its holy trace in you, even
if I did not believe who you are, then what I just witnessed
would have convinced me."

Tsorreh drew her hand away. Emptiness pulsed faintly, the loss now muted.

Sandaron frowned. "I have never heard of such a thing. The *alvara* are passed on at the death of each generation."

"So I had been taught. I never expected it to come to me, although through my father, I am indeed of the lineage of Khored." Could she—dare she?—speak of what she had done and who now bore the *te-alvar*?

"When I was in prison," she went on, her voice shaded with hesitation, "certain of the approach of my own death, my greatest fear was that—Khored's gem"—the words came awkwardly—"should not perish with me. Or, worse yet, fall into the possession of Qr."

"The Scorpion priests are everywhere now," Sandaron agreed. "They crowd out the old orders, taking over temples. I've never heard of such a blatant assault as this one on Silon, but it doesn't surprise me. It's only a matter of time before all Gelon worships that one god. Until then, what affair is it of ours how many idols they bow to, so long as they stay in their own country?"

"Qr is more than an ambitious sect," Tsorreh said. "Perhaps once it was one among many, serving those who felt drawn to it. Scorpions are natural creatures, not evil in themselves. Now a far darker power works through them." She watched his expression. "Through the—gift—I sensed many things. A shadow lies upon the Golden Land, an intimation of far worse to come. Does not this"—she touched one fingertip again to his chest—"speak to you of the ancient enemy? Of Fire and Ice, waking after all these years?"

He looked away, but not before she caught the glitter of rose-gold beneath his skin.

She had made a terrible mistake, giving the *te-alvar* and all the danger that came with it to Zevaron. She had thought only of the need to keep the petal gem safe, not of what she might be inflicting on her only child. Or what the passing of the *te-alvar* might mean in the larger sweep of events— Khored's war fought anew. The gem had come to her and had been her responsibility.

"You fear for the one into whose care you entrusted the *te-alvar*," Sandaron said. "Perhaps in ordinary times, the danger would be slight, but now—with Cinath's ambitions out of all bounds, with Meklavar, that once stood against the ancient evil, in chains . . ."

"My son will not fail us. He is strong and resourceful. Khored's gem will teach him what he needs to know, even as it revealed those things to me. The period of adjustment may be difficult, but if I survived it, so can he. He will do what I—I could not. If only it had come to someone more worthy if only—"

"Shh, Tsorrch . . . Tsorreh san-Khored. Tsorreh *te-ravah*."

Taking her hands, he bent his head and kissed them. She could not remember having been touched with such reverence.

"You know my name, so far from home? I was but a second wife and then a captive of war, exiled and forgotten."

"You were never forgotten, my *te-ravah*. We heard of your capture. Some said it was a rumor put about by Gelonian agents to dishearten us. I thought you must have been killed. Forgive me, if I had known you were so near—if I had—"

Tsorreh found Sandaron's words discomforting. "I would not have you or anyone else risk your own life for me."

"Marvenion was right. It is not safe for you in Gelon, even if the Ar-King and all his minions still believe you dead."

"The priests of Qr know otherwise," she said, sighing, "because of Lycian, Jaxar's wife. She may be a vain, silly woman, but she has influence in court. Cinath will surely know by now."

"We must get you out of Gelon and safely to Durinthe as fast as possible. The longer our journey, the more chances for discovery. That means the river."

"What about Bynthos? Should we not wait for him? What if he looks for us and we are not here?"

Sandaron's face hardened. "He can look after himself. Perhaps he is not yet done with being a monk."

"He is a friend, whatever else he may be."

"Then ask yourself if he would want you to risk your freedom—your life—which he fought to save."

"You are right, I suppose."

"Our way will take us in the same direction, toward the temple," Sandaron said encouragingly. "We may meet him on the road."

Tsorreh did not want to go any closer to the Lady temple and the agents of Qr, but she admitted they had no choice. Returning overland the way they had come would take them back toward Aidon, and whoever those mounted men were—soldiers or Silon city patrol—they must know about the trail and were surely watching it.

The donkey had remained where they left it, placidly nibbling on foliage. They continued slowly, minding the donkey's pace, down the trail as it joined the main road. Heat simmered up from the earth. It didn't take long for Tsorreh to turn their conversation back to Meklavar. She asked about the fate of her people, where they were now and how they coped after the fall.

Sandaron said, "Those of us in exile have always formed communities, if only for the comfort of hearing our own language and celebrating our own holy days. Even tasting of our own foods."

"Yes," she answered, wanting to giggle. "The Gelonian penchant for drenching everything in olive oil becomes tedious over time. How long have you been here?"

"I left Meklavar soon after the city fell. Cinath"—Sandaron drew a breath—"exacted retribution for the attack on Thessar."

The Ar-King had put his oldest son in command, perhaps thinking that the conquest would bring glory with relatively little risk. Under pretense of surrender, Tsorreh's stepson Shorrenon, heir to the Meklavaran throne, had made a desperate attempt to take the Gelonian prince with him into death. Thessar had survived.

"It was not safe for those of us . . . to remain in the city." Sandaron broke off at the approach of a shepherd whistling to his dogs as he strode away from Silon.

As they passed the road leading to the Lady temple, greasy billows drifted up from the compound, as if the fires still smoldered fitfully. Scorpion banners hung from the walls. There was no sign of Bynthos, and Tsorreh wondered how he had fared. He had fought well at the Aidon pier, so his time as a monk had not erased the skills of a seafaring captain.

Sandaron and Tsorreh entered Silon through one of the poorer-looking gates, where Sandaron paid a nominal entry tax. As he counted the coins, the clerk glanced nervously in the direction of the smoke. A handful of people, bent under heavy sacks, stood in line inside the gate. They scurried back as a half-dozen armed men, mounted on onagers, pushed their way through the gates and onto the road leading to the Lady temple.

Silon was much smaller than Aidon and lacked that city's great hills. It was laid out in haphazard fashion, with narrow, twisting streets. Tsorreh peered at the livestock pens and warehouses, the taverns, the corner shrines to gods she'd never heard of in Aidon. Sandaron sold the donkey at one of the stables and then distributed the donkey's packs between them.

"It's not far now," he said as he stopped to dispose of several items of clothing and gear. Some he offered at shops, but others he gave to beggars. Each time Sandaron exchanged a few words with a shopkeeper or tavern owner, he came away looking grimmer. "The situation isn't good. What we saw at the gate is happening all over the city. People are on the edge of panic. The city masters are doing their best to keep things calm, but they don't have enough guards to deal with the fighting at the Lady temple and also secure the city's borders. Passage on a boat will be hard to find."

"We have come this far," Tsorreh answered, trying to keep her voice light. "We got past the fugitives, and then the soldiers were called back to Silon. Nobody stopped us sneaking past the temple, and we made it through the gates. Surely we are destined for drowning."

Gray laughed, and the tension in his features lifted. "We will try the wharves, then, and see what they have to offer us."

Sandaron and Tsorreh arrived at the waterfront just as a small contingent of city guards were setting up barricades across the principal piers. One of the guards shouted that no boats were to take on passengers. The people at the barricade pressed forward, and from the riverside, others cursed and cried out their protests. Tsorreh remembered other crowds back in Aidon, their quicksilver shifts of mood, the sudden heat, the madness hanging in the air like an invisible pall.

And a sense beyond sight or hearing of long, jointed limbs with claws, reaching across the sky . . .

"Tsorreh?" Sandaron had taken her arm and now bent toward her. "Are you unwell?"

Tsorreh was shivering so hard that only his firm grip on her arm kept her from falling. "A moment of dizziness, no more. It will pass."

"Lady Amber, do not lie to me. What you once carried still exerts its influence . . . its protection. I too sense something hanging over the city, perhaps over all of Gelon. A shadow, a swarm. I think it has lain quiet for a time, but no longer."

"We must leave Gelon." She turned to look him full in the face.

"Aye, if I have to steal a boat to do so. Our best course is downriver. Rivermen often tie up there, beyond the notice of the wharfmaster's agents."

They cut back toward the river, where they followed the path used by barge oxen. The way was little more than a ditch, wide enough for two oxen to walk abreast, and often caked with dung. Several times, they met teams drawing their boats upriver. Well beyond the city, they passed piers shaded by willowy, water-loving trees, but saw no boats. Toward the end of the day, Tsorreh felt like one of the barge oxen. She was stronger than when she'd left Aidon, but the dangers of reaching Silon had drained her.

In the growing dark, they emerged from the ox-ditch to a stretch of flat land. A small tributary fed into the Serpan and on its near side, a light flickered. Tsorreh blinked, trying to convince herself it was really there. A short distance further, she made out the shape of a boat. Its prow had been pulled up on the bank. A man stood beside it, holding a lantern. At their approach, he lifted it. "Took you two long enough."

Tsorreh could not mistake that voice, that stocky build. That grin. It was Bynthos.

She rushed forward, the pack thumping against her spine. Mud squelched under her feet. "What are you doing here?"

"Providing thee with a boat, my lady. It seems thee and thy friend Gray have need of one."

"This will take some explaining," Sandaron said dryly.

"Sail first, talk later."

Tsorreh felt a prickly chill over her skin. Bynthos would not have abandoned the Silon temple, not as long as there was any hope of salvaging it. "What happened?"

In the gloom, his face tightened.

"I am sorry." She wanted to say more, to promise an end to such atrocities. But she could not in honesty do so.

Bynthos recovered himself. "The night won't last forever."

Tsorreh pushed the boat into the river, laboring alongside the men. The ooze, dank and odorous, clung to the craft so that at first it was like trying to shift a wall of mud. Then, capriciously, the sodden ground released its hold and the boat floated free. Panting, she splashed after it. Sandaron grabbed her around the waist and lifted her over the side. She landed beside a pile of cloth sacks. The boat smelled of fish and rope and riverweed. It rocked as Sandaron heaved himself over the side. Bynthos followed a moment later.

Bynthos guided the boat to the center of the river, navigating by the currents. Remembering her near-drowning and the sheer power of the rushing water, Tsorreh crouched lower in the boat and held onto the sides so tightly her knuckles hurt. The boat rocked sickeningly. Sandaron was doing something to help Bynthos, but she could not tell what. She could barely focus on the planking a few feet from her, growing dimmer with the last fading of the light. Although she knew it was irrational, she imagined the darkness of the night river swallowing them up, drawing them *down down down*, sucking the air from their lungs and the warmth from their flesh. And this time, there would be no water spirits to save her. They had answered the *te-alvar's* call, not her own—

"Lady Amber?" Sandaron bent close to her. His breath touched her face.

"It's nothing. I'm not accustomed to boats, that's all."

"I think it's rather the river that distresses thee," Bynthos put in, "and not this sound craft. See how merrily she rides in the water? The current carries us without effort."

It was true. Tsorreh could feel the change, the lightness in the boat's motion. She sat up and inhaled the wind, moist and clean.

"There now, get some rest. I'll take first shift," Bynthos said.

The moon had risen, reflecting off the river's surface like a thousand streams of silver. Bynthos himself was a shadow against that brightness as he settled into his post. He seemed easy and contented on the water. Tsorreh tried to find comfort against her own fear by watching him.

Sandaron slid down to rest against the side of the boat opposite from Tsorreh. He placed his sword across his thighs. "We should sleep while we can."

Tsorreh curled up on the softest of the sacks. Now that she was actually lying down, her body throbbed with weariness. The boat rocked and the river sang to itself. As soon as Tsorreh closed her eyes, the river reached for her with invisible fingers. Her thoughts coursed together like the currents that carried her. She wasn't fully awake, nor was she dreaming. Beneath the wooden bottom of the boat, depths stretched dark and cold and vast. She sensed the river in all its power flowing ... joining other waters ... Something stirred in those abyssal plains, lightless and ancient ...

She jerked upright. Her heart yammered against her ribs. The river wind blew cold across her face. Trembling shook her. It must be due to her own exhaustion from the days of running.

"Can't sleep?" Sandaron's voice was velvet in the river-dark.

Tsorreh was on the edge of denying that anything was

wrong, then stopped herself. Sandaron would know if she lied to him.

He shifted, wrapping her in his arms. The warmth from his body seeped into her like perfume, like twilight. "Better now?"

"A little." She turned so that her cheek rested against his chest. His heartbeat was steady and strong. Breath whispered through his lungs. Her own pulse slowed to his.

"My soul longs for thee," he sang the words from the *Te-Ketav* in his rich baritone.

> *"As a gazelle in the wilderness,*
> *As an eagle in the heights,*
> *As a willow in the snow."*

She drifted through the borderlands of sleep, as the boat glided down the moonswept river, as the river melted into the sea. She could not remember when she had been held like this, when a man's song had hummed through her bones like streams of gold.

Drowsiness lapped at her, tinged with awareness of Sandaron's strength, the heat of his body. His breath touched her hair and she felt it shiver like a cascade through her skin, her breasts, her belly, between her thighs. She wondered what would happen if she tipped her head back and pulled his face down to her. What his hair would feel like between her fingers . . . his lips on hers . . .

Let it go, she told herself with a tinge of regret. *Such thoughts are not for you.* Such foolishness it would be, such hopeless delight. What could come of it but heartache? Her life had never belonged to her and never would.

Chapter Eleven

BATHED in the bright Isarran sun, Tsorreh rested her elbows on the stone balcony outside her quarters in the royal palace. Upon her arrival in Durinthe two months ago, she had been given a suite of spacious chambers, but she was not yet accustomed to such splendor. Brilliantly hued frescoes covered the walls, so unlike the softer Meklavaran colors and hangings, or even the whitened walls of Jaxar's mansion.

I am a bird in a jeweled cage.

After the first days, she had made a number of attempts to interest her kinsman, King Ulleos of the House of Rynthos, in an alliance, but each time he'd deflected her. He refused to discuss Isarran help for the liberation of Meklavar. She had not yet recovered enough from her ordeal, he'd say, meaning that military and political matters were best left to men. Beyond his surprised but courteous welcome, he had no idea what to do with her. She was too well placed in the royal lineage to be ignored, and too outspoken and stubborn to adapt herself to the perfumed customs of the court. She wanted to discuss strategy against Gelon, to analyze news of the Azkhantian war and piracy on the Denariyan seas. Ladies of the Isarran court did not concern themselves with such things. She had yet to find a way to change his mind.

Somewhere in the vast, interconnected maze of court-yards, Sandaron was training with the Isarran officers. Ulleos had thanked him for escorting Tsorreh, then quietly dismissed him as yet another Meklavaran exile, a person of no standing or importance. Tsorreh could not fault Sandaron for bowing humbly and then finding ways to make himself useful. She wished she could disguise herself and join him on the training field. Anything would be better than day after day of gilded idleness.

As for Bynthos, he spent his days at the docks. Each time they spoke, Tsorreh expected he would tell her he had found work on a ship bound for the Mearas or the spice lands of Denariya, but so far that had not happened.

Tsorreh rubbed her arms, feeling the dryness of her skin. If she complained, a flock of maids would coax her into yet another milk bath and rub her body with sweet almond oil. The first such bath had been heavenly, the third tedious, the tenth unendurable.

She could not continue like this, or she would go mad. If Ulleos would not aid her, then she must find allies elsewhere. Yet if she forced a confrontation with her cousin and revealed her intention of leaving his court, he might make her even more of a prisoner than she was already. It had been a mistake to come here instead of returning to Meklavar, but she could not have known that at the time.

Behind her, slippered feet whispered on the wooden floor. She turned to the wide, opened doors. Faranneh, one of the senior attendants and herself a noble lady of the House of Gamaroth, bowed. "My lady, His Majesty requests your presence before dinner."

Tsorreh arranged her features into a pleasant smile. "I am at my cousin's disposal." Doubtless, she would be expected to present herself painted and plumed, swathed in linen and pearls and gold embroidery. With a stifled sigh, she resigned herself.

"What is the occasion, do you know?" At least, there might be music.

"I believe the ambassador from Azkhantia has returned."

Azkhantia? Ulleos had sent an embassy to forge an alliance between Isarre and the horsemen of the steppe. That would be greatly to Isarre's advantage, whereas a similar pact with Meklavar would pose considerable risk. Regardless of the outcome of the Azkhantian negotiations, Tsorreh might learn something of value to her own cause.

"What is his name? How soon can I meet him?" Tsorreh hurried to the clothing chest. The interior smelled of sandalwood and citrus. She lifted out the plainest of the gowns, cream-colored linen worn over a skirt of a slightly darker hue, embroidered in copper-thread along the neckline. "Will this do?"

"Ah, my lady!" Faranneh shook her head to hide her smile. "All the entertainments of the court cannot please you half so much as a political debate. And the gown will do very nicely with the gold and amber pectoral." She went to get the jewel chest.

"The ambassador's name?" Tsorreh called, pulling off her ordinary dress.

"Leanthos. I don't know much about him, other than the obscurity of his family and the length of his absence. Will that appease your curiosity for the moment, so we can return to the matter of your dress?" Faranneh lifted out the heavy pectoral with its ovals of polished amber.

"Why should it surprise anyone that I am more interested in the fate of my country than the latest fashion in sleeves?" Tsorreh said. "I will have more than a few questions for this ambassador."

"My lady, you must not draw such untoward attention to yourself! I know it is difficult for you, having been a prisoner in Gelon for so long, but you must try—"

"Enough! I can dress myself perfectly well. As for the pectoral, I would rather not distract the ambassador with all that glitter. I want him to answer my questions, not admire my breasts."

"But—"

"I promise I will not embarrass myself. I was *te-ravah* in Meklavar and I know how to behave. Also, I would like it very much if Sandaron were present, for I value his judgment. Would you be so kind as to arrange it or must I speak to my cousin the King?"

"No, no, I will inform the chief councilor of your wish." Faranneh backed away before Tsorreh could issue any more outrageous demands, replaced the pectoral in the jewel case, and scurried from the room.

With spirits lightened, Tsorreh slipped into the gown. Faranneh would have suggested matching brocade slippers, but after everything she had been through, Tsorreh refused to wear anything on her feet that was not both comfortable and durable, in this case low boots of suede.

Tsorreh inspected her image in the polished steel mirror. Her hair, arranged into seven plaits and tied together, was tidy enough. The Isarran sun had darkened her skin, but rest and good food had softened the curves of her cheekbones. She thought of Sandaron and glanced at the pot of kohl, then pushed it away.

She found Faranneh waiting outside the door, along with two attendants. They formed a procession down the broad, tiled steps and across one of the many courtyards to the main part of the palace. Tsorreh had to moderate her pace to allow the ladies in their flimsy sandals to keep up.

The royal court chamber was large and airy, its walls covered with gilded mosaics. The king's chair, carved of a grayhued wood set with mother-of-pearl, occupied its usual place beneath a skylight at the far end. Isarran kings did not customarily hold forth from a raised dais.

The most important courtiers and advisors had already entered. Many of them were related to Tsorreh, either through her mother's family, Arandel, or the king's own House of Rynthos. She recognized a senior military advisor and two naval officers, and silently vowed that this time, she would not keep silent on the matter of Meklavaran independence.

Sandaron stood at the door, talking with the guards. His skin was still flushed from exercise in the heat, but his hair had been slicked back, as if he had dunked his entire head in the washing basin. Tsorreh suspected from the friendly manner of the guards that most of them had sparred with him and respected him.

Ulleos entered a short time later, received the traditional honors, and seated himself. Two of his personal bodyguards took up their positions to either side. The Isarran king was a rangy, angular man, ruddy-haired like many of his nation, his beard shot with white. Years of worry had incised deep lines between his jutting eyebrows. He wore a three-quarters-length robe of fine linen. Because Isarre was formally at war with Gelon, he went armed with a scabbarded two-handed sword as well as the usual dagger. His only ornament was a single pearl threaded on gold wire through one earlobe.

At the king's gesture, Tsorreh came forward and settled herself on a stool to one side. Although it had taken some diplomatic maneuvering to convince him of her interest in court proceedings, there had been no question about her right to attend, as a member of a royal Isarran House.

"Well then," Ulleos said to his chief councilor, a dignified Rynthos lord named Rhessan, "let us welcome home our ambassador and hear of his adventures among the warriors of the steppe."

There was a stir at the far end of the room as the guards opened the doors. Tsorreh's line of sight was blocked by the crowd, so that at first she could not see the men who entered. Offering civilities, the courtiers drew back to let them pass. First came a palace officer, sword held at a ceremonial angle. The white-haired man who followed must surely be the ambassador, he looked so travel-weary. That was hardly surprising if he had journeyed all the way to Azkhantia and back. He moved as if his knees pained him. There was a second man at his shoulder, one who carried himself with the taut alertness of an assassin. Tsorreh had seen that same coiled vigilance in Cinath's Elite Corps. A pace or two behind them, dressed also in plain, trail-worn clothing—

Tsorreh noticed first the red-blond hair, caught back in a knot, the skin freckled from sun and roughened by wind . . . those alert, pale-green eyes. No, it was not possible. *Danar, here?*

"A Gelon!" someone cried. One of the king's guards placed his hand on the hilt of his sword. Rhessan gestured for the guard to hold where he was. Ulleos lifted one finger and a quartet of guards moved deftly into position. The ambassador was saying something, bowing low to the king.

Danar jerked to a halt. He stared at Tsorreh. Blood

drained from his face, leaving his skin milk-pale beneath his freckles. His mouth dropped open. He looked, Tsorreh thought, as if he had seen a ghost. For all he knew, that's what she was.

If Danar was here in Durinthe, *where was Zevaron?*

The ambassador concluded his salutation and Ulleos responded with a speech of welcome. When Leanthos gestured Danar forward, the muted commotion died down. Everyone wanted to hear what this foreigner had to say. Still looking dazed, Danar managed a deep bow. Tsorreh recognized the gesture as the greeting of a noble to one of equal rank but greater age.

"I present to you Danar of Aidon, son of the Lord Jaxar and nephew to Cinath-Ar-Gelon," Leanthos said. "He has come to make a treaty with Isarre." Murmurs of amazement and skepticism rustled through the chamber.

"We will consider his proposal presently," Ulleos said. "What of your mission, Leanthos? What of the Azkhantians? Where are *they* and *their* offers of help?"

Leanthos shook his head. His thin shoulders sagged. Ulleos did not look greatly disappointed. An Azkhantian alliance would have been an extraordinary feat of diplomacy. The horse people were notoriously insular and had never concerned themselves with troubles far away. They had problems enough of their own, defending their lands against repeated Gelonian incursions.

In the pause, the king's councilors began whispering among themselves again. "How dare a Gelon come among us?"

"He looks innocent enough, but that's just what a spy would do . . . gain the ambassador's trust, get close to the King . . . lure us into foolhardy actions on the basis of lies!"

"Spy . . . or assassin?"

"How do we know he is who he says he is!" another put in. "Out there on the steppe, he could have made up any story he wished and how would Ambassador Leanthos determine the truth?"

Tsorreh did not think Ulleos would execute Danar out of hand, not without investigating his story. His next command, she was sure, would be to lock Danar away in an airless, oven-hot cell until a decision could be reached.

"If I may, cousin," Tsorreh spoke up. "I spent four years in Aidon in the house of Cinath's own brother, Jaxar. This is indeed his son. More than that, he holds no favor in his uncle's eyes."

Zevaron! howled through the back of her mind. *What has become of my son?*

"Yet it cannot be mere chance that in a land as vast as the Azkhantian steppe, the very Gelonian noble known to you encountered my own ambassador," Ulleos said dryly.

"Is it any stranger than my sitting here now?"

"I suppose not. Well, let this Gelon approach."

Danar came forward, halting a good distance from the king's chair. He was still very pale, but if he trembled, Tsorreh could not see it. He bowed again, then lowered himself to kneeling. By his act of vulnerability, he commanded the attention of the assembly.

"I present myself to you, O King. As my friend Leanthos said, I am Danar son of Jaxar of Gelon. I am willing to swear by any god you name that I mean no harm to any person in Isarre. I have come here of my own will to make common purpose with you. The vainglorious ambitions of Ar-Cinath-Gelon, whom I am ashamed to call uncle, threatens people of good will everywhere."

As Danar spoke, his voice gained in strength and authority. The chamber had stilled. "You ask what I said to Leanthos, back at the Azkhantian *khural*, when he sought my death? I said to him what I say to you now, O King. Our nations should not be enemies, but allies and trading partners. By the breath of my soul, I pledge myself to restore Gelon to a nation worthy of the blessings of its gods, a nation of justice, of learning and prosperity. A nation at peace with its neighbors."

"How do you propose to fulfill this extraordinary vow?" Ulleos asked in the astonished pause that followed.

"By becoming Ar-King myself. My ancestors chose their rulers from the royal houses on the basis of merit, not ambition and deceit. Loyalty must be earned as well as rendered, and Cinath has betrayed the allegiance I once owed him. Against all the bonds of blood and honor, he has sought my death and that of my father, his own brother. It is by his vicious will that I am outlawed, sent into exile. I have no love for him, only for my people."

Ulleos frowned. "You would have us pour out our own blood for your throne? Did you ask the same of the Az-khantian chiefs?"

"I did, and they refused me," Danar admitted with an engaging grin.

Ulleos threw his head back and laughed. "Well, you do not lack in candor."

"Only humility, Your Majesty. It is the fault of my education, no doubt."

"We will hear your entire story in good time, Danar son of Jaxar, Prince of Gelon. Meanwhile, be as our guest, but do not lay your hand to any weapon or venture where you should not, or all your fine words will not save you."

Danar got to his feet and bowed again. Only then did he look directly at Tsorreh. She could not read his expression.

Ulleos gave a few brief commands to dismiss the audience, and for his advisors to meet shortly in council to hear the entire story.

"As for you, cousin," Ulleos said to Tsorreh, "you had best come along. I do not want to imagine what sort of trouble you will get into, left to yourself, and what other secrets you have been hiding." He rose, sending the court into a flurry of bowing, and swept from the room.

Tsorreh pushed her way through the crowd to Danar. No one moved to stop her.

Danar still bore a look of stunned incomprehension. "You're alive. How is this possible?"

"Lycian's poison was not as effective as she intended."

He flushed, swallowing hard. "She visited you in prison."

The assembly was breaking up, courtiers milling in different directions. Two of the king's guards remained nearby, still watchful.

"Gods." Danar lowered his voice. "If only Zevaron—he believed you were truly dead this time. It almost broke him. It *did* break him."

"Tell me where he is!"

"He was alive and well when I left him—"

"*Where?*"

A courtier, one of the Rynthos cousins, bumped Tsorreh from behind, then apologized effusively before bowing on his way.

"In Azkhantia. He—"

Tsorreh noticed that Rhessan was watching her and Danar with an intent expression. She cut Danar off. "This is no place to talk." She tried to compose herself as Danar was escorted away from her and back through the public doors.

Zevaron was safe, that was all that mattered. But why had he stayed in the steppe and not come to Isarre with Danar?

A short time later, Tsorreh took her place in the king's council chamber. The central table was a work of art, cedar polished to a high gloss and inset with a map of the known world in mother-of-pearl, ebony, and rosewood, with accents of serpentine and turquoise-bright faïence. She traced the outlines of the southern Firelands with one fingertip and thought how easy it was to destroy things of beauty.

Ulleos sat at one end of the table, flanked by Rhessan and his closest advisors, most of them Rynthos kinsmen. Tsorreh and lesser councilors were ranged to either side, with Danar and Leanthos at the far end. Two armed guards, the same who had watched Danar so closely in the court chamber, stood nearby.

Leanthos detailed his journey in a polished, stylized manner. He was clearly accustomed to giving flowery speeches. Tsorreh did not suspect him of outright deceit, only of shading the facts to his own benefit. Adventures could be narrated in many ways, from the most ordinary happenings to a progression of increasingly astonishing events. Self-aggrandizement seemed to be the rule everywhere.

Leanthos and his assistant, Phannus, had made their way to the Azkhantian border, evaded Gelonian patrols, and approached the nearest clan. They'd presented their case for an alliance, but the chieftain had insisted that no one clan could act alone in such an important matter, and had sent them on to the yearly Gathering. When Leanthos described how the nomads attacked and destroyed a Gelonian outpost, Tsorreh noted not only his respect for their fighting prowess, but his regret at not having enlisted their help.

The other incident of note along the trail was the encounter with Danar and Zevaron. The Azkhantian leader, a woman, had enforced a truce until they arrived at the *khural-lak*, the place of summer Gathering, where the inevitable confrontation between Isarran ambassador and Gelonian exile took place. Danar would have another version of the story, she was sure, along with Zevaron's part in it, but the outcome was that Leanthos had become convinced of Danar's sincerity. When the Azkhantian chieftains refused an alliance with Isarre, Danar had departed for Durinthe with the ambassador.

It had taken them longer than expected to make the return journey. The Gelonian outpost had been but a small part of a concerted assault upon the steppe. Gelon was pushing hard toward the north and east, so Leanthos and his party had been forced to detour to the south, toward Meklavar. Gelon was building ports on both sides of the Sea of Desolation. Tsorreh was puzzled, for she had been taught that those waters were poisonous, an enduring aftermath of the battle between Khored of Blessed Memory and the armies of Fire and Ice. This was apparently not the case, or else the Gelon feared the displeasure of the Ar King more than they feared the old legends.

Throughout the recitation, Ulleos listened intently, elbows on the table, chin resting in one palm. He let Leanthos spin out his tale, his only reaction being the occasional narrowing of his eyes. When Leanthos had finished, he asked Danar, "What can you add to this?"

"When I left Aidon, the situation for my father was very bad," Danar answered. "There were accusations of treason and then arrests. We thought that Lady Tsorreh had died in prison."

"I have heard that part of her story." Ulleos glanced at Tsorreh. In his eyes, she read the unvoiced question of how she had escaped.

"My father feared for my life," Danar went on, "and sent me from the city with Zevaron—Lady Tsorreh's son—as my bodyguard, and so we came to Azkhantia. One of the tribes brought a very strange object to the Gathering—a stone-drake like those described in Father's books. To the nomads, it was taboo. They made everyone who touched it undergo ritual purification."

Danar's tone suggested his disbelief in such superstitious customs. "It meant something more to Zevaron. He became obsessed with it, with finding out where it had come from. He convinced the chieftains to let him investigate, and Shannivar—the woman who led the Golden Eagle party— went with him. The shamans were full of prophecies and warnings, none of which Zevaron heeded. In the end, they decided the stone-drake carried a curse and so Zevaron would take the curse away with him."

Tsorreh's heart hammered in her throat. "Where did he go?"

"North and east, to the mountains up there."

The mountains where the comet crashed to earth. According-ing to scripture, the physical prison of Fire and Ice. Her vision went pale.

Ulleos turned to Tsorreh and said, not unkindly, "Your son will be well enough. He has a native guide and the Az-khantians know how to survive on the steppe."

She nodded, unable to speak. There was nothing she could do for Zevaron except to entrust him to the Source of All Blessings, the wisdom of the *te-alvar*, and his own luck.

The king's advisors proceeded to an interrogation of their own. The military men wanted details of the Gelonian incursions and the fighting strategies of the Azkhantian horse people.

"This news presents us with an unanticipated opportunity," Ulleos said. "My agents have reported that the garrisoning of Gatacinne has recently been reduced. Cinath's attention turns elsewhere. He seems to not have learned the lessons of his ancestors—that it is impossible to conquer the steppe. He will pour out the blood of Gelon in the attempt. And we may seize the chance to take back Gatacinne."

Ulleos gestured, indicating dismissal of everyone except a few of his councilors. Tsorreh asked his leave for a private interview with Danar. Sandaron, as her countryman, would act as her escort. She let a mother's natural concern, her hunger for word of her son, flavor her plea. Ulleos agreed, provided Danar remained under armed guard through the palace.

Chapter Twelve

FARANNEH was scandalized that Tsorreh intended to hold a private audience with two men, one of them not even remotely her kin.

"It is for me alone to determine my chaperonage," Tsorreh reminded the waiting-lady. "I appreciate that you speak from concern for my reputation, but I have traveled with one of these men and lived in the same household as the other. They are known to me. Moreover, I am not some sheltered virgin whose only value is her chastity. I am the *teravah* of Meklavar, and if I say I will meet with these two men on matters of my country's welfare—or a hundred men, all armed to the teeth and mounted on giant crimson snakes—then *no one* has the authority to prevent me!"

Faranneh, having been chastised twice in the same day, withdrew without further comment. A short time later, Sandaron presented himself at Tsorreh's quarters. Danar's guards looked uneasy but did not protest when she instructed them to remain outside.

"Let's sit on the balcony," Tsorreh said. "If we speak quietly, I do not think we can be overheard."

Once they were settled on chairs carried from the sitting room, she confronted Danar directly. "Tell me about

Zevaron—everything you can remember since you left me in the Temple of Ir-Pilant."

She sensed Sandaron's understanding of her emphasis on the word, *everything*. How had Zevaron, as unprepared and ignorant as she had been, received the *te-alvar*? She wanted to know if he had understood what was happening to him. What exactly did he seek in the North, and had the petal gem prompted him to remain in Azkhantia? Zevaron might have said nothing about the *te-alvar*, but Danar was a good observer, well trained by his scientist father, and might have noticed significant details without understanding them.

"You know what it was like just before your arrest." Danar's green eyes darkened like the sea under a clouded sky. "Cinath suspected everyone, even his own family, *especially* his own family." Tsorreh nodded. "Then we received word of your death. Zevaron, he—when he saw your body, he went mad, I think. He hates Cinath more than I thought possible, and over the years my uncle has made many enemies."

Regret stung Tsorreh, that she had not found a way to let Zevaron know she still lived.

Sandaron stirred, the subtle lifting of his chest in breath, and she felt a pulse of warmth from him. He, at least, did not blame her. The story was not yet over, and these sorrows were part of a greater tale. The tightness in her throat eased. *Teharod . . . wisdom.*

"I still don't understand," Danar said. "How could Zevaron have been mistaken about your death? Surely, if there were even a whisper of breath in your body, he would have noticed, he was so desperate."

Tsorreh had no memory of that visit or of anything between when she lost consciousness in the cell and when she found herself drowning in the Serpan River.

"Some potions bring the victim to the brink of death," Sandaron commented. "The life force sinks so low that breathing and pulse become undetectable. And even so"—cutting off Danar's protest—"we may never understand why one person succumbs and another does not. Perhaps the power of the river revived Lady Tsorreh when no ordinary means could."

"I do not remember much of that time," Tsorreh admitted. "The monks of the Lady of Mercy pulled me from the river. I was too weak and confused to leave their compound for several days. But that is behind us now. Tell me what happened next."

"Zevaron and I fled Aidon. My father insisted."

"Lord Jaxar—he was well—and still at liberty?" *Not imprisoned in a dank, noisome hole as I was,* she prayed, *for that would mean death for a man in his poor health.*

Danar looked away, his mouth tight. "He was alive, but for how much longer I cannot say. His strength declined rapidly without your care. Now he has lost both of us and is shut up with"—his voice quavered on the edge of fury—"with my stepmother and her incessant nattering about Qr."

Tsorreh and Sandaron exchanged glances.

"God of Forgotten Hopes, may my father never learn what she did!"

Tsorreh paused, letting him recover before pressing on. "What happened then?"

"We escaped from Aidon. It wasn't easy—we had to fight our way out. Zevaron was wounded and was very sick for a time. Delirious, raving all kinds of nonsense. From the wound going bad."

From the te-alvar *waking in him, as it did in me.*

Tsorreh permitted herself another quick look at Sandaron. She had found someone who in some measure shared her experience. She was not alone.

"It was fortunate for Zevaron," Sandaron observed, "that he had a friend to help him."

"What else could I do?" Danar looked discomfited by the praise. "Leave him to die or be captured by my uncle's men? I would not treat an enemy that way, and Zevaron had saved my life more than once already. Perhaps we were not friends at that time, but we became so."

Tsorreh found her voice again. "Nevertheless, I thank you. What then?"

"Isarre made the most sense as a destination. I remembered you had kin here and I thought it would be the safest place for Zevaron. You must understand that at the time, he was in no condition to decide. I did the best I could for both of us. Once Zevaron was able to ride, we headed overland, but we wandered too far into Azkhantian territory. Shannivar and her party found us. That was right after they'd destroyed a Gelonian outpost and they were quite naturally wary of strangers."

"This Azkhantian woman, this Shannivar," Tsorreh said. "You've mentioned her before. I know so little about those people, only their success in resisting Gelon. So their women ride to war, as well?"

Danar grinned. "Shannivar does."

"The steppe nomads are horse people and archers," Sandaron put in. "Except for sword fighting, a skillful woman can hold her own with the men. They are trained from childhood and boast that they can ride before they can walk."

Tsorreh thought that unlikely, but did not say so.

"She's not the only warrior woman among them," Danar added, "but I think she must be one of the best. Certainly, no one rides better. She has this black horse—I swear he has wings, the way he flies over the earth. She and Zevaron have a—a bond. Perhaps I should not say so, except to let you know he is not without friends."

Tsorreh considered the possibility of a liaison between the heir to Meklavar and a nomad woman. The courtiers would be outraged, as would her Isarran relations. Let them sputter and groan! Zevaron would never be happy with a timid wife. A woman who could ride and shoot and swing a sword, would she not be the ideal mate in these desperate times?

"When Zevaron saw the stone-drake, he determined to seek its source?" Sandaron interrupted her musings.

"What exactly is a stone-drake?" Tsorreh asked.

"It's a rock formation, the size and approximate shape of man but with the features of a lizard." Danar's face lit up with the enthusiasm Tsorreh remembered well. "The scholars of Borrenth Springs say they are the result of lightning striking a salamander as it rests upon volcanic rock."

Laughing, Tsorreh raised her hands. "You truly are your father's son."

"How can I not be curious about such wonderful things? At any rate, most of the clansmen regarded the stone-drake with suspicion, but not Zevaron. I've never seen a man so stubborn. He wouldn't leave it alone, even when the shamans placed it under taboo. They put him through the purification rites not once but *twice*. He said the stone-drake was a sign of something dangerous up north. He insisted the only way to be sure was to go there himself."

Did Zevaron have any idea how foolhardy it was to venture into such a place? Surely the *te-alvar* would have warned him. *Or perhaps he went at its command.*

"The chieftains didn't believe him," Danar said, "but they were just as happy to have him take away the curse. Especially after the prophecy."

In the uncomfortable silence that followed, Tsorreh forced her dry lips to move. "What prophecy?"

Danar's brows drew together. "I don't remember it all, only this part:

> *"When the heir to gold is drowned,*
> *He returns with treasure.*
> *When the heir to light goes to the mountain,*
> *He will not return."*

Tsorreh understood all too well who the *"heir to the light"* was. *"The mountain"* must be where the white star—the comet—had crashed. *Source of All Blessings, protect him!*

Sandaron grasped Tsorreh's hand. His fingers laced with hers, tightened. Held.

"But it's all nonsense, isn't it?" Danar said. "Metaphor and folklore? How can a drowned man return anywhere, with or without treasure?"

"Many things can affect the interpretation of prophecy," Sandaron replied. "We live in a time when the old certainties no longer hold," meaning that she, Tsorreh, had survived the transfer of the *te-alvar* and still lived. Not only that, she still bore lingering traces of its power.

What else might be possible?

A morsel of hope flickered to life in Tsorreh's mind. Zevaron was not alone. This warrior woman of the steppe, this

Shannivar, had gone with him. Perhaps the situation was not so dire, after all.

They talked longer as Danar recalled things Zevaron had said, the details of their journey, the fighting ways of the Azkhantians, and the excellence of their horses. He described how Leanthos had issued a formal challenge before the chieftains, how Zevaron had stepped in when Phannus took his master's place in the combat circle, and how Zevaron had fought the assassin to a standstill. Then Leanthos had had to face Danar by himself.

"Leanthos must have been terrified at the prospect of doing his own fighting," Sandaron said dryly.

"I could have killed him," Danar said, "but what would that have accomplished? You've seen Leanthos. It would have been outright murder. The only way to achieve anything of lasting value—to open communication—was to refuse. I think that decision, more than all my fine speeches, convinced him that I meant what I said."

Tsorreh had no doubt of Zevaron's fighting skill, a combination of his early training and his years on a Denariyan pirate ship. Now she felt a dawning respect for the young man before her, who chose not to use his strength against a weaker man. What might Gelon become under such a leader? Could he put an end to constant warfare, purge his country of the Scorpion god's influence, perhaps even give the conquered territories back their freedom?

Reluctantly, Tsorreh drew the conversation to a close. She wanted to know more, but Danar's guards could not be kept waiting in the hallway indefinitely. They would already have plenty to report on the length and secrecy of this audience.

After dinner, Tsorreh delayed returning to her own chambers and the ministrations of her ladies. Instead, she sought the gardens, where she wandered along the mirrored pools through the sweetness of the night-blooming *rohallis*. She lowered herself on a marble bench in one of the larger courtyards. Light lingered like a film of mist along the western roofline. She sighed, remembering evenings atop Jaxar's house, taking notes for him as he studied the heavens, discussing the nature of celestial bodies and the laws governing their movement. Together they had watched the white star grow from the faintest smudge to a streak of brilliance, until it disappeared to the northeast, in the direction of Azkhantia.

We thought the worst had happened when Meklavar fell. The world is a larger and more perilous place than we ever imagined.

Footsteps broke her reverie. Sandaron sat on the bench beside her. She ached at his nearness. They were not private people, free to follow the yearnings of their hearts, but guardians of something far greater. At least, one of them was.

After a time, Sandaron said, "He is no ordinary man, your son."

"I worry for him, now more than ever." Words spilled out, hot and raw with anxiety too long suppressed. "What Danar said—the northern mountains—the prophecy—"

"Zevaron is protected, even as you were. If the evil woman's poison could not end your life when you had only the traces of power, how much stronger must your son be?"

"He bears the heart of the Shield, yes. Can it alone defeat a power great enough to snatch a comet from the night sky and send it crashing to earth? Khored assembled the seven petals because *all* of them were needed—and now my son goes to the enemy with but a single one! Do you not see—this stone-drake Danar spoke of—an unnatural thing of fire and earth—it is like the creatures described in the *Te-Ketav*, in the *Book of Khored*? Fire and Ice is rebuilding its armies."

"That is my thought as well." Sandaron moved in the moon-kissed dark, turning to face her. The warmth of his body caressed her skin.

"Consider Danar's prophecy," he said. "The heir to light—to Meklavar—has indeed gone to the north. It is time for the *te-ravah* to return to her people. Not to lead a hopeless and bloody insurrection. Not to waste her strength in a worldly struggle that neither side can win. To gather together what has been dispersed."

To reassemble the Shield.

But how, when the keeper of its heart was so far away, venturing into the very stronghold of the enemy? *What better time,* came the answer, and she could not be sure if the voice was her own, or Sandaron's, or that of some deeper, vaster intelligence, *to resurrect the powers of Light?*

She did not know if she had the power in herself and in the lingering traces of the *te-alvar* to accomplish such a task. She could not do it alone. But she was not alone.

"You are Teharod, the fifth gem." She began to count on her fingers. Her breath steadied with each phrase. "And there is Zevaron. I believe that the Cassarod gem is still in that family, most likely with the older son, Ganneron. I met the younger brother in Aidon and there was no trace of its presence in him."

Sandaron nodded. "The *alvara* of Dovereth and Shebu'od were still in Meklavar when I left. Shebu'od had passed to a collateral lineage and a few of them intermarried with my cousin's family. What became of Dovereth, I don't know."

"Just when we are in most need of its virtue of truth! All we have to do is find an honest man. Perhaps we should consult this new prophet, Iskarnon."

"I don't think it works like that, or I should be far more wise."

You are more wise than you know. You have become my anchor, my rock.

"What about Benerod, lost long ago?" She forced herself to speak. "Or Eriseth?"

"Eriseth," he repeated. "All my father knew was that the heirs had emigrated to Denariya."

For a long moment, neither said anything. Eriseth embodied steadfastness, persistence, loyalty. Eriseth would have endured, even in Denariya. As for the lost gem of Benerod, she could only pray that in time some sign of it would emerge.

The truth hung unspoken in the night air, that only another guardian stood any chance of discovering who now bore the blue gem of Eriseth. She was a guardian no longer, and a woman would be easy prey on the long route to the spice lands, to pirates, brigands, or simply desperate men who would not hesitate to take advantage of a single vulnerable traveler. Even accompanied by Sandaron, she would be a liability. He, on the other hand, could travel fast and fight hard, and he knew how to make allies anywhere. Meanwhile, someone must begin the search for those *alvara* still in Meklavar. That much she could do.

"I feel like a fool," Danar said, sighing dramatically.

"Surely not." Tsorreh speared a chunk of orange-fleshed melon. Sandaron stared into his cup of minted tea without any discernible reaction.

A week or so after Danar's arrival, the three were taking breakfast together beside the fountain in one of the garden courtyards. The air was cool and pleasant, and Faranneh had been persuaded to maintain a respectful distance.

"I came here, made all those ridiculous speeches, and have ended up a court parasite," Danar continued.

"What did you think would happen?" Tsorreh said. "You command no fighting men or ships. Your good will and promises are as much value to Ulleos as . . . well, good will and promises. It's not likely that the people of Gelon will rise up against the Ar-King when they hear you are now on friendly terms with Isarre."

Danar pushed away his untouched plate of fruit and honey-nut pastry. "I'm no good to anyone."

"Not wallowing in self-pity, you aren't," Sandaron pointed out.

Danar winced. "If you see a way I can be of use, then speak plainly. I might as well have stayed in Azkhantia."

"We do not always see things clearly, least of all our own actions," Tsorreh said.

"You have brought us information we did not have before," Sandaron pointed out. "We now know where Zevaron is."

"Danar is right about one thing," Tsorreh added. "None of us should remain here in idleness, no matter how luxurious. Least of all me."

"I thought you came here to be safe among your kins-men," Danar said.

"At first, yes. Those who are hunted need a measure of safety in which to recover. I confess I had hoped to make a military alliance to free Meklavar, but I was foolishly naïve."

"Not foolish," Sandaron said, an instant before Danar's protest.

Tsorreh smiled. "At any rate, my sojourn here is now over." She turned to Danar. "Will you come to Meklavar with me?"

Danar looked astonished. "Yes! I mean, of course. But I don't see . . . yes, I do." He smiled broadly. "Can you imag-ine the confusion at home if the royal heir were to lead a rebellion at the side of the Queen of Meklavar?"

"It would mean death for both of you." Sandaron said.

"Rest easy, that is not my intention," Tsorreh said. "But I see no purpose in either remaining here or abandoning Danar to morbid self-doubt."

Sandaron was right that a public arrival in Meklavar would be suicidal. The governor, assuming it was still old Anthelon, might not execute her and her companions, but he would certainly send Danar back to Aidon in chains.

"The effort to retake Gatacinne," she mused aloud. "Might that not divert Cinath's attention sufficiently for a small party to reach Meklavar?"

"It might, especially if that *small party* were already skilled in avoiding notice," Sandaron said.

"Land or sea?"

"Let us consider the situation." With a finger dipped in wine, Sandaron traced a rough outline of the coast on the table. "If I were Ulleos, I would wait until Isarre's land forces were in place and then lead the navy myself. Gelon still has a powerful naval presence, but the ocean is wide, with much room to maneuver. The sea route is also a shorter passage."

"Is it likely Ulleos will succeed, then?" Danar asked.

"That is the spirit in the barracks," said Sandaron. "The King would not commit his resources without a good chance of victory. He knows that if he gambles and loses,

Cinath will use Gatacinne as a base to push deep into Isarre, perhaps to Durinthe itself."

"If we wait until Gatacinne is back in Isarran hands," Danar said, "the port will be open to us. We can go by sea that far, then retrace Lady Tsorreh's path south and east across the Sand Lands. You see," he added with a grin, "I remember the tale of your escape. But I don't know how we will get a ship."

"Bynthos!" Tsorreh and Sandaron exclaimed together.

"I don't understand. Where would Bynthos find a ship if there are none to be had?" Danar said, for he had not yet met Bynthos and had no idea of the former monk's resourcefulness when it came to watercraft.

"Where would Bynthos *not* find a ship?" A smile hovered at one corner of Sandaron's mouth. "Even a small merchant vessel will suffice. You will head east, following in the wake of Ulleos and his navy. They'll clear the way for you, not only of Gelonian warships but of pirates and scavengers."

As the conversation drew to a close and their plans took shape, Tsorreh tried to sound hopeful. Inside, her heart was sore.

You, Sandaron had said. Not *we*.

PART TWO:

Danar's Leap

Chapter Thirteen

A SHIP, a trader in incense, salt, and copper, departed for Tomarziya Varya in Denariya with the next tide. With Gatacinne still in Gelonian control, the sea was the only trade route open, down the western coast of the Fever Lands and through the perilous straits called the Firelands, then north to Denariya itself. Sandaron departed without a word of farewell.

Danar dreamed of Tsorreh weeping. He knew why she wept, even though she would never admit it. He had known since the moment he had walked into the Isarran court.

He also realized that he was no longer in love with her. When she had arrived at his father's house in Aidon, she had seemed as radiant as the Star That Brings in the Day, as kind as the Kindler of Hearts, and as mysterious as Moon-Dancer. He, on the other hand, had been young and miserable, beset by his tyrannical stepmother and worries for his father's health. In truth, Tsorreh had been only a mortal woman, not half the pantheon of Gelonian goddesses, only a fellow human creature pressed almost past her limits. She had been as much in need of a friend as he.

Danar's escape from Gelon, his friendship with Zevaron, the passage through the Azkhantian steppe, and all that had happened there, had tempered him. Once he had fancied himself as a follower of the Remover of Difficulties, but the God of Forgotten Hopes might have been a more apt choice. Now he did not know what he believed. He trusted the words that flowed so easily from his mouth, words of hope and reconciliation. He trusted the impulse that had stayed his hand when Leanthos challenged him to a duel.

He trusted what he saw with his heart as well as his eyes. When Tsorreh looked at Sandaron, she glowed like an ember about to burst into flame. Whatever happened now, with Zevaron off on a hopeless quest so far away, with upheaval in Aidon and war brewing here in Isarre, Danar would always have the memory of seeing his friend happy.

The days limped by as Ulleos made his preparations to recapture Gatacinne. Soldiers drilled in the fields outside the city. Women rolled bandages and prepared healing tinctures. The land force departed, and ships were requisitioned and equipped.

At Tsorreh's request, Ulleos granted permission for her to go riding every day, with Danar as her escort. Danar thought the king was glad to have them occupied, and the exercise did both of them good. The months in Azkhantia had hardened Danar's body and increased his ease in the saddle. At first, Tsorreh was a poor rider, but she practiced with such determination that her skills rapidly improved.

Every day they rode down to the harbor. The riverwharves of Aidon were tame and colorless compared to this swath of kelp-laced sand. The sea smelled bitter and salty and urgent. Here Tsorreh introduced him to her friend Bynthos. With his clothing, his weathered skin, and the way he knotted his hair, the former monk looked like any seaman. Danar glimpsed a hint of longing in the older man's gaze when it fixed on the expanse of waves. The poets of Borrenth Springs called the sea the Lady Without Mercy. They said it forgave nothing, taking all and everyone forever to itself.

As the time for the navy's departure neared, it would become increasingly difficult to obtain a private vessel. Bynthos made arrangements with a ship setting out for the Mearas before it could be requisitioned. He warned that it wasn't much, just a fishing boat that had been modified for longer hauls and greater cargo. The quarters would be cramped, but the craft was sound enough. It was to hide offshore and return for them after the navy departed.

Danar and Tsorreh rode out to watch the morning tide, as had become their custom. They left the city shortly after sunrise. The good horses had gone with the land force, leaving only a handful of aged or unsound beasts. Danar's mount was blind in one eye and had gaits as rough as an onager's, and Tsorreh's mare wheezed at the slightest exertion. One of the horse-boys accompanied them on a donkey.

The night before, they had each prepared saddlebags filled with necessities, and Tsorreh had divided what money and jewels were rightfully hers, to be carried on their persons. She wore a loose Isarran gown and a sand-colored cloak, and a dagger hung from her belt, one Danar had not seen before. He suspected that Sandaron had given it to her. It was a puny thing compared to his own long knife, strapped in a leather sheath to his thigh, but a more practical weapon for a woman her size. Tsorreh's other preparations included two notes left in her quarters. One was addressed to Ulleos, although he would not receive it until after the fate of Gatacinne had been decided. The other went to Rhessan, appointed by Ulleos as regent. Privately, Danar did not think Rhessan would regret their absence or track them with any great vigor. He had seen the sour looks the councilor had given Tsorreh.

They halted to let the horses breathe at the top of the rise looking down over the village. The harbor was almost empty, for the few remaining fishing craft had already set out.

Tsorreh pointed across the gray-blue water. "Bynthos has not failed us!"

Danar peered at the boundary between sky and water. A ship, stout and unlovely, had just rounded the headland into the mouth of the bay. Tsorreh nudged the old mare with her heels and they rode down through the village, the horse-boy on their heels.

Two fisherwomen, who had been loitering on the dock beside a moored dinghy, sprang into action as the riders approached. One lowered herself into the dinghy and began loosening the ropes while the other gestured for them to hurry. They spoke a patois of Isarran and a dialect that Danar did not recognize. He understood them enough to gather that Bynthos had arranged for them to take him and Tsorreh out to the ship.

Tsorreh handed her reins to the horse-boy, along with a silver coin. Danar unstrapped the saddlebags and passed them down to the woman in the boat. After helping Tsorreh into the dinghy, he almost fell into the harbor himself as the craft shifted under him. Cackling in glee, the second fisher-woman grabbed his arm and yanked him onboard. Greasy, fish-smelling water filled the bottom, but a sideways plank served as a rude seat.

The dinghy moved away from the dock. The water had looked smooth enough from land, but the craft tilted and swayed alarmingly. Within a few minutes, Danar was hold-ing on to the side of the boat, wishing he hadn't eaten breakfast. Tsorreh smiled at him, looking quite at ease. Meanwhile, the fisherwomen never missed a stroke.

Sea-tanned faces peered down at them as the dinghy came alongside the Mearan ship. One of the fisherwomen shouted a greeting, and a rope ladder was lowered. Tsorreh leaped from the rocking dinghy to the ladder. Several sail-ors, their faces stretched into wide, broken-toothed grins, lifted her over the side.

Praying he would not disgrace himself, Danar gauged the distance and jumped. His fingers closed around the knotted rope. A wave dashed against him, almost breaking his hold. Salt water stung his eyes and nose. Sputtering, he grabbed for the next rung and pulled himself up.

Bynthos was waiting on deck, wearing seaman's dress. A smile creased the corners of his eyes. "Welcome aboard the *Riamanha-Ka*, my lady, my lord."

Perhaps it was the effect of seawater, but Danar's stom-ach already felt calmer. The ship that had looked so un-gainly from afar felt blessedly steady beneath his feet.

Danar knew little about oceanfaring vessels beyond what he had read in his father's library. This one had a large mast with an ordinary-looking squarish sail. A second, smaller sail angled into the wind. The deck had been scoured clean, and everything on it, from ropes to oars to unrecognizable canvas-wrapped bundles, was neat and orderly. A half-deck extended from the rear of the ship, covering a cabin or two. On their approach, in between bouts of sickness, Danar had noted openings for oars, but far fewer than the numbers of a Gelonian warship or those Ulleos had taken out. This ship, he surmised, traveled primarily by sail and not human sweat. Yet he saw activity aplenty, men doing complicated things with ropes, on their knees scrubbing wooden surfaces, or carrying barrels down the open hatch. They seemed to be in the last frenzy of activity before departure. More small boats pulled alongside, and crates packed with jars of oil and honey were added to the cargo of dried apricots, coral, and sea-jade.

"Where is the captain, that I might thank him?" Tsorreh asked.

Bynthos grinned and sketched a bow. "Thee will want to change from those wet clothes. 'Tis warm here in harbor, but the ocean winds blow hard."

Danar glanced inside the tiny cabin before Tsorreh swung the door shut. There were no windows, only thick oiled cloth, and the space smelled pleasantly of tar and salt and some kind of soap. When Tsorreh emerged a short time later, she had changed her Isarran garb for calf-length drawstring breeches and a long shirt with a sash that went around her waist twice.

The ship turned toward the open sea, rising eagerly to the waves. Danar gazed over the gray-green expanse. The wind teased his hair and brought heat to his cheeks. It blew away the last touches of his seasickness.

Bynthos pointed to Danar's sodden boots. Danar tugged them off and handed them to Tsorreh who, grinning, took them back into the cabin.

"Now that you're barefoot like a proper seaman, you'd best pull your weight," Bynthos said.

"I have no skill," Danar admitted, uncertain of what use he might be. He knew a great deal about poetry and politics, but almost nothing about the practicalities of getting a ship from one place to another. He summoned up his most eager expression. "Show me what I am to do."

"And me, as well," Tsorreh said.

When Bynthos looked as if he would protest, she adopted an expression that Danar had come to know very well. With a shrug of surrender, Bynthos set one of the sailors to teach her rope mending.

The days rolled by like waves, each with its own rhythm. The Mearan crew were small, dark men, curious and shy. They knew a few words of Gelone and Denariyan, besides the patois the fisherwomen had spoken. They regarded Danar as a slightly dimwitted younger brother, showing him with gestures the best way to accomplish his work, for the ship was under-strength and every pair of willing hands was welcome.

Tsorreh worked at repairing the fishing nets with which they caught most of their food, and took her turn at the endless cleaning and scrubbing. From time to time, one of the crew would bashfully offer her a trinket, a piece of carved whale-ivory or shell.

Bynthos steered the ship along the coastline and the occasional cluster of islands. The Mearans were the most skillful of all sailors at navigation by stars, but too many nights were clouded for that method to be reliable, and they dared not risk becoming lost. With any luck, Gatacinne would be back in Isarran control by the time they arrived.

Danar gradually found a place among the sailors, amusing them with his attempts to make jokes in their language and occasionally diving off the side to swim alongside the dolphins. Growing up by the Serpan River, he had learned to swim as a child and was puzzled that few of the Mearans had that skill. He did his share of rowing whenever the sails lay slack. This was the one task Bynthos refused to allow Tsorreh to try. She watched the men, bending and pulling in the still air, with a curious, pensive expression, as if she were wrestling with memories.

At night, as the ship rode at anchor, Danar and Tsorreh sat on the deck and told stories. The Mearans hunkered around them to listen.

"What does *Riamanha-Ka* mean?" Tsorreh asked Bynthos.

"It's Mearan," Bynthos said, as if that explained any oddity. They were speaking Gelone among themselves.

"*Boat That Stinks*," suggested Danar. He affected a scholarly tone. "The *Ka* indicates the stink."

"It docs *not* stink," Tsorreh protested, laughing. "I spent yesterday scrubbing the deck!"

"The holds stink," Danar insisted.

"All holds stink," said Bynthos, "even ones on Mearan ships."

At this, they all laughed, even the Mearans.

"What does the *Ka* really mean?" Tsorreh asked Danar when the laughter died down.

Danar shrugged but Bynthos answered: "It is the presence of the greater ocean that joins all water, or so the Mearans have told me. Whether this is a real ocean that lies beyond the Inland Sea or one more spiritual in nature, I cannot say."

As Danar leaned on the railing, the sun poured warmth over his shoulders. The sky above was crisp, almost painfully clear. Below, the waves looked more blue than gray. His gaze wandered toward land, safe and stable, but it had disappeared behind a haze.

One of the Mearans, stationed at the lookout post on the mast rigging, called out. The wind tore away his words, but not the urgency behind them. He pointed, not in the direction of Gatacinne but southeasterly. Danar struggled to make out the blurred shape—one, perhaps more. Behind him, Tsorreh set aside the sail she was patching and stood up.

"Can you see anything?" she asked.

Danar shook his head, wishing he had his father's farseeing lenses.

Bynthos scrambled aloft. Clinging to the mast ropes, he shaded his eyes with one hand. Above the splashing of the waves, Danar heard cursing. "Gelonian warships!"

The safety of the open water vanished. Danar had not felt such an intense sense of peril since Zevaron had spirited him out of Aidon. Even when they'd encountered the Azkhantian war band, he had not been without resources—

his words, the nomads' honor, his dedication to ending Cinath's mad conquests. Here on the wide, pitiless water, he had nothing.

Shouting orders, Bynthos raced to the steering oars. Danar rushed after him, eager to do whatever he could. He joined the Mearan sailors as they hauled on the lines. The sails creaked, catching the last breath of wind as the ship answered reluctantly.

Everything now depended on whether the Gelonian captains had spotted the *Riamanha-Ka* and if they were of a mind to investigate. Even if the Mearan vessel had been seen, perhaps it would be dismissed as a small trading vessel of no importance.

The *Riamanha-Ka* settled into the new course. Bynthos went aloft again, peering for what seemed like an eon into the hazy south. Finally he came down, more slowly this time.

"They're following," he told Danar. "At least, one of them is. Pray to whatever god protects you that the wind holds."

The Gelonian ships would have banks of oarsmen, most likely slaves. The *Riamanha-Ka* could not hope to match their speed, and once they closed . . .

"Lady." Bynthos laid one hand on Tsorreh's arm. "Best stay out of the way."

Out of the corner of his vision, Danar saw her fingers curl around the hilt of her dagger, Sandaron's gift that never left her side.

"That won't be much use in a fight," Bynthos said.

I won't be taken a second time. Danar read her thoughts on her determined face, for they were his own as well.

God of Forgotten Hopes! Danar prayed fervently, including any of the hundred other Gelonian gods who might be listening. *Be with us now!*

When the crew scrambled to their oars, Danar took one, too. The grueling work gave him the sense of doing something, instead of waiting passively for his fate. The coxswain shouted out the rhythm as the men hauled on their oars. Danar pulled and stretched, pulled and stretched. His mus-

cles ached and then burned. Blisters and abrasions tore
open the skin on his palms. How long they could maintain
the pace, Danar could not guess. They were strong and fit . . .
and desperate. And undermanned.

Sweat trickled down Danar's temples and along the
sides of his neck. His shirt was already sodden. His breath
came hot and hoarse. He struggled to keep the pace, to not
miss a single beat. His shoulders twinged with each stroke.
A glance told him that the warship with its ranges of oars
men was gaining on them. Soon it would come alongside
with grappling hooks and swords.

Around him, the others rowed like madmen. Beneath
their swarthy complexions, their faces were as red as if fire
had touched them. Sweat slicked their hair to their skulls.

The next time Danar looked, the Gelonian ship was
much closer. The prow was long and narrow, its metal-
capped point shaped like the snout of a dragon. He made
out the doubled ranks of oars clearly now. Water dripped
and flashed as the blades lifted.

This should not be happening, Danar thought numbly,
His own people should not be his enemies.

At the steering oar, Bynthos spat out curses. Danar
heard Tsorreh's voice, taut and desperate: "What can I do?"

"The men need water—"

Tsorreh raced across the deck. A moment later, she was
moving down the line with a bucket and cup from the rain-
water barrel. Steadying her hand on each man's head, she
lifted the cup to his lips. The men rowed and gulped and
rowed.

Tsorreh reached Danar. Her touch on his face was surprisingly cool. He drank without slackening his pace. When
the cup was half-empty, he tilted his head back for more.
She poured the rest of the water over his sweat-slick back.
His pulse, which had gone ragged, steadied. New vigor
flowed through his muscles. He grinned up at her as she
dipped the cup and offered it again to him. Then she continued down the lines. He kept rowing.

Danar felt the ship rise beneath him, as if carried on an
immensely powerful swell, a tidal wave like the ones writ-

ten about by Irvan of Solis. For a moment, as the *Ria-manha-Ka* tilted, he saw only sky. Then the wave passed and the ship dropped into the trough.

The Gelonian ship came into view, even closer than before. Bynthos shouted orders to stow the oars and prepare for boarding. Muscles leaden, Danar set his oar aside with the others. They had only a few weapons, mostly knives that would be no match for Gelonian swords.

Tsorreh rushed to Danar's side, her dagger gripped in her hand. He had never seen her face so set, so desperate. He wondered if she meant to use the dagger on herself, rather than be taken prisoner again.

Suddenly the *Riamanha-Ka* trembled in the grip of a huge wave. Tsorreh lost her balance and fell against the railing. Danar rushed to steady her. At first, she did not respond. She was staring over the railing. Something was moving in the water, something huge and pale, but not a dolphin or whale. It seemed to be passing beneath the *Ria-manha-Ka*, heading in the direction of the Gelonian ship.

If this were the end, Danar prayed that the Master of Waters would receive them gently.

Leaning far over, Tsorreh called out in the holy language of her people. Danar knew enough of that tongue to catch her meaning: "O spirit of the water! May you be blessed now and forever!"

A pale, curved dome, like a gigantic pearl, pushed up through the waves. Higher and higher it rose. Sheets of foam-laced water poured off the emerging figure. Danar gazed dumbfounded at an enormous bearded man, broad-chested and muscular, rising from the water. Tangled sea grasses streamed like a mane over the shoulders of what must surely be a monarch of the sea people. His skin was mottled gray and green, and marked by scales. His face was human enough, except for the lidless eyes. In them, Danar saw both ferocity and intelligence.

The sea-king raised one massive hand in salute, not to Danar but to Tsorreh. Words rang through Danar's mind as if they were shouted aloud: *"Hail to thee, O mother twice reborn! O woman who speaks of the singing stars!"*

Tsorreh had journeyed over this same ocean, reading

aloud the poetry of the *Shirah Kohav*. Truly, Danar thought, the Mearans were right. All water was one. She must have prayed for a merciful death, and had been answered.

"No rest awaits you beneath the waves, O woman. The prophecy written before the dawn of time must be fulfilled."

"What prophecy?" she screamed into the wind.

"What aid would you ask of the sea?"

"If ever the words of my people brought you joy, then help us now! Our enemies pursue us and we cannot outrun them!"

The waters lifted the sea-king even higher. The pearls woven into his mane and beard clicked like bones in the wind. Those enormous eyes regarded her, then turned to Danar. He was a particle blown by a storm, but she was the mountain against which the waves crashed and failed.

"To the citadel must you go, but for a sojourn only. Tarry there not, lest all the living waters perish."

Then the sea-king was sinking, as if sucked down by a slow, inexorable current. Danar thought he saw the ghost of a smile before the waters closed over the massive head. The whipped-froth surface swelled as if the ocean were a colossal beast arching its back. The shape that moved beneath it was no longer shell-pale but dark, a creature of the abyss.

The ship lifted again, but gently. The winds subsided into breezes. Danar tipped his head back, his face toward a sky now an intense, cerulean blue. Sunlight bathed him, penetrating him with its warmth.

Gradually he became aware that the ship was traveling at great speed, although the last of the seamen had lain down their oars and were, like him, savoring the soft air. He ambled to the far side of the ship to see the Gelonian pursuers as mere specks on the horizon. Within moments, they disappeared as if the ocean had swallowed them up.

They traveled on, lulled by sweet-scented zephyrs. Languor seeped into Danar's body. He wanted nothing more than to sleep. Bynthos slumped to the deck, his arm still wrapped around the steering oar. Tsorreh had curled up like a kitten beside the railing.

He was weary, so weary. The deck was warm. It rocked gently, soothing away the aches of exertion. There was nothing to fear, for the Gelon were far away. The sky was clear, the winds benign. He would sit for a little and regain his strength. For just a moment . . .

Danar jerked awake. The hypnotic rhythm of the ship's motion had given way to a sharp pitching. The deck lurched and tilted under him, suddenly dropping away. His stomach roiled in protest. He clambered to his feet and steadied himself against the rail. Around him, the other seamen were returning to their tasks.

The sun, which had been well overhead, now dipped toward the western horizon. Traveling east, they had outrun the day. The strange stillness of the air had disappeared, and stronger gusts tugged at Danar's hair.

"Land ahead!"

The line of haze before them resolved into a crescent of sand rising to eroded hills. Arms of headland embraced a sheltered bay. Foam marked the edge of a breakwater where the waves crashed against the rocks. A village nestled in a cleft in the hills, rows of white and tan buildings, red tile roofs, and gardens extending toward the neat harbor.

"We'll put in before sunset," Bynthos said. "We're almost there."

As Danar watched, the coast grew nearer. The buildings glowed in the slanting light, defined by long shadows. Bynthos stood at the steering oars, angling the ship toward the piers. The crew sang, and everyone shared a mood of jollity and relief.

But where exactly were they?

Chapter Fourteen

BYNTHOS guided the *Riamanha-Ka* alongside the out-ermost pier, and the men laid down their oars. The ship rocked gently, as if content to rest from its labors. The sun, near setting, slanted across the wooden planks and pilings, softening the scars of years and hard usage. Boats, most of them fitted up for fishing, crowded against the moorings. The shadows of their masts were long and wavering, follow-ing the contour of the shore.

Danar studied the pattern of dark on dark. Something was odd, out of place. Bynthos, too, was glaring at the water. A shout brought their attention. A group of villagers, eight or ten most likely, were headed their way.

"Your appearance may lead to difficult questions," Byn-thos said. "I do not know how far north we've come," mean-ing how close to Gelon-held territory and whether word of the hunt for Danar might have reached this far.

Danar and Tsorreh hid inside the cabin, listening to the voices of the village men above the boom and hiss of the surf. Danar tried to visualize the coastline, the harbor and village, the boats making their way toward the *Riamanha-Ka* . . . the deck beneath his feet, the shadows across the clean-scrubbed wood . . . shadows across the water . . .

Yes, that was it! *The shadows across the water . . .*

One of Danar's tutors, trained at the academy at Borrenth Springs, had been an avid collector of maps. As a consequence, Danar had been forced to memorize large portions of the coastline of the Inland Sea.

Abruptly, he came back into himself. "I know where we are." Tsorreh bent toward him, one eyebrow arched in question. "The sun sets in the west, so the shadows should point *toward* the shore, not across. These shadows run *parallel* to the land," he explained. "That means the coastline here runs east-west, not north-south. The village is to our south."

Tsorreh frowned. "We're near Gatacinne, then?"

"No, I'm pretty sure we've gone well beyond, headed northeast, and are now in the Occeldir Inlet—"

Before Tsorreh could respond, Bynthos swung the door open. He nodded to Danar. "You've figured it out, have you?"

"Occeldirin?"

"Aye, though there's not a man alive who'd believe how we got here." Bynthos told them that there was no word out of Aidon of a reward for Danar's capture. Moreover, the town merchants were eager for new goods. The Gelon had extended their territory beyond their usual outposts, and requisitions had put a heavy strain on local supplies of food and building materials. It was rumored that the Gelonian engineers planned to build a canal between the Sea of Desolation and the Inland Sea. Cinath meant to create another, faster trade route to the Denariyan spice lands.

Despite the legends about the poisonous waters of the *Mher Seshola*, the Gelon had apparently been able to cross it by boat and had established a settlement and shipworks on the north shore. In their own fashion, the Gelon had renamed the Sea of Desolation; it was now the Dawn Sea, referring both to its location east of Gelon and Cinath's hope for a new trade route.

"Madness," Tsorreh murmured, "to set out on such waters."

"Nothing endures forever," Danar said to Tsorreh, "or so the scholars tell us. Alkalinity and other factors can be modified by natural processes. Perhaps your Sea of Desolation was lifeless once, but time has healed it."

She gave him a dark, unreadable look. "There was nothing natural in the poisoning of those waters."

Together they devised a cover story for himself and Tsorreh. Danar would present himself as a Gelonian noble and Tsorreh as his servant. If they could make their way to the northern shore of the Dawn Sea, they should be able to buy passage to Meklavar.

"I could do it," he said. "It won't be hard to act sufficiently arrogant."

First, however, business must be attended to. Danar went ashore with Bynthos. They wandered through the open-air markets, sampling the local food, a nutty grain simmered with hot peppers, cumin and raisins, dried salted squids, and figs so ripe and tender they melted in his mouth. He bought some to bring to Tsorreh. Soon Bynthos had struck bargains with both buyers and sellers. Honey and oil were in particular demand, and in exchange the villager merchants offered Denariyan peppercorns, silver filigree, and sandalwood.

While loading triple-wrapped sacks of peppercorns onboard, Danar paused for a moment beside Tsorreh, watching the line of surf. The sun warmed his shoulders. The same golden light shone on his city, on Tsorreh's city, on Zevaron and Shannivar and all the friends he had made on the steppe, perhaps even on his father, if he was still alive. He felt linked to those he loved by sun, by sea, by memory.

Bynthos came on deck, and Tsorreh walked over to him. They stood together, facing the mouth of the harbor and the open ocean. Danar, glancing at them, was struck by how the days under the open sky had erased the captain's paleness born of study and prayer. If the monk lingered anywhere in the seaman's weathered features, Danar could not see it.

Tsorreh said, "My friend, I think the sea has captured you again."

Bynthos rested his forearms on the rail, his hands loose, his gaze on the stretch of gray-green water. "She is not done with me yet."

They stood together in silence, as if they had no words of farewell. Another pair of friends might say, *Thank you for everything you have done for me*, or *Perhaps we will meet again*, or *May the gods watch over you*.

Without taking her eyes off the ocean, Tsorreh said, "*Ka.*"

Once the cargo was unloaded and the new goods safely stowed, the crew rotated through shore leave. Danar had thought to hire a local guide and donkeys, but chance brought him into contact with a caravan heading toward the Dawn Sea. After arranging to join them, he set about procuring native clothing for Tsorreh. The Occeldrini were a thin, dark people, and Tsorreh looked very much like them when wrapped in a woman's flowing cloak and headscarf.

The next morning, the *Riamanha-Ka* set sail again, and Danar and Tsorreh headed east with the caravan. They traveled slowly, their speed limited by the laden donkeys. The caravan route curved between steepening hills, their stony slopes cut by gullies. The land turned sere and dry, the brush sun-browned, the trees twisted, as if they had lost the struggle to wrench themselves from the bony soil.

At last, toward the end of one day, they crested a pass and looked down the long slope leading to a vast plain of water. Light sheeted off its surface, reflecting the colors of dusk. A Gelonian settlement had grown where the caravan road ended at the shore. Beyond it stretched a patchwork of yards and warehouses. Several boats lay moored at the piers. They went down into the bustling harbor, where Danar learned of a ship setting out for the Meklavaran shore the next morning.

So far, Danar had relied on his accent and appearance to avoid questioning. It now became clear that anyone seeking passage across the Dawn Sea needed proper authorization. Danar handed Tsorreh his saddlebags, thrust his chest out, and strode up to the officer in charge.

"I require accommodations on the next ship headed south," Danar announced in precise, educated Gelone. "I believe one sails within the hour."

The officer turned from where he had been conferring with several artisans, moving with a lassitude that bordered on insult. Danar knew his type; competent enough but lacking the necessary patronage to secure a more desirable post or the initiative to further his career through boldness and hard work. By the weathering of the man's skin, the thinning of his hair, and the slightly large fit of his leather armor, this service had not been kind to him.

"Then *I* require identification," the officer said. "If it is sufficient, then passage may be arranged as is convenient." By the man's twanging accent, Danar guessed he had been raised in a provincial region near Ayford and come up through the ranks.

Danar lifted his nose a fraction higher. "The orders concerning my travel arrangements should have preceded me. My uncle's couriers are usually quite efficient. I suggest you examine your records more carefully."

The officer hesitated for an instant, enough to confirm that the man could not read.

"It is of no matter," Danar said carelessly. "A military man such as yourself understands the importance of missions that can be conducted only by trusted family members. My uncle will see you well rewarded for your perspicacity."

Another slight but no less gratifying pause ensued before the officer recovered himself. "And your uncle might be . . .?"

Danar bent close, imbuing his voice with confidentiality, "Ner-Haslar-Varan."

No such person existed, of course. Rather than name a real general, Danar conflated the names of one of his old bodyguards and an oil merchant's son, suitor to a maidservant in his father's household. Nevertheless, the officer turned five shades paler.

"My lord, of course there is no question! If—if I can offer any other service—"

"Quite unnecessary. My servant is accustomed to my requirements." As Danar proceeded past the officer, he paused. "I shall make sure my uncle receives word of your cooperation. What name shall I send for his commendation?"

"Amon, sir! Amon of Lesser Ayford!"

Danar and Tsorreh went aboard. The ship was of classic Gelonian design, its sleek lines contrasting with those of the *Riamanha-Ka*. There were two masts but no side rails, only a low wooden curb. Although oar holes ran the length of both sides, there were far too few men to man the oars. Likely, all available able-bodied workers had been conscripted for the shipworks.

They set off with the small crew straining at the oars. Once in open water, the breeze picked up nicely. The blue and white sails rounded in the wind. Waves rolled across the surface of the water. The ship leaped forward.

Tsorreh stood quietly beside Danar. Perhaps her bearing was out of keeping for a servant, but Danar welcomed her company. When he glanced at her, he thought bits of the sun had gotten into her eyes.

She said, "It's hard to believe I'm going home."

Toward midafternoon, the sky clouded over. The temperature dropped noticeably. The breezes, which had blown so steadily, turned fitful. The sails rippled as the winds shifted course and the captain struggled to keep the ship properly positioned. Waves crashed together, as if the currents could not decide their direction but ran every which way. After a few minutes of this, the winds would steady and the ship would leap forward, its passage smooth until the next bout of gusts.

The erratic changes in sky and waves alarmed Danar. The river he'd swum in as a child had currents, sometimes hard and swift, but he had never seen them change so unpredictably. He licked his lips and tasted something—not salt as he expected, but metallic. He turned to Tsorreh. "You'd best get within."

The wind changed direction and the ship staggered beneath their feet. Half the crew went rushing about in response to the captain's orders.

"Danar, I am as safe out here as I would be inside," Tsorreh said. Her chin lifted in a gesture he recognized.

One of the masts creaked under the onslaught of the wind. To the south, great charcoal-dark clouds were piling up at furious speed. Sullen with rain, they blanketed the sun even further, except for a moment, when a chance shift of wind in the heights admitted a ray of thin yellow light.

Danar glanced up to see the sail straining, the lines taut. He murmured a prayer to the Master of the Sea and turned back to Tsorreh. "Please!" He shouted above the worsening storm. "This is no place for you—leave the sailors to their work!"

With a nod, Tsorreh retreated to the cabin. Moments later, the wind rose to a shriek. The clouds swirled and billowed, streaking the sky. All traces of the ray of light vanished.

Within an hour, the ship was pitching so violently that the timbers screeched under the strain. Water sheeted over the deck, making the planks slick. Footing became treacherous. The captain raced the length of the ship, shouting orders. The storm grew wilder, as if driven by demonic forces.

Just as Danar made up his mind to offer his assistance to the captain, Tsorreh burst from the cabin. "Stay inside!"

She shook her head, and he realized that the terror of being enclosed must be more frightening than facing the storm.

The water parted, the waves crested to either side, and the ship plunged sickeningly downward. The next instant, the hull hit the bottom of the trough. It shuddered with the impact. Gray spume shot upward.

"Hold on!" Danar reached for Tsorreh with one hand while anchoring himself to the nearest mast with the other.

Another wave, practically on the heels of the last, caught the ship sideways. Tsorreh slid on the slick deck, tripped on the low curb, and toppled over the side. Danar threw himself down at the edge of the deck, clutching the wooden curb to keep from going overboard himself. The water below was a shroud of foam-laced gray.

She was gone. And it was his fault.

Danar raised himself up and dove over the side. Once past the turbulence of the surface, the sea became clear, almost pellucid. Gray light fell in slanting rays, as if the water provided its own illumination.

He glanced down. The seafloor was already closer than he expected. In the shifting light, he glimpsed a human form trailing dark, braided hair. It drifted downward, toward a pile of wreckage on the bottom. Kicking strongly, he followed.

A short distance lower, the debris resolved itself into a boneyard. Not even in his father's most arcane books had he ever seen such, massive arching ribs and eerily misshapen skulls that came from no creatures he knew. They glimmered in the wan light, sickly pale. If these were monsters, then they were giants of their kind.

Danar had no time to spare wondering, for already his chest was beginning to ache. He didn't have much time left. Tsorreh had disappeared behind a pile of disarticulated skeletons. He kicked again and pulled himself through the water with his arms.

There she was, drifting into the shadows cast by the monstrous remains. As he strained toward her, he saw what looked like an ordinary horse skeleton lying among a half-dozen of its fellows. Tsorreh came to rest, graceless and inert, beside it. Bubbles streamed from her nose and mouth.

Danar gave one last push and reached out. The gray-lit water swirled, distorting his vision and making it difficult to judge distances. Then his fingers closed around her outstretched arm. Her wrist felt fragile, too slender for life. She came easily into his arms, as if the sea had no will to keep her. Her eyes were closed, her expression peaceful.

Suddenly she gave a convulsive start. Her eyes flew open, charged with fear. He held her fast. Her arms and legs paused in their frantic thrashing. Clearly, she recognized him.

Danar kicked again, pushing for the surface, but his muscles responded sluggishly. When his lungs cried out for air, he clamped his lips shut. Tsorreh tugged on his arm, indicating that he should release her. For an instant, he hesitated, fearful that she could not swim. She jerked harder. This time, her determination won him over. The moment he let her go, she shot upward toward the light.

Danar gathered himself to follow her. His feet thrust through water—and then caught on something. His first thought was that his foot had snagged in the wreckage. He shoved with his free foot but could not budge. If anything, he had the sensation of being drawn deeper.

He reached down to feel what held him. The horse skull gleamed, as if it had turned to mother-of-pearl. Something winked, emerald bright, beneath its vertebral column. Despite the agony building in his lungs, he paused in his attempts to break free. He twisted, coming around for a closer look.

A human skeleton stretched across the sea floor, half-covered by the muck. It was twisted where the horse lay across it, the rider most likely trapped when his mount fell. From the distortion of the posture, the poor man must have died in agony. Bits of corroded metal covered parts of the skeleton. The rest of the gear and clothing had long since rotted away.

Bony fingers closed around Danar's ankle. In horror, he opened his mouth. Air streamed forth, gone past recovery. He kicked again. The bones clamped tighter, the slender phalangeal tips digging into his flesh like iron spikes. He reached down to pry the dead man's fingers open. Faster than Danar could follow, the skeleton stretched out its other hand. Again came that wink of impossible green.

The skeletal hand struck his chest. The blow sent him reeling, spinning away. His foot came free. He heard a noise like splintering bone, distorted by the water.

Darkness edged his vision. In the distance, light shimmered. It beckoned him, but lead weighed down his muscles. Sensation faded from his hands and feet. The water no longer felt chillingly cold. In an instant, perhaps two, he would surrender to the craving for breath. Water would inundate his lungs. The light would dim until all turned to endless night.

A rushing sound filled his ears, bringing a peculiar tranquil clarity. The thought that even now he was sinking into the eternal void had no power to terrify him. All was ended, all his disappointments, all his fears.

Receive my spirit, O Remover of Sorrows. He opened his lips to welcome death into him.

But no water poured into his lungs. It rushed past him,

now warm and soft and, most surprisingly, infused with the same light he had seen in the jewel-bright glint on the skeleton's hand.

Around him and through him light flared in every shade of green, from the first tender shoots of springtime to the flash over the ocean at sunset, from high summer's foliage to the faceted glitter of emeralds. Never before had he felt such a sense of exuberant well-being. The light nourished him, fed new strength into his failing muscles, and eased the burning in his lungs.

With a crashing surge of whiteness, he burst into the air. His head broke the surface, sending frothy water in every direction. His chest heaved, sucking in air. Above him, thunder crackled in the distance.

Treading water, Danar glanced around for Tsorreh. A short distance away, he spied the Gelonian ship. The seamen were pulling someone out of the water, someone whose long black hair streamed wetly down her back. Above the splashing of the waves and the rumble from the clouds, he heard her cry out, "No, go back—he's down there!"

Danar began swimming for the ship. His arms and legs propelled him powerfully through the water. A few minutes later, he reached the ship and climbed up the ropes lowered for him.

On deck, one of the sailors was awkwardly wrapping a blanket around Tsorreh. When she saw Danar, she thrust the crewman aside and ran to Danar. Her arms around him felt chill and clammy. "I thought I had lost you!"

"*You* lost *me*?" He began to say, "*If I had let you drown, Zevaron would kill me—*" but thought better of it.

"If I hadn't—hadn't been so foolish," she babbled, "if I hadn't come back on deck—it would have been all my fault if you—"

Her loss of composure almost undid him. To cover his embarrassment, he took the blanket and shoved it into her arms. "Get yourself dry. I have enough to explain as it is," meaning why a Gelonian noble would risk his life for that of a servant. After a moment's astonished pause, she hurried away. Another seaman brought Danar a blanket, and he made sure to laugh heartily and comment on how refreshing a swim it had been.

By the time Danar joined Tsorreh in the cabin, his legs were shaking. The tranquil confidence from the green brilliance had faded, leaving him on the edge of nausea. Tsorreh rose from where she had been sitting on the floor. She grasped his shoulders and guided him to the single seat, a wooden plank attached to one wall.

She peered into his face, examining him closely for an uncomfortably long time. "I think you'd better tell me what happened."

"You fell in. I went after you. We both survived. I think shock is s-s-setting in . . ." Despite his best efforts at control, his teeth chattered.

With a *tsk!* of exasperation, she rubbed his hands between hers. Her skin, which had felt almost icy before, now warmed him. At last, she gave him another sharply measuring look.

"Benerod," she said with a nod.

"What?"

"The green gem of healing and compassion, one of the seven that make up the Shield of Khored. I sense its power in you."

And she began to tell him what he had been given.

Chapter Fifteen

PAUSING for breath, Danar gazed down the sloping, rock-strewn hillside that led to the city of Meklavar. Although the worst of the disorientation seemed to be over, he did not know what he would have done without Tsorreh's guidance in those first days after receiving Benerod's gem. Most likely, he would have gone mad. He thought of Zevaron's mysterious illness as they fled Aidon. That had been no natural malady but the disorientation—the utter collapse of reason—as the crystal roused to life.

They had just emerged from the barren lands north of the city, Danar on foot and Tsorreh on the scrawny donkey that was the best available when they'd reached the far shore of the Dawn Sea. Before them, the ancient citadel of Meklavar shimmered in the light, its walls and towers stark against the volcanic cliffs. From its highest towers, he reckoned, the Dawn Sea might be visible on a clear day. To the west, where the sun was now setting, peaks rose in jagged rows. A garrison dominated the area outside the main gates, a palisade encircling rows of unadorned wooden barracks. Beyond a perimeter of bare earth lay livestock pens and a village.

Shielding his eyes, Danar strained to see the contours of the Var Pass, gateway to the spice lands of Denariya. "Shall we arrive at the city gates before dark?"

"I think we should not try tonight. For all we know, the gates are locked at sunset. We might draw attention to ourselves simply by arriving past curfew."

Danar stared at the outlines of low buildings, yards for livestock, and a few pitiful garden plots. "We'd best seek lodging in the village."

"And news as well. Before the fall of Meklavar, Viridon was head of the House of Cassarod. I do not know if he himself possessed the red *alvar*, the one that embodies courage, although I presume so. I encountered his younger son, Setherod, in Aidon, and I am certain it was not in his keeping. Either Viridon never had it or he passed it on to his older son."

"Ganneron, yes. You said he might know of the other two—Shebu'od and Dovereth, right? They stand for purple and strength, and yellow and truth."

"You remember your lessons well."

"I am my father's son," he replied.

"And that must surely give us cause for hope."

"I grew up with the hundred gods of Gelon. These are simple by comparison, with only seven sets of colors and attributes."

The smile faded from her face. "I don't think there's anything simple about them. But let us not borrow trouble, debating which system is more complicated."

The village was very much as Danar had expected, ramshackle buildings smelling of the sheep and goats in the pens, of strange spices, smoke and grease, and raucous with a dozen different tongues. At Tsorreh's insistence, they entered an inn that, while not of the poorest quality, was hardly luxurious. Danar suspected, by the pointed lack of curiosity as they found places in a corner of the common room, that very little of what transpired in this establishment was legal. No one here would willingly attract the attention of the authorities.

As they ate, Danar sifted the mood of the patrons, catching references to a prophet who might be a rallying point for rebellion, accusations and excuses regarding the Meklavaran governor, and the price of Mearan amber. He suspected that Bynthos would have a great deal to say about the latter. There was less grumbling about Gelonian rule than he'd expected, although many of these men were local laborers working on various projects, including improvements to the road over the Var Pass. Once he thought he heard a comment about Qr, but the conversation passed on so quickly, he could easily have misunderstood.

Once in their chamber, for which they had paid double the price of bedding down in the common room, Danar felt it safe to ask Tsorreh what she had observed, but she silenced him with a gesture. The walls were thin, and they could clearly hear footsteps in the corridor outside.

Inspecting the straw pallet that passed for a bed, Tsorreh sniffed in disapproval and picked out a bed-louse. They both made themselves as comfortable as possible on the wood floor. There was very little room, barely enough for Tsorreh to curl up next to Danar. She might have been his little sister. The sounds from the common room died down and the timbers of the inn creaked softly.

"Danar . . ."

"Mmm?" He rolled over, easing the pressure of his hip-bone on hard floor.

"I think . . . it's not as bad as I had feared. I don't think conditions . . . are as harsh as they once were." The last time Tsorreh had seen her home, it had been in flames, its defenders dead or dying.

"We should be careful," Danar said, "until we know who is trustworthy." There had been strangers aplenty in the common room, men glad to exchange gossip for a drink or two.

"I think it's safe to enter the city with the morning traders. We must arrive early, as the gates open two hours before dawn, or as they did when I was last here. We'll make our way to the markets of the lower city. The men I want most to contact live—lived—in great houses up on the *meklat*, but I cannot tell what might happen if we tried to pass through the King's Gate. Assuming"—she lowered her voice—"it still exists."

Sleep came for Danar slowly, but it came deep. He awoke to the sounds of Tsorreh moving about the room. A faint light showed between the shutters. She set something

down on the single, rickety chair. Danar discovered it to be
a pitcher of water, clean enough and cold. He splashed his
face, scrubbed cheeks bristly with several days' growth, and
raked damp fingers through his hair. He had no illusions
that these measures improved his appearance, not that anyone in this district would care, but he felt better.

A short time later, they joined a stream of traffic heading
through the garrison gate. Men pushing carts rubbed shoulders with women bent under enormous baskets, and trudged
beside laden donkeys and camels, or strings of goats. Here
and there, Danar heard a voice shouting out in Gelone.
Through the rising dust, he glimpsed the glint of armor or
spearpoint, or the outline of an onager-pulled chariot.

Gelonian guards watched the people entering the city.
Danar dared not let his gaze rest on them for more than an
instant or two. These men might appear bored from having
been posted to such a distant city, policing a population that
was already subdued, but they were trained soldiers. Anyone who voluntarily attracted their attention was either
foolhardy or dimwitted.

Inside the gates, a single avenue led to the market
squares and mercantile districts in the lower city. Danar
stayed close as Tsorreh edged to the outside of the stream
of traffic. Once free of the throng, they headed down a side
street. From his own youthful misadventures, Danar recognized the signs of decay, the cracked and begrimed paving
stones. Two men in dark, shapeless clothing came their way,
heading toward the market. Danar tensed. His hand went
to the hilt of his knife. The larger of the two glared at him,
eyes narrowing. His companion shook his head and muttered in Denariyan. Danar let out his breath when the two
men passed.

Tsorreh was trembling, her breathing fast and light. Danar cursed himself for expecting that once they'd made it to
Meklavar, everything would be fine. This was her city, but
not her world. He had known her as a captive and servant,
but in truth she had lived most of her life as an aristocrat.
In fact, so had he. What did he truly know of these streets,
of desperate poverty? If Zevaron had not stumbled upon
him that evening outside a tavern in Aidon's most crime-

ridden district—or rather, come roaring out of the darkness like The Thunderer himself—Danar would surely have been killed or kidnapped and held for ransom. He'd been a fool to venture into such a place in all his finery and then to have gotten stinking drunk. Well, none of those things was going to happen now.

"We've got to get out of here." Gently, he took Tsorreh's arm. "Let's check the King's Gate, shall we?"

As they retraced their steps back through the square, the *meklat* rose above them like a fortress within a walled city. It looked to Danar as if the enormous terrace had been hewn from the side of the mountain. It would be scalable by Gelonian siege engines, but not easily taken. The wall that bounded its edge was clearly intended for defense, and the stairs narrowed as they ascended. The stone of the walls was cracked and blackened in places.

The King's Gate had once spanned the top of the stairway, but if any part of it had survived the fall of Meklavar, it was long gone. Instead, a Gelonian soldier guarded each side of the opening, and more stood in a line across the lowest stair. They were checking each person who tried to pass, turning many away. Those they allowed through were either well-dressed in Meklavaran style or else wearing Gelonian armor.

At the sight of the soldiers, Tsorreh's body went rigid. She halted abruptly, then backed away. Danar hurried after her, certain they would attract attention, but no one called out for them to stop. The people they passed had the air of those who had learned to keep their noses out of what did not directly concern them.

Just as they neared a more heavily traveled intersection, they heard a clamor ahead. Danar's understanding of Meklavaran wasn't good enough for him to gather anything more than a riot in the making. He grabbed Tsorreh's hand.

"No," she said when he would have pulled her back, "I need to see—to know—"

Through a sudden parting of the crowd, Danar glimpsed a man standing on a platform, exhorting his listeners with lifted arms. In his dust-colored robe, with his unkempt beard and hair, he looked like a madman. Even at a distance, Danar felt the hypnotic pull of the man's speech. Power resounded through the bronze-toned voice.

Behind Danar's breastbone, the gem of Benerod came alive.

The next moment, cries of alarm interrupted the speech. Gelonian soldiers poured into the plaza. Their armor glinted in the sun. Danar thought he saw the shaven head of a Qr priest among them, but there was no time for a second look. The audience rapidly disintegrated into a mob. Shouting and shrieking, half the crowd turned to flee. Others pressed toward the speaker, perhaps so entranced they had lost all sense of danger, or else bent on protecting him from the soldiers.

"Iskarnon! Iskarnon!" The cry was taken up throughout the crowd.

A woman rushed past Danar and Tsorreh, yelling, "It's the Prophet—"

"Aiee! Soldiers!"

"Gelon scum!"

"Run—hide! Run for your lives!"

The next moment, Danar lost sight of the Prophet. He and Tsorreh were surrounded, hemmed in on all sides by struggling bodies. At the same time, the Gelon would not be able to move quickly through the throng, with people pushing and shoving in different directions.

"I've heard enough," Tsorreh said. "Let's go!"

Danar scrambled to keep up with her as she threaded a path through the milling crowd. Where he saw only an unbroken mass of bodies, she managed to slip through an opening that was not there an instant before. Within moments, she brought them to the edge of the throng. Here luck deserted her, for she bumped into an elderly woman with enough force to send both of them staggering.

"Your pardon—" Tsorreh began, speaking Meklavaran.

"*My lady?* Can it be?"

The other woman was modestly dressed, her snowy hair covered by a cap of the same black and white printed cotton as her long sleeveless dress. She could easily have been Tsorreh's great-grandmother, by the wrinkling of her face. In one hand, she clutched a basket covered by a faded blue cloth. The other hand flew to her cheek. Eyes bright as bits of diamond blinked away sudden tears.

"Otenneh?" Tsorreh gasped.

"Come with me!" The old woman rushed off with surprising vigor. Tsorreh followed without a moment's hesitation. Danar had no choice but to go along.

Shortly, they reached a district of modest shops. In contrast to the market square, the few pedestrians here looked well-dressed and dignified in demeanor. They glanced surreptitiously at Danar with his reddish hair. In this city of gold-hued faces, his fair skin, even though tanned by the better part of a year of travel, clearly marked him as Gelon.

The old woman hurried inside one of the shops and latched the door behind them. Parchment scrolls and bound books lined the shelves to either side, while a central table displayed open volumes and beautifully colored drawings. Danar inhaled the scents of parchment, paper, and ink. His father would have loved this place.

Otenneh bustled them through the shop and beyond a canvas curtain to a room that was barely larger than a closet but furnished with a table and low, cushion-lined benches. An elderly man emerged from one of two doorways. Tsorreh flung her arms around his neck, then embraced the woman as well.

"It is—it cannot be—it is you!" he said.

"We thought—" the woman began.

"We heard you were a hostage in the Gelonian capital," the old man said, with a glance at Danar that was not entirely friendly.

"So I was, and have since been to Durinthe." Tsorreh sounded almost too overcome to speak. "I'm home thanks to my friend . . ." Here she hesitated, perhaps wondering if it was safe to let them know who Danar was. Despite their evident devotion to her, these people owed him no loyalty.

"Issios." Danar gave the name of his father's steward. He was getting good at thinking up aliases, names so familiar that he would respond naturally to them.

The next moment, all three began speaking again in such rapid and idiomatic Meklavaran that Danar could follow only the most general sense. He gathered that the two were only recently married, and that the old man tutored the children of noble families and his wife managed the bookstore. There was some lively discussion about a library being safe, at which news Tsorreh looked relieved. Danar recognized her own story, her capture and transport to Aidon. She skimmed over her escape from Gelon and said nothing of the *alvara* or Khored's Shield. She did, however, mention Sandaron, although the old couple didn't know who he was.

"And the young *ravot*?" Otenneh asked with a trace of hesitation, as if she feared that Zevaron had perished in some dreadful way and her question might arouse renewed grief.

"I believe he is well, if far away," Tsorreh reassured her. "We were separated when the Gelon attacked Gatacinne, but he found me in Aidon quite by chance. It's scandalous, I know, but he'd spent those four years on a Denariyan pirate ship!"

The old woman looked shocked, but the man chuckled. "That young scamp! He was probably safer among brigands there than here in Meklavar."

"From Aidon, I went to Isarre," Tsorreh continued, "while Zevaron and Issios ventured to Azkhantia, hoping to enlist them as allies. When they parted, my son remained with a party of their best warriors."

"Even better," Otenneh said crisply, "for not even the Ar-King can reach him there."

Tsorreh pulled away from another round of embraces and prayers of thanksgiving. She spoke slowly so that Danar could understand. "I forget myself. I have performed only half an introduction. This is my tutor, Eavonen"—to which the old man sketched a bow with an inclination of his head—"and my nurse, Otenneh, who came here with my mother from Isarre." Her voice caught in her throat, and Danar thought, *She thought they were dead. She thought everyone here she loved was dead.*

Danar bowed formally. With a nod, Otenneh disappeared into the back of the shop.

"Eavonen, if you are tutoring at the great houses, you must have free access to the *meklat*," Tsorreh said.

The old man slipped a cord from around his neck and held out a coin-sized copper token. "These are issued by the governor."

"My husband's old councilor, Anthelon!" She peered at the image on the token. "I did not know he was still alive."

"He took the conquest of the city very hard." Otenneh came back with a tray bearing a pitcher, cups, and a plate of honey-soaked pastries. She began pouring and handing round the drinks. Danar took a sip and found it to be minted water, and very refreshing.

"Not that he has much power," Otenneh added. "General Ner-Manir-Thierra is the one who gives the orders."

Manir! Holy Sower of Mischief! The general's deceased wife had been a cousin of Danar's mother. More than that, Danar could not remember a time when Manir had not been his father's friend, despite Jaxar's being much older. For a time, before Manir's military career had strained their relationship, he had spent many evenings playing castles with Jaxar, discussing books and philosophy. Manir would recognize Danar instantly, no matter how well disguised.

Danar wrenched his thoughts from what would happen if Manir should lay eyes on him. He must be careful not to attract attention. But he would accomplish nothing by hiding.

"I don't think Anthelon would dare to sneeze without the general's permission," Eavonen commented dryly.

Cup in hand, Otenneh lowered herself to one of the benches. "Perhaps Anthelon was able to temper Prince Thessar's moods—well, the less said about *that one*, the better—how vindictive he was in those first years, the delight he took in exacting his revenge. Ah! 'Twas a blessing *ravot* Shorrenon did not survive and you, my dove, were safely gone."

Too ashamed to meet the eyes of these people, Danar bent his head. How could they fail to regard him as an enemy, blood kin to those who had oppressed them and still did so?

My uncle did this, and my cousin. My people waged this war. A pulse of green swept through him, whispering, *All shall be set right in the right time.*

All would be well, he promised himself, because he would make it so.

"There is no one so lost that he cannot be redeemed," he heard Tsorreh say. "Is that not what the holy texts teach us?"

At her words, Danar caught a fleeting hint of reverence in the eyes of Eavonen and Otenneh. Did they hope Tsorreh had returned to lead her people to freedom? To get them all killed in a futile gesture of glory? He thought he knew the Meklavaran temperament from all the books he had studied, but now he saw that he had understood nothing.

". . . and there will be a time for reckoning, for the healing of all harms," Tsorreh finished. After an awkward pause, she shifted to a new topic. "I have heard very little news of home. What is the standing of the great houses?"

"After the fall of the city, there were pockets of resistance," Eavonen said, carefully not looking at Danar. "Anyone Thessar suspected was executed. Every noble family lost at least one member." He went on, mentioning names Danar did not know.

Tsorreh's face tightened as she listened to tales of men killed and their children sent away, into exile or slavery, this house shut up or that one given over to another family, others cowed into loyalty.

"And what of Cassarod?" Tsorreh ventured to ask when Eavonen's recitation waned. "Is it true that old Viridon died?"

"Ganneron is now head of that house," Eavonen replied. "I am not sure of the fate of his younger brother. He had gone abroad, or so it was said."

"I must speak with Ganneron of Cassarod," Tsorreh said, "although I do not know how I might enter the *meklat* in my present state."

Otenneh slipped one arm around Tsorreh's shoulders. Tsorreh was a small woman, but Otenneh was even smaller. "My dear lady, that is no problem at all. Eavonen and I may live here behind the bookshop, but as I told you, he tutors for the noble families above. A little soap, some decent clothes, my token of passage in your hand, and you may pass as his assistant without question. *That one*, on the other hand"—with a flicker of her eyes, she indicated Danar—"may take some explaining."

"That won't be necessary," Tsorreh said. "You"—she turned to Danar—"are staying here."

"I can't let you—" Danar began, ignoring Eavonen's scowl.

"You can. You will!" Tsorreh cut in. "I did not come home to be *safe*. Besides, I have a task for you here."

"What shall I do, then?" Danar muttered, taken aback by her peremptory manner. "Sit here and rot?"

"You will make yourself useful."

"Useful? How?"

"By learning something!" Without waiting for his reply, Tsorreh turned to her old tutor. "Eavonen, you must have histories of the city and genealogies. Also a copy of the *Te-Ketav*. Those should keep Dan—Issios occupied for at least a few hours."

Otenneh bustled Tsorreh into the back of the house while Eavonen went about the shop, selecting books. Danar managed to wrestle his temper back under control. He'd just seen a side of Tsorreh's character he hadn't known before. Why should he be surprised? These were her people, her city.

When Tsorreh emerged, Danar barely recognized her. She looked poised and aloof in a long sleeveless vest of red-patterned cotton, over full trousers just a shade more intense. Her hair had been plaited and knotted on the back of her head with red ribbons. A copper passage token hung on a chain of the same metal around her neck.

The smile she gave Danar held both warmth and regret. "I am sorry to impose such a demanding task on you and then abandon you to it. Please understand that I would not do so if the need were not great and if I did not have the greatest confidence in you."

Danar stilled a protest at her praise. She spoke rightly, for his scholarly training had been thorough. His tutors had often expected him to do meticulous research in a foreign language, too.

She came to him and clasped his forearms, almost as a soldier might. "We must be prepared for a long and arduous search, one that lasts years perhaps." Her gaze softened and he knew she was thinking of Sandaron's quest, how remote the possibility of success, and yet how much depended on steadfast determination. Could he, who had not even the hardship of long travel to contend with, do less?

He managed a smile. "Can this"—with a glance at the piles of books—"be any less arduous than my father's lessons in astronomy? Or yours in classical Denariyan literature? At least, my understanding of Meklavaran isn't as dreadful as it was before you came."

"No, indeed! Seriously, you will be on your own for much of the time, just as I will be pursuing my own part of the search." She did not add that she trusted him to keep at his work without supervision. He was, after all, an adult.

Eavonen cleared his throat. "We must be off. I am already late to hear the first recitation of the day."

It seemed only a blink of the eye later that Danar found himself in the back room, seated in front of a pile of bound volumes with a Gelone-Meklavaran dictionary at his side.

Chapter Sixteen

DANAR remained in the living quarters behind the bookshop for the rest of the day. Customers entered and left, and Otenneh went out for a time, warning him not to open the door. Around midday, when the faded calligraphy was beginning to blur in his sight, the old woman brought him a platter of lentils and spicy greens with coarse grained flatbread and a flagon of watered wine. She sat beside him as he ate.

"Now then, who are you really? And don't say *Issios*. I'm not such a fool to believe that's your real name. If it were Isseus, I might think you had Isarran blood."

"Tsorreh wants to keep my identity secret—" he began.

"Then not another word!" Otenneh slapped her hands on her knees, cutting him off. Her lips compressed into a puckered line, but Danar caught the gleam of approval in her eyes. She gathered up the empty dishes and left him to his efforts to understand the complexities of five generations of Meklavaran kings.

Later that afternoon, Danar jerked alert from his studies at the sound of a Gelonian accent. He froze, hardly daring to breathe, acutely aware that only the thickness of a canvas curtain lay between him and discovery. Over the pounding of his heart, he overheard a man speaking halting Meklavaran, inquiring whether the shop had any scrolls in Gelone. Otenneh answered, her voice respectfully low as she listed a number of titles, including the Cilician *Odes* that Tsorreh loved so much.

Why didn't she just send the man away? Danar fretted for the transaction to be over, but Otenneh seemed in no hurry. Neither did her customer, who left with not only the *Odes,* but several other scrolls as well. She had a business to run, and must appear enthusiastic in obtaining the patronage of her city's conquerors.

"Oh, yes," the man might even now be saying to his fellow guards, *"that bookshop? Not much in the way of decent literature, but a very nice proprietress. Very obliging. Happy to have my custom. Gave me a good bargain."*

As the last twilight faded, the smells of garlic and mint wafted from the kitchen. Danar set aside his books, rubbing his temples and the knot between his eyebrows. Eavonen came in, moving as if his joints pained him. Tsorreh was not with him.

Danar's pulse stuttered. His mind roiled with questions: *What had happened—if she were still—if they had—if someone—*

"She is well," Eavonen said as he lowered himself onto one of the benches.

The kindness surprised Danar. He had thought the old man did not like him because he was Gelon, although he had not the slightest doubt of Eavonen's love for Tsorreh.

"Did she—" Danar paused, wet his lips, and stumbled through translating his thoughts into Meklavaran. "Did she find the one she sought?"

"Ganneron san'Cassarod? Yes, she obtained an audience with him. When I finished my duties, I called again for her, but she had been invited to remain as a guest of the house. She thought it better to accept. For the time being, at any rate."

Danar's spirits plummeted. He had assumed they would stay together, guided by Tsorreh's knowledge of Meklavar and the Shield. He had not anticipated being left on his own with no idea what to do next.

As Danar struggled to compose himself, Otenneh came

bustling in from the kitchen. For an old woman, she possessed surprising energy. Danar didn't think she ever stopped moving, but then, if she had had the care of Tsorreh as a girl, she would not have known a moment's idleness. Now she put her hands on her hips and glared at her husband. "What have you done with Tsorreh?"

"Taken her where she will be safe!" the old man replied. "And in far greater comfort than we can offer her."

"Ah. Lord Ganneron, as I expected." Otenneh nodded, as if it were the most natural thing in the world for Tsorreh to enjoy the best accommodations in the city.

"She has left you in our care," Eavonen said to Danar, "and bids you to familiarize yourself with the history of her people, in particular the lineage of Khored of Blessed Memory."

Danar thought he had been doing that, but refrained from saying so.

"The boy can't stay indoors all day," Otenneh put in, giving Danar an appraising look. "We'll have to devise a disguise."

"He might pass for Isarran if his hair were darker," Eavonen suggested.

"His nose is the wrong shape."

"Is it? It's smaller than mine, you mean."

Danar wanted to laugh at hearing the couple argue with such affection. His father and Lycian had fought regularly—or rather, she had shrieked and he had ignored her. "I don't want to place you in any danger," he said.

Otenneh replied, somewhat tartly, "Then why don't you remove yourself from Meklavar?"

Danar gestured to the pile of books and mumbled that Tsorreh had given him work. She had not merely supplied him with a pastime or a way of improving his understanding of written Meklavaran. She had meant for him to search for specific information. Two *alvara* were still unaccounted for. Their last reported whereabouts were here, in the city. Yellow Dovereth, yes . . . and purple Shebu'od. To Danar's relief, neither Otenneh nor Eavonen pressed him on the issue, but went about their own business.

In the days that followed, Danar applied himself to the texts. The material wasn't any more demanding than what he had been assigned throughout his growing years. Jaxar had valued scholarship as a necessity as well as a pleasure. As hard as Danar tried to immerse himself in the search for the two missing *alvara*, he could not entirely dispel the feeling of being vulnerable and isolated. In moments, he even felt abandoned. Most of the time, he did not have the heart to venture outside, even when Eavonen deemed it safe.

His doubts disappeared when Tsorreh reappeared two weeks later. From the back room, where he had finally managed to concentrate on tracing the lineage of the heirs of Dovereth through six generations, Danar sensed an approaching presence. Benerod's emerald gem pulsed as if charged with lightning. He was already on his feet, an emotion stronger than courage rushing through his veins, when he heard two sets of footsteps and Tsorreh's voice in the bookstore.

Caution vanished. Danar yanked aside the canvas curtain and rushed into the shop. There she was, dressed in typical Meklavaran women's clothing, this time brown silk that turned her skin to the color of sun-touched caramel. A pace behind her stood a man of middle years in a knee-length tunic of indigo brocade over narrow trousers. His shoulders were rounded like a scholar's, and his jaw was tight. There was no question in Danar's mind that this man was Ganneron san'Cassarod, bearing the name of both the house and the *alvar*.

Ganneron stood for a moment as if stunned. His scowl melted into incredulity and then recognition. *Benerod,* his lips moved silently. "The lady told me," he said aloud, "but I did not believe."

In those few words, Danar heard an entire history. Ganneron had been prepared to receive his family's heritage, but had thought the transfer no more than an antiquated ritual. It was easier to accept the truth if you had not spent your entire life believing something else.

Tsorreh turned to Danar. "Have you discovered anything?" *About the other two gems?*

"Only a little, and that information was very old. Come, I'll show you." In the back room, Danar pointed out the passages in one of the older bound volumes, its parchment pages stiff with age.

"My father spoke of how the lineages were broken," Ganneron said, reading over Danar's shoulder. "You did well to have found these references."

"I have some small training as a scholar," Danar replied.

Now they had located three *alvara*, including Teharod's pale rose of wisdom, although no one knew what dangers Sandaron endured or when he might join them in Meklavar. But surely, there was reason to hope that the others were hidden rather than truly lost.

They talked for a time longer, discussing what Danar had found and suggesting avenues for further research. When at last Ganneron indicated that they should be on their way, Danar longed to go with them, although a man so obviously Gelon and not known to the occupying authorities could not be openly welcomed into the mansion of one of Meklavar's ruling families.

Tsorreh must have read all this in Danar's face. "I have been thinking how you might make a place for yourself in the city. You have done a marvelous job with this research, and Lord Ganneron and I will pursue it, but we must have other, more current, sources of information. What if another guardian were walking the streets and neither one of us knew?"

"You think I could detect such a one?" Danar asked.

Ganneron said, "Even as you and I did, once we were in each other's presence. It is not very likely that you would cross paths in a city this size, but Lady Tsorreh and I agree that it is not good for a young man to remain indoors and physically inactive for long periods of time."

"I confess I am not enamored of the prospect," Danar said. "But how can I go wandering about the city? Won't people question what I'm doing there?"

"You cannot masquerade as a soldier, but you speak adequate Meklavaran"—and here Tsorreh smiled—"and you can read and write it as well. Not every Gelon knows even that much of our language. Many might trust a countryman over one of us."

"They think we all mean to deceive them," said Eavonen, "and most of the time they are right."

"I could hire myself out as a translator, you mean?" Da-

nar considered the idea. "I don't know the city well enough
to be a guide, and I would need different clothes."

"Eavonen and Otenneh can help you with both." Tsorreh took a small leather bag from her pocket and held it
out. Danar heard the soft metallic clink as the contents
shifted.

Ganneron gestured to the door. Tsorreh shot Danar a
parting glance. Then she was gone.

Following Tsorreh's suggestion, Otenneh helped Danar to
buy clothing that, while not as fine as what he had worn in
his father's house, was still good enough to set him apart
from the beggars. He wore his knife in its leather sheath,
but not ostentatiously. Within a short time, Danar had
learned the location of every major marketplace, the inns
and stables within the city walls and in the encampments
outside, and most of the brothels. Every aspect of life was
tainted by the presence of the conqueror, the cost of the
tribute sent to Aidon, and the tariffs levied on every load of
goods transported through the Var Pass.

A block of warehouses and other buildings facing the
largest market square had been turned into a second garrison, and other structures had been leveled to create a defensive perimeter. Danar kept well clear of the garrison, so
as not to attract attention.

He had a second reason for avoiding the location, for a
short distance away stood a Qr temple. He could not tell the
building's original purpose, but the banners bearing the insignia of the Scorpion god looked fairly new. No Meklavarans approached the temple. Knowing Tsorreh's strong
faith, Danar could not imagine any of her countrymen looking kindly on the god of a foreign invader.

The Gelonian soldiers didn't show any interest, either.
They had their own gods, Protector of Soldiers and Bringer
of Fortune. A few might even pray to the Remover of Sor-
rows, who brought peace at the end of a painful struggle.
What need had they for Qr, even if it were favored by the
Ar-King?

When Danar remembered how Lycian had poisoned

Tsorreh, Lycian who was devoted to the Scorpion, he felt a sickening uneasiness at the presence of the temple.

As days blended into weeks and then months, Danar cultivated the habit of stopping by this tavern or that one, being moderate in both his spending and his consumption of the local barley wine, or the potent rice wine that came up the pass from Denariya. He posted himself near those establishments patronized by his countrymen, mostly infantry and animal handlers. Only the highest-ranking officers were housed with Ner-Manir-Thierra in the royal palace in the Upper City, as the Gelon called the *meklat*. Foot soldiers barracked in the garrison, but even the meanest of them had coin to spend in the city. As a result, Danar soon had enough steady work to move into lodgings of his own, a narrow room above a bakery. He kept the name Issios and affected a faint Isarran accent.

The drinking places outside the city walls were the cheapest. There, Danar could nurse an ale for several hours while he looked for customers. One afternoon, as was his custom, he settled himself at a rickety table outside one of the less disreputable taverns with a chipped pottery beaker of something that tasted vaguely of hops and alcohol. He recognized a few of the local regulars, drinking away what few coins they'd earned or stolen overnight. Wincing at the edgy taste of his drink, he sipped slowly. He was beginning to regret having spent anything on this camel-swill. It made *k'th*, the fermented mares' milk of the Azkhantian nomads, taste elegant.

Danar looked up at the sound of Gelone spoken with a Westriver accent. A dozen soldiers, newly arrived, by the condition of their boots, had entered the outdoor area. The Westriver man wore the token of a lower-grade officer.

"What a backwater!" one of them grumbled. "Can't eat that muck they call food, not a drop of decent grape wine in sight and, to make matters worse, can't make out one word in ten of the local gabble."

"Yar. Those natives mumble something fierce when they're not cursing us outright. Landlord! Bring drink!" The second soldier began pounding on the table, which looked as if it might disintegrate with each blow.

"He won't understand you," Danar said in Gelone. "Or if he does, he won't let on. Please, allow me." When the proprietor poked his head out the door in response to the clamor, Danar politely requested, in Meklavaran, the best of the barley wine for everyone, adding that no expense should be spared. At that rate, these Gelon might get something halfway decent, even if it wasn't what they were used to.

The man with the Westriver accent sipped his tentatively, then tipped his beaker and gulped. His larynx worked convulsively as he swallowed. He set his drink down and smacked his lips. "Not ale, but it'll do. Thank you, friend."

Danar inclined his head with a half-smile. "Just arrived?"

One of the others groaned. The Westriver man shook his head. "Three days ago, our team crawled into this godsforsaken place. Protector of Soldiers, who would have thought it? Three days and three stinking nights."

"Double shifts," one of his men added.

The others responded with more groans and, "On the lookout for—"

"Should you be telling me this?" Danar broke in.

The man who'd done most of the groaning looked away. The Westriver fellow said with a conspiratorial wink, "Why not? Keep an eye out for us, there'll be something in it for you."

Danar permitted himself a smile of discretion.

"Gods." The fourth soldier stared glumly into the hollow depths of his beaker. "We've had nothing fit to drink since we left Verenzza. Nor anything fit to eat."

"Cheer up," Danar said, "it could be worse."

"Yar," agreed the second, "we could be in Azkhantia!" At this, his comrades nodded agreement and took a long draft of their drinks.

"Not too bad, this stuff," one of them said. "What d'you call it?"

"Barley wine," Danar said.

"Not even any decent grapes," another mumbled as he took another swig.

"Could be, on those hills we went through," the Westriver officer mused. "I could come back here, once the war's over, and terrace them properly . . ."

The conversation revolved around vineyards until the tavernkeeper brought out a pitcher to pour another round of drinks. Danar declined his with a quick shake of his head. The Westriver officer set aside his second beaker, still half-full. His expression shifted to one of watchfulness. He wouldn't tell his men how to spend their off-duty time, but neither would he let them get themselves into trouble. Instead, he let them grumble while he stayed relatively sober.

The men drank, and the officer watched, and Danar pretended to drink. After a time, Danar eased into his usual pitch, implying that he could provide not only guide and translation services, but connections of other sorts. With a roll of his eyes, the officer indicated that his men wouldn't be going anywhere but to their lodgings.

"Still, it's good to see a friendly face and have a civilized conversation. My men'll catch the language, at least enough not to be cheated blind every time. Meanwhile, we know who we can trust." The officer sketched a gesture toward his own chest. "Irvan of Westriver."

Danar opened his mouth to say that his father knew an Irvan who was a scholar in Aidon. "Issios"—he searched for some suitably large place—". . . of Roramenth."

"Ah, Roramenth. Plenty of foreigners there. Isarran blood, have you?"

Danar shrugged and Irvan nodded in agreement of the insignificance of such things.

"So, Issios of Roramenth, if my men have need of your services, where would we find you?"

"Not here, not usually of a morning," Danar agreed. "But you might try The Two Sheaves. It's by the Well of Four Waters. You'll find that one easy enough; it's where the drovers bring the onagers."

"Two Sheaves. Sounds more like a bakery."

"They ferment the grain. Barley, of course, and rice."

"Rice wine?" Irvan lifted his eyebrows; Denariyan rice wine was an expensive luxury in Aidon. He dug in his belt pouch and offered Danar a Gelonian coin, generous but not overly so. "Thanks for the tip."

Danar slipped the coin into his own belt. "It's been awhile since I was home. Not much news reaches us here."

"That I'll believe, but life goes as it will. You know Prince Thessar's dead?"

The question was a test, with the accompanying too-casual glance. "In Azkhantia? Yes, may-his-memory-inspire-fear-in-all-transgressors, that much we did hear. Who's heir now, Prince Chion?"

"Eventually, though he's not yet been formally confirmed. There's a brother—not Chion's, his father's—so the issue's clouded. Some favor that one, although he's said to be a cripple without ambition. What difference does it make? We serve the one whose backside warms the Lion Throne."

"May the reign of Ar-Cinath-Gelon be everlasting," Danar said, lifting his beaker to mask the relief washing hot and naked through him.

My father still lives.

Chapter Seventeen

AS the days swung toward Danar's third winter in Meklavar, the seasonal rains set in. The first winter had been a sodden misery, and the second one not much better. He had never imagined the place could be so cold. Meklavar lay far to the southeast of Gelon, but it was also high in the mountains. Slush had buried every street, and the damp wind cut through layers of clothing. The only time he'd felt warm was when he practiced sword and unarmed fighting with Irvan's men. At least the city seemed quieter, or perhaps so mired in mud and slog and misery that no one had the energy to make trouble. The number of beggars seemed to increase every day. The soldiers grumbled as always.

Watching the rain slant down from his vantage under the overhanging eaves of a tavern, Danar thought of Zevaron. If the winters were bad here in Meklavar, how much worse might they be on the steppe? He wondered where Sandaron was, somewhere in Denariya where it was hot all the time, hot and dry, and how could one man or even an entire army find a single person in such a broad, diverse land? Maybe it was all fruitless and he'd be stuck here, waiting uselessly, until his bones turned to mildew.

Danar rubbed his chest and felt the subtle, reassuring pulse of the green gem. His doubts eased. Despite Tsorreh's warning that the search might take a long time, he had not expected it to be years. Waiting had always been difficult for him, but that was no reason to lose hope. Eriseth's quality was steadfast endurance. Such magic would not be easily lost, even in a place as wild as Denariya.

At least Danar and Tsorreh had found one critical petal gem, for all the good it did anyone. It had taken them over a year to trace the lineage of Shebu'od, and at this rate, they would all be doddering oldsters by the time they found them all. It had taken Danar's genealogical research, Ganneron's trading contacts, and a dose of extraordinary good luck to locate the current guardian, penniless and living in a lower city house that had been badly damaged during the conquest. Forrenad was an elderly man, frail and somewhat wandering in his wits. Shebu'od's attribute was said to be strength, but Forrenad did not seem to have received any benefit from its influence. Although Ganneron had taken Forrenad into the Cassarod household, the old man's health had not improved. Forrenad's only relative was a niece, orphaned in the battle for the city. Tsorreh was already training the girl to receive Shebu'od's gem, a violation of tradition that clearly shocked Ganneron.

Sighing, Danar handed his beaker of mint tea, now tepid, back to the barkeep. Just beyond the shelter of the eaves, mud slicked the paving stones. His woolen cloak, bought from a used-clothing seller with his own money, had enough natural lanolin to smell like unwashed sheep in weather like this, but it kept out the worst of the wet. The morning had worn thin, and the number of people hurrying about their errands had dwindled. Gelonian patrols, their oiled-leather capes draped like soggy sheets around their shoulders, continued on their rounds. As luck would have it, the rain let up just as he stepped into the street.

Danar had reached the central market square when he heard the rhythmic footsteps of men moving in formation. He scurried out of the path of the soldiers, hunching his shoulders so he looked like any other city dweller. Gelon passed him, row after row, perhaps a hundred in all. Their expressions were grim, their eyes focused. They meant business, not idle display. Something must have happened.

Danar had heard no rumors this morning, nor in the past few days. The city had been relatively quiet. There had been no sightings of Iskarnon the Prophet since the rains of this latest winter began.

The bulk of the soldiers headed for the city garrison. The rest divided into patrols, four in each instead of the usual two. Within a very short time, the soldiers dispersed to their posts.

Bystanders began moving back into the market square. Vendors replaced their wares. Street urchins scampered between carts and barrels, snatching up whatever small items had fallen. As the rain lessened, more customers came, anxious to be about their business before another downpour.

Danar adopted his most nonchalant demeanor as he sauntered over to the nearest stall. It was sturdier than most and therefore more resistant to the rain but also more difficult to move in a hurry. Under the awning, an overturned bench had once held rows of pottery, jars and plates, cups and small trays. The goods now lay in a heap on the pavement. Much of it looked damaged. Danar bent to pick up a cup that was only slightly chipped and handed it to the harried-looking owner. The man paused in his stream of muttered curses to accept the cup.

"What's the news, friend?" Danar asked, using a lower-class Meklavaran accent.

The pottery man's face twisted even tighter. "Naught to do with us, though we'll bear the brunt of it. Look at this! A month's work gone! And for what? Some courier comes riding into the outer garrison and look what happens. How's a man to make a living?"

"Aye, it's a hard life." Danar shook his head in sympathy. "I wonder what got them so stirred up. Azkhantia's a long way off and I've never heard of the Denariyans taking sword to anyone they could trade with instead."

"We'll find out soon enough." With a nod, the man returned to his salvage, a clear signal the conversation was over.

Turning away, Danar lifted his gaze to the sky. Through a gap in the lower clouds, he caught a glimpse of sky. Thunderheads billowed above. A wave of restlessness shivered through him. His mouth went dry, as if the sky had sucked all the moisture out of him. The muscles of his shoulders threatened to cramp, but he could not wrench his gaze away. A pang lanced through his chest.

He remembered standing on Victory Hill in Aidon with Tsorreh not long after her arrival in his father's house. She had looked up at the sky with an expression of horror and fascination. Now, as then, something moved in those shifting layers of storm and light, something pale as ice and black as ashes. Something was gathering in the north. When Danar squinted up at the sky again, however, the clouds looked normal.

Near the far edge of the square, he glimpsed Irvan at the head of a double pair, moving briskly toward the King's Gate. Perhaps later in the evening, Danar might find the officer and buy him some rice wine in exchange for gossip.

As had become his custom, Danar paused for a cheap breakfast, Denariyan rice and lentils mixed with onions, steamed in folded leaves. He chewed slowly, letting the spices warm his mouth. He hadn't eaten meat in a couple of weeks, whereas back in Aidon he had eaten it every day. Idly, he wondered if his father's health might not have benefited from simpler food.

As he licked the last morsels from the leaves, the back of Danar's neck prickled. His first thought was that he was being watched. He glanced around, but saw nothing out of the ordinary. The market was as full of vendors as it was going to get, which wasn't very, and customers were already haggling over the best of what was offered. Before long, Danar thought, the whole city would be living on rice and lentils.

Yellow, bright and evanescent as a single ray piercing an overcast sky, brushed his mind. He flinched as if someone had struck him from behind. The old woman selling the rice balls regarded him warily. He felt as if the masks of his disguise had been momentarily lifted, leaving him exposed.

Yellow . . . and truth . . .

His pulse leaped in his throat. With an effort, he kept his expression calm and his movements careless as he searched his surroundings. The sense of another *alvar*, near enough to taste, vanished.

Dovereth! And so close! Danar clamped his teeth together to avoid screaming in exasperation. He knew from his first meeting with Ganneron that he could not detect another Shield gem except at very close range. And now he had let one of them slip through his grasp. Maybe it wasn't too late . . .

He quartered the market, then traced its perimeter, pausing to concentrate on that inner trace, but found nothing. Dovereth's guardian had disappeared without leaving a clue to his identity.

Danar muttered a curse he had never dared use in his father's house. There was nothing more to be done, except to let Tsorreh know that the Dovereth gem was still in the city. Surely, some news was better than none. The best way to send a message was through Eavonen. A visit to the bookshop would be pleasant. He'd been so busy working, so preoccupied, that he hadn't seen the old couple in months. He found, much to his surprise, that he missed them.

A short time later, he paused on the bookstore threshold. The door was locked, which was unusual. Alarmed, he rapped on it with the back of his knuckles. A moment later, it cracked open. Otenneh stepped back to admit him. When he tried to greet her properly, she made a hushing gesture and pointed to the back room. Curious, Danar followed her.

Tsorreh jumped to her feet, her skin flushed in the light of the oil lamps. She made a movement toward Danar, and he knew she would have embraced him were it not for the presence of Eavonen and a pair of grim-faced Meklavarans. Clearly, Ganneron had sent them as protection. Although Danar could not see any weapons, he had no doubt they were armed. This time, Tsorreh wore the dress of a household servant, a sleeved tunic over narrow trousers. A coif of the same nondescript gray cloth covered her hair. The effect was one of anonymity, turning her into a person of no importance. One of the Meklavarans was dressed as a minor noble, the other as another servant.

To fill the awkward moment, Danar bowed, Meklavaran-style. Tsorreh's cheeks paled. Her eyes, he now noticed, were too bright.

"Sit down, lad." Eavonen's voice was grave.

Danar lowered himself to the nearest bench. "Why, what has happened? Have you heard from Sandaron?"

Tsorreh sat beside Danar and took one of his hands. "No," she said in a low voice, "this has nothing to do with him. The news is from Aidon."

Aidon?

"Danar, I'm so sorry."

The room turned chill. Danar's heart sounded unnaturally loud in his ears. He remembered the moment of unexpected joy at hearing his father still lived, lived against all reason and expectation. How long ago had that been? Two years? Longer? He'd just met Irvan. That time belonged to another age, to another son. To someone else.

"How?"

"His heart must have given out. At least, there has been no talk of foul means." Tsorreh's voice sounded distant, as if it came from the far end of an enormous, echoing chamber. "It happened some months ago. Your uncle is dead as well—"

"Cinath, too?" That could not be by chance.

"Yes, and your cousin Chion has claimed the Lion Throne. Your father's death cleared the path for him to do so without challenge."

Chion!

"More likely, he saw his chance," Eavonen said.

"Or created it," muttered the Meklavaran in noble dress. "From everything we know of him, he's twice as bad."

My father dies and the skies are full of evil omens . . . my cousin has committed the most heinous of murders, patricide . . . Danar could not summon even a morsel of grief for Cinath. The only surprise was that he had lasted this long before someone—the Qr priests, his own ambitious son—*gods, even my stepmother, for all I know!*—decided he was of no further use to them.

He found himself on his feet. "I must go home."

"We cannot risk you." Tsorreh's fingers closed his.

"There is no one else who can hold my cousin accountable," Danar protested, "no one else who has the legal right."

"No, child!" Otenneh sounded genuinely distressed. "Think what you are saying! To return now would surely mean your death. Listen to my lady!"

"You do not understand," Danar said. "Cinath was feared, even despised in certain quarters, but he was once a strong Ar-King. No one doubted his fitness to rule. Chion is ruthless and clever, but he has never commanded the respect of the noble families. He's a fool if he thinks they'll accept him simply because of his blood."

"He speaks truly, *te-ravah*." The second Meklavaran faced Danar. "We have heard reports of riots in the streets of Aidon. The major cities of Gelon on the verge of civil unrest."

Danar began pacing. One dreadful suspicion after another seized his thoughts. He felt as if he were about to jump out of his skin.

Chion—not a fool—his father's son—but he killed his own father—must have planned—had Qr played a role in it?

If Chion had a hand in Jaxar's death—

The green gem ignited within him. Verdant light swept clear the jumble of his thoughts for a moment. With a wrenching effort, he forced himself to stand still. To speak rationally, even if he did not feel that way. Too much was at stake.

"*I* can unite them," Danar said. "I can and I must."

"Then all the more reason for you to remain here," said the first Meklavaran. "With any luck, Ner-Manir-Thierra will be recalled and we'll have our first real chance at freedom."

Danar whirled to face the older man. "You think only of your own petty, provincial concerns! There's more at stake here than an ill-conceived rebellion!" His words were hateful, but he couldn't help himself. Rage numbed the pain he could not face. "What does Meklavar matter, compared to an empire spanning a hundred Meklavars? Or are you so narrow in vision, so heedless of anything beyond your own noses, that you think the fate of the entire world depends on *Meklavar?*"

"I'd expect no less from a pampered Gelonian pup!" The Meklavaran glared at Danar, fists clenched at his sides. In another moment, he'd throw a punch.

Danar wished he would.

"A Gelon," Tsorreh interposed, "who is under my protection."

The Meklavaran rocked back on his heels. "My lady, you can't seriously—"

Danar burst out, "I can fight my own battles!"

"Enough." Although Tsorreh spoke the word quietly, the entire room fell silent.

Danar couldn't speak. He could barely breathe. He lowered himself back to the bench with what dignity he could muster.

"Enough," Tsorreh repeated. She shot Danar a look that was at once piercing and compassionate. She saw his anger, his alarm at the suspicions roiling in his mind, the impossibility of his grief. Danar thought of all she had lost—husband and grandfather and stepson, and her own mother long ago. Now Zevaron was somewhere on the steppe, and there was no word from Sandaron. And Jaxar—she had loved Jaxar as a father.

"Danar, you had best come with me back to Lord Ganneron's house. You should not be alone at a time like this." Tsorreh's eyes were filled with an expression so kind, he thought his heart would shatter. "Your father has died. You need to mourn him. Everything else can wait."

He tried to speak, to declare that he would do so, but in the proper time. Gelon needed him now. He could not allow Chion to claim the throne. Then it came to him that he was no longer just his father's son or his country's heir apparent. He was the guardian of Beneroth, and he was not free to follow his own desires.

He started shaking and could not stop. His throat was tight and congested with feeling. No sound emerged.

Tsorreh took his hands, drawing him to his feet. Her fingers were hot, as if with fever, or perhaps he himself had turned to ice.

Shock, he thought distantly, and then: *I cannot afford to be weak.*

Tsorreh's touch was so gentle, he could have broken away with a sigh. Together with Otenneh, she pulled the cloak worn by one of her guards over his shoulders and took away his knife in its carrying sheath, saying it would only create an excuse to detain him. He did not understand why that mattered. Otenneh massaged something into his hair. Someone said, "He'll do," and then the second Meklavaran slipped a silk cord around his neck.

There was no reason not to go with Tsorreh. She had known Jaxar. She had walked the paths of grief, and at a time when her people needed her—as much as his needed him now. It must have been agony for her to have been a captive of her enemy, with her own loss so raw.

Danar recovered himself a little as they emerged into the brightness of the day. The covering of clouds was already breaking up. He must pretend to be a servant walking respectfully behind his master. His body sagged, as if it had not the strength to endure the weight of his grief. It wasn't hard to round his shoulders, lower his head, and let the Meklavaran in noble dress take the lead, to ignore what he saw and heard around him, as if his only purpose in the world were to trudge along. No one tried to speak to him.

His pulse sped up as they approached the King's Gate. He felt half-naked without his knife, but there was no help for it. His disguise was minimal, just a cloak and whatever coloring agent Otenneh had rubbed into his hair. Tsorreh did not seem to be worried. He must trust that as a servant he would be ignored, invisible.

The guard at the entrance to the stairs had been doubled, but they did not check for identity beyond the passage tokens. They were looking for weapons, not specific individuals. Finding nothing beyond the small jeweled dagger that the first Meklavaran handed over, the guards waved them upward. The dagger, Danar noticed, was not returned.

The stairs narrowed as they neared the top, where the wooden gates had been burned and never replaced. Soot still streaked the stone walls. Beyond them rose the towers and spires of the palaces. Many of them looked untouched, but others here and there showed damage. One building dominated the *meklat*, a palace grand in scope and peerless in execution. Banners bearing the insignia of the Lion Throne hung to each side of the elaborate formal entrance.

They ascended to a city that was far less populated than the markets and tavern districts below. There were no beggars; almost everyone here seemed to be either a noble, a servant, or a Gelon. A pair of Qr priests with cloth bands bearing the scorpion insignia wrapped around their shaved heads came into sight. Tsorreh tensed but then the priests turned aside and headed for one of the palaces, taking no notice of her.

Their destination proved to be an elegant, modest-sized house a short distance from the palace. By the time they had crossed the entrance hall, Tsorreh no longer meekly followed the men. Passing them, she strode through the arch at the far end. Two servants, one a steward by his dress and bearing, stood aside respectfully as she proceeded into a second hall. A third hurried to open a door for her.

Danar followed Tsorreh through a series of corridors to a back part of the house. Unlike Gelonian homes, this one had no central courtyard, nor any outdoor gardens. The winters here were bitterly cold, so that even the meanest hovel wrapped itself around its hearth.

Tsorreh waved Danar through a door and closed it behind her. There was no lock. The room was furnished for sitting, much like the one behind the bookshop but on a more luxurious scale. With a sigh, she dropped to a bench upholstered in garnet velvet. "Come, sit by me. Would you like wine?"

He stayed where he was. The air was too thick. He did not know how to negotiate the magnitude of his feelings. He had never lost anyone this dear to him, for his mother had died when he was still an infant. Zevaron's grief had been terrifying in comparison to his own.

Somehow, he could not tell by what means, they began to talk, circling their way through ordinary topics. The first time Jaxar's name was spoken, Tsorreh blinked and looked away, but by the fifth time, she was weeping openly.

He sat beside her on the bench and put his arms around her. Her face, hot and wet, pressed against his shoulder. His body rocked with her sobs. His own eyes were dry, as if his tears could flow only through hers.

At last she straightened herself, wiped her eyes, and

poured a cup of wine for each of them. This time, Danar did not refuse. He had not expected his father's death to come as such a shock. Jaxar had been so very ill when Danar and Ze-varon had fled Aidon. A miracle—and Tsorreh's Meklavaran medicine—had prolonged Jaxar's life even this long. Now the worst had come, all his unacknowledged fears realized, and he could do nothing. Nothing but let his friend weep for him.

"It will not always be this hard," she said, setting down her wine cup still half-full. "But for the moment . . ."

For the moment, duty. Only he did not know where his lay.

A gentle knock sounded and, a moment later, the door cracked open. Danar caught a fragment of whispered con-versation, concluding with Tsorreh saying, "I'll be there shortly."

The door closed with a snick of the latch. Tsorreh stirred on the bench beside Danar. "It seems we have run out of time," she said. "I had not planned—I would not have cho-sen this way, but perhaps it is an unexpected blessing."

"I don't understand." How could any of this—his fa-ther's death, his cousin's murderous schemes, the looming threat of anarchy at home . . . the insistent distraction of Benerod's gem—be considered a blessing?

"I had not thought the end would be so soon," she went on with infuriating patience, "or I would have waited to bring you the news. Forrenad cannot last much longer. The physician says an hour, perhaps a little more. I must go—to be there when the—when the—"

She took his hands once more and this time hers felt cool, her touch hesitant. She had never been easy speaking of the *alvara*, and the intensity of the last hour—or had it been more?—had affected her.

"Danar, I would like you to witness the transfer. We are trying something new, for the heir is a young woman, as well prepared as we can make her, in the presence of those who have taught her. I think it might help you as well. To put things into perspective, I mean. Each of us, in the normal course of life, comes to bear an *alvar* through the loss of someone we love."

Except Zevaron, who thought you dead. Except me, who never knew Benerod's heir.

"So we are a fellowship of mourners. It is not so different to lose a father or grandfather while taking up the burden of a Shield gem, as what has happened to you."

They did not face assassination and civil war at home, Danar thought, and then: *Tsorreh's city had fallen—Thessar was enraged and vindictive—she'd been unable to speak of Meklavar's suffering.*

He hung his head. "I do not know what good I can do, but I will come." Tsorreh looked as if she would reply, but said nothing.

The feeling of being utterly adrift subsided. Danar's body knew what to do; his heart beat and his lungs took in breath. His muscles flexed as he ascended two flights of stairs. Another corridor led to a wide door, polished wood that gleamed softly. The green crystal pulsed like a second heart in his chest. His skin tingled as if a feather had brushed the back of his neck.

The room beyond was amply proportioned and furnished in Meklavaran style. Oil lamps, some of them with mantles of pieced colored glass, cast warm light from their alcoves on the walls. Intricately patterned Denariyan carpets cushioned the floor. Ganneron sat in a chair instead of the usual bench, a chair with carved armrests and a matching footstool on which a gray striped cat slept. To one side, a man sat in a smaller chair. Wrapped in blankets, he looked withered and gravely ill.

Also present was a woman about Danar's age, dressed like the invalid in an unadorned black robe. She held herself with such poise, she needed no jewels or bright colors to draw the eye. The women of Meklavar tended to be small and light-boned, but this girl was almost as tall as Danar. He wondered if she had been trained in archery and horsemanship as well as dancing.

The servant who had waited just inside the door withdrew. For an instant, no one moved.

The room hummed with power. Danar could almost see the play of energy and color—Cassarod's ruby light from Ganneron, a tenuous thread of violet from the old man, a radiance of green from himself. From Tsorreh came a listening, a waiting, an aching echo of gold. She might no longer bear the heart-stone of the Shield, but she held its memory.

Tsorreh went to one of the two empty seats, indicating that Danar should take the other. Ganneron turned to Danar and said, "I am sorry to hear of your father's passing. He was never an enemy to us. May his memory be a blessing in times to come."

"Thank you," Danar said, adding on impulse, "sir."

A smile ghosted the corners of Ganneron's mouth. "I am not *sir* to you, except in the sense I am your elder. Here we make no distinction based on rank or race, for the fellowship in which we have been enlisted makes us equal."

There followed a lapse in the conversation, the silence marked only by the stertorous breathing of the invalid, Forrenad. Danar was surprised the old man was still upright, for the effort of drawing in and then expelling each breath seemed almost beyond his strength.

Danar glanced at the young woman, sitting so tall and still, her hands folded in her lap, her face tilted downward. The nearest lamp was to one side and slightly behind her, so that shadows muted her face.

"It is time," Tsorreh said.

"I . . ." Forrenad roused himself with a brittle energy, like a candle's guttering flame. "I am ready."

The girl knelt before the old man. The affection with which she took his hand moved Danar unexpectedly.

Forrenad coughed, struggling to breathe. Ganneron supported him on one side and Tsorreh on the other. Tsorreh looked hard at the girl, a frown shading the skin between her brows. The girl nodded. With her two hands, she raised Forrenad's to his chest.

"Let it go," Tsorreh murmured. "You have carried this burden long enough. Give it over, so that you may rest."

"Let me bear it for you." The girl's voice was light and gentle.

Heat battered Danar's skin. A distant, thudding rhythm blanketed all other sound. Under the girl's fingertips, under his own, Danar felt the parchment dryness of Forrenad's skin, the texture of a few sparse hairs, the arch of ribs. Cartilage softened—

*And then he could not see or hear or touch. Water boiled
around him, chill and steaming. It blinded him. It flooded
him. Once more, fleshless bones shackled his ankle, pulling
him down, down, down into the lightless depths. Now, as
then, green-tinted brilliance blazed, piercing the surging currents.*

*He was the source of its emerald effulgence, and he was
also the tide on which it lay like a fleck of jeweled foam.*

—cartilage softened into mist. A nugget of purple light,
like the dimmest, deepest star, emerged.

Aged fingers, a laboring heart, a mind almost at rest,
called to it.

Young fingers, a strong heart, a mind keen and eager,
called to it.

The *alvar* of Shebu'od answered.

Danar sensed the moment when the gem broke free, the
instant later when it became part of the girl's body. There
was no sense of penetration or of invasion, only relief and
violet heat searing the blood.

Danar's pulse slowed from its hectic pace. Trembling
seized his muscles and then subsided. His vision cleared. He
no longer felt faint.

The girl wavered where she knelt. Without thinking, Danar caught her in his arms. She was heavier than he expected, a density of muscle and bone and spirit. Her hair
smelled of sandalwood. Then she lifted her head and looked
directly at him. He was struck by the gold-limned softness
of her skin, the mouth now in repose but expressive all the
same, the eyes full of fire.

Marisse . . .

A swirl of color-tinged power touched his mind: *Danar.*

His heart opened as if they had always belonged to one
another. The light in the room took on a quality like sun-
infused glass. Its sweetness drenched him. Grief diminished
like the ebbing of a wave. It would come again, but the
memory of this moment would fortify his spirit.

Ganneron lifted Forrenad as if the old man were a child,
so light, all fire fled. Tsorrch stood beside him, resting a
hand on his bony shoulder. Forrenad breathed with painful
hesitation.

"Stay with her," she said to Danar, and followed Ganneron from the chamber.

In Danar's arms, Marisse stirred. "I should be . . . with him . . . at the last."

It would not be long now. Danar could not think how to say that she needed all her strength to adapt to the *alvar.* He heard his own voice: "He has already said good-bye."

She shuddered, and for a terrible moment, he wondered if he had offended her. Clearly, Tsorreh had prepared her to receive the petal gem. She must have warned Marisse that the old man would not survive, that in the usual course of events, the *alvara* were transferred only when the bearer's death was imminent.

If Marisse raised her eyes to him, he would see the tears he had yet to shed for Jaxar. If she touched her tongue to honey, its sweetness would fill his mouth.

Was he thinking clearly? Was this sense of union an illusion born of sorrow and the strange powers of the *alvara*? Was this usual when multiple petal gems came into proximity?

Did it matter?

"Hold me," Marisse said, and the world became right.

Chapter Eighteen

DANAR opened his eyes at the sound of the door latch clicking open. He and Marisse had fallen asleep in each other's arms, cushioned by the discarded blankets. Somehow, they had ended up drowsing and talking in turns. A connection flowed between them, nurtured as much by their shared understanding of grief as by the contact of their bodies.

He lifted his head as Tsorreh entered. The light from her oil lamp fluttered like moth wings across the walls. She touched Marisse's shoulder.

"Oh!" Marisse cried. "I must have fallen asleep."

"That is the best medicine of all," Tsorreh said. "How do you feel?"

"Just startled, I think." Marisse glanced at Danar and colored. "And a little embarrassed." She began clambering to her feet, lost her balance, and sat down again. Danar smiled at her momentary awkwardness.

"Take it slowly," Tsorreh said. "Let Danar help you to a chair. We must sit before we can stand."

"And stand before we can walk, as it is written, and walk before we can run." Grimacing, Marisse took Danar's hand. He restrained himself from kissing her fingertips. She wavered to the nearest chair but did not release Danar's hand.

"It will pass," he said, "the disorientation, I mean."

Tsorreh lifted her lamp to examine Marisse's face. "The worst is over already."

"*You* were sick for weeks," Marisse pointed out, hastening to add, "I meant no discourtesy, *te-ravah*."

"You spoke plainly, child. That is all. Yes, I was much more ill than you are or than Danar was. You must remember that I had no idea what had happened to me. I was unprepared, and there was no one with me who could explain. I could not allow anyone else to undergo that, not if I could prevent it. I did what I could for you. I see now the benefit of having another guardian as a helper."

Marisse's fingers tightened on Danar's.

Tsorreh looked thoughtful. "You two are something new, bound not only by what you safeguard but by something greater. Perhaps grief. Perhaps the polarity of being male and female. I wonder if even Khored of Blessed Memory could have foreseen this. Until I myself . . . I had not known it was possible for a woman to inherit one of the Shield gems. There is nothing to suggest it in the holy writings. We know only of Khored and his brothers. In your case, Marisse, you are not only of the lineage, but you had a certain sympathy of mind, having nursed Forrenad. He might not have been willing to surrender his *alvar* to anyone he loved less."

"As it was," Marisse said, "we were almost too late."

"This was lost for generations and yet it found its way to me." With his free hand, Danar touched his chest where the gem of Benerod rested. "In Gelon, I worshipped the Remover of Difficulties. Perhaps he is only an aspect of your Most Holy One. Or perhaps this *alvar* knew when it was time to be found."

"Perhaps it sensed what stirs in the north." Marisse bit her lip. "The ancient enemy, whose true name no man knows."

"Then it may be a woman who discovers its secret and masters it," Danar said.

A knot of traffic had gathered at the King's Gates, where the narrow opening provided an easy checkpoint. One of

Irvan's men was arguing with the guards, insisting that his right to go *down* took precedence over all the people wishing to come *up*. Danar remembered the man from their first encounter, the one who'd found an endless stream of things to complain about. Politely but firmly, the guards informed him that who went through the Gate and in what order was their business, not his. If the man had any sense, he'd spend his time petitioning the Protector of Soldiers or any other god in the pantheon who bestowed patience, or he'd still be waiting when the next day dawned.

Danar offered his own private thanks to the Bringer of Fortune and stepped forward. He nodded a greeting to Irvan's man. "Corren, isn't it?"

"You've a good memory on you, lad." The soldier's eyes flickered to the knife strapped to Danar's thigh.

Danar adopted a pose of careless waiting. "Been here awhile?"

"Hmmph! If I didn't know better"—Corren lowered his voice—"I'd say yon lummock was in the pay of the natives."

"And you've got better ways to pass the time."

Corren drew Danar aside. "Captain's running us all ragged. We was supposed to get reinforcements from home. Instead, a whole company's been pulled out."

"Rotten luck, but maybe the poor bastards have worse in store. Where are they headed? Or is that a secret?"

Corren snorted. "Azkhantia, most like."

Danar's eyebrows lifted. So Chion was pursuing his father's ambitions on the steppe. Then he must be secure at home. Before Danar could say anything more, the guard at the Gate indicated that one of them should proceed.

"Go on," Danar said. "I'm done for the day. I can wait." As he watched Corren hurry down the stairs, he thought, *That should do it.*

The next day, Danar went to see Irvan in the city garrison. The office was cramped, little better than a closet, and the desk was a slab of wood propped on a folding campstool.

"Corren says you have business of your own that takes you to the Upper City," Irvan said. "Your affairs are your own, you understand? I don't care if they're strictly legal, only that they're done on a regular basis."

"That's right."

"I've need of a courier I can trust—one of us"—meaning Gelon—"and I can't spare the men."

Danar composed his features into an expression of thoughtful consideration. "It might be best if you didn't entrust anything of a sensitive nature to me. I wouldn't want to be responsible—"

"I have more than enough routine messages." Irvan made a dismissive gesture. "Or do you suppose one of the rebel faction would rob you of a livestock feed requisition?"

"No, no, of course, if that's all you need. But tell me, *is* there a viable 'rebel faction'? I haven't seen anything that well-organized."

"Then you've been keeping to the better districts. Things have been quiet this winter, but if that prophet fellow shows his face . . ."

"It's said he favors springtime appearances, but it isn't wise to put too much credit in that. Why borrow trouble needlessly?"

"Exactly," the captain agreed, although his expression remained grim. "Look, check in every morning around this hour and see what I have for you. I'll have a special passage token for you in case there are any questions. There will be payment, as well. Your usual rates?"

"Of course." Danar knew perfectly well that a courier would be worth much more, but preferred to let Irvan think he was getting a bargain. It was enough that he now had a legitimate reason to come and go into the Upper City. And to see Marisse.

The next morning, Danar presented himself as agreed. Irvan wasn't at the garrison, but his aide handed Danar a stack of messages. One was a secured packet that not only bore a seal but required an answer. It was for General Manir, once his father's friend and one of the few people who could recognize Danar.

Danar stared at it for a long moment. *Of course, it would be. It's too much to hope the Sower of Mischief would look the other way. But I may get the better of him yet.*

One of the guards at the King's Gate checkpoint recognized Danar and nodded him through with only a cursory glance at his token. Danar went about delivering the other messages first, wondering if he could sneak in a visit to Ganneron's house, but decided not to attempt it until he had finished his tasks.

When Danar arrived at the royal palace, General Manir's headquarters and residence, his hands were empty except for the sealed packet, and he was acutely aware of the dampness of his palms. He wished there were a back entrance or some household steward he could deliver the packet to without showing his face inside.

Coward. Yet if he were seen and recognized, he might never come out again. He had not yet seen Marisse.

Danar set his chin, took a deep breath, and marched up to the formal entrance. The pair of Gelon guards to either side of the doors eyed him. Despite everything, he could not bring himself to think of these men as his enemies. The lineaments of their features, the cut and color of their tunics, the style of their weapons and armor, all evoked a feeling akin to nostalgia.

He halted at a respectful distance and greeted them in Gelone, remembering to put a Roramenth twang into his vowels. The senior of the two guards gestured for him to approach. He inspected Danar's passage token, then nodded. "You're new. So they're using civilian couriers now?"

Danar affected a shrug. "Shorthanded, I guess. I'm grateful for the work."

"Where are you from, boy?"

"Roramenth."

"I thought so. Well, what do you have there?"

Danar held out the packet. "I'm to take back an answer."

"Hmmm," said the senior guard, squinting at the inscription. "This'll go first to Lord Porlon." He handed it to his partner, who disappeared into the interior of the building at a sharp clip.

Minutes passed, and Danar felt at loose ends. The guard's posture and expression did not invite conversation. And all the while, Marisse was so close ...

Danar wrested his thoughts back to the task at hand. He

had played the country bumpkin for so long, he'd forgotten his early years of discipline. Jaxar had trained him for public life. Playing this role was no more difficult than listening to speeches at court.

Eventually the second guard returned. "Lord Porlon's aide says they're all in meeting with the general, for how long only the God of Loquacious Fools knows."

The first Gelon said, "All right, lad, take an hour for yourself and then check back. You don't look like you often get to see the sights up here."

Danar did not need to manufacture a smile.

"An hour only, mind. I'll not be keeping the answer all day. Now off with you! There's no use in your cluttering my view."

Danar forced himself to proceed sedately until he turned a corner, and then covered the remaining distance to Ganneron's house at a racer's pace. A manservant, fortunately one who recognized him on sight, opened the door of the side entrance.

Light from a high window spilled across the hallway. Marisse stood there, facing a servant girl, cloths folded over her outstretched arms. Several enormous baskets sat at their feet. They had most likely been counting the linens just back from the laundry.

At the sound of Danar's voice, Marisse looked around. The light shone full on her face, giving her skin a pearly glow. He rushed past the man at the door and took her into his arms, linens and all. Behind him, the girl giggled. He didn't care. The only thing that mattered in the world was Marisse, her arms tight around him, the faint sandalwood scent of her hair, her cries of delight.

She pulled away and he saw the brightness of her eyes. "I didn't think I'd see you so soon!"

"Nor did I!" It was absurd to feel such joy, but impossible to feel anything else. "I mean—that I could come . . ." He stumbled to a halt. It was enough just to look at her.

She shoved the linens into the girl's hands. "We'll finish later. Tell Lord Ganneron that Danar is here and we'll be with him shortly."

Blushing, Marisse twined her fingers with Danar's. They

hurried down the hallway, passing work areas, scullery and pantries.

"Just a moment," Marisse murmured as she drew Danar into a shadowed alcove. "Just for us."

Before he could answer, she slipped one hand around the back of his neck, pulled his head down, and kissed him full on the lips. Her strength, a wash of Shebu'od's purple light, rushed through him, to be met and joined with the green from his own breast. For a long moment, he couldn't breathe. Her mouth was like fire on his; it was as if she kissed his heart as well as his lips.

I didn't . . .

". . . know I felt this way?" she finished, breathing into the space between them. Her words caressed his skin, another kiss. "How could I not?"

Was love possible so fast, so deep? Or was it some effect of their being guardians of the petal gems?

"I wish . . ." he breathed into her hair.

I wish I could run away with you. I wish there had never been an Ar-Cinath-Gelon to bring your city down in ruins. I wish Fire and Ice had never existed . . .

She drew back far enough to meet his gaze. "Does it matter?" When he did not answer immediately, she went on, "Has there been *anything* like us—like our love—since the world began?"

To that, he had no answer but to kiss her again.

After a time, an instant or an hour he could not tell, they went to find Ganneron. The older man greeted Danar with grave courtesy. If he read anything in their bright eyes and the slightly breathless tone of their speech, or the mirrored brilliance of their *alvara*, he forbore mentioning it.

Chapter Nineteen

CLOUDS rumbled across the skies, rain pelted the rooftops, and gradually winter crept to an end. Danar's life settled into a new routine as, gradually, the intensity of his grief lessened. He presented himself to the city garrison each morning, even though Irvan often had nothing for him, or only one or two brief tasks. There were no more packets for the general, at least none that could be sent by civilian courier.

Within the walls of Ganneron's house, Danar explored an intimacy of mind with Marisse. This work, more than anything else, helped ease the pain of his father's death. It was clear to everyone, even Tsorreh, that the bond between Danar and Marisse was by far the strongest of the three. Tsorreh insisted that they must not rely on that but must each develop a firm connection with the others. More than once, Danar had wished Tsorreh still carried the *te-alvar*. She brought the three of them together with tact and grace, but these were human attributes. There should be more, a loom to weave them into a single tapestry.

Danar spent his mornings working with Ganneron and Marisse on different ways to balance the energies of their *alvara*, using color as their guide. Once or twice, Danar had caught a flicker of some other hue, yellow perhaps or even blue, as fleeting as a bird swooping out of sight. Then it was gone, with none of the others having noticed, and he could not be certain whether he had imagined it.

Danar recognized the natural affinity between the attributes of Cassarod—courage—and Shebu'od—strength. Even their colors—red and purple, respectively—were related. He did not know what part the healing powers of his own crystal's powers might play. When he confessed his doubts to Tsorreh, she said, "Healing is not the sole attribute of Benerod, although it is the most compelling. When one is wounded or ill, one has little use for philosophy."

They were sitting together over cups of minted tea after a morning session. She had turned the sitting room into a study. Scrolls and books, some of them very old by their worn covers, covered the side table and several chairs. Unlike the disorder of Jaxar's library, not a single document had been placed on the floor.

Tsorreh reached for a bound volume, flipped through several pages, and ran one fingertip down the calligraphed text. "Here, in the holy writings, we learn that justice has no meaning without mercy."

"I'm not sure I understand. The Giver of Justice and the Lady of Mercy are entirely separate."

"What is strength, if there is no wisdom to guide it? What is courage without compassion?" She leaned forward. "For that matter, what are any of these qualities when used to further deceit instead of truth? Without the steadfastness to carry them through?"

In his mind, the six *alvara* framed a single crystal, Khored's own gem, whose attribute was unity. Unity and purpose.

Slowly Danar nodded. "Put that way, the Shield makes sense."

"As does life itself." She paused. "It does not strike me as accidental that Benerod's gem should come to you."

The days warmed with the ending of the rains. The sun, which had cast gray promises through the clouds, now turned golden. Danar strolled through the market, a mosaic of carts and booths, livened by the bright colors worn by both men and women at the approach of the spring festival, the first harvest of barley.

Foreign merchants joined the local farmers and craftsmen, for the ending of the rainy season had opened the trade roads over the Var Pass. The men clustered around a wooden-wheeled cart looked Denariyan. The leader wore full trousers of striped silk and carried a long curved knife tucked in his wide multicolored sash. His skin, several shades darker than that of the Meklavarans, gleamed like oiled copper.

Danar waited until the last customer had finished bargaining for a length of cloth. Unlike the garish silks worn by the trader, the fabric was a subtle caramel hue, thick and soft. It looked very much like Azkhantian camel's hair.

"Good day to you and a profitable market," Danar said.

The trader paused in rearranging the rejected yardage and smiled at Danar.

"This is very fine." Danar brushed his fingers along the nearest roll of fabric, feeling the softness of the nap. It was indeed camel's hair.

"Is the cloth not pleasing? I assure you, it is of the finest quality, as warm and durable as it is beautiful."

"No, nothing's wrong, it's just . . . I'm sorry, I thought you were Denariyan."

The trader's dark eyes gleamed. "Indeed, but my"—he used a word that most likely meant *family* or *company*—"trades mostly with the horse nomads. We bring them sandalwood and frankincense, spices and tea. Since they do not venture beyond their own territories, such goods as they produce"—and here he indicated buttons carved from bone and some green mineral, perhaps jade—"are all the more valuable because of their rarity. Alas, those days are gone. These are the last I can offer at the old price."

Danar kept his voice light. "Then good fortune in their selling, friend."

"Ah, I see you are no stranger to bargaining."

"I am no stranger to the steppe, either," Danar said in trade-dialect.

"Your pardon," the trader responded in the same language. "I took you for a Gelon, and those folk are not welcomed in the north."

Relenting, Danar pretended interest in the stone buttons. They were not jade, but green-tinted amber. "Isarran."

"Ah, then. Your people are not unknown to us. One or two traveled under the protection of the Golden Eagle some three years past, but the war-lady would not let us speak with them."

That would have been Leanthos ... and Shannivar. "It's a pity your business no longer takes you to the land of the horse people. I believe such goods"—indicating the green amber—"would fetch a good price in Durinthe."

"No one accuses the sons of Bahariya of cowardice, but some things not even the most courageous can face." The trader hesitated for a moment and glanced around to make sure they could not be easily overheard. "We used to travel under the countenance of the Reindeer clan—you know of such things? Like the passage token you wear around your neck? Two summers ago, only a few of the clans would honor it; they said the Reindeer clan, of the far north, had failed to answer a summons of the chieftains at their yearly council. It was said they had massacred their neighbors—Snow Bear, Ptarmigan, Silver Fox, I do not know what more. I have traveled among the tribes for two tens of summers, first as a boy in my father's caravan and now as master of my own. I have never broken their customs, but have always dealt fairly with them. Now they tell me that no outlanders are permitted. What is a man to think? A few of the Golden Eagle clan traded for my steel arrow points and what weapons I had. They bade me go in peace, but what they meant was I would find none in Azkhantia."

Something is rising in the north ... But where was Zevaron? And Shannivar, of that same clan of the Golden Eagle?

"I have—had friends among the Golden Eagle," Danar said.

The trader's eyes hooded, like those of bird of prey. "Your friends must look to their own, as must we."

Danar expressed interest in the amber pieces, using the sale to regain his composure. He felt it only right to recom-

pense the trader in some way for his news. The amber was
costly, so after a little haggling, Danar settled on a small
teardrop that might be set in silver as a gift for Marisse.
Even after its purchase, he had enough money left from
Irvan's latest commission to make a deposit with a jeweler.
Humming an Isarran tune, Danar pocketed the amber and
headed toward the Street of Dancing Rings in the district
of the metal-smiths.

Danar's path took him obliquely across the lower city
and through one of the lesser, poorer markets. A small audience had gathered there, blocking his view.

"On the sands, a vision came to me . . ." The words were
distorted over the buzz of the crowd, but the speaker was
unmistakably male. His voice rang with passion.

As Danar moved closer, the speech became easier to understand: "And I beheld an army gathering in the north . . .
creatures of frost and flame, stone-drakes, ice-trolls, and . . ."

Recognition stirred. Jaxar had drilled Danar in the mem-
orization of texts and Tsorreh had continued that education. The speaker quoted the *Te-Ketav*, the most revered of
the holy writings of Meklavar.

"*I saw rivers boiling,*" the voice soared, answered by the
murmur of the crowd. "*Mountains crumbled before my
sight! I tell you, my brothers, I saw them melt like glass!*"

"Did you hear what he said?"

"A sign! It is a sign from heaven!"

"*I saw blood run thick and hot across the living earth!*"

"The Prophet!" cried a man at Danar's shoulder.

"He speaks—he has returned . . .!"

". . . come to lead us to freedom!"

Iskarnon! Who else could summon such reckless hope?

"And I heard a voice crying out," the Prophet was
screaming now, every word ringing through the square, his
voice filled with awe and rage. "'*Awake, awake, O sons of
Meklavar! Arise, O brothers of Khored!*'"

"Ahhh . . . ." shivered through crowd. They were like tinder yearning for a spark.

"The shadow of the Scorpion crushes the Golden Land!
Its poison spreads everywhere—even to these sacred
mountains!"

"Down with Gelon! Death to the invaders!"

"Free Meklavar! Free Meklavar!"

Someone shouldered into Danar, a burly man a hand's width taller and correspondingly broad, a smith or a drover. Hands strong as iron dug into Danar's shoulder.

"Here's one of the scum now!"

Danar's captor thrust him through the crowd, who were now hooting and jeering. In another moment, they would turn on him like wolves starved for blood. His Isarran disguise would not save him. They were too many and too angry, even unarmed.

Danar's hand went to his knife, but it would be of little use, except to enrage the crowd even further. He glanced around wildly, hoping to catch sight of Irvan's squad, one of the patrols—

The smith jerked Danar to a halt, then spun him around. A fist the size and hardness of a horse's hoof collided with the side of Danar's head. His vision went wild and white. He lifted his hands to defend himself, but they were coming at him from all sides. He might handle one or two, but not a dozen at once. Someone else hit him in the ribs. A kick landed on the side of his leg just missing his kneecap.

Danar's eyes streamed tears. His breath caught and his ribs stung where he had been hit. The smith would throw him down, there in the dirt at the Prophet's feet. There would be a pause, maybe a flurry of words. Not enough to clear his head, not enough to get to his feet. Not enough to break free. The mob would seize him. He would feel the first dozen blows, but not even that many if they stoned him.

Behind his breastbone, the stone of Benerod flared. Green heat shot through him. No healing power could save him now.

Hands propelled him into a clear space. Someone stuck out a foot and Danar tumbled to his knees. He caught himself on one hand. The smith held on to his other arm until the last moment, so that Danar's weight wrenched his shoulder joint. He barely felt the hardness of the pavement, the edge of a stone slicing open his skin.

Through tear-blurred eyes, he squinted up at the Prophet, standing immobile and silent. He saw a face, lean and dark from seasons in the wild. Saw a ragged gray robe, tangled hair, red-rimmed eyes widening—

Yellow light filled Danar's skull. It shot downward through his body. Green pulsed in response, hot and strong. He felt himself turned to glass, unable to contain so much radiance.

Yellow. Yellow for truth. Yellow for Dovereth.

Somehow Danar found himself on his feet again, wavering and dizzy. He blinked and his vision came clear. His gaze locked on that of the man facing him. He saw the flare of recognition and then of madness.

Behind him, the crowd hissed and shifted like a nest of serpents.

Danar saw only the man before him and felt only pity, that any man should awaken to the power of a Shield gem alone and untutored. If Iskarnon had gone mad, it was no wonder.

Danar's breath came fluidly, despite the hot, sick pain in his ribs. He held out his hands. *You are alone no longer . . . we are brothers in the light, heirs to the Shield . . .*

Who speaks to me? Who?

I do . . . we do. Those of us who bear the same heritage . . . Khored's own . . .

Blood of my enemy, you lie!

No, Danar thought, and called on the emerald-hued radiance. It filled him, spilling over the boundaries of flesh and mind until it bathed the ragged man before him with Benerod's healing and wisdom.

A change swept over the Prophet's face like a breeze clearing the sky of smoke. A flush rose to the sun-parched cheeks, but the alteration in those dark eyes moved Danar unexpectedly. He saw in rapid succession astonishment, recognition . . . relief. Returning sanity gentled the contours of the weathered face.

Alone . . . I have been alone with my visions for so long . . .

Shouting fractured the moment. Behind Danar, men howled, elbowing one another aside. He heard the rhythmic tramp of men in unison, commands shouted in Gelone, then a woman's shriek. Above the clamor, steel shrilled.

"Seize him!" a man shouted in Gelone.

Iskarnon stood like a man transfixed, even when his followers screamed at him to flee. The smith rushed up to Iskarnon, pleading with him to save himself. The Prophet turned to go, but it was too late. Gelonian soldiers had pushed their way through the scattering onlookers. They came at him from three sides as more armed guards moved into position.

The *alvar* bond broke. Recognition fled from Iskarnon's eyes. His mouth twisted into a snarl. Anger blanketed the place where only a moment before had dawned a fragile understanding.

Liar! Traitor! Spy!

Danar shouted, "No, don't—" and then the Gelon rushed over him like an ocean wave. He stumbled, barely catching his balance as he scrambled out of their path. Adrenaline hummed along his veins. The air rushing through his throat reeked of blood and dust. In another instant, he was going to be violently sick.

"There, lad."

Danar startled at a touch on his shoulder—the good one, fortunately. The voice was vaguely familiar. "Corren?"

"Let's get you out of here and that lump seen to." The Gelon propelled him away from the center of the square where the soldiers had rapidly established order. "Did us a favor, you did, holding that scoundrel until we got here."

"I didn't—" Danar protested.

"Least we can do is patch you up. Here you go, then." Corren took Danar's good arm and propelled him out of the market square. Danar stumbled along, too stunned to resist.

All he could think was, *They've taken Iskarnon—they'll kill him! I've lost Dovereth again.*

Pavement blurred. Buildings and people elongated, flitting in and out of Danar's sight. He heard fragmented phrases in Meklavaran, in Gelone, in Denariyan.

What good will the Shield be without Dovereth's truth? How am I going to make things right?

Then he was thrust out of the day and into a closed space, smelling of men and leather and steel oil. And old blood, he realized. And fear.

Hands grasped his head, turning his face this way and that. Broad fingers poked at the sore place on his temple. "As miserable as you feel, you young pup," someone said, not unkindly, "you'll be in even worse shape tomorrow, once those bruises swell up. Still, you're lucky that thick skull of yours is still in one piece."

"He's well enough, then, eh?" That was Corren.

"He'll live."

Danar sat in mute wretchedness as the tonsorial—or perhaps the man was a priest of the Protector of Soldiers—bathed his head in water that smelled pleasantly of an astringent herb. Arnica, he thought. The aroma helped clear his senses. Nausea receded, but not the throbbing pain where he'd been struck. His shoulder ached, although it felt sound enough. He'd been lucky to escape without a dislocation.

The tonsorial shoved a cup into Danar's hands. Danar took a sip and sputtered at the bitter taste. He forced himself to drink, accepting the vileness as just punishment. The stuff made his eyes water anew and sent shivers through him.

"Good strong ale, that's what the lad needs," Corren said.

"That's precisely what he should *not* have, not with a head injury like that," the healer retorted. He scowled at Danar until the cup was empty except for a layer of sludge at the bottom.

"Please tell me that's all," Danar croaked.

The healer chuckled. "*He'll* be all right."

Already both Danar's vision and his nerves felt steadier. He got to his feet. "My thanks, good friend."

"Exactly where do you think you're going?" The healer put one hand on Danar's shoulder.

Now that Danar stood erect, his balance once again firm, he topped the other man by a good half-head. Gently he removed the healer's hand. "Thank you for your services, but—"

"If you go roaming around as if nothing had happened to you, I won't be able to help you! *You*—" The healer spoke to Corren, spinning Danar around and shoving him into the soldier's arms. "Take him back to the barracks and make him lie down. Tie him to a bunk if necessary! And make sure he doesn't fall asleep! And *no ale!*"

No amount of protesting on Danar's part could dissuade Corren from following his instructions. "Not that it's proper for a civilian such as yourself," Corren muttered as they crossed the narrow yard and entered a building filled with three-tier bunks and ranks of wicker chests, "but Captain Irvan would have my ears—not to mention other portions of my anatomy—if anything happened to you."

"Something *has* happened to me," Danar protested as Corren shoved him down on a lower bed near the far wall. "I've been detained against my will."

The light was dimmer here than outside, but not enough to hide Corren's determined expression. Danar sighed and lay down. The mattress was only canvas-covered straw, but it smelled faintly of sun and some kind of herb, a vermifuge most likely. As soon as he lay still, Danar felt every bruise and outraged joint. The effect of the healing draught faded, leaving a deep, demanding lethargy. He closed his eyes, promising himself it would just be for a moment.

Through fragmented dreams, Danar wandered across a landscape that must surely have come straight out of the Prophet's vision. Drought and frost had blasted all color from the barren earth. As far as he could see in every direction, withered grasses covered the flat, unchanging land. Overhead, ice clouds obscured the sun with a pallid gray shroud. He shivered, although he felt no cold.

A distant rumble sounded above the thud of Danar's heart. Unlike true thunder, the sound did not rise and diminish, but increased steadily. Now he saw, in the far distance, a shadow stretching across the horizon. With each passing heartbeat, it became larger and darker.

Danar braced himself for the oncoming surge. It was near enough now so that he could make out individual shapes—horses, hundreds of them, running at full gallop toward him, and on their backs, men brandishing bows and wearing the distinctive garb of the steppe nomads. Their war cries sounded like those of birds of prey.

They were almost upon him. Crimson-laced foam spattered the jaws of the horses. The eyes of their riders were also red, as if filled with blood. Although Danar could not understand their words, so distorted were the sounds, their chanting rattled through his bones: *"Gelon will burn! Gelon will burn!"*

They rushed past him, leaving dust as pale and glittering as ice.

The raucous sound of men's voices wrenched Danar alert. He threw one arm over his face, setting off a rush of pain that jolted him fully awake. After a moment of confusion, he realized he was in the barracks of the city garrison, and he had no idea how much time had elapsed.

Moving gingerly, for he had more sore muscles than he had thought possible, Danar got up. Corren was nowhere in sight, but the barracks were filled with men, some in armor, some laughing, some rummaging in the wicker chests.

One of them, an older man in a sweat-stained tunic, approached Danar. "You're Irvan's man, then?"

"Yes, I was brought here—"

"All right are you, then?"

Danar resisted the impulse to check the lump on the side of his head. He tried to look healthy.

"You'll be off, then?"

"Yes, thanks for everything."

Outside, the day was well advanced, judging by the length of the shadows. Danar passed clumps of soldiers, tending to leather gear and weapons and a dozen other tasks. He hurried from the garrison toward the King's Gate. Pedestrians hurried by without greeting one another. He wanted to stop and ask what more had happened, if Iskarnon was still alive and where he had been taken, but decided that such questions might be too dangerous. Nevertheless, his mind roiled with uncertainty. Would General Manir, either directly or through the local governor, Anthelon, use the trial and execution as a brutal reminder of who ruled here?

Was there anything he could do to stop it?

Chapter Twenty

IN Ganneron's house, they gathered in the room where they had first met, their chairs drawn close as if against an approaching storm. As Danar related the events in the market square, Ganneron's face turned grim and then distant. His fingers dug into the carved arms of his chair, leaving his knuckles bloodless. Tsorreh closed her eyes when Danar said the name, *Dovereth*, but betrayed no other sign of emotion. Danar finished his story and answered their questions, dismissing his injuries as of no consequence.

Marisse stirred, white-cheeked. "What is to be done?"

"General Manir will not listen to me," Ganneron said. "None of us"—meaning the Meklavarans, even those from noble families—"has any influence with him."

Tsorreh began moving restlessly about the room. "If we could argue that this is a purely domestic issue, that whatever offenses Iskarnon has committed, they are against his own people, not Gelon . . ."

"Ner-Manir-Thierra will not listen to such reasoning," Ganneron said.

"No. But Governor Anthelon might. These are, after all, his own people."

"With all respect, *te-ravah*, Meklavar is no longer the city your husband ruled. You have asked me to speak plainly, and so I shall. Anthelon may have been great once, but now he is only a feeble old man with no power of his own."

Tsorreh paused in her pacing. "Anthelon is a man who has lost his purpose. I remember him well from Maharrad's court. His strength was always to serve, not to direct. Now he will serve *me*."

Ganneron closed his mouth.

Marisse said, "Lady—*te-ravah*—that would—then he would know you have returned—that you are alive—and if the Ar-King learns—" Tsorreh's look silenced her. She bent her head. Not in shame, Danar thought, but in anticipated grief.

"Anthelon will not betray my presence here," Tsorreh said. "He may be old, as Ganneron says, and weak out of a desire to do good, but he has a true Meklavaran heart. Maharrad trusted him, and I shall do no less." She strode from the room with such determination that not even Ganneron voiced a protest.

A servant maid tapped timidly on the door, then entered and replenished the oil in the lamps, lit them, and ghosted from the room.

"I should have gone with her," Danar muttered at exactly the same time as Ganneron said, "The fault is mine. This is my house. I should have stopped her. Now it is too late."

"Stopped her?" Danar said incredulously. *Not even Lycian could break her. Not the river. Not the Dawn Sea. Not Qr.*

Danar heaved himself to his feet. Marisse was sitting very still, watching him. He dared not meet her gaze as he stated his intention to learn what he could from Captain Irvan or his men.

Ganneron went to attend to his own affairs while Marisse accompanied Danar to the door. He kept trying to think of what to say and could come up with nothing. In the foyer, she took his face between her hands.

From his chest came a pulse of warmth, and he could not tell which *alvar* had generated it. He felt himself bathed in a steady emanation of strength. It was not her own, any more than the healing and compassion of Benerod belonged to him. The magical attributes were theirs on loan, to use for purposes beyond their own.

And yet, in ways he had no words to express, she *was* his strength. She would always be his strength. As he would always be hers.

Captain Irvan looked surprised when Danar presented himself, but if he thought Danar ought to rest, he did not mention it. "I've no work for you today," he said, looking harried and distracted. "Or rather, none I can give you."

"Can you tell me what's going on?" Danar said. "I know the Prophet was arrested, but . . ." He let his words trail off. "Is there news from home?"

Irvan set his lips together and looked even more unhappy. Danar decided to leave it at that.

On the third day, when Danar arrived at Ganneron's house, Tsorreh had returned from her errand. She and Ganneron, but not Marisse, were sitting in the room given over to their training sessions. As Danar greeted Tsorreh, he saw the shadows like bruises around her eyes, the tension in her shoulders.

"No good?" Danar asked.

"Anthelon tried. He thought—and I agreed—that he must not appear too eager in this regard. Our arguments must be dispassionate and reasoned."

"We must not reveal how important Iskarnon is." Ganneron's eyes glinted as if to say, *I knew it would not work.*

"As long as there was any hope," Tsorreh explained in a tone of gentle admonition, "I had to remain close by, to be available for advice and discussion, or to calm Iskarnon in the unlikely event of Anthelon's success. It would have been too dangerous to send word."

"We should not quarrel among ourselves," Ganneron admitted.

After a moment's pause, Danar said, "Tsorreh is safe and back with us. We must not give up."

"If you have any suggestions, speak them," said Ganneron. "We can hardly break Iskarnon out of wherever Manir is holding him by force."

"Why not? He's in the palace, isn't he? And Tsorreh knows it well."

"He could be in any of a dozen secure places," Ganneron protested.

"Then we will discover where he is."

"Even if by some wild chance we found out, he would be under heavy guard." Ganneron shook his head. "The only result of such a rash plan would be more of us in the clutches of the Gelon."

Danar refused to relent. "Manir won't execute him in secret, will he? He'll want everyone in the city to witness what happens to those who defy Gelonian rule. He'll make the execution as dramatic as he can."

"It might be done, if we knew where and when. And if we were very, very lucky." Ganneron rubbed his chin thoughtfully. "Afterward there would be no place we could run to, either here on the *meklat* or down below. The hunt would be in full force and no place would be safe, not even this house."

"If we could reach the Temple, we could follow the path I took out of the city," Tsorreh suggested.

"Yes, but getting there would be the problem. All the approaches would be guarded. I'm sorry to keep repeating myself, *te-ravah*, but we don't know where—or when—or even *if*—the execution will take place. Iskarnon may not survive that long."

Tsorreh paled. "Anthelon said that Manir's men were still interrogating him."

If Iskarnon weren't already crazy, he is now, Danar thought. "We don't have much time—" He broke off at the sound of footsteps outside the door, too heavy to be the maid's.

A man's voice rumbled, the words indistinct. Ganneron stiffened.

Danar scrambled up from his chair, positioned himself in front of the door, and slid the knife from its thigh sheath. Resistance was lunacy and he knew it. What could he do against trained soldiers with swords?

Die fighting, or die without lifting a hand to defend those you love?

"No, don't—" Tsorreh gestured for restraint.

There was no other way out of the room. As Danar drew

in a breath, he heard something he did not expect from the other side of the door: a woman's voice, speaking Denariyan. The man said something and then Marisse's voice answered.

The next moment, the latch clicked, the door swung open, and Sandaron stepped into the room. A nimbus of pale rose light bathed the older man's form. In response, Benerod's green light filled Danar's breast. And here was Ganneron's crimson and Marisse's velvety purple. Behind her, blue shimmered like a cloudless sky.

Sandaron took another step into the room, revealing a second woman behind him. Even before his eyes took in the sight of her, Danar felt her in his heart, in the currents of color and power.

She was tiny, smaller even than Tsorreh, and wrapped in a garment like a waterfall of pleats the color of sunset. Here and there, gold threads glinted in the fabric. Her skin was dusky and kohl rimmed her eyes. A tiny ruby in one ear caught the light like a droplet of blood.

"Put up your knife, my friend," Sandaron said to Danar.

"Gray! Sandaron!" Danar shoved the knife back into its sheath. Drawing from the years of training in formal protocol in his father's house, Danar performed the proper introductions, except for the unknown Denariyan woman. It was really Tsorreh's place to do so, but she stood as one transfixed. Her eyes seemed to have too much light in them.

Taking Tsorreh's hands in his, Sandaron raised them to his lips, first one and then the other, then bent to whisper something in her ear. A high color swept her cheeks.

"You are most welcome," she said, struggling for composure, "and your companion as well. We did not know to expect you."

"I thought it best not to send word, lest the news of my coming fall into unfriendly hands."

"Will you not introduce the lady who bears the steadfast attribute of Eriseth's gift?"

"Lady Tsorreh," Sandaron said, shifting to a more formal mode, "I have the honor of presenting *Dir* Jenezhebre of the Court of the Jade Dolphin in Tomarzhya Varya."

"Your Majesty." The Denariyan woman glided into the

center of the room. She inclined her head, touching the fingertips of her right hand first to the point between her dark brows, then her lips, and finally extending her cupped hand.

"I wish I could offer you a better welcome," Tsorreh said. "Nevertheless, I am glad you are here."

"*Dir* Jenezhebre," Sandaron said, "allow me to present Danar son of Jaxar of Aidon."

Danar found himself bowing as well.

"It is as you told me, wisdom-keeper," the Denariyan woman said to Sandaron. "Here is the heart of compassion, known to my own people as the Serene Serpent. There stands the guardian of courage, and I have already met the soul of strength."

With each phrase, the room pulsed with rainbow light. Danar's head reeled with it. He no longer felt weary or in need of food.

"Five *alvara*, all in the same place," Marisse exclaimed. "I do not think such a thing has happened since the days of Khored of Blessed Memory."

"Sandaron, how did you find the *dir*?" Tsorreh asked.

"It is a long story."

"One that doubtless will require not only time but wine," Tsorreh said with a smile.

"Much wine, yes. Briefly, then: in my work in Aidon, helping those of our people who needed to resettle, I often had cause to contact my counterparts in Denariya. They advised me regarding the oldest Meklavaran enclaves throughout the spice lands. Through the elders of those communities, I was able to trace even older lineages. By this time, my activities had come to the attention of the Court of the Jade Dolphin."

Tsorreh glanced at the Denariyan lady, who said, "It could well be said that *we* found *him* and not the other way around."

Danar suspected that if Sandaron had not wanted to be found, then his presence would yet remain unnoticed.

"But did you not—" Marisse said shyly. "Your pardon, lady *dir*, but did you know what it is you bear? Did your family prepare you?"

"After our own fashion, yes."

"We would not have returned so quickly without the skilled travel arrangements of the Court of the Jade Dolphin," Sandaron added.

Jenezhebre looked around the room. "Five we are, but where is the sixth? Where is the truth-seeker? Have you not yet found him?"

"We ... did," Tsorreh replied. From one syllable to another, the elation of a moment ago drained from the room. "Please sit down, all of you." She waited while they did so, keeping her gaze on Sandaron as if he were an unwavering star. "We found Dovereth's heir, or rather, Danar did, just before he was arrested by General Manir's men."

The muscles of Sandaron's jaw clenched and released. Jenezhebre's calm expression did not change, however.

"It's Iskarnon, the prophet we've heard so much about, the one the Gelon have been so eager to apprehend," Ganneron said, although the name could mean nothing to the Denariyan lady. "They're sure to execute him."

"I tried bargaining with Governor Anthelon, but it was no use. He has no power to help us. I'm afraid you've returned to us at a dark time." Tsorreh lowered her gaze to her hands. Her back was painfully straight, as if she held herself upright by the force of her will.

"This news is indeed grim, Lady Amber," Sandaron said, but with such kindness that Tsorreh looked up and gave a faint smile. "Yet I fear it is not all we must face. You may not have heard, for news travels faster on Denariyan ships than overland. Your general may be the least of our troubles."

"What do you mean?" Ganneron asked. "What news?"

"A new war-leader has arisen in Azkhantia. By all accounts, he has united the northernmost clans, by conquest if not persuasion," Sandaron answered.

"So?" Ganneron made a derisive noise. "Let the tribes make war on one another! If they draw the Ar-King's attention away from Meklavar, so much the better for us!"

Danar winced inwardly. How easy it was for these people to talk about Gelon as the enemy, forgetting that it was *his* homeland.

"The north is where this war-leader began," Sandaron said, "but he is not content to rule there. It does not require the gift of prophecy to read the meaning of the rumors. This war-leader aims for dominion over more than the steppe. His forces are on the move, pressing to the south and west."

Danar closed his eyes, wishing he could as easily shut out the memory of the ravening horde. It had not been a figment of his concussed brain, but a true vision. He had not spoken of it, partly out of fear that putting it into words would give it power, but mostly because he wished it were only his imagination.

"...and how can you have received such news before anyone here knows it?" Ganneron was saying.

"My family trades widely across the known world, even to the Fever Lands and the farthest reaches of Azkhantia," Jenezhebre replied. "In recent years, we suspected some change for ill. At first, we heard rumors only, such as are told at crossroads, but nothing to the detriment of our trade. More of our agents were turned away where they had once been welcomed. The bonds of friendship and fair dealing no longer held. Some of our people, those who journeyed the farthest north, did not return at all. My own son was one such." She paused. Her expression, which had been animated and serious, now reflected nothing.

"I'm so sorry," Tsorreh said with feeling. Danar thought that, had they been alone, she would have reached out and taken Jenezhebre's hand. Perhaps she might have spoken of her own anguish at being parted from Zevaron.

"The Azkhantians are ferocious warriors," Ganneron said, returning to the topic, "none better. And effective against the best Gelon can muster."

"In small bands, yes," said Sandaron, "and in terrain where they can use the speed of their horses and the skill of their archers to best advantage. It's said they use the shape of the land—the hills and gullies, the rivers—to wear the enemy down. It's not like them to venture out of their familiar territory. They've always let the Gelon come to them."

"Maybe they got fed up with having to repel one incursion after another," Ganneron persisted. "Or maybe this new leader is capable of forming the tribes into a single fighting unit. If so, that man is our ally, for we share a common adversary."

"No," Danar said. "They are bent on vengeance against Gelon, but they will sweep us up in their war."

"Let them go where they will," Ganneron said, as if he had not heard. "We have our own business to attend to."

"This is our business," Tsorreh said. "And our adversary is not Gelon."

"How can you say Gelon is not our enemy?" Ganneron demanded. "You who suffered so much during the fall of our city? You who were Cinath's prisoner for so long?"

"Am *I* your enemy?" Danar faced the older man. Marisse put out a hand, a plea for him to moderate his tone, but he did not relent. The issue had to be settled, for if Ganneron would not accept him because he was Gelon, then the Shield could never be truly united.

"You are not like the others," Ganneron admitted, "not like Cinath and his kind."

"I am exactly like them!" Danar shot back. "I am Gelon and cannot be anything else. And I love my country as much as you love Meklavar. The only difference is that my uncle was corrupted by his ambition." He reined in his temper before fervor led him to justify Cinath's lust for power.

"Danar." Tsorreh spoke quietly, yet the sound of his name calmed him as no command could. "No one believes you unworthy of the gem of Benerod. You and *dir* Jenezhebre have demonstrated that the honor and burden of guarding the *alvara* belong to all peoples, not just Meklavar.

"And Ganneron, Danar is not trying to excuse the horrible things Cinath did. In our own righteous anger, let us not lose sight of what we are doing here and why we have come together. Cinath may always have been ruthless and acquisitive, but another force moved through him, one that twisted his pride into arrogance and greed, and *that* is our real enemy."

"Qr," Danar said, and heard Sandaron echoing him.

"Qr and what lies behind it." Tsorreh nodded. "The shadows cast by Fire and Ice stretch across every land, and Qr is indeed Gelon's version. When Meklavar fell, I fled the city and so did Sandaron. The Shield had already been weakened over the centuries as Benerod and Eriseth were scattered. Without the heart-stone, the center itself was lost.

As the Shield fragmented even further, Fire and Ice gained sufficient strength to pull down a comet from the heavens and destroy its earthly prison. Cinath may have followed his own craving for power, but he served a far more dreadful purpose."

At these words, Ganneron flushed. Sandaron looked grim. Even Jenezhebre's serene expression faltered.

"This Azkhantian war-leader may be a hero to his own people, but that does not automatically make him a friend to us," Tsorreh concluded.

"His success can hardly be an advantage if we must traverse a land torn apart by war," Marisse spoke up. When Ganneron shot her a sharp look, she stood her ground. "Are we not here to gather all the petals of the Shield and then unite them with the one who bears its heart? And has he not gone into the northern fastnesses of the steppe? If this war-leader and his followers occupy the intervening territory, it will be a perilous journey for us to reach him. Or for him to come to us."

"Yes," Sandaron said, "that was my thought as well."

Ganneron did not answer. Perhaps he had assumed the Shield would be united here in the land of its birth, in Khored's own city. He probably had never ventured beyond the walls of Meklavar, being a city man. As Leanthos had been.

As I was.

"There can be only one reason why the Azkhantian clans have banded together, against all their history and custom," Danar said. "We must consider the possibility"— he could not bring himself to say *certainty*— "that Zevaron is their leader."

Tsorreh turned from Danar back to Sandaron. Color drained from her face.

"Danar, what do you mean?" Marisse asked, moving protectively toward Tsorreh. "Why do you say such a terrible thing?"

"I had a dream," he said, "a vision shown to me by the *alvar* I bear, of a horde of horsemen, thundering toward me. I don't think they were entirely human. They were screaming, '*Gelon will burn!*' but I do not think I would have been given such a revelation if it did not directly bear on our purpose," meaning unifying the Shield to combat Fire and Ice. "And now you tell me the vision was real, that such a horde exists."

Marisse gave a cry of dismay. Tsorreh looked appalled. The lines bracketing Sandaron's mouth deepened. Only Jenezhebre seemed unsurprised, her eyes calm with Eriseth's steadfastness.

"The steppe is vast and its people thinly distributed," Ganneron said, shaking his head. "It goes beyond credibility that one man known to us—an outlander to the horse tribes, at that—would rise to such prominence."

"Danar makes a good argument," Jenezhebre cut in. "The Azkhantians do not possess the temper to unite in such a fashion. Fighting on a large scale comes to them only of necessity, for the land is so poor and the seasons so harsh, they have not the luxury to neglect their herds. Drought or pestilence or even an overly cold winter can leave a clan in a precarious and vulnerable state."

"Zevaron would never—" Tsorreh cried. "Even if—no, he knows what is at stake! He is a leader, not a warmonger. The *te-alvar* will have taught him, even as it did me. It has to be someone else."

"Yet it is the only explanation that makes sense," Danar insisted. "The Azkhantians have never coordinated militarily. Having watched their summer Gathering, I can understand why. It took the entire council of chieftains to decide even minor matters. They had to consult their shamans on what to do with the stone-drake and *they* took days to come up with a prophecy that no one understood. Sower of Mischief, can you imagine running an entire army that way? No wonder they never tried to invade Gelon before."

Danar prayed to the Light-Bearer to sweeten his tongue. "Lady Tsorreh, when Zevaron believed you dead, it almost destroyed him. I think he stayed alive only out of hate."

"I know." Her voice sounded papery, a ghost.

"And then when you died *again* . . ."

She closed her eyes. The room grew so still, the others hardly seemed to be breathing.

"Tsorreh, I am Zevaron's friend. I love him as a brother.

He saved my life and I, his. But this I swear to you. He would have given anything, sworn allegiance to any power, given himself to any master who offered him what he most deeply and darkly craved—the destruction of Gelon."

"If he loved you in return," Tsorreh cried, "how could he do such a thing? Yes, Gelon gave birth to Cinath and his wretched sons, and that abomination of a Scorpion god. But people of goodness and integrity also live there—your father and you, and many others I met. I hate what Cinath and Manir have done, but I cannot condemn an entire people for the crimes of a few."

Ganneron threw his hands up. "This is idle speculation. We have no way of knowing who the war-leader is. And even if we did, what is to be done about it? We are only five. Without Dovereth's gem, we cannot move forward. We should focus our energies on the problem before us, not that there's any chance of freeing the Prophet now that he's in Manir's clutches. We'd do better planning how to smuggle a new heir into prison before he dies—and who would we get to do that?—or how to salvage the *alvar* from Iskarnon's corpse. Or what we will do if Dovereth is truly lost to us."

The prospects Ganneron described were so bleak that for a long moment, no one said anything.

"I think . . ." Marisse spoke hesitantly, breaking the silence, "that it does not matter if *ravot* Zevaron is this war-leader. He is certainly on the steppe. The Azkhantian horde still stands between him and us." No one contradicted her. "For the Shield to be restored, either he will have to come to us, or we to him."

Ganneron looked as if he were forcibly restraining himself from burying his face in his hands.

Jenezhebre shook her head. "The steppe is too big. We cannot simply venture north in the hope we will somehow encounter him. Even with my family's trading connections, the obstacles would be too great."

For a long moment, Danar could not answer. In the place behind his eyes, he felt the rising of a multihued dawn, pale rose and crimson, deep purple shading into sustaining blue. Again came the vision of the ravening horde, and this time he understood why he had such faith in what he'd seen. The images did not arise from a bruised and fevered brain or from his own fears. The *alvara* sensed their missing heart. Their united power reached across a distance far greater than their separate limits.

"Is it possible he might know we have come together, through the *te-alvar*, and find his way to us?" Marisse asked Tsorreh. It was as if she had read Danar's mind.

Tsorreh made a helpless gesture. "I don't know. I don't think I would have."

The situation was impossible. In a bizarre twist of thought, Danar hoped he was right about Zevaron leading the Azkhantian horde because it would make him so much easier to find.

"If Khored's gem is also beyond our reach . . ." Jenezhebre said.

"Then we must get it back," said Marisse.

Jenezhebre looked at her as if she had lost her wits, but Sandaron smiled. Ganneron said, "For that, we'll need Dovereth, as I've pointed out, so we're right back where we started."

All our hopes hinge on liberating Iskarnon, Danar thought. *I'm the only one Manir might listen to . . . if he doesn't send me back to Aidon to face execution.*

The meeting broke up as Tsorreh and Ganneron made provision for the new arrivals and Danar bid Marisse goodbye. If she noticed how distracted he was, she made no mention of it. Already his thoughts were rushing ahead to what he must do, the arguments he might use . . . and all the things that could go wrong. But he had no other choice. Action was needed, not more empty words.

Chapter Twenty-one

LEAVING Ganneron's house, Danar burst out onto the street. He must not think what he was doing. The slightest hesitation now might paralyze his resolve. He must simply act. What he intended was neither rational nor prudent. It could well end in disaster. If he paused to consider, he would come up with a hundred arguments why he could not—*should not* do it. All he knew was that there was no other way.

Danar covered the distance to the royal palace so quickly that it seemed no time had elapsed. With a twinge of unease, he noticed a pair of priests, devotees of Qr by the scorpion insignia on their headbands. As they passed him, one of them broke off what he was saying to glance in Danar's direction. Danar pretended he hadn't seen their interest, sharp and penetrating.

Two officers stood watch at the front door. One, who knew Danar, held out his hand for the expected message. Danar took a deep breath. "I am to see General Manir in person."

The officer who did not know Danar frowned. "We don't have the authority to admit you. All messages must go to our captain for approval. Is this on behalf of—who did you say? Captain Irvan?"

"I'm here on my own behalf," Danar said. "Let General Manir himself decide whether he will see me. Tell him that I thank him for the annals of the Denariyan pirates, although it was many years before I was old enough to appreciate them."

Although the two officers looked skeptical, one withdrew into the palace while the other remained on watch. The glare he gave Danar told him that the slightest misbehavior would be quickly dealt with. Danar returned the man's gaze with as much composure as he could summon.

The first officer returned a short time later. Guarded amazement replaced his former expression of mistrust. "You are to come up directly," he told Danar. "I will escort you."

The palace had once been a majestic structure by Meklavaran standards. Like Ganneron's house and the other buildings here on the *meklat*, it had been constructed of stone quarried from the mountain. The labor involved, not to mention the narrowness of the *meklat* compared to the open hills of Aidon, encouraged small but well-proportioned structures, rather than sprawling edifices in the style of Gelonian architecture. The general's offices were up a single flight of wide stairs and halfway down a hallway. Danar's escort exchanged a few words with two guards stationed outside before ushering him into the chamber beyond.

Danar had only a moment to take in the size of the room, the central table serving as a desk, and the man now looking up from where he sat on the far side. Years had bleached the brightness from Manir's red hair and incised lines around his eyes and between his brows. At a flicker of those granite-gray eyes, the man at Danar's elbow withdrew, closing the door behind him.

Manir waited, his jaw set but his expression otherwise unreadable. Danar moved forward a step, then two, then four, and halted. Manir seemed not to be breathing, he was so still.

Danar cleared his throat. "It's been a long time, sir."

Slowly, Manir got to his feet. His leather breastplate and belt creaked with the movement.

"Jaxar's son ... *Jaxar's son!*" Manir moved around the

table with astonishing speed. He clapped his hands to Danar's shoulders. "Where have you been, you young scoundrel? We thought the worst when you disappeared from Aidon! Cinath, may-the-glory-of-his-memory-never-fade, gave out that you'd taken the coward's flight"—meaning suicide—"but I never believed it. Not *Jaxar's son!*"

Danar managed a smile. "It was best to let the world think I was dead. At least, my uncle wouldn't be sending assassins after me. Nor could he use me as a hold over my father."

Manir released Danar. "You've learned a thing or two since your fifth birthday."

"I hope so. Sir, I would not have come out of hiding if Gelon's need were not so great. Like my father, I have no political ambition for myself, but I would not see our country in flames." He paused. "I've been running errands for one of your captains. I hear the soldiers talk. I've also heard the rumors from Azkhantia."

"When I was a young officer, it was said that one good veteran knew more of what was happening than all the generals combined."

"We both know that nothing like this new war-leader and his horde as ever arisen before. Chion cannot effectively counter this threat."

"You'd better sit down, Lord Danar." Manir drew up a second chair beside his own. On the table, he spread out a map, with Gelon drawn in the center, its borders traced in Cinath's colors, royal blue and purple. The shores of the Inland Sea had been delicately shaded in indigo, Denariya in orange, and the Var Mountains in gray. Across the steppe, featureless on this map, stretched a series of markings in dark red. They formed an arrowhead aimed directly at Aidon.

"The Azkhantian horde, although some of these sightings are rumors only, and others are too old to be trustworthy," Manir said, running his fingers over the pattern that bore an uncomfortable resemblance to droplets of blood. "That's what they're calling it. The demon warlord and his horde." Something in his voice hinted that he had heard other rumors as well. He leaned against the wooden back of his chair and regarded Danar. "Of course, it's not certain he'll ever leave the steppe. It's said that his own people are fighting him."

"If they really are his people," Danar muttered.

"If you have more information about this horde, I would hear it." Manir lifted one gray-flecked brow. "Or do you no longer serve the Golden Land?"

"Does that mean following the orders of an incompetent usurper?" Danar shot back.

The moment hung, leaden and breathless, over them.

Danar leaned forward. "I've let Chion rule without challenge because, until now, it mattered little whose backside warmed the Lion Throne. This"—with a gesture at the map—"is the biggest threat Gelon has faced in our time, or our fathers' time or *their* fathers' time. I can't stay safely hidden when so much is at stake."

Manir waited. Danar plunged on, "Under the law, my claim is as valid as my cousin's. We occupy equal rank in the succession. But unlike him, I will not sit back and let the danger come to us. The time to counter such an enemy is not when he is camped at the gates of Aidon. It is now."

"Are you asking me to support your claim to the throne?" Manir kept his tone neutral.

"Chion and I can sort that out in the proper way once Gelon is safe. I need your help to keep this Azkhantian warlord where he belongs. If we fail, there won't be anything left for either Chion or me to rule."

Manir looked thoughtful. "If I acknowledge you as a legitimate claimant, is it your intention to march on the steppe?"

"To intercept the horde, yes. Our border patrols and a few free clans won't be able to stop them. But with the forces at your command, we stand a chance."

"My orders are to hold Meklavar. Even if everything you say is true, I can't abandon the city. It's full of rebels and troublemakers. My agents say they breed like goats. We'd leave behind a second battlefront and a city in chaos."

"Not if you left Meklavar in friendly hands, under a ruler the people would readily obey, one willing to make an alliance, or at least a truce, with you."

"Who? Not that old man, Anthelon. Without us to put teeth behind his words, he'd be deposed in a day."

"No." Danar took a deep breath. "I mean the rightful heir to Meklavar. The *te-ravah*, the wife of the city's last King."

"She's dead."

"She's alive. Here in the city. And willing to become our ally." Danar meant *my ally*.

"Well now." Manir gave Danar a level, appraising look. "This is either the most inspired piece of statesmanship I have witnessed since your father was last at court, or we have both utterly lost our minds."

Danar had a feeling it was both. "I would like nothing better than to discover that everything I have told you is a delusion."

"You're suggesting that I take it upon myself to reverse years of Gelonian rule. Meklavar has become part of our empire."

"Meklavar will never be anything but an insurrection waiting to happen. These people want their own country back, and one way or another, they will have it. The only way to leave a city that will not turn on us is to place it back into the hands of its rightful ruler. And not as governor, either, for a governor rules at the pleasure of the Ar-King. Tsorreh san-Khored will not answer to the Lion Throne, but if she agrees to not retaliate, she will be true to her word."

Danar thought he'd gone too far when Manir did not respond at first. Then the general nodded. "If only Cinath had realized the nature of Meklavar, far too many good men would not already have died."

Danar looked down at his hands, not the hands of a soldier, but not those of a pampered princeling, either. "If you believe me, if anything I have said makes sense to you, then help me. If not . . . if you are Chion's man before you are Gelon's, then I am in your power."

As Manir rose, the legs of the chair scraped on the stone floor. One knee joint popped as he straightened. "I serve Gelon," he said in a voice gone husky. "I believe you do the same. But I am no kingmaker. I do not have the right. I will not put a sword to the throat of Chion-Ar-Gelon, may-he-eventually-attain-the-wisdom-of-his-ancestors, but neither will I murder a prince of Gelon for the convenience of an arrogant bully."

For a long moment, Danar could not speak. His hands felt cold. "You are a man of honor."

"I am a soldier of Gelon."

Danar wished Zevaron could be here, could see this man and hear his words. "Then you had best escort me to Aidon, that my claim may be tested."

"So I should," Manir said with a hint of a smile, "and should any questions be asked regarding—oh, whether I had deserted my post—I have an answer, one that is grounded in historical precedent. You have claimed to be the rightful Ar-King. Who am I to disagree? I have taken you under my protection or into my custody, depending on the interpretation, until the matter can be decided."

"Still, there is a risk to you."

"There is an even greater risk to Gelon if I take no action. Besides, I am not exactly in favor in court, or why would I be dispatched to this remote place inhabited by the most recalcitrant people the gods ever created? Your father, may-peace-be-ever-with-him, used to say that what is convenient and what is right are rarely the same thing."

"I remember him saying that." Danar felt a pang of loss, but it quickly subsided. "He also used to say that our ancestors, the men who founded Gelon and made it great, dedicated themselves to doing what was right. I don't think my uncle liked to hear that, except in praise of all the *right things* he had done. The bonds of family kept my father safe for a time, but once Cinath suspected him, his friends would have fared no better."

"And I was indeed your father's friend." Manir paused, and when he spoke again, his tone was lighter. "We might return to Aidon by way of Azkhantia. In my military judgment, a more direct route would not be . . . prudent."

Danar bent over the map again. "How should we proceed? What is your advice, General Manir?"

"We must count on resistance from the free clans. They will not suffer us to freely enter their territory."

Some among them might remember Danar with good

will. He had impressed the Council of Chieftains, Tenoshi-nakh in particular, even though at that time they had not been willing to support any foreign venture. "Or perhaps they may speak with me. I have traveled among them by their own leave, and that is not a bad beginning."

"So that's where you went after you vanished from Aidon. You're truly your father's son if you could get the Azkhantians to grant you the freedom of their lands—you, of Cinath's own house."

"It did take some persuasion," Danar conceded. "And I had help."

Manir's eyes narrowed but he did not ask.

"I will leave the details of the campaign to you, who have knowledge and skill in such matters," Danar said. "Now I must bring news of our agreement to the Queen of Meklavar. As a token of our good will, I wish to restore her countryman, your prisoner—Iskarnon, called the Prophet."

For a moment, Danar thought Manir might refuse and the whole scheme would come crashing down like a house of twigs. Then Manir chuckled and shook his head.

"If the goal of this entire interview has been to effect the release of that madman, then I salute you."

"Actually, my intention is to prevent him from becoming a martyr. We need Meklavar united and peaceful, not boiling over with insurrection."

"That much is true. Well, Lord Danar, this Iskarnon is of no use to me. He knows of no conspiracies, or at least he is not coherent enough to divulge them. I have held him this long only because it was equally foolhardy to execute him. You have solved that problem for me. Do you think he is rational enough to obey his Queen?"

"I cannot vouch for his sanity," Danar admitted. "I have not yet spoken to him. But Tsorreh san-Khored is a remark-able woman. We will see what she can do with him."

"She has your confidence, I see. If she has managed to stay alive, despite all rumors to the contrary, make her way back here from Gelon, and hide herself from my agents, then she indeed possesses considerable resourcefulness."

Manir strode to the door and spoke a few words to the guard stationed outside. Returning to the map, he and Danar discussed route by which the Gelonian forces might reach the borderlands of the steppe. Much depended on how far the warlord had advanced and the vigor with which the remaining Azkhantian tribes impeded him.

They were still deep in their analysis when a pair of soldiers entered, dragging Iskarnon between them. The Prophet showed no obvious signs of torture, but his hair and robe were filthy, and the skin beneath the layers of grime was ash-gray. Wide, unfocused eyes stared blankly ahead. He seemed too stunned to struggle and too weak to stand.

At Manir's command, the soldiers placed Iskarnon on a bench just inside the door. Breathing through his mouth to manage the smell, Danar went to the prisoner. The guards tightened their grip on Iskarnon's shoulders, causing him to wince visibly.

Danar crouched down until his eyes were level with Iskarnon's. Through the stupor glimmered the faint, clear yellow of Dovereth's gem. It was all but extinguished, it had been so encrusted with doubt and despair.

Poor, tormented soul. The visions bursting from a newly acquired *alvar* would have been terrifying enough if one were among friends. But if one were alone in the desert, if the stories about Iskarnon were true, or in the hands of enemies . . .

"*Friend,*" Danar wanted to say, "*you are not mad. The things you see and feel are real. I have seen and felt them, too.*"

From deep within Danar's chest, radiance blossomed like an emerald sun. He placed the palm of one hand against Iskarnon's chest. Ribs moved under roughened skin. Dark eyes cleared as the miasma of fear thinned, allowing a moment of true sight.

Benerod's gift, Danar thought, was not meant to make life comfortable or convenient, but to reach those in darkness beyond all other light. Compassion illuminated truth, and truth brought reason.

Iskarnon wet his cracked lips and whispered in Meklavaran, "Who are you?"

"A friend," Danar replied in the same language. "One

who understands." Rising, he grasped the hands of the prisoner. "I will take you now to a place of safety. Your *te-ravah* awaits. Will you allow me to take you to her?"

"I never sought to harm anyone," Iskarnon said, his voice breaking.

"Yet much ill can come from the best intentions." Manir spoke from behind Danar. Clearly, he had learned enough Meklavaran to follow their conversation.

Iskarnon was too debilitated to walk far, so Manir arranged for a curtained litter, such as those used by the ladies of Gelon when they wished to travel discreetly. Manir agreed with Danar's request that the litter bearers be Meklavaran and that no Gelonian soldiers accompany them. On the following morning, Manir would present himself at Ganneron's house to formally declare his intention of restoring the rule of the city to its Queen. Once that was done, there would be no turning back. Chion was sure to hear of it, but Manir seemed as determined as ever to throw his support behind Danar's plan, no matter what the consequences to his own career.

With that, the audience came to a close. Manir bowed to Danar, a general's abbreviated salute, eloquent in its restraint, respectful but not subservient. Danar had entered the palace as a fugitive, accused of treason and who knew what else. He had risked much, relying on his judgment of Manir's character and their shared ideals. The magnitude of his success left him dizzy with relief. He felt exhilarated, jubilant, intoxicated, but not with his rise to power as claimant to the Lion Throne. His mind swam with images—Iskarnon, healthy in mind and body—the Shield glowing in rainbow brilliance with each new addition—Marisse laughing for sheer joy—Tsorreh happy, Zevaron restored to them—and the shadow of Qr lifted from the Golden Land. He felt as if everything that had happened up until now— his father's teaching, his narrow escapes, his friendships, his hopes—had prepared him for this moment.

Danar nodded to the guards outside the door and started down the corridor when a prickle of unease brought him to

a halt. He glanced back in the direction of Manir's office.
The guards showed no sign of alarm. Was he imagining
things or was this a symptom of the euphoria of success?

From the opposite direction of Manir's doorway, either
from the interior of the palace or some back stairway, a Qr
priest stepped from the shadows. Danar sensed what the
man was even before he recognized the distinctive robe,
bald skull, and scorpion-emblazoned headband. In his
breast, the stone of Benerod felt icy. His belly quivered and
his heart raced. He should run, he should hide. He should
be anywhere but here. Something terrible was about to happen.

During the moment Danar had stood, immobile and
shot through with premonition, the guards had admitted the
Qr priest. The door closed behind him.

Walking back to Manir's office was one of the hardest
things Danar had ever done. The guards regarded him, cautious but polite, but would not let him pass.

Danar scarcely understood their refusal, but they had no
idea what had transpired. As far as they were concerned, his
interview was finished and he must make another appoint-
ment if he wished to speak with the general again. The two
soldiers seemed to be hallooing from so great a distance,
their speech turned to tendrils of fog. Before him, the door
rippled, as if mere wood could not contain what was happening inside.

Silently he called out to all the gods of men, the ones he
knew and those from unknown lands, to any divinity that
might be listening. *Help me!*

A verdant ember ignited within Danar's chest. Power
surged through him, green intensifying into white and then
fracturing into rainbow brilliance—Shebu'od's purple
strength shading into the ruby courage of Cassarod, deepening into the wisdom of pale rose Teharod, and sustained
by the clear blue of Eriseth's endurance. Distantly came an
echoing pulse of yellow, Dovereth's truth. Danar had no
idea how that melding was possible, but he sensed it could
not hold, not without the unifying purpose that was
Khored's own gem.

He thrust himself between the guards, shouldered the

door open, and rushed into the room. Swirling currents of white vapor thickened the air. Danar's body felt as thick as clay, damp and inert. The unexpected denseness of the mists made movement impossible.

The Qr priest stood with his back to the door, one arm raised. With the splayed fingers of one hand, he seemed to be gathering up the streamers of white . . . or sending them forth.

Manir bent over, his body heaving. The ribbons of power linked the priest's hand to Manir's chest. Danar could not tell if Manir saw him, so wild and frantic were the general's eyes. Then Manir's skin turned gray as he clutched his heart. All his former vitality vanished. He barely kept his feet.

A power beyond Danar's own will propelled him forward. He crouched, gathering himself to punch through the thickening mists. His feet pushed hard against the floor as he braced himself. Then he leaped forward, reaching out with his arms.

He collided with the priest and grabbed him around the hips. Together they slammed into the carpeted floor. Danar landed on top, the priest belly-down. The priest writhed and jerked, flailing. Danar grabbed one of the priest's arms near the wrist. Using a wrestling move, he tried to twist the arm up and between the other man's shoulder blades. The priest's skin was slick, not with sweat but something colder and more slippery. It felt like a thin coating of ice.

The priest lashed out with his feet, found purchase on the carpet, and flipped over so that he now faced Danar. His face contorted, but with rage or terror Danar could not tell. The priest's eyes were the color of mud, flat and lightless, surrounded by gleaming rings of gray.

Benerod's gem pulsed like a second heart in Danar's chest. With a sudden, deadly certainty, he knew that the priest had not only sensed the *alvar*, but hated it, despised it. Would stop at nothing to destroy it. Tsorreh had been right to fear them.

Eyes rolling up in their sockets, the priest arched his back like a spring of steel. The movement threw Danar off-balance. The man's muscles strained and his joints creaked. His breath hissed between clenched teeth. His skin was no longer icy but furnace-hot. Sweat dampened the scorpion headband.

The air around them condensed. Vapors flowed together, taking on greater substance as they spun out from the priest's body. Those that touched Danar vanished in puffs of green-tinted smoke.

The priest groaned. The scorpion insignia on his brow wavered in Danar's sight as if it, too, struggled . . . to come alive? To flex those weirdly articulated legs, to spread its pincers.

The vaporous streams grew denser and stronger. He must do something! Throttle the priest into unconsciousness? Kill him with bare hands?

Did he have a choice?

For an instant, the air no longer churned with fumes and ice vapor. It shone like candlelight through a peerless emerald. A sense of deep well-being suffused Danar. His heart steadied from its frantic rhythm. No evil could touch him nor any harm come to those within Benerod's compassionate sphere.

The priest's body relaxed from its spasm. He opened his mouth, wider than Danar believed possible. His jaw must have gone out of joint like a snake's. No breath came from his mouth, no sound.

The air ignited into colorless brilliance. Lightning shot along Danar's nerves. Thunder roared in his ears. His vision went blank. He felt his muscles wrenching at his bones, his bones cracking, his blood charring into dust. . . .

Chapter Twenty-two

"DANAR? Danar?" The infuriatingly persistent voice was that of an older man, one he should know. Memories tantalized him, from a time when he was much younger. He expected to be called *son* in the next breath.

The man spoke again. "No, leave him to me. Let him come out of it on his own." Another voice answered from across the room. The first man said, "Stop fussing. I'll be fine. I've had enough of priests! And I want every single one of those Scorpion-worshippers in irons within the hour."

Danar's eyes wavered open. In a rush, he came back into himself. He was lying on his side, his head and shoulders cradled against the general's body as if he were a child. He remembered being carried up to his room after an evening's play in these same strong arms.

As Danar pulled himself to sitting, he felt surprisingly well, perhaps as a lingering effect of Benerod's healing. Manir clambered to his feet, drawing in his breath with the effort, then held out a hand to help Danar rise. "You all right, lad?"

"But you, sir—did he harm you? The priest?"

Gray tinged the general's sun-reddened skin. "Shook me up a bit, but don't tell them," with a nod in the direction of his men, who were now carrying away the body of the priest. One guard remained, a man of middle years but lean and fit looking, with watchful eyes and a somber expression. Danar didn't recognize him, only the ribbon insignia of the general's personal staff.

Manir waited until the door closed, leaving only his bodyguard. The general swayed on his feet and, waving off any aid, lowered himself into the nearest chair.

"We can speak in front of Runar," Manir said with a faint tug at the corners of his mouth that might have been a smile. "He's seen me through worse." He leaned back in his chair and closed his eyes. The gray was already fading from his face. "Now," he said, his voice deceptively casual, "suppose you explain to me what just happened."

"A priest of Qr attacked you."

"By attempting to wrench my heart from my chest from several yards away?" Manir did not open his eyes, but his voice dropped in pitch. "I may have been within a minute of explaining my sins to the Remover of Sorrows, but I know what I saw."

"It's difficult to explain," Danar said with a glance in the direction of the guard. "I don't really understand it, myself. Why would a priest of any of our gods want to eliminate the Ar-King's own general? That would be—"

"Treason as well as murder. My thought, as well. Why would the Scorpion-lovers attempt it?" Manir lifted his head and regarded Danar with unflinching directness. "Perhaps time will reveal the answer to that mystery. But Aidon politics do not explain why the priest took one look at you and fell down in a fit, or what you were doing back in my office."

Benerod.

"I came back—I'd forgotten something," Danar explained, "and I saw him menacing you. He was using some kind of magic. I tried to knock him out of the way, thinking that would break his spell. I have a little skill in wrestling, as you know. You taught me the basics in my father's house. The priest must have hit his head on the floor."

"Such things do occur," the general agreed, clearly unconvinced.

As they spoke, a thought grew in Danar's mind. The Qr

priest could not have known of their conversation or Manir's decision to accompany Danar to the steppe. The priest had been surprised, shocked even, at the presence of an *alvar*. So the attack on Manir had been for some other purpose.

He remembered what Tsorreh had said about the ancient enemy, the foe not only of Meklavar but of all the living lands. If Tsorreh's surmise were right, and Fire and Ice intended to remake the world, then it would have to destroy Meklavar and its legendary Shield first. What better way to weaken Meklavar than to remove the man who oversaw the Gelonian occupation? Even if Chion did not retaliate with even more brutal measures than before, Manir's death would surely provide the opening for a rebellion. Most likely, even more of the old aristocracy, including those most likely to have come into possession of the *alvara,* would be executed. Fire and Ice would use Qr to destroy the remnants of Khored's Shield. The agents of Qr did not know about the gathering of the *alvara* and their guardians. They must never find out.

Danar felt how tight his face had become, the painful clenching of his jaw. Manir was watching him obliquely, waiting for him to say more.

My father's true friend is now my ally. I must take care never to abuse that trust.

"Whatever the goal of the Scorpion priests, they must not interfere with our own plans," Danar said. "I have preparations to make and a prisoner to restore to his own people. This attack has convinced me even more of the rightness of our scheme. I hope you feel the same way, sir"—correcting himself—"General Manir."

"Lord Danar, I am at your service. We cannot yet know the full import of these events, but I believe they are related."

"As do I."

"Then go, take away your prophet, and let there be an end to that particular species of trouble. We will have enough without him."

*   *   *

Iskarnon climbed into the litter without protest, leaned back against the cushions, and closed his eyes. They set off, Danar walking alongside. The exercise loosened his muscles, but also brought his attention to a twinge in one knee. He'd be sore tomorrow, but on the whole he had come through the encounter with the priest very well. He thought he heard the sound of sobbing from behind the swaying curtains, but he could not be certain.

As Danar expected, they were met with some fuss at Ganneron's door. He dismissed the litter, then managed to persuade the obstructive woman servant to admit him and this foul-smelling, begrimed stranger who could not even stand unaided.

"Stop this racket at once!" Ganneron burst into the entry hall while they were still arguing. The moment he approached close enough to sense the aura of Dovereth's gem, he halted.

Iskarnon lifted his head. It seemed to Danar that a wash of ruby light—Cassarod's courage—infused the Prophet's wan features.

"He needs rest," Danar said. "And food."

"And a bath," the woman servant added tartly.

"Go then and prepare it!" Ganneron snapped. As the servant scurried away, he slipped one of Iskarnon's arms over his own shoulders. "Come on, then. We'll take him up the back stairs. How did you mange to break him out?"

"I had some influence with Manir," Danar said. "I'll tell you the whole story when we're all together. The others, they're still here?"

"My house is big enough for us all. There's still some risk of arrest, but less than if Sandaron or the Denariyan woman went wandering about the city."

Danar felt a measure of pity for any ruffian foolish enough to take on Sandaron. He would not be surprised if Jenezhebre carried a weapon or several under the pleated layers of her dress, and was expert in their use.

Together they maneuvered Iskarnon through a doorway that led to a back corridor and the landing of the stairs. Iskarnon took on a measure of strength, perhaps from realization that he was once more among his own people, but more likely from the proximity of two other *alvara*. He was able to take most of his own weight, although he needed help in ascending the stairs.

Danar and Ganneron bathed Iskarnon, attempted to comb his hair, gave up, and then dressed him and helped him to bed. The same sharp-tongued woman servant trimmed the Prophet's hair quite short before dosing his scalp with a pungent lice ointment. She hovered over him, spooning broth into his mouth.

Tsorreh and Marisse were waiting outside the door. Marisse threw her arms around Danar's neck. At that moment, he realized how close he'd come to never seeing her again—if he'd been wrong, if Manir had not been the man he remembered, if the Qr priest had succeeded, if a dozen other things had gone wrong....At the time, he had not considered the danger, focusing solely on the task at hand. Relief now swept through him, leaving him breathless.

The moment Marisse released him, Tsorreh grabbed Danar by the shoulders. "What were you thinking?" With each phrase, she gave him a shake. "You have no right—no right at all—to risk yourself—and Benerod's gift!"

Danar struggled to speak, but the words would not come.

"To go to Gelonian headquarters—to Manir himself!" Tsorreh raged. "He could have laughed in your face and then butchered you alongside Iskarnon. We would have lost two *alvara* for nothing!"

Stung, Danar shot back, "*You* went to Anthelon."

"The danger was to myself alone!" Tsorreh released him. "Besides, Anthelon was once a trusted advisor to my husband. The situations are completely different."

"No, they're not. Manir was my father's friend, and I've known him since I was a child."

"Men change, lad," Ganneron said in a temperate tone. "You took a terrible risk, but I am more happy than I can say that you succeeded."

Danar hesitated, but only for a moment. "It was not such a hopeless cause. A man does not rise to General Manir's rank—or retain the friendship of my father—without integrity. Manir's loyalty is to Gelon, not to Chion."

"That is as it may be," Ganneron said, his expression

deepening into a frown. "But why did you say nothing to us beforehand?"

"Would you have let me go?" Danar said.

Ganneron made a pacifying gesture and said, "By whatever means, you've managed to restore Iskarnon to us. Let that be an end to it."

"It is not the end!" Tsorreh insisted, her voice rising. "Now Manir knows who and where we are! Danar, you have put us all at risk."

The door jerked open and the woman servant stuck her head out. "Quiet, all of you! This man needs rest. Go take your yammering elsewhere!"

"Don't trouble yourself, Harannah," Ganneron said mildly. "We'll be off. Please continue your excellent nursing care." With a gesture, he indicated for the others to proceed toward their meeting room.

When they were reasonably private again, it was Danar's turn to take Tsorreh by the shoulders. He was gentle, his touch intended to calm instead of restrain. His heart went out to her for the losses she'd sustained and her desperate fears for them all.

"These are not safe times," he said, looking into her eyes. "Events summon us from our hiding places. They demand that we take risks." He paused, seeing in her eyes that she understood. She was afraid, as were they all, but she was of the line of Khored.

As I am of the royal line of Gelon, the blood of Ar-Kings.

"Taking those risks has won more than I hoped," Danar added, now that she was calmer. "I have brought to you, my sister and friend, more than the bearer of the last of the six lesser *alvara*. My gift to you and to Zevaron, may we soon be able to tell him, is your city."

She frowned, a fleeting shadow across the smooth expanse of her forehead. "I don't understand."

He wanted to laugh, except that it would wound her. "General Manir recognizes that I have a legitimate claim to the throne of Gelon. He released Iskarnon on my command. And on my command, he is now preparing to turn Meklavar over to its rightful ruler. That is you, *te-ravah*. Tomorrow morning, he will come here to tell you so himself."

Tsorreh inhaled sharply. Marisse clapped her hands.

"He wouldn't just march out of the city," Ganneron said. "Not when the Ar-King commanded him to hold it."

"Of course not," Danar agreed. "But when the heir to the Lion Throne *then* commands him to defend Gelon—and has made an alliance with a ruler the people of Meklavar will accept—is it not his duty to obey? That's why Manir will recognize the *te-ravah's* authority and why he and his men will be escorting us to the north. To find Zevaron."

"What!" Ganneron looked ready to strike Danar. "Place ourselves in the hands of the tyrant-general? Are you insane—or have you plotted our deaths all along?"

"How dare you accuse Danar of treachery!" Marisse stepped between them. A sudden heat suffused her cheeks. Her voice rang like steel. "It was he, not you, who saved the *te-ravah's* life in the *Mher Seshola.* He, not you, who kept Zevaron alive and out of Cinath's reach. He, not you, who discovered Iskarnon and brought him to us. If he truly meant us ill, would he have done any of these things?"

"How is this possible?" Tsorreh wondered.

"How is any of it possible?" Danar said. "You are twice dead, twice reborn. I am the keeper of Benerod's gem, lost all these years in the Dawn Sea. Sandaron found Jenezhebre, the one person in all Denariya we needed. In such a world, anything can happen."

"You are full of surprises," Tsorreh said. "But then, you are Jaxar's son."

Feeling a little embarrassed, Danar turned back to Ganneron. "There is yet another reason to trust Manir's loyalty. He owes me more than patriotic duty, for I saved his life this day."

"Indeed?" Ganneron asked.

When Danar told them what had happened with the Qr priest. Tsorreh's expression darkened. "I hope your General Manir is prepared to move quickly."

Even though Iskarnon was apart from the others, the stone walls hummed with the proximity of so many *alvara.* If five had seemed a miracle, six were even more so.

Danar felt no need to return to his old room above the bakery. Doubtless the landlord would sell whatever was remaining, just a few pieces of clothing and toiletries. Instead, he sat with Iskarnon. Benerod's gem knew where it was most needed, or perhaps Danar found being with the sleeping man restful. It seemed to him, with that more-than-vision, that as the hours passed, the yellow light of Dovereth grew stronger and clearer.

When Iskarnon roused, Marisse brought some soup and stayed while Danar fed him. She had the gift of sitting quietly, filling the room with her presence. Iskarnon accepted her without question. From his expression, however, he was not so sure of Danar. Perhaps he remembered seeing Danar in the crowd just before he was arrested.

Danar set the spoon down in the bowl. Iskarnon stared at him, but it was not the blank, unseeing look of the insane.

Iskarnon blinked. "I know you."

"Friend," Danar said, somewhat awkwardly, "you are safe with us. We have been looking for you for a long time."

"Have I been dreaming? It seemed to me that I wandered in a wilderness while the towers of my city blackened and fell into dust. Everywhere I looked, I saw ashes. Now I lie in this pleasant chamber in a soft bed, and before me sit a woman of my own people and a man of our oppressors, a man who calls me *friend*. Am I dead, and is this the life to come?"

Danar glanced at the spoon in his hand. "Do the dead eat soup in your afterlife? They don't in mine."

Marisse giggled, sounding so carefree that Iskarnon's face lit up in a crooked smile. He looked as if he had almost forgotten how.

Manir presented himself at Ganneron's house the following morning. He brought only four guards and he left them outside, an action that conveyed more than a hundred fine promises, even though Ganneron was still clearly unhappy about having armed Gelon stationed outside the door.

Ganneron had prepared the largest room in the house as an audience chamber. For Tsorreh, he had brought out a huge carved chair, somewhat reminiscent of a throne. He had wanted to arrange seats for the others, but Danar prevented him, saying that it was to everyone's benefit to preserve Manir's dignity. It was to Tsorreh, and not an assortment of disreputable-looking Meklavarans, that Manir intended to pay his respects.

Tsorreh had dressed herself in the same sleeveless vest and trousers as on her first visit to the *meklat*, and she carried herself with regal poise. Marisse was less talkative than usual, and the quieter she got, the more imperturbable she looked. Jenezhebre seemed to treat the upcoming audience as a trade negotiation, with an expression of studied unconcern. To the casual glance, Sandaron also looked at ease, his hands very still, his expression calm. He kept his weight balanced on both feet, and as he studied the room, Danar knew he was memorizing the exact distances and angles for attack or flight.

The audience began with official salutations and all the proper formalities. Manir still had time to back out of his commitments to Danar, but by his presence, he reaffirmed them.

Manir addressed Tsorreh in accented but clear Meklavaran, and Tsorreh welcomed him in fluent Gelone. Both had clearly rehearsed their speeches. Tsorreh listened with solemn attention as Manir recited the phrases that passed on governance of the city. Only a slight heightening of her color hinted at her emotional state. Through the connection between the *alvara*, Danar sensed a kaleidoscope of reactions from the others—willingness to suspend judgment from Sandaron, relief from Marisse, lessening skepticism from Ganneron. It struck Danar that Jenezhebre's determination to listen, the way she measured each syllable with a trader's ear for deception, might serve them best.

When Manir finished, it was Tsorreh's turn to speak. She tilted her head to one side in the way Danar had come to know well. "I do not know that we can ever be friends," she began.

Manir's expression betrayed nothing of his reaction. Danar, however, was surprised. *Friendship* had nothing to do with the freedom of Meklavar. What was she doing?

"You are responsible for much sorrow and even more misery among my people. This does not produce an atmosphere of trust." Her mouth, which had been hard, now softened. "Yet I believe you have served your Ar-King to the best of your very considerable abilities. Who can say what you might have done if the rule of this city had been left entirely to your own judgment?"

She paused. Manir waited, motionless. *Trust her,* Danar urged silently.

Tsorreh nodded, as if Manir had, by his refusal to defend his actions, passed a test. "Danar tells me that you mean to lead your men to the defense of your own country and that you wish to leave behind a Meklavar that, if not friendly, at least does not pose a second threat."

"Lady, that is so." Manir's gaze flickered to Danar and then back to Tsorreh.

"In surrendering the rule of this city, you forfeit any right to dictate what actions I will then take. Beyond my promise not to attack Gelon, that is. For example, I might choose to retain or dismiss anyone currently serving in an official capacity."

"That is of course your prerogative, Your Majesty."

She dipped her chin, accepting the Gelonian version of her royal title.

Jenezhebre stepped forward. "*Te-ravah*, I am a stranger to your city, but I have a good deal of experience in trading matters. If you would have my advice on the good ordering of the transition of power, you would take care how many officials you replace. It is true that some of your own people are seen as foreign puppets and therefore not to be trusted. But they also have knowledge of many things necessary to the welfare of the city. Trade, for instance, and the policing of criminal activity. It will avail no one to relieve the streets of soldiery at the cost of public security."

"I will consider the matter," Tsorrch said.

A harmonic in her voice told Danar that she already had a plan. He wondered if she meant to ask Manir to leave behind a contingent to help maintain calm.

Tsorreh spoke again, sketching out with Manir the best way to make the public announcement. Such an event required preparation, and besides, the *alvara* guardians could not depart the city immediately. Iskarnon was in no shape to travel. Danar did not know if Marisse could ride, although he had no doubt that Jenezhebre, like all her people, was a hardy traveler. Manir was looking considerably relieved, even hopeful, when he bowed again to Tsorreh and took his leave.

The moment Manir had left the chamber, Tsorreh sprang up. "Lord Ganneron, is your brother Setherod still in Aidon?"

"No, it was too dangerous for him after your trial and everything that followed," he replied. "He's been living in Verenzza, where foreigners attract less attention."

"Even better, for he is on the seacoast and in easy reach of a ship. You must summon him home immediately. We will have need of him, as the heir to your family and proof that the line of Cassarod has endured. What is left of the great houses must give the city stability—not to mention hope—during the transition."

"I will send word to him this hour." Ganneron delivered a short bow and left the room.

Tsorreh watched the door close behind him. "Marisse, will you and Jenezhebre be so kind as to attend Iskarnon? Tell him what has happened. He must understand that Meklavar is now free, that his visions have been fulfilled. You can do that gently, yes?"

Marisse inclined her head. "*Te-ravah*, it is not we who give him strength and steadfastness, but what we serve."

When they were alone, Tsorreh's regal bearing faltered. With a breath like a sob, she took a step toward Sandaron, then checked herself.

"You did it," Sandaron murmured. "Ah, my *teshura*, I would not have believed it of anyone else."

"No, not me. Not me alone. And . . ." she swallowed, "it is not over."

"You think Manir means to betray you?"

"Manir does not worry me." She returned to her chair. "It will take me some while to establish order in the city and to convince the people to accept those I designate to act in my stead. It would be cruel to ask Anthelon, even if he had the credibility with our people. I do not expect him to live much beyond his release from office. Indeed, I suspect he has stayed alive only because he believed, however mistakenly, that he accomplished some good. Setherod will be a better choice. If all goes well, he will arrive at about the time Iskarnon is fit to travel and peaceable conditions in the city are assured."

Tsorreh pointedly had not invited either Danar or Sandaron to sit. They stood before her like vassals before a monarch. Danar had the sinking feeling that she was marshaling every advantage of distance and authority to present a decision neither man would readily accept.

"Danar, it was difficult for me to consider what you said about Zevaron," Tsorreh went on, "about him being the Azkhantian war-leader. The notion was at odds with everything I know about him, but I have since had time to reflect. The truth is that I may not understand my son nearly as well as I had thought. With the exception of that brief time at Jaxar's house, I've had no contact with him since the fall of Gatacinne. I know only a small fraction of the things that happened to him in that time, things that must inevitably leave their mark upon a person's character. I did not want to believe he could so hate Gelon that he would conquer an entire people to destroy it."

Her voice trailed off, but as much as Danar wanted to offer consolation, her expression forbade any expression of sympathy. Sandaron's mouth tightened but he did not speak.

"It is possible that Zevaron has nothing to do with this horde, that he has remained in the northern fastnesses. But there is this: the horde comes from the north, from where the comet landed." She ticked off the points on her fingers. "The comet was drawn from the heavens and directed at that specific location by the forces of chaos—Fire and Ice— and its Gelonian manifestation, Qr."

She paused, her eyes glittering with a perilous fervor. Her voice dropped in pitch but gained in strength.

"If Fire and Ice commands this horde, directly or indirectly, *why is it headed for Gelon?* Gelon is its pawn. There is no reason to subjugate it by violence when it could be

easily controlled through Cinath. Or Chion, or whoever in-
herits. The priests of Qr will see to that."

Danar nodded, following her argument. The agents of
the Scorpion god had been tightening their grip on the
Aidon court for years, drawing the Ar-King and the most
powerful court nobles under their influence.

"Fire and Ice would drive its army here to Meklavar, its
ancient enemy."

With a sharp inhalation, Sandaron lifted one hand to his
chest. In Danar's mind, fire flashed green.

"There can be only one reason why the horde advances
on Gelon instead. You yourself said it, Danar. Zevaron
leads it, and he believes me dead." She swallowed, blinking
hard. "He would not betray everything we cherish and
place the living world in such peril . . . except for me. I
should have found a way to let him know I had survived! At
the time, it seemed the best way to keep him safe, then I had
no choice. He and Danar had already fled Aidon."

"Are you saying that Zevaron has entered the service of
Fire and Ice?" Sandaron spoke what Danar feared.

Tsorreh's face had gone hard, her eyes lightless. Danar
could not look at her any longer. "More likely, Zevaron believes that Fire and Ice can be forced to serve *him*."

"Yes," said Sandaron, "with the power of Khored's gem,
he might well believe that."

"Therefore," Tsorreh went on, "I must accompany the
party going north. If my son is obsessed with vengeance
against Gelon, it is because he believes Cinath had me
killed. He will not believe anyone who says otherwise. The
only thing that will convince him is seeing me alive."

"You think you can talk him free from Fire and Ice?"
Sandaron said. "If he has given himself over to it, then he
may be lost to us—to you, no matter what you say to him.
Men have been enslaved by the ancient enemy, but none
have ever freed themselves. Danar, help me to persuade
her."

You are no longer part of the Shield, Danar wanted to say
to her. But she had not died when she relinquished the *te-
alvar.* Could it be that the god of Meklavar had further
work for her?

"I do not know," she said, her voice dropping. "I know only that I must try."

"Surely Danar can tell him—or I," Sandaron protested. "He'll believe a countryman—and both of us bearing *alvara*."

Tsorreh shook her head. "He might not, if grief and suspicion and the craving for revenge have eaten him up. He doesn't know you, and Danar is a Gelon. Hatred can blind us to even those we love."

She's right, Danar thought. From the moment Zevaron had set eyes on the stone-drake, he had been a man ensorcelled.

Sandaron made a slight movement, as if he would go to Tsorreh, but her posture still enforced the difference in their rank, her terrible separateness. "*Te-ravah*, I tell you plainly, you must not risk yourself on a hopeless cause."

Her chin lifted fractionally. "Do you dare say that to me—tell me what I must or must not do?"

Sandaron did not flinch. "I am, as I have always been, your friend. Once you trusted my judgment of the dangers ahead. Will you not do so now?"

She lifted her shoulders. Her voice had lost none of its resolve. "Silon was a long time ago. We must save Zevaron. And if my son is gone, then we must save our world."

PART THREE:

Shannivar's War

When the city lies in shadow,
A fire burns in the snow.
Blood flows across the steppe.
The horse gallops on the edge of a knife.

When the heir to gold is drowned,
He returns with treasure.

When the heir to light goes to the mountain,
He will not return.

When the woman finds what is lost,
She gives it to the stranger.

Thus the gods have spoken to us.

—Azkhantian prophecy

Chapter Twenty-three

"THE Mighty One will not see you," said the creature with marble-pale eyes, the thing that had once been a rider of the steppe. The words were spoken with a chilling flatness. The clan totems stitched on the quilted vest were unrecognizable with filth, the colors muted like winter slush. Behind him rose a blanket of impenetrable fog, slowly advancing over the landscape.

Shannivar daughter of Ardellis tightened her fingers around her bow. Tension hummed along the opalescent wood, and she imagined the bow yearning for release. It was not an ordinary bow, but had come to her from the Mother of Horses, Tabilit herself.

Already, the lush grasses of high summer were fading, green and gold bleaching to the color of dry bones. A single hawk hovered far overhead, a black shape against the gray sky, but no marmots rustled the grasses. Even the familiar whine and buzz of insects had stilled. The nearness of the enemy drained all life from the land. Yet in the three years Shannivar had defended the territory of the horse people against these eerie marauders, she had never set eyes on what lay behind the bank of mist.

Moon by moon, the dense vapors had advanced, and no one knew what they concealed. They swallowed up all but the tallest hills. Unlike normal fog, the wind had no effect. The fog shone with a faint, sickly light, as if ice could smolder like embers. On even the darkest nights, its cold gray luminescence shrouded the horizon.

Was the mist a cover for an army of monsters, things that could not bear the sun, or was it itself the adversary? No one knew, although from time to time straggling riders, tattered remnants of a decimated clan, would carry tales of lands over which the mist had passed. In broken whispers, they told of ash and shattered rock where once feathergrass had flourished. Not a trace of life, not even an insect, stirred across the mounds of whitened cinders.

The forerunners of the mist were visible enough, creatures such as the one before her, mounted on emaciated, terrified horses. Band after band of them had run before the mist, how many clans she could not tell, only that when they fell, more kept coming. Only in the past few moons had she and her own riders been able to visibly diminish their numbers.

Zevaron led them. She had seen him emerge from the mist, issue commands to his enslaved men, and return again. If only she could speak to him . . .

The emissary's horse trembled as if it had been driven past endurance, past sanity. Its hide had once been chestnut and was now laced with oozing, white-rimmed burns. It stood, legs splayed wide, tail clamped against its withered rump, head lowered to its knees. It gulped air through nostrils crusted with dried blood.

Beneath Shannivar, Eriu stood like a rock. Once the stallion had been solid black. Now white streaked his mane and fetlocks. He, too, had been blind, pale-eyed like the creatures of Zevaron's army, but when he had stumbled free of the wall of colorless light, Tabilit had healed his eyes, and time and patience had restored his courage.

Zevaron, who had ridden Eriu into that unknown place of mists and magic, had not been so fortunate. He was no longer the man she loved, whose child she had borne, the son who was nearing his third birthday.

The creature that had once been a man jerked on his horse's reins, pulling the tortured animal's head up. The horse's nose pointed skyward as it attempted to escape the pressure of the bit on its torn, bleeding mouth.

A spear, tipped with backward-curving spikes, pointed at Shannivar. "Go. He will not see you."

"I will not give up. Tell him that."

Shannivar shifted her weight, nudging Eriu with one knee. The black pivoted, supple beneath her. Another shift and a touch of her heels sent him from a walk into a gallop within two strides. His speed sent a thrill through her, as it always did. *My Eriu.* She unstrung the bow and slipped it into its case beside her left knee. *My wings.*

The others were waiting for her beyond the rise. Here the grasses were still fresh enough to provide grazing for the horses. Zaraya of the Badger clan held Shannivar's son in the saddle in front of her. Shannivar had met Zaraya when she rode the Long Ride at the fateful summer Gathering four years ago. Zaraya was not an especially skillful fighter, but she was the best rider. If anything happened to Shannivar, there was no one she trusted more than Zaraya to get her son to safety.

Shannivar's son, Chinggis, waved his arms. "Mami!" he cried in his high, clear voice.

Zaraya laughed. "I told you, little eagle, that your mother would come back." She was not a handsome woman, having the broad cheekbones and flat nose of her clan, but her kindness made her beautiful.

Shannivar took the little boy in front of her own saddle. Some things had not changed, despite the terrible fog and Zevaron's horde. Children still must learn to ride as soon as they could walk, to care for their horses, and to mind the herds that were the wealth of the clan.

Chinggis laced his stubby fingers in Eriu's mane. The black cocked one ear backward in recognition.

"No luck?" Shannivar's cousin, Alsanobal, shifted in his saddle, easing his bad leg. Broken in a raid on a Gelonian fort, the thighbone had healed crooked, but not so badly as to interfere with his being able to ride and shoot. More importantly, the injury had sobered him from his former recklessness. With his father's death, he was now chieftain of Golden Eagle clan, although Shannivar led the war party.

Shannivar shook her head. "Not this time."

Rhuzenjin, another warrior from the Golden Eagle clan, frowned. He looked uncomfortable standing beside his horse, a sour-tempered grulla mare borrowed for the day because his best horse had pulled a leg tendon in the last skirmish. Although not her blood kin, Shannivar thought of him as a clansman. Born into the Rabbit clan, he had joined Shannivar's own Golden Eagle when his mother married there.

"I said it was no use trying to talk to him," Rhuzenjin said. "We've wasted time we could have used in better ways."

"No harm was done," replied Zaraya evenly. "It was worth a try."

"How many times does the outlander have to say *no* before you believe it?" Rhuzenjin said to Shannivar. "He is not the man you knew, if he ever was."

Shannivar saw no purpose in pursuing the old argument. In the end, Rhuzenjin might prove right, but that time had not come. She kissed her son's cheek, settled one arm around his body, and nudged Eriu into an easy trot.

Their present encampment lay a solid hour's travel from the mist. It was one of several, for Shannivar had not wanted to consolidate all her riders in one place. The trail tents and picket lines had been dismantled, the horses saddled, and the pack animals made ready. Riders stood in clusters or hunkered beside their mounts, talking quietly or playing at knucklebones. The last of the cookfires gave off thin wisps of smoke, and cups of buttered, salted tea were being passed around.

Tarabey, son of the old chieftain of the northern Ghost Wolf clan, trotted his horse forward to meet them. His face had the pinched look of constant strain and his eyes narrowed from habit. "A bright day to you, Shannivar warleader."

Politely she responded, "May your horse never stumble."

"The riders are ready for your command."

"Then bring the wing-leaders to me. We have a battle to plan."

Tarabey, Zaraya, and Alsanobal rode through the horsemen, signaling to the other war captains. Dust spiraled upward as their horses moved in response to their riders.

Shannivar had known for some time that the enslaved riders were but a means to clear the way for the strange mist. In recent days, however, scouts reported their numbers were diminished. Perhaps Zevaron was no longer able to force enough men into his service to replace those lost in battle or exhaustion. In the past moon, Shannivar's forces had been able to slow the expansion of the mist by preventing the human vanguard from advancing. This allowed those who could not fight—the very old and very young, along with the flocks and herds on which their lives depended—to flee.

For all these gains, they were running out of room. The mist might move only a little at a time, but move it did. Eventually, the remaining free tribes would be driven to the Gelonian borders. She did not doubt the Ar-King would take full advantage of the situation. This mist and whatever lay inside it would finish what Gelon alone could not accomplish.

Shortly, Tarabey, Zaraya, and Alsanobal returned with the other war captains. Shannivar addressed them: "We must find out what lies beyond the mist and how to defeat it. Until now, their Azkhantian slaves"—she would not say *allies*—"have cleared the way, but there are too few of them now to block us. With luck, we can break through."

At first, it had been difficult to attack the captive riders. With the exception of very limited livestock raiding, the riders of the steppe did not make war on one another. The bitter cold of winter, the drought of summer, and the loss of herds through predation or disease were enemies they all faced. For all they knew, these strange, white-eyed creatures had once offered them hospitality, the bonds of salt and *k'th*. They might even be kin.

They are lost to us, she thought, and saw in the faces of her own riders that very same thought.

"We will pass through their midst like a heated knife through butter," said Tarabey, and the others smiled.

Chapter Twenty-four

THEY set out shortly before dawn, with Zaraya remaining in camp with Chinggis. She had not protested being left behind, for her strength was not in battle. Instead, she advised Shannivar on how best to prepare the horses and how to feed them parched barley mixed with camel butter to strengthen their hearts for battle.

Shannivar rode Eriu at the head of the war party, with Tarabey, leader of the Ghost Wolf clan, on one side. Alsanobal, leader of Shannivar's own Golden Eagle clan, rode on the other. Golden Eagle's best archer, Jingutzhen, also accompanied them. Shannivar had pointedly not included Rhuzenjin. He might be her own kin-by-adoption, but he had no wish to endure his constant questioning. She let the captains choose their own riders, balancing numbers against the need for speed. Everyone understood that enough must be left behind to continue the resistance should this expedition fail.

The horses settled into a ground-covering trot. One of the riders, an older man from the Rabbit clan, began to sing. Within a short time, others had taken up the chant-like melody. Shannivar recognized it as a variation of Saramark's Lament.

Like every child of the steppe, Shannivar knew the legend. When Saramark's chieftain husband was wounded by the Gelon and unable to lead the men into battle, the clan faced annihilation. Saramark took up her husband's sword and led her warriors. One woman had turned disaster into triumph. It was Shannivar's favorite story, one she never tired of hearing.

"May the strong bones of my body rest in the earth," the Rabbit clan man sang, and the others answered, *"Ayay, ayay!"*

"May the black hair on my head turn to meadow grass." *"Ayay, ayay!"*

"May my bright eyes become springs that never fail." *"Ayay, ayay!"*

As much as she loved the song, Shannivar could not lift her voice with the others. Her heart had risen up in her throat, leaving her mute. If she failed, there would be no meadow grass, no ever-fresh springs, no rest for the strong bones of her body. What then would become of Chinggis, her son?

Tabilit, Mother of Horses, Lady of the Sky! Ride with me now!

The mist appeared as a darkness stretching across the horizon. At first, the sight filled Shannivar with despair. How could she, or any mortal, triumph over such vastness? The singing faltered and then died.

Shannivar lifted one arm and drew her riders to a halt. She squinted, trying to make out details. On this day, the spirit of her clan totem, the Golden Eagle, granted her keen sight. The mist was wide but finite. Her courage rose as she saw that it had not eaten up all the land as it passed. It might be possible to ride around the mist, to strike at its flanks.

She touched Eriu with her heels, and he moved forward. The mist grew rapidly in size as they approached, as if it hastened to embrace them. The land was gently rolling, the soil dry. Shortly, the vanguard of the mist riders came into view. Dust billowed up behind them, obscuring the base of the mist wall.

Shannivar drew her bow from its case beside her left knee. Without slackening speed, she strung the bow and nocked an arrow. The other riders did the same.

"Do not forget," she cried out so that all could hear her. "No matter what they once were, these are not our own people. Not any longer! They are slaves to *Olash-giyn-Olash*, that would crush the life out of Tabilit's green earth! We fight now so that our kin, our friends—our children!—may not suffer the same fate!"

Shannivar settled herself more deeply in the saddle. Eriu snorted and arched his neck, one ear pricked back at her. She risked dropping the reins on his neck to lift one hand in signal.

"Wait!" She wanted to see what formation the approaching riders would assume. As best as she could see through the dust, they remained spread out. They were riding in a long, ragged row, one or perhaps two riders deep, not the masses she had first faced. Once or twice, a new burst of dust marked where a horse stumbled and went down. If their mounts were in no better shape than the ones she'd seen the day before, they could not sustain a fighting pace.

Shannivar slowed Eriu, so that her captains came alongside. "Stay together—punch through the line! Then divide into three wings—Golden Eagle and Snow Fox with me, the others split—Ghost Wolf, Rabbit, Black Marmot to the left—Falcon, Antelope, all the others, to the right. Hit them side-on—keep them from turning on us!"

She felt rather than saw Tarabey's fierce grin. "We'll hold the tent flap open!"

Then her captains fell back, shouting commands. Alsanobal took charge of the Golden Eagle riders, but Jingutzhen remained with Shannivar as her strong right arm.

She shifted her weight and Eriu shot forward like an arrow loosed from her bow. Behind her, the sound of the running horses was like thunder. Eriu skimmed the ground, drawing well ahead of the others. His mane lashed her chest, driven by the wind of his passing. She heard voices raised in the battle cries of each clan. In her own chest, she found only silence.

Shannivar could see the mist riders clearly now. The line

was drawing together, closing ranks. The foremost lashed their horses into a shambling gallop. Spear points gleamed.

She took aim at one of the riders in front. His vest was a dull red and he rode a brown-and-white spotted horse. Eriu flowed beneath her, unfaltering. The bowstring, released, sang in her ears. The mist rider toppled from his saddle. The spotted horse stumbled to its knees and was quickly swallowed up by the dust.

Another mist rider went down, and then another. Shannivar set a second arrow to her bow. Then a rain of arrows streaked down toward her from the sky. A shriek, suddenly cut off, came from behind.

They were almost upon the mist riders. Shannivar thrust her bow back into its case and drew out her curved bronze sword. At her signal, Eriu veered, changing leads in midstride, toward a gap that had just opened in their ranks.

The two lines of horsemen collided with one another. The war cries of the men and the squealing of horses mixed with the pounding of hooves and the clash of swords.

Eriu shot through the opening. A mist rider spun his horse around to follow, but he was too far away and too slow. Shannivar saw his arm cock back, the glint of sun on spear, the powerful cast. Like the shadow of a striking snake, the spear hurtled toward the horse beneath her.

Shannivar swung her sword in the direction of the oncoming spear. She caught the point on the edge of her blade. The momentum of her strike deflected the blow, but the impact shocked up her arm and almost caused her to lose her balance. She dug her knees into Eriu's sides and regained her seat.

Another rider turned toward Shannivar, closer than the last. With a twist, he reached down beside his right knee and whipped out a sword. It was long, with a pale, icy sheen. Shannivar's blade was shorter, and bronze was softer than steel.

The rider reined his horse, a dust-colored dun, directly into Shannivar's path. Ropes of bloody froth dripped from the dun's mouth. Ears pinned back, eyes wild and yellow-rimmed, it barreled toward Eriu.

The two horses crashed into one another. The collision

almost knocked Eriu, smaller and lighter, off his feet. Squealing in rage, he recovered. The dun went past and began to turn. Shannivar felt Eriu's spine hunch an instant before he lashed out with his hind feet.

The dun staggered, head thrown up, hooves churning dry earth. By some feat of horsemanship, the rider not only stayed in the saddle but drew his bow. The horse steadied itself just as the rider nocked an arrow to his bowstring. At this distance, he could not miss.

Suddenly the rider arched backward. The shaft of an arrow pierced his neck. The dust swallowed him up. The next moment, Jingutzhen booted his horse alongside Shannivar, bow in hand. He looked grimmer than she'd ever seen him. He gestured toward the mist. It was even closer than before, towering above them, a wall of seething gray and white. It smelled of charred stone and old ice, snow at the bitter end of winter, of death in the starless nights, and the howling of wolves, the taste of famine and of fear.

Eriu pranced sideways, clearly unhappy about the stench. But he was a warhorse of the steppe. He would go where she asked, when she asked.

Jingutzhen was beside her, the Snow Fox clansmen somewhere behind. She heard Alsanobal's war cry and knew that her horsemen had broken through the line of the mist riders. She raised her sword. Eriu leaped forward as if he were one of her arrows.

The mist wall loomed in front of them, twenty paces away.

Eriu lengthened his stride. Wind clamored in Shannivar's ears. Her heart was no longer ice-touched or her mind beset with fears. The wild, fierce battle pride of the Golden Eagle swept away all else.

Ten paces . . .

The surface of the mist glistered like winter sun on ice that had melted and frozen too many times. The clansmen roared behind her.

Five paces . . .

Two . . .

With a shock of searing cold, Shannivar burst through the wall and into the mist.

Whiteness surrounded her, a world bleached of color. Eriu's hoof-falls sounded like ice shattering. For the first time, he faltered. She touched the reins and drew him to a walk. As the other riders crossed the boundary, they cried out in alarm. Their horses snorted and whinnied.

The mist closed behind them, flowing along the fissured, frost-laced earth. Shannivar's mouth filled with the taste of snowmelt, of dawn, of unshed tears.

Zevaron, my heart, father of my son! Where are you?

"War-lady, what is this place?" Jingutzhen asked. He so rarely said anything, his question carried even greater weight. He spoke for them all.

It is what awaits us all if we fail. She could not say so aloud. A daughter of the Golden Eagle did not show her fear.

"This place is not our enemy," she said, loud enough for them all to hear. "Pay it no heed, and do not waste your arrows on vapors. We will press on until we find the ones we must fight."

"Aye!" came Alsanobal's raised voice. "The war-leader speaks the truth!"

Shannivar gathered the reins and Eriu broke into a trot. Mist swirled and darkened. For an instant, she saw a shadow like that of a bear, easily twice the height of a mounted rider. Its head swung from side to side, as if questing a scent. The damp air clawed at her throat. Then the vapors twisted and rolled, and she could not be sure she had seen it at all.

The riders drew closer to one another. No one wanted to risk becoming separated in such a place. The horses followed where Eriu went, even as the men looked to Shannivar's lead.

She sensed the end of the mist wall before they reached it. The chill eased, and the vapors turned translucent. To either side, she noticed shapes of slightly darker gray. Something huge and white loomed in her path.

Shannivar's breath caught in her throat. Habit and training kept her in the saddle, her weight centered, one hand on the reins, the other bracing her sword. She looked up—and up.

Ice-troll!

The monster was no bear, but a thing of macerated ice. Its hide reeked of sodden ashes and had an odd, unstable texture. Enormous shoulders and forelegs sloped back to stumpy rear legs. The skull tapered to a snout so narrow that the bifurcated fangs jutted out at angles. It would have been impossible for the creature to eat, but Shannivar did not think it needed ordinary food.

A man straddled the hump where neck met ridged spine. He was as pale and rigid as if he had been carved from glacial ice.

The troll reared up, massive paws churning the air, opened its ill-shaped maw, and let out a bellow. When it crashed back to earth, the impact rattled Shannivar's teeth.

Eriu slowed, stiff-legged. Shannivar shifted her weight just as the troll lunged. Eriu spun on his hindquarters and sprinted out of reach.

"The eyes!" she shouted to her riders. "Aim for its eyes!"

She signaled for them to break, half to each side. Bowstrings twanged, and arrows found their marks along the ice-troll's shoulders. Most of the arrows fell away like straw. Only one lodged in an eye. The feathering was that of the Golden Eagle clan.

The ice-troll reared again, this time to its full height, revealing sickly, luminous patches on its exposed belly. The man atop the ice-troll lashed his mount with a whip like braided ice. He raked the beast's sides with spurs that sent gouts of thick, pale-blue liquid streaming over the rounded arch of its ribs. Bellowing again, it pawed at the arrow shaft.

Lesser creatures appeared at each side of the troll. A pack of stone-drakes moved forward at an undulating lope, their eyes animated by a dull red glow. Shannivar had seen one of their kind, but it had been frozen like an eerie rock formation. It had disturbed her even when she had believed it inert and powerless. She could not mistake the malevolence of the creatures rushing toward her.

A horde of winged snakes rose hissing into the air. Their bodies writhed as they dodged the Azkhantian arrows. The wan overhead light glinted on their needle fangs. They breathed out green-tinted vapors that turned the arrows to powder.

From behind the ice-troll came a sound like thunder, only it did not fall away. Instead, it increased with each passing moment, a growling thrum as if the earth itself were being pulverized. The man on the ice-troll gestured to the monsters, urging them to attack. He dug his spurs into the troll, and it lurched toward the nearest riders.

Shannivar screamed out a warning. Jingutzhen, in the lead, tried to wheel his horse out of the path of the troll. There was no time to draw her bow. "Go!" she cried to Eriu.

Within one stride, the black launched into a flat-out gallop. He ran with his head low, his ears pinned tight against his neck. Like one of her own arrows, he flew toward the troll. The man on its shoulders looked down. For a terrible moment, his gaze locked with Shannivar's.

Zevaron.

He gave no sign of recognition, although she was only a pace away. Chance favored her, for she was coming up on the troll's blind side. Too slow, the monster swung around, but not before Shannivar spotted the smooth, unarmored hide behind its knees.

Shannivar shifted her weight and touched Eriu with one heel. He responded, swerving to pass behind the troll. Shannivar took her sword in both hands, braced her knees against the saddle, and tightened the muscles of her torso. She send a silent prayer to Tabilit that she would not be unseated. A moment later, as Eriu pounded past, her blade slashed into the ice-troll's hamstrings. A sound like shattering ice rent the air. The troll screamed, its voice harsh and metallic.

Eriu's momentum carried them past the troll and toward the oncoming army. Shannivar guided him back toward her own riders. He tucked his hindquarters and circled, but even the most nimble horse could turn only so fast from a gallop.

Two gigantic six-legged beasts emerged from the clouds of ice dust. Their bodies resembled those of the woolly rhinoceros, the *ildu'amar* that Shannivar had hunted with the clansmen of the Snow Bear, but these creatures were gargantuan by comparison. Whitened horns slanted back from their snouts to their massive skulls. Dense, matted hair covered their bodies. Shannivar glimpsed the shadowy outlines of several more, swaying as they approached. Their footfalls sent tremors through the earth. The foremost dipped its head, dug its horn into the bleached soil, and ripped out a ragged-edged trench. Colorless flames burst forth from the overturned soil, crisping what was left of the grass. Instead of ash, the flames left oozing patches. A gust of air carried the taint of decay.

The next moment, Shannivar found herself in the midst of a handful of smaller creatures, somewhat akin to the stone-drakes but four-footed. Jagged spines ran the length of their hunched backs, and the edge of each spike glistened wetly. Screeching, they circled her. The nearest pair crouched, forked tails lashing, jaws gaping wide to reveal gullets that glowed like sulfurous mud. They had no eyes, only rows of parallel slits cut across their brows.

Eriu's stride faltered. Shannivar's hands had gone numb from the blow against the ice-troll, and lines of fire laced her wrists and shoulders. It was all she could do to keep hold of the sword. She could not manage the reins at the same time.

Winged snakes darted overhead. Hissing, the largest one plunged toward her. Its sinuous body shot through the air like an obscenely bloated arrow. Shannivar had no space to maneuver and scarcely any time to think.

Eriu, be my wings!

When she touched him with her heels, the black's ears flicked forward. He shifted from a slowing, hesitant canter back into a gallop. The plunging serpent streaked past, narrowly missing Shannivar's knee. She did not see it crash. Its cry was lost in the roiling tumult behind her.

From the howling clamor on the far side of the ice-troll came a human scream, and then another.

Eriu flexed his back, bringing his rear legs under him. Shannivar leaned forward so that her weight was poised over his forequarters. With a powerful thrust, he tucked his front legs. Horse and rider soared. The blasted earth lost its hold on them. For a long moment, they became creatures of air and light.

Eriu cleared the nearest slouching, fork-tailed creature and landed hard but in balance. Shannivar slipped her sword back into its carrier and grabbed her bow. She was taking a terrible risk, changing weapons, but she needed the longer reach of her arrows. She sent Eriu on an oblique path back toward the ice-troll. The monster was staggering on three legs, heaving its body from side to side as if trying to dislodge the arrow in its eye socket. Gouges marked where Zevaron had spurred it. Blue ichor trickled down the crevices in its hide.

The troll threw back its head and bellowed again. The sound was pitched higher than before, a cry of mindless pain and frustration.

Shannivar drew even with the troll as she set an arrow to her bowstring. With a shift of her weight, she slowed Eriu's pace. She bent her bow and sighted along her arrow. Up . . .

. . . to where Zevaron clung to his seat atop the wildly swaying troll. He looked down. This time, she saw the flicker of recognition in his eyes. He *knew* her.

Her fingers froze on string and arrow.

Then the moment was gone. The ice-troll reeled back, forefeet clawing the air, head thrown up. For a moment, it teetered on its one sound hind leg. Then its flesh seemed to soften, its bones to melt. Its head flopped sideways. No sound issued from its mouth.

Eriu swerved out of the way only a moment before the troll slammed into the earth. As they raced past, Shannivar glanced down at the irregular mound that even now was dissolving into wetly gleaming pulp. Elation and hope filled her. She had not expected to destroy the ice-troll, only to hamper it. Whether by the arrow in its eye or the severing of its hamstrings, it had perished—this monstrous, gigantic thing could be killed!

Seeing no sign of Zevaron, Shannivar tore her gaze from the sight. Eriu pounded toward one of the stone-drakes that had become separated from its pack. Beyond it, Shannivar spied a knot of Azkhantian riders. She loosed her arrow. The tip disappeared below the drake's jaw. The drake fell to its knees, clawing at its neck. The shaft splintered and fell away. The creature heaved itself to its feet, but Shannivar had already passed it.

Bodies littered the frost-brittle earth, many of men and horses, only a few of the mist creatures. Shannivar's elation at the death of the ice-troll vanished as she realized she'd lost half her riders. Those that remained looked dazed, as if they had been battling nightmares. Alsanobal was trying to rouse the Golden Eagle men. She did not see Jingutzhen among them.

"Out! Get your men—get out!" Shannivar whirled Eriu toward the enemy. Behind her, she heard the sound of fleeing hoofbeats.

Tabilit, guard them!

With that prayer, she faced the horde of Ice and Fire. She could no longer see the fallen troll. A pair of horned behemoths shuffled toward her. Their stumpy feet sent up clouds of glittering ice dust. Stone-drakes and fork-tails loped, yowling and chittering, in their wake. Behind them came more of the horned beasts and white-shadowed shapes that Shannivar could not yet make out. The earth trembled beneath Eriu's hooves.

The black slowed to a prancing trot and arched his neck. Shannivar reached into the case beside her left knee for another arrow. She took her time in aiming, waiting for the moment when one or the other of the behemoths swung its head to the side, so she would have a clear shot at its eye.

The roaring and rumbling, the screeching and howling of the oncoming mass deafened her. Their stench filled her nostrils. Heart racing, mouth dry, she held firm. Her shoulder muscles burned with the strain of holding the bow to its maximum tension.

There . . .

She did not hear the twang of the bowstring as she released it or feel the wind of the arrow's passage. The horned beast in front of her staggered and went down. A cry like a thunder-crack rent the air. It rattled the bones of Shannivar's skull.

Eriu shook his head and pulled at the bit. Shannivar held him in place. Something was emerging from the ice-dust, something that caused the other horn-beasts to shuffle out of the way and the lesser monsters to pause in their attack. They cowered and scuttled backward, opening an avenue . . .

A man walked there. A man of Fire and Ice.

A man of shadows.

At the sight of him, Shannivar's courage faltered. She could face anything, but not him. Not after she had squandered her only chance to put an end to what he had become.

She loosened her hold on the reins. Eriu pivoted on his hindquarters and sprinted after the Azkhantians.

Chapter Twenty-five

THE wall of mist rushed past and then Shannivar and Eriu burst into the brightness of day. Her heart thumped so loudly, it almost drowned out the sound of Eriu's hooves. They emerged into an open space between two groups of milling horsemen. Shannivar could not tell what was happening, nor did she care. It was enough to be among human riders and not the horrific army she had left behind. The other clans—Rabbit, Black Marmot, Falcon, Antelope— yes, they were all here. She had no time to count, to determine how many had fallen.

"Run!" she shouted.

They ran. Their horses, eyes rimmed with white, needed no urging. Hooves pounded over the frost-burned earth, scrambling for speed and yet more reckless, frenzied speed.

After a time, Eriu galloped raggedly, no longer in his silken floating gait. Much as Shannivar wanted to keep going, to ride until the entire steppe lay between her and the mist, she gave the signal to slow to a trot. Sweat ran in rivulets down Eriu's shoulders. His ribs heaved like bellows, drawing in air. The other horses were just as blown. They must walk until they were cool or risk becoming broken in wind. And in spirit, too, after what they had endured. The men, as well—*We must survive to fight again.*

One of her riders, a Golden Eagle clansman, reined his mount beside hers. Blowing foam from its nostrils, the other horse jigged and tossed its head.

Shannivar glanced at her clansman. "Jingutzhen—is he with you?"

Slanted eyes narrowed and lips pressed together in a line. The rider's skin, normally the dark-honey shade of the steppe people, paled.

Shannivar thrust aside the rush of grief. Jingutzhen had died a hero's death. He had met a glorious ending. What more did any Azkhantian warrior want, in the end? There would be time for the proper respect, not just for Jingutzhen, but for all those who did not return on this day.

"I would speak with Tarabey of the Ghost Wolf clan. Send him to me." To Shannivar's ears, her voice sounded thick, as if her throat had swollen up.

A few minutes later, Tarabey jogged his horse beside Eriu. The black laid his ears back and looked as if he might snap at the Ghost Wolf horse. That he did not was an indication of his fatigue. Shannivar grabbed a handful of mane and tugged. He relaxed.

Tarabey waited for Shannivar to speak.

"How many of your men dead?" she asked.

"Four. Those riders—those man-creatures—"

"Servants of the mist?"

"Yes. Even creeping things have more will to fight."

"Did you kill many?"

Tarabey ducked his head and pretended to focus on the spot between his horse's ears. He did not need to say aloud that it would have been a waste of arrows. It had been sufficient to hold them back, to keep the way clear for Shannivar's return.

The memory of Zevaron's face, a shell of glacial ice surrounding a colorless flame, rose up in Shannivar's mind. She'd had a clear shot. She could have ended it then. Now Jingutzhen was gone, her own kinsman, the archer who'd saved her life. Jingutzhen and how many others? How many others would yet perish, all because she had hesitated for one fateful moment?

This was no time for guilt or recrimination. It was her

responsibility to find a means to victory. She could not do it by human prowess at arms. Arrows alone could not defeat ice trolls and horned monsters.

She needed new weapons. New allies.

By the time Shannivar's party arrived at the encampment, the horses were flagging, even Eriu. She massaged his salt-crusted hide with a plait of dried grass until he sighed in contentment, then hand-fed him grain from her precious store before turning him out to graze. He wandered over to his favorite companion, a caramel sorrel mare with a white blaze. She was the last foal of Shannivar's old soft-gaited mare Radu and still too young for hard riding. In these days, no serviceable horse could be spared, and the mare's presence calmed Eriu. Shannivar had not yet given her a name.

"Shannivar?"

She turned at Rhuzenjin's approach.

"Shannivar, are you all right? You're not hurt?"

"No," she replied, "only weary in spirit. I will join you shortly."

Sighing, Rhuzenjin melted back into the twilight.

For long moments, Shannivar watched the horses, their heads lowered, blowing away chaff as they searched for the few remaining tufts of grass. They were hardy steppe horses, able to survive on the poorest fare. By the time Shannivar returned to the center of camp, her mind had steadied. The solace of horses had restored her, as it always did.

Dusk lengthened the shadows as the missing were counted and named, the injured tended, fires kindled with dung chips, and food prepared. Rhuzenjin brought out a store of *k'th*, the fermented milk of mares. Shannivar had no idea where he had found it. She suspected Tarabey's wife, Ythrae.

In silence, they ate a meal of parched barley simmered with a few shreds of dried gazelle meat and wild onions. Afterward came the usual buttered tea.

In the absence of an *enaree*, Shannivar rose to recite the funeral prayers. The gathering grew still, even Chinggis where he sat on Zaraya's lap. Shannivar lifted one of the skins of *k'th* to honor the transformation of the spirit, in the milk and in the slain.

> *"Let these warriors return to you, O Tabilit,"* she chanted.
> *"Let their pure spirits rise up to your Sky Kingdom,*
>   *Carried by the wings of the Golden Eagle.*
> *Guided by the sure wisdom of the Snow Fox,*
> *In the path of the fleet Antelope, the cunning Marmot, the*
>   *intrepid Ghost Wolf.*
> *Let them take their places with the chosen ones.*
> *Let them sit at Onjhol's strong right hand."*

She placed the spout to her mouth and moistened her lips with the pungent *k'th*. She would take no more, lest there be not enough for everyone.

The *k'th* was passed from hand to hand. Everyone, even those who had not ridden against the mist and its army, took a sip. Zaraya dipped a finger into the spout and then offered it to Chinggis.

Shannivar thought, *My son is a true clansman.* She went to him, took his hand, and led him to the horses.

Silent and solemn, he waited beside her as night blurred the shapes of the grazing animals.

"See that one with the white blaze? She will be yours."

"What's her name?"

"You must discover that for yourself."

"Does she have a mami?"

"Yes, she was Radu. Don't you remember her?"

A nod in the silence. The earth smelled of dust and rising dew and the tired animals. "And a papi?"

"My own Eriu."

"A papi like mine?"

Mother of Horses! Chinggis was not the only child to be raised by only his mother and her kin, so the question of his father's identity had not yet arisen. "No, little eagle. Not like yours."

After a time, the child's silence changed. He was tired but had already learned not to complain. Shannivar picked him up and carried him back. She gave him to Zaraya, who

took him off to the tent that they shared with Shannivar.
Then she called together the captains and leaders.

"The mist horsemen are no longer an effective fighting
force," she told them. A few of them grunted in agreement.
One or two smiled. "Do not think that means we have any
advantage against what follows them. Today we saw what
lies behind the wall of mist. Those creatures, not the mist-
riders, are the real enemy, and they are more deadly and
more powerful than anything we know. *They* are not easily
killed by our arrows." She lowered her voice. "They poison
the very land over which they march."

Shannivar sensed their dismay. These men and women
were worn down by moon after moon of combating a relentless enemy, only to face one that was nearly invincible.
Not only that, they had just lost their strongest archer.

"We cannot fight this army in the ordinary way," Shannivar drove home her point. "They are not creatures of blood
and flesh. We were able to bring down a few, and then only
by luck."

"What are we to do, then?" asked the Rabbit captain.

"We need help," she answered. "What our arrows and
swords cannot accomplish, our *enarees* must."

At that, their spirits lifted. Every one of them had been
tested by their clan shaman in the ancient ways. The *enarees*
possessed powerful magic and even more powerful sight.

Shannivar outlined her plan for gathering the *enarees* into
a new council, a council of war. For generations untold, they
had dreamed their smoke dreams and uttered their enigmatic
omens. The time had come for them to defend the steppe.

"The *enarees* will not answer your summons," Rhuzenjin
objected. "When have they ever fought at our side against
the Gelon? Bah! Everyone knows they are half-women,
half-men, neither one thing nor another! They will cower in
their tents while the rest of us die."

"Not all of them are cowards," Shannivar insisted. "Bennorakh journeyed with us to the land of the Snow Bear
clan, and that was no mean feat."

"What would you propose?" Alsanobal said to Rhuzenjin. "That we continue on as we have, losing more riders
with every encounter until none of us remain?"

"Of course not! We must buy time—"

"Have you heard nothing of what is coming—the *things* in the mist?" Tarabey cut Rhuzenjin off. Around the circle, those who had been in that battle muttered in agreement.

Rhuzenjin faced Alsanobal. "If we cannot stand against such a foe, then we must seek help elsewhere."

"Where?" Shannivar asked. "Isarre is too far and the Denariyans are traders, not warriors." She did not add that Mcklavar had never possessed any significant military resources. Zevaron might have found a way to summon their help, but Zevaron was worse than lost. She must not think of him now.

Rhuzenjin was saying, "We could make alliance with Ar-Chion-Gelon."

Silence fell away into shock and then outrage. Someone cursed and another cried, "Traitor!"

Shannivar held up her hands for calm. "Let Rhuzenjin explain himself! Only then can we judge his plan."

"How dare he suggest that we deal with the stone-dwellers?" another captain snapped.

"No other people compares with Gelon in armed prowess," Rhuzenjin rushed on. "We all know that. Look at how many others, great in their time, have fallen or are near to ruin. The Ar-King is known as *The Scourge of Isarre*. Mcklavar, famed for its sorcery, succumbed as well. It is only because we Azkhantians are the mightiest warriors in the world that we have held them off. I tell you, we can join with Gelon, not as supplicants but as equals. We need not concede anything to them, and their armies will strengthen our own."

"Are you saying we should allow them to march across our lands," Tarabey asked in a strained voice, "the lands we and our fathers and our fathers' fathers have kept free by our own blood?"

"*And* our mothers," his wife, Ythrae, put in. She was normally so quiet that everyone looked at her in surprise.

"If that is how the battle must be fought, then yes! Does it matter, so long as the Gelon take the brunt of the fighting?" Rhuzenjin glanced around the assemblage, seeking some sign of support for his argument. "Shannivar, you know that not all of them are treacherous and degenerate. You thought well of Danar, didn't you? Remember how forcefully he spoke at the Council of Chieftains? Did they not respect his words? Would he not treat honorably with us? And where there is one praiseworthy man, there must surely be others. He was of the royal line, did he not say so?"

"Everything you said about Danar is true." Shannivar had admired the Gelonian youth, with his modesty and courage, but neither did she hold any hope that Danar could help them. For all she knew, he was either too far to help, a captive in his own land, or dead. "He was driven into exile by Ar-Cinath-Gelon, his own kinsman. We cannot rely on his being able to speak for us before the Lion Throne."

Rhuzenjin drew in a breath between clenched teeth and straightened his shoulders. "Military force is not the only weapon Gelon can offer us. They have their own magic, some of it more powerful than anything our *enarees* can summon."

Shannivar shivered, as if icy claws dug into her back.

"What have the gods of Gelon to do with us?" Alsanobal said. "We worship the Mother of Horses and Onjhol, Father of Battles."

"Where are Tabilit and her consort, then?" Rhuzenjin demanded. "Why have they not reached out their hands to aid us in our most desperate need?"

Around the circle, men hung their heads. No one answered. Shannivar closed her eyes. *The gods will not answer because I was given a task and I failed.*

Rhuzenjin was talking again, a low, insistent cascade of words, describing a power so great that all the Golden Land had fallen under its sway, a power ancient and sagacious and utterly without human weakness. Again a chill brushed Shannivar's spine. What little she knew of the Gelonian pantheon did not inspire her trust, but this was something sinister.

"Let the gods of Gelon stay in Gelon," one of the riders muttered.

"We want none of their kind—or the Ar-King's armies—here."

"Rhuzenjin has had his say," Shannivar said, cutting off

further discussion. "Let that be enough for this night. We will consider his proposal."

"You are all set against me!" Rhuzenjin cried, rising from the circle. "You are determined to see the last Azkhantian child, what's left of our herds, our elders, and our sacred places, all swallowed up by that monstrosity to the east. Tabilit's silver ass, are you blind? Or are you too stubborn to ask for help, too stubborn even to live?" Red-faced, he strode into the night.

One of the Golden Eagle men, who was a friend of Rhuzenjin, began to rise. Shannivar restrained him with a gesture. Like a rebellious colt, Rhuzenjin needed to sort things out for himself.

The discussion then shifted to who would go in search of the *enarees* and where they were to assemble. Partly out of deference to Shannivar as war-leader and partly from logistical advantage, the consensus settled on the *dharlak*, the summering-place, of the Golden Eagle clan.

By the time everything had been decided, Shannivar ached in every joint and muscle. She stared at the dying embers while the others drifted off to their rest. Traditionally, a war-leader was the first to rise and the last to depart; because she was a woman, she must do all these things and more. Gritting her teeth, she heaved herself to her feet.

Rhuzenjin emerged from the shadows, a sheepish expression on his face and a *k'th* skin in his hands. Shannivar gave him an encouraging nod.

"You did not drink your share," he said.

It was the duty of the war-leader to go without, to see to the needs of her warriors first. "No."

He offered the skin. "I saved a little for you. For good fortune. Safe passage, Shannivar."

"And a bright day."

She raised the spout to her lips and tipped it back. With a laugh, Rhuzenjin squeezed the skin. Tangy *k'th* gushed into her mouth. She took two big gulps before the skin emptied.

"My thanks."

"None are ever needed from you."

Chapter Twenty-six

AT first light the next morning, the encampment broke up. Those best able to fight, including Tarabey and Ythrae, would stay behind to harry the mist army as best they could. They would choose their own leader until he fell, and then another, and then another. The rest would disperse, riding fast to the summering-places of their own clans.

Shannivar herself would lead the search for Bennorakh, the *enaree* of the Golden Eagle. Zaraya would ride with her to help care for Chinggis, along with Rhuzenjin and a few others.

Alsanobal insisted on taking one of the most dangerous territories, that of the Ptarmigan clan, which had already been swept by the mist army. The clan leader, Kharemikhar son of Pazarekh, had been his good friend, and in these time, loyalty crossed clan boundaries. Shannivar had not seen Kharemikhar since the *khural* four summers ago when he struck Eriu during the Long Ride. His was not one of the clans that had answered her call to battle.

As Shannivar bid good fortune to her cousin, she did not know if she would ever see him again. They had wrestled as children, raced their horses, and competed in archery. As a youth he had been foolhardy and boastful but never cruel. Shannivar had teased him that his big red horse would be the death of him, but it was the horse and not Alsanobal that died at the Gelonian fort.

The party set out at a moderate pace, using remounts to rest the horses they had ridden in the battle. To the delight of her son, Shannivar rode the sorrel mare with Chinggis on the saddle in front of her, and they played at choosing a name for the mare. Rhuzenjin kept so close to Shannivar that it was impossible to hold a conversation that did not include him.

Once Shannivar called a halt, they turned their weary horses out to graze. There was a little grass and a muddy pond, but steppe horses were not finicky about water. Zaraya took charge of the camp, while Shannivar put up the women's tent. After that was completed, she sat cross-legged in front of it on a folded blanket.

Chinggis crawled into Shannivar's lap. The skin around his mouth had turned pale with fatigue. He was growing fast, but had not reached his third year. She rocked him gently, crooning the old lullaby about the horse with the velvet back. His body felt soft and heavy in her arms. Before she had finished the song, he was asleep.

Zaraya came up and squatted on her heels beside Shannivar. She studied Chinggis with the same measuring care she would use for a colt pushed too hard and too soon, but she did not say anything. Both women understood that in these times, even very young children must harden or they would die.

Shannivar tightened her arms around her son. She met Zaraya's clear, unflinching gaze. Something loosened in Shannivar's chest and she thought how long it had been since she'd had a female friend. Ythrae, although kin, was too shy. Zaraya was quiet, but she was not shy.

If anything happens to me, there is no one I would trust more with my son.

After carrying Chinggis into the tent, Shannivar took her turn at the cooking. If she'd been a man, she would have expected a woman to prepare the meals. What did it matter now who did which work? Food and hot drink were as needful as riding foremost into battle. She had set the parched grain and dried meat to simmer when Rhuzenjin joined her. Smiling in a friendly way, he asked how Chinggis fared.

"As well as any child of a warrior," she replied with the usual phrase. Until now, Rhuzenjin had expressed little concern for the boy. His resentment of Zevaron's son had overshadowed the protectiveness that all Azkhantians felt for their children.

"I have arnica tea," he said diffidently. "If you permit, I will steep it with butter. When the boy wakes, it will ease the pains of the trail."

"I thank you for your gift," Shannivar replied. If he wanted to make amends, she was happy to accept, especially when it would benefit Chinggis.

Rhuzenjin prepared enough arnica tea for Shannivar and Zaraya as well. Shannivar sipped hers, feeling the warmth and medicinal qualities of the drink soothe the aches from the battle. She wondered if a preparation might also be helpful to the horses, who had no language to express their discomfort.

They ate with little conversation beyond the necessities. Sleep would be their best remedy. When Chinggis roused, Shannivar gave him a little of the tea. Rhuzenjin brought her more and she finished it before creeping into the tent where her son and Zaraya were already asleep.

This was no ordinary dream. Shannivar had traveled the paths of Bennorakh's smoke enough times to recognize a vision, a sending. Now she walked over earth as barren and colorless as that beyond the wall of mist. Her hands were empty. By some trick of light, she could see only a few feet in any direction. All else was gray, not the seething currents of the mist but a dull and uniform nothingness. Although naked, she felt no breath of air moving over her skin. Her heart grew more heavy with each step. Sorrow weighed upon her. She felt as if she were the only person in the entire world, eternally alone, eternally seeking. . . .

A tracery of uncertain light resolved itself into a horse of silver against the formless gray. Its rider was blurred, as if seen through a film of tears.

Shannivar dropped to her knees. Her face came within

an inch of the ground. She dared not look up, dared not speak. For what seemed an eon, she crouched there, barely able to breathe, awaiting whatever punishment the goddess saw fit to administer.

Daughter . . .

In Shannivar's heart, hope flared and died. She did not deserve such gentleness, such love.

Daughter of the Golden Eagle, why do you turn your face from me?

Startled, Shannivar dared to look up. The horse stood before her, radiant with inner light. On its back sat a woman, ageless in her beauty.

"Mother of Horses, have I not failed you? Have I not lost your favor by my own weakness?"

How have you done such a thing, you who have loved me since you first heard my name?

Zevaron, she thought. Even here, in this dream, she could not forget his face. So cold, so remote, as if bitterness had hollowed him out. Had she seen something there, some memory of what they had shared? Or had she only *wished* to see?

"I—I couldn't—"

The silver horse pawed the ground with one gleaming forehoof. Tears gleamed in Tabilit's eyes.

You were not given a heart so that you might turn away when it calls to you. We will not speak of what might have happened had you chosen differently. That is one story. This is another. New events have been set in motion.

Shannivar's breath shuddered through her chest. "What am I to do?"

Awake, then, and do what must be done . . .

Awake . . .

"Awake! Shannivar, wake up!"

Shannivar jerked her eyes open. The interior of the tent was dark, except for a blue tinge from where the door flap had been pulled aside. A man crouched beside her, visible only as a dark shape in the dim light. He grasped her by the shoulders and shook her. Acting by reflex, she broke his hold, rolled away, and came raggedly to her knees. The knife she never went without slipped into her hand.

"Shannivar—no, please! It's me!"

Rhuzenjin.

"I've come to help." He ducked his head, turning half-away from her. "To help you find where they've taken—to find your son."

She knew without having to lay her hand on the rumpled blanket that it was already cold. A short distance away, Zaraya snored lightly.

Chinggis was gone.

Outside, the encampment lay still. The last embers from the cooking fires had dwindled into ashes. A near-full moon cast a pall across the heavens, heralding high summer and the Moon of Mares.

Roaring filled Shannivar's skull, rage and fear and things she could not name. Her belly roiled and she reeled on her feet. Cold sweat dampened her clothing.

Rhuzenjin followed her from the tent. She whirled to face him, knife still in hand. Her body felt thick and sluggish, but her nerves shrilled with fury.

"Who took him?"

"I don't know! I was on my way to the latrine pit when I saw them." He was talking too fast, as if he could calm her with a torrent of words. "Three riders, that's all. I didn't recognize them. Listen, it's not hopeless. They have only a small head start. If we go now, we can catch them."

Shannivar's heart was hammering and her thoughts jumbled together with the fading shards of her dream. The abduction of her child—of any Azkhantian child—was beyond comprehension. The people of the steppe cherished their children. No horseman would ever harm a child, not even the son of his most hated enemy. The moon and the sun might more readily change places, or day turn into night.

Who could have done such a thing?

She looked down at the knife still in her hand. Rhuzenjin had not stolen her son. If he had meant her any ill, if he had harbored any bitterness because she had chosen Zevaron instead of him, then he would not have brought her the news so quickly.

"We should wake—bring others—Zaraya—" Shannivar's words echoed oddly in her mind. She turned back toward the tent, but Rhuzenjin grabbed her arm.

"There's no time! Come on!"

Rhuzenjin had already saddled two horses, Eriu and his own grulla mare. Her body moving from long habit, Shannivar pulled on her boots and jacket, and gathered her weapons. She fastened the cases for her sword and her bow and arrows to the saddle, took a handful of mane, and swung up on Eriu's back. She hated to run him hard, so soon after the foray into the mist, but there was no other horse that could match him.

"Which way?"

Rhuzenjin pointed southwest. Toward Gelon.

She squeezed Eriu with her calves. He moved from a walk to a trot, as willing as if he'd spent a month at pasture. As they left the encampment, Shannivar heard the sorrel mare's whinny. Then all sound fell away in the rush and clatter of galloping hooves.

They passed the sentry lines, but no one hailed them. They might as well have been ghosts, or else the sentries had fallen into the same sleep as Shannivar. The horses raced on, sure-footed and nimble. The moon cast enough light for their quick eyes.

The night sped by them, grasses and hillocks blurring. Rhuzenjin kept his eyes on the ground, guiding the grulla mare without hesitation. Here and there, Shannivar made out recent signs of several horses, but she was no tracker. She needed an enemy she could see. And touch. And kill. Anger helped clear her senses, as did the wind on her face, the feel of a horse beneath her.

The black put a foot wrong and recovered himself with a jolt. Shannivar nearly lost her balance. The edges of her vision went jagged, like the surface of a storm-whipped lake. She grabbed the pommel and steadied herself. His next few strides were rough, and she feared he'd injured himself, bowed a tendon or was otherwise lamed. Her stomach clenched. But soon he was running as he always did, as if he had wings.

They rode on, as the night swung toward sunrise. Shannivar's queasiness lifted, although her mouth still tasted as if she had drunk too much *k'th* the night before. She should have at least let Zaraya know what had happened, but it was too late now. Ribbons of brightness spread across the eastern horizon. The grass shimmered in the growing light. The land sloped upward and the horses slowed, breathing hard.

Rhuzenjin took the lead, following a game trail. The ground turned rocky, hillsides cut by erosion gullies. They rounded the shoulder of a hill where wind-twisted scrub blocked the view until the last moment. Shannivar would have proceeded cautiously, wary of a trap, but Rhuzenjin forged ahead.

The trail fell away sharply. A glen opened up below them, a pocket of willows and blue sage fed by an underground spring. Two tents occupied the central flat area. Despite their unfamiliar design, they looked as if they could shelter three or four men, sleeping close. The earth between the tents had been trampled and stones piled up to make a fire pit. A little ways distant, a half-dozen onagers drowsed in a makeshift corral of green-cut willow.

Onagers. Cursing silently, Shannivar slipped her bow from its case. *The two of us against eight Gelon. Six, if we're lucky.* The odds would be in their favor if only they'd brought other riders with them. If only she hadn't let Rhuzenjin rush her away, if only she hadn't felt so disoriented, as if the night had stolen her will. But there was no help for that now. She and Rhuzenjin might be on their own, facing greater numbers, but they were Azkhantian warriors.

She took an arrow and held it ready, planning her attack. She did not know which tent Chinggis was being held in. They were not here to kill Gelon but to rescue her son, and their best chance was to attack hard and suddenly. Perhaps a diversion might work . . . stampeding the onagers . . . then a fast charge, Rhuzenjin to break down the topmost rails and frighten the onagers, she to shoot the Gelon as they emerged from their tents. They would have very little time before they were noticed.

She explained to Rhuzenjin, who didn't like her plan.

"We don't know what they'll do if we attack outright. We can't risk them threatening Chinggis." He glanced pointedly at her bow. "There's another way. See, they're still asleep. They haven't even set a watch. We can leave the horses here and sneak into their camp."

He pointed out a route that would allow them to get almost to the camp without being seen. There was only a short distance when they would be visible to anyone emerging from the tents.

"With luck, we'll find Chinggis without waking anybody," Rhuzenjin said.

Chinggis wouldn't cry out. Shannivar had trained him well. He was already a warrior, as were all children of the steppe. If they could get him out of the camp without confronting the Gelon, without risking him being killed in the fighting . . .

Still, Rhuzenjin's plan rankled. Azkhantians did not *sneak*. Azkhantians attacked, bold and proud.

Shannivar very much disliked leaving Eriu behind. It was like cutting off one of her own legs. Yet she could not see any better way. She relaxed her hold on the bow, replaced it in its case, and jumped to the ground. She hesitated over taking the sword. If she had to carry Chinggis, she was not sure she could manage a sword at the same time. Its weight might slow her too much on the uphill flight.

Rhuzenjin had dismounted also. "Leave it," he said, as if sensing her thoughts. He buckled his own sword in its sheath on to his belt. "You see to the boy. I will take care of you both."

Shannivar's chin jerked up. He meant well, but his words stung. She did not need any man's protection, certainly not Rhuzenjin's. But there was too much at stake to indulge in foolish pride. While her archery might be better than Rhuzenjin's, the bow was of little advantage in close fighting. She was as capable as any woman with the sword when mounted, but on foot she could not match a man's greater muscular strength. It was better to stick with her advantages, her speed and smaller size. The knife tucked into her boot would have to be enough.

She glanced in the direction of the camp. "Let's go."

They followed the route Rhuzenjin had indicated, sprinting across the exposed portions, waiting breathlessly in each next cover. There was no sign of alarm from below. The camp might have been deserted, except for the onagers. The silence disturbed her. She could not believe the Gelon thought themselves invulnerable to attack on the steppe. This stillness might mean a trap. Or it might be just more of their arrogance.

Now only a short distance separated them from the nearer tent. Water-bushes would screen the rest of their approach, or almost all of it. Rhuzenjin nodded to Shannivar in an encouraging way. She pointed to him and then to the onager pen, then made a gesture of scattering. He nodded agreement.

Rhuzenjin headed down to the onagers. He turned his head once or twice toward the tents, then slipped the bars on one side from their supports. The onagers flicked their long ears in his direction. At Shannivar's signal, he rushed at them, waving his arms and shouting. Braying, the beasts bolted for the opening. They burst into the space between the tents. One broke into a ragged gallop, heading out of the camp. The others milled around, snapping at one another. Apparently, they were as bad-tempered as camels.

Shannivar raced for the tent, approaching it from the back. The thick canvas smelled faintly of smoke, not ordinary woodsmoke but something unfamiliar and uneasy-making. She paused, hardly breathing, and listened. The only sounds were Rhuzenjin's shouting and the noise of the onagers.

She drew her boot knife. Moving in stealth, she crept around to the front of the tent. Instead of the usual door flap, which would be properly secured during the night, a loosely hanging piece of lightweight fabric covered the opening. She swept it aside and plunged into the dimly lit interior. Strips of carpet covered the ground except for the center, where a spindly, three-legged brazier stood on the naked earth. A hint of warmth clung to the air, and smoke issued from vents in the lid.

Shannivar moved deeper inside, straining to make out anything besides the dimly glowing brazier. Her eyes were slower than usual in adapting. She tried to breathe shallowly, but could not avoid the smoke. Her eyes stung and would not focus properly. A rushing noise filled her ears, muffling the sounds from Rhuzenjin and the onagers.

The smoke wound itself into gossamer ropes, pulling her down. Her knees threatened to give way and send her toppling. She tried to turn back, but her muscles would not obey her. The carpet rippled beneath her feet like a stream in flood. She swayed and almost lost her balance. The only thing solid was the hilt of her knife.

From behind Shannivar came a brighter light, as if she were standing at the edge of the circle of firelight, looking outward. A gust of fresher air, the same gust that must have ruffled the door flap, brushed the nape of her neck. With another silent prayer, she gathered her strength and threw herself backward. The lightweight door panel ripped under her weight. She fell heavily, landing on her back. The next moment, the cool sweet breath of morning washed over her. Half-sobbing, she drew it into her lungs as she struggled to her feet and tried to focus on the scene before her.

The onagers had run off, leaving a circle of churned earth. A man in a belted white robe stood in front of the second tent. Shannivar could not make out his race or features. Smoke clung to him. No, it *shrouded* him. He seemed to have too many shadows, and those were elongated, misshapen. She thought he must surely see her, but he gave no sign. She tightened her grip on her knife and hazarded a glance around the camp.

"Rhuzenjin!" Her voice sounded as hoarse as a raven's. Her chest ached from the smoke.

Where was he? Where was her son? Except for herself and the eerie robed figure, the place appeared to be deserted.

"Gelon! Gelon!"

Suddenly the camp boiled over with armored soldiers. They rushed out from behind the second tent and the nearest sheltering woods. Within moments, they had encircled her.

Chapter Twenty-seven

STILL fighting the effects of the smoke, Shannivar sank into a defensive posture. Her breath rasped, harsh and raw, in her throat. She might by luck and speed prevail over one or two of these men, but their height and the greater length of their swords were too great an advantage. And there were so many—far more than the six or eight she'd expected.

Where was Rhuzenjin?

The Gelon formed a circle around her, holding their swords level. Shannivar searched for a weakness in their ranks and saw none. They were disciplined, steady. But they did not move in on her. They seemed to be waiting, but for what? A signal from the man in the robe?

"Shannivar! Put down your knife! Don't fight!"

Between the surrounding Gelon, she spotted Rhuzenjin. He was standing beside the robed figure, holding Chinggis in his arms. The boy's head rested on Rhuzenjin's shoulder.

Shannivar did not lower her knife. Even dazed from the smoke and the residue of whatever drug Rhuzenjin had given her last night, and at a loss to understand what had happened, she dared not surrender her only weapon.

"Please listen!" Rhuzenjin called to her. "It's not what you think!"

"What's going on? Have you sold yourself to Gelon?"

In answer, he glanced at the robed man. The blurring effect had lessened, so that Shannivar now made out a bald head with a band bearing a stylized insignia. An insect? A scorpion—the Gelonian god, Qr! So this was what Rhuzenjin had been up to with his talk of *other gods*! Unable to persuade her with words, he had resorted to treachery.

"Betrayer!" she shouted. "Darkness visits my eyes, that ever I looked upon you in friendship! May Tabilit show you mercy, for if you come within reach of me, arrow or sword, your next breath will be your last!"

"Shannivar, please! You don't understand!" Rhuzenjin elbowed his way through the circle of soldiers.

He halted less than the length of her arm away, so close that she could kill him and still have time to engage the first Gelon, were it not for the child in his arms. Sweat shone on his brow. His eyes were dark with emotions she could not read.

"Take your son," he pleaded. "He is unharmed, only asleep, I swear it. Take him, and all three of us will go free."

She stared at him. The robed man—the Qr priest—lifted one hand, and the soldiers lowered their swords. Lowered them, but did not withdraw.

The knife hilt felt slippery in her palm. Her mouth went dry. "I don't understand any of this." But she did, in the sick churning of her belly. She understood too much.

"I'll explain everything. But not here. Just give me your knife and all will be well. Chinggis will wake soon and want his mother. They'll let us go, I promise. We'll ride north where we can be together, safe from this war that has nothing to do with us."

She waited so that Rhuzenjin would believe she was seriously considering his words.

"From the moment of our birth," Shannivar's grandmother had said, or perhaps it was Saramark herself, she of the fabled lament. *"We walk in the shadow of our own death. To die in glory is not so bad a thing."*

On Rhuzenjin's shoulder, Chinggis stirred. He made no sound, but his eyes opened. Shannivar held out her empty hand. "Give him to me."

The boy lifted his arms as she swung him onto her hip. His hands grasped her vest. He wrapped his legs around her waist. With a twist, she could shift him to her back, trusting that he would cling there like a burr. They had played hours of riding games together.

She watched slantwise as Rhuzenjin leaned toward them.

Just a little closer . . .

Snake-quick, she brought up the knife and pressed the point to Rhuzenjin's throat. He was too surprised to react effectively. "If you value your worthless life, you will tell them"—with a jerk of her chin, Shannivar indicated the Gelon—"to drop their swords and back off."

"I don't—they don't answer to me."

"Then they will watch you die."

"Aii! Shannivar! It wasn't my idea, it was the priest—"

The Qr priest remained motionless, refusing to interfere. Rhuzenjin was nothing to him, no more than a tool to lure Shannivar here. If she followed through on her threat, she would kill a man she had once thought a friend. Then she would still have to fight her way out of the camp and to where they had left the horses. She did not think she could do it alone, let alone with a child on her back.

"Why?" she demanded. "Why did you do it?"

"It was the only way we could be together." Rhuzenjin swallowed hard, his larynx working against the tip of her knife. He could have fought back, possibly even disarmed her. Hope and desperate longing pinioned him to the spot. "They said you would not be harmed so long as you came with me. They wanted you out of the way."

The riders of the steppe were as grass in the Moon of Icefall compared to the armies of *Olash-giyn-Olash*, of Fire and Ice. She must pose a separate threat or the priests would not have bargained with Rhuzenjin.

Poor Rhuzenjin. Shaking her head, she eased the knife away. The tip left a spot of blood on his skin.

They might kill her anyway, the soldiers and the Scorpion priest. They probably would. But she would not be the cause of a single needless Azkhantian death.

His eyes widened, one moment shadowed with loss, then

next wild and white-edged. The change startled her, but it also granted her an instant's warning.

Rhuzenjin strode back the way he had come, through the narrow gap in the ranks of the Gelon. As he cleared the lowered swords and came even with the soldiers themselves, he swerved toward the nearest, grasped the hand holding the sword, and twisted. Before the startled soldier could react, Rhuzenjin wrenched the sword free and, without reversing it, rammed the hilt into the solar plexus of its former owner. He turned on the next two Gelon, slashing across one's arm hard enough to cause him to drop his weapon, and driving the tip of his sword under the edge of the breastplate and into the belly of the other.

Shannivar tightened her grip on Chinggis, praying he would hold fast, and darted after Rhuzenjin and the opening he had created. With the weight of the child, she was slow and off-balance, and her knife was no match for a longer blade. To either side, the Gelon reacted. They had been focused on a single opponent in the center of their circle and had counted on the reluctance of a mother to risk her child. But they were trained fighters, accustomed to the lightning action of battle. Quickly and efficiently, they moved to close ranks.

The Gelon stabbed by Rhuzenjin fell, his body a barrier to his neighbors. The other Gelon bent over, fumbling for his fallen sword. Shannivar lunged at him, raising her knife in an upward sweep. She caught him in the neck.

Together they burst out of the circle, then Rhuzenjin spun around to face the Gelon. The nearest were only a pace or two away. There was no time to discuss strategy. Shannivar left him to his glory and sprinted for the trail.

Before she'd run very far, she realized how hopeless the situation was. The distance was too great. Her initial burst of speed quickly faded. She was a rider, not a runner. Her body was accustomed to long hours in the saddle, not races on foot. She would never make it to the horses in time. The Gelon had already engaged Rhuzenjin. He could hold them off for only a few moments longer. Then they'd be after her.

Shannivar's feet slipped on the loose dirt. The weight of her child staggered her. Her lungs burned with each labored breath. She fought to stay upright and moving, praying she would not stumble.

Above the yammering of her pulse, Shannivar heard a piercing whine coming from the camp. The buzz and chitter of many-legged flying things filled her skull. Without a conscious decision, she stumbled to a walk. Her muscles no longer throbbed. They felt sodden, like rain-drenched clay. Chinggis whimpered in her ear, the first sound he had made.

Not sure what she would see but dreading it nonetheless, Shannivar turned back. In her flight, she had come a short distance up the trail itself. If she'd only kept going, she might have made it.

On the patch of ground between the tents, bodies lay jumbled and graceless. Some of the remaining Gelon were on their feet, hunched over, their hands clamped over their ears. Rhuzenjin was not among them. Only the Qr priest stood erect.

Slowly he raised one hand and pointed at her.

The air turned thick, like spring mud. She had thought she knew magic, the chants and dreamsmoke visions of the *enarees*. What happened next was utterly alien to the clan shamans, and utterly horrific. Her feet began moving of their own accord back toward the camp, one shuffling step after another.

With all her will, she fought to stop herself. She struggled with each gasping breath, each morsel of strength. Chinggis buried his face in the curve of her shoulder. He trembled, clearly too frightened to make a sound. His silence tore at her heart and filled her with renewed desperation. Cold sweat trickled down the sides of her body. She tried to dig her toes into the ground, to lock the muscles of her legs.

It was no use. The priest's spell was too strong.

If only she could throw herself backward or twist to the side . . .

She managed a pause in her forward motion, but no more. The next moment, her weight shifted and the other foot dragged itself forward. No matter how hard she resisted, each reluctant, shambling step brought her closer to the priest. It was getting harder to breathe, to even think.

*Tabilit, Mother of Horses, Lady of Life, help me! Onjhol,
Sky Father, help me!*

She glanced down. Only a pace ahead, a splinter of rock
the length of her forearm protruded above the dust. She
had scrambled over it in her flight and never noticed it.
Now it leaped into sharp focus. It was solidly fixed and had
not budged when she'd stepped on it.

Shannivar allowed the priest's spell to pull her forward.
Instantly, the pressure eased. She could breathe again. Her
body resumed its slow progress toward the camp.

Just before she reached the rock, Shannivar hugged
Chinggis against her body. She dug her feet into the loose soil,
against the edge of the rock, immobilizing her feet. The rest
of her body kept moving. With a jolt, she fell to her knees,
narrowly missing the rock. Pain lanced through her knees, but
she managed to keep her balance and to hold her son close
against her body.

Rage contorted the priest's face. His outstretched fingers
curled as if grasping an invisible rope. Even at this distance,
his knuckles shone like polished bone. Slowly, he twisted his
clenched fist.

Shannivar rocked on her knees. A vise as strong as Denariyan steel gripped her chest. She struggled to draw a
single breath. A whisper of air flowed through her upper
chest, but no more. Tears blurred her sight. The skin of her
face smarted and then flared into fiery agony.

Chinggis was trembling even harder than before. Shannivar felt his body against hers, the softness and the promise
of strength. She glanced down at his face—the eyes that
were so like his father's, the cheeks still round with baby fat,
the mouth that had already learned the discipline of silence.

*Farewell, little eagle. We will meet again in the Pastures of
the Sky, where you will sit at Onjhol's strong right hand.*

No matter what happened now, she promised him,
Olash-giyn-Olash, the Shadow of Shadows, would not have
him. Nor this Scorpion priest, nor the Fire and Ice that Zevaron had spoken of, though they were all one malevolent
entity.

Shannivar still held her knife in one hand. She knew a

dozen ways to kill without pain. He was so small, it would not take much strength.

Let the Scorpion priest work his spells. The riders of Azkhantia did not surrender to outlanders. Her son would die free. And so would she.

Grayness clawed at her, sullen and hungry. She had lost all sensation in her lower body. In another moment, she would not be able to wield the knife. She must not delay.

Mother of Horses, be with me now! Give me strength!

A riot of discordant sound swept over her—the howling of a winter storm—someone chanting in a vile, indecipherable tongue—the clatter of racing hooves—the neighing of horses—

Tabilit, coming for her?

No, wait! She was not ready, she had not finished her last, dreadful act. If she failed him, Chinggis would be taken captive. The Shadow of Shadows would defile him and warp him, even as it had Zevaron.

Swirling whiteness saturated Shannivar's vision. Within a few heartbeats, it blinded her. Her heart stuttered. She could no longer feel her skin or the breath in her lungs. Her muscles felt as unresponsive as sodden wood. Across a great distance, she heard a child wailing. Something pulled at her arms and then a weight lifted from her.

Gathering the tatters of her will, she tried again to move. Her entire body had gone numb. She could no longer tell if she still held the knife, although she feared that both the weapon and her son had been taken from her. By concentrating as hard as she could, she received the vague impression of hard earth beneath her knees, of movement around her. Men, she thought. She caught a phrase or two of their speech, not enough to understand what they said, only to recognize the language—Gelone.

Another voice joined theirs, slower and darker. The sound sent quivers through Shannivar's belly. Acid raked the back of her mouth. Her belly churned under waves of nausea, a revulsion as much of spirit as of flesh. She seized upon the stomach-sickness as she would grasp the hand of a comrade. In her mind, she imagined it growing in intensity, inexorable. It was a healthy response, a rejection of all that was poisonous and unnatural. Her body shook with increasing frenzy. Her joints creaked. Stones jabbed into her knees.

She welcomed the pain. It cleared her senses enough to make out what the men were saying.

"If our spy was telling the truth, she's the war-leader." This man's voice was forceful, with the arrogance of habitual command, but higher in pitch than the slow, dark one that had terrified her. "We have no orders to take prisoners, let alone a hellcat and her whelp."

"You will obey me in this."

Trembling racked her body even more strongly than before. Whatever fate the Qr priest intended for her, a quick death on a Gelonian sword would be better.

She came back to herself a moment or two later, not just in her thoughts but with a fragmentary returning awareness of her body. With an effort, she managed to shift her weight to one knee. Her fingers tingled as she stretched them and then curled them into fists.

Hope flared. The priest's attention had been distracted by the argument. His control over her wavered. Pain and nausea had helped her to throw off the worst of the spell. If she used all her strength, she might be able to get to her feet.

The Gelonian commander and the priest were still talking. ". . . in herself, she is nothing of value," the priest was saying, ". . . the babe has Meklavaran blood."

"What of it? Is that a reason to place our mission at risk?"

"The horse people have never made alliance with outlanders." The priest's voice turned oily and even more frightening. "Nor do the sorcerers of the south trade on the steppe. They leave that to the wretched Denariyans. So tell me if you can, captain, why a woman with sufficient standing among the clans to be named war-leader would bear a half-Meklavaran child?"

Shannivar's vision cleared. In a single flickering glance, she took in the camp, the disposition of the soldiers, the robed form of the priest, and the officer with his dust-cloaked armor. She gauged the distance to where Chinggis lay inert in the arms of another soldier. Her heart steadied and her lungs opened, freely drawing in air.

"The brat is no threat to us or if he is, that is easily removed," the Gelonian captain said. "I don't see what difference his parentage makes."

"Which is one of the many reasons why *I* am giving orders and *you* are obeying them."

Shannivar heaved herself to her feet. She managed not to cry out at the pain as she wrenched her muscles free from the spell. By luck or by Tabilit's hand, she came up balanced and steady.

"Holiness, my men are soldiers, not nursemaids."

"Let the woman tend him, then."

"Too dangerous . . . they fight like demons, all of them."

The Gelonian captain turned his head toward Shannivar. Perhaps it was by chance or the rhythm of the debate. Or perhaps with his soldier's instinct, he sensed her struggle to break free. Before his hand reached his weapon, she was already lunging toward the soldier holding her son.

The priest shouted, not in Gelone but in a language Shannivar did not recognize. The syllables reverberated through her skull, blanketing all other sounds. Her breath clotted in her chest. She juddered to a halt as if an invisible hammer had smashed both her knees. Her heart convulsed, radiating lightning-bright spasms. The echoes of the priest's command spun down like thunder. Earth and sky slipped sideways.

She labored to draw a single gasp, battling the dimness that lapped at her sight. In vain, she tried to summon the nausea that had previously returned her to her body. Nothing made the slightest difference. This new ensorcellment gripped her like an eagle clenching its prey. She could not even tell if she was still standing.

A shape approached her. She knew it was a man, although she could not discern his features. Bending forward, he took up the hands that might have once been hers. She felt a tugging, a sensation around her wrists.

The world moved past her, sometimes smoothly, sometimes in jerks and starts. Sounds brushed her: men's voices, the snort and clatter of animals, then a high-pitched mewling. Nothing touched her. Nothing stirred her emotions in the slightest.

A face bore down on her, looming larger and larger until she could see nothing else. Haltingly, she realized that it was not like her own, not like the others she knew. The skin was too pale under its flush of ugly red, as if smeared with blood. The eyes did not reflect Tabilit's starry cloak but instead gleamed like orbs of ice.

Set above those inhuman eyes, in a band of folded, sweat-grimed cloth, crouched a many-legged form. Its tail ended in a hooked barb that she recognized as poisonous, and its oversized pincers seemed to move, its head to turn in her direction. The next moment, surely, its eyes would come alive. They would glitter in triumph and in hunger.

The moment never came. The scorpion remained an image. The man whose brow it marked was speaking now. She felt his words as an unendurable weight on her mind.

"Show me the father of that child . . ."

I will not, she thought even as she found herself, as if in a fever dream, in the wooded dell where she had first seen Zevaron. She had just been chosen as war-leader and was still fresh from the fight at the Gelonian fort, so she had not been kindly disposed to two outlanders camping on the steppe without leave. In the underbrush, she had made out the shapes of two horses and there, camouflaged by the dappled shade, were two men. One was Gelon, young. His red-gold hair and milky skin betrayed his race—*Danar!*

No! Shannivar raged silently at herself. *Do not think his name! They must not know he is alive! Do not remember—*

Memories rose up in on her nonetheless, relentless, but the scorpion-man had not asked about Danar. His focus was on the Meklavaran, the one who had fathered Chinggis.

Look away! she urged herself. *Look anywhere but at him!*

The grove glowed in Shannivar's vision, as vivid as if she looked on it now. She felt the warmth of the day on her face, the muscled bulk of Eriu beneath her, the smooth wood of her bow in her hands. In the pit of her belly, the kernel of her soul, she knew the Qr priest also saw these things. He felt everything she did. But he could see and feel and hear only what she did.

If only she could close her eyes and stop her ears! She

tried and tried, but it was no use. She had not done so *then*, so she could not do so *now*.

She had ridden into the outlanders' campsite with the fever of battle humming through her bones, and grief still fresh and bright in her breast. Those days had brought her so close to death, to life, to glory.

Get out! she raged at the silent, inexorable watcher. *These things were mine to do, mine to remember!*

The second outlander—*Zevaron!*—had stepped forward. He moved like a cloud leopard, lean and fit and proud. Slanting afternoon sun illuminated his features, the skin that was so close to the amber of her own. His eyes were strangely shaped, his shoulder-length hair as dark as Eriu's coat. The memory of that meeting gathered power with every unfolding detail. It was impossible to erase the sound of his voice or the light in his eyes. So many times in the past years, she had revisited these moments until they had become engraved in her soul.

"We come in peace," he had said in lilting trade-dialect.

"You are no Gelon," she had pointed out.

He had paused, his dark-lashed eyes flickering away from hers and then back again.

A pang stung Shannivar, like the bright point of an arrow as it pierced her through. She felt the presence of the Qr priest, his humid breath on her neck.

"No," Zevaron was saying in that quiet, resonant voice, the voice that still sang through her dreams. "I was born in Meklavar, in the mountains far to the south. My name—"

No! No! If only he had hidden it from her! If only they had never met, or he had pretended to be an ordinary trader—Denariyan—anything but who he was!

Yessss . . . The scorpion's pincers rattled.

Mother of Horses!

"—is Zevaron." Her traitor memory rolled relentlessly on. "I am the only living son of Maharrad, the last king—what we call the *te-ravot*—of the city."

The prince of the city! Exultation flared in the mind of the scorpion-man. *This child is of the royal line.*

Shannivar reeled under the raw avarice streaming from the priest's mind. For a moment, the pressure on her thoughts eased. She hung like a tattered rag in the wind, wrung out and violated.

"... we must be sure ..." Someone spoke aloud now, in Gelone, she thought.

More! The voice rioted through her head. *There must be no question of the child's lineage.*

If she had had any control over her physical body, she would have screamed as the scorpion seized her again. In memory, she felt her body, whole and strong. Her skin tingled with Zevaron's nearness. It was night now, the air ice-edged, the sky ablaze with hanging curtains of color. The inside of the *jort* smelled like home with its willow lathes and felted camel's hair, the pots of cedar paste and myrrh. She felt herself moving into his embrace. Her skin still remembered the imprint of his body against hers. She had never ceased longing for this night to come again.

Zevaron's breath was in her throat. Her body rocked with the power of his racing pulse, so strong and fast that it seemed they shared one heart. Gold shimmered just beneath his skin, and she thought that surely Tabilit had gathered them both in her embrace, that this night, this joy, could only be the gift of a goddess.

With a spasm of disgust, Shannivar wrenched herself away from the intoxicating memory. The lovemaking had been a covenant between the two of them, with only the Mother of Horses as their witness. This vile thing, this priest of Qr, had no part in it. His presence desecrated the very memory.

Colder than blizzard ice and far more sharp, a promise crystallized in her mind: *I will kill him for this.*

Chapter Twenty-eight

THE Qr priest released his hold on Shannivar's mind. Her body jerked as she came back into herself, but her strength was gone. When she dropped to the pebble-studded earth, the impact shocked the air from her lungs. She lay there, struggling for breath. One glance told her that she was no longer in the encampment with its flat area for tents and easy forage for horses. The Gelonian party had stopped in the lee of a rocky outcrop midway up a long, eroded slope. The soil here was poor, the grasses withered.

She had no memory of how she'd gotten here, although from the rope around her bound hands and the ache in her thighs, she must have walked many miles. Her feet were bruised and sore. By the angle of the sun, most of a day had passed, perhaps more.

Around her, soldiers were setting up a camp. Shannivar spied an onager and Rhuzenjin's grulla mare. One of the soldiers wrestled a howling, squirming child from the onager's saddle.

Chinggis!

Shannivar heaved herself up to a sitting position, just as her son punched the soldier squarely in the nose. The soldier cursed and cuffed the boy hard enough to send him sprawling. Before she could react, another of the soldiers hauled her to her feet. For an instant, they stood, almost touching. He was a head taller than she, but Azkhantians had never measured valor by height. Dust and a smear of dried blood marked the Gelon's face.

"Don't try to run," he said in Gelone.

Shannivar tried to look confused as she answered in trade-dialect, "I don't speak your language." She feared he would either not understand or else would take her statement as defiance. She'd heard enough stories of how Gelon treated their prisoners.

"No run," he said in heavily accented trade-dialect. "Understand?"

She glared at him.

He grabbed her vest and shook her, lifting her to her toes. "Run, boy dies. Fight, boy dies. Captain not like—*boy dies*. Understand now?"

"Un-understand." She glanced toward Chinggis, slumped at the feet of the soldier and trying hard not to cry. "Let me go to him. I will make no trouble. Please."

"Fine. If priest says yes." His voice sounded less gruff. Perhaps he was relieved at her cooperation.

Shannivar offered no resistance as he tied her feet as well as her hands, looping the cords so that even if she managed to slip her wrists free, she would have to crawl rather than run and could not get very far without attracting attention. She sat as she was left, praying the passage of time would clear her head.

The Qr priest withdrew into the first tent to be set up. The same soldier who had struck Chinggis carried the sobbing child inside.

After a time, the Gelonian guard returned with a handled bowl of hammered metal piled with gray-brown mush. Without explanation, he untied the loop between Shannivar's wrist and ankle ropes so that, by lifting the dish to her mouth with both hands, she could feed herself. She eyed the food. It smelled like grain, wheat perhaps, pounded into coarse flour so that it could be cooked quickly. Using her fingers, she scooped up a mouthful. It was unsalted, with an earthy undertone. Mixed with the grain were bits of undercooked dried beans, but no meat. By the time she finished, warmth spread from her stomach to the rest of her body.

"My thanks," she said, holding up the empty dish as far as her bonds would allow.

With a grunt, the soldier took the dish and hooked it by the handle through his belt. He then retied her and settled in to guard her. Shannivar adjusted her posture to ease her aching knees. Watchful, the Gelon followed each small movement. He made no comment, and Shannivar guessed that any attempt at conversation on her part would be met with silence.

She had been fed, which meant that her captors intended that she should remain alive and able to travel. Clearly, the Qr priest had a purpose for Chinggis . . . and here Shannivar's gorge rose. She forced herself to appear calm, her expression betraying nothing of what she felt. The Gelon was watching her too closely.

Chinggis, then, as the son of his father and the heir to Meklavar, had value. Or did the priest have his own uses for the child, apart from those of the Ar-King's men? The Gelonian captain had argued with the priest.

None of it made any sense. Who knew what notions infected those who dwelled in stone?

Think!

They were being kept alive, she and her son, and they were being taken west. Toward Gelon. Zevaron had said that his mother, the widowed Queen of Meklavar, had been brought as a slave to Aidon.

But I am no such royal captive. What would the Ar-King—or the priests of the Scorpion god—want with me?

Shannivar jerked alert at a wailing cry from the priest's tent, followed by a shout and then a series of orders bellowed in Gelone. A few moments later, a soldier rushed from the tent and hurried over to Shannivar's guard.

"He's sent for her. Now."

"I told you he would." The guard untied the loop connecting Shannivar's ropes and pulled her to her feet. "Priests know as much about nursemaiding as you do about horses."

With a snort, the soldier took hold of Shannivar's bound wrists.

"Speak trade-dialect if you want her to understand," the guard said.

"Savages."

The guard shrugged and made as if to accompany them. The soldier waved him back. "I can handle one trussed-up native woman. If she acts up, the priest can do his spells on her again."

Another howl of childish fury issued from the tent. Shannivar shuffled behind the soldier, moving as fast as she could without tripping. The last thing she wanted now was escape. Her abhorrence of the priest couldn't keep her from her son.

The soldier pushed her inside. The interior of the tent seemed strange, without the usual Azkhantian furnishings. The priest sat on a folding chair, the wood cut into an intricate lattice to lighten its weight. He held Chinggis across his knees, trying to wrap the boy in ribbon-thin straps of leather. Red-faced and frantic, Chinggis flailed his arms and legs. He let out another cry of protest. Shannivar saw his desperate, failing strength. He had been trained in the ways of the steppe, but he was only a little boy, alone and terrified.

I will kill the priest for this, too.

Shannivar held herself immobile, lest any trace of her fury show. She could do nothing at this moment. She must wait for an opportunity, and while she did, her revenge would grow deep and hot.

The priest noticed her. He loosened his grip on Chinggis, who twisted free and hurled himself at Shannivar. She managed to lower herself to her knees, although with her hands tied she could not wrap her child in her arms. He threw his arms around her neck and broke out into wild sobbing.

"Hush, hush, my little eagle," she murmured in Azkhantian. "All will be well. We are together now."

The next few minutes tangled together, with the priest giving commands, the soldier struggling to free Shannivar's hands, and Chinggis fighting any attempt to separate him from his mother. Finally Shannivar was allowed to hold him, stroking his back and rocking.

Chinggis calmed, his sobs subsiding into hiccups and then sighs. Shannivar became aware of the taint hanging in the air. It was part physical, the same smoke that had almost overcome her in the first camp. Under it, she sensed a reek that was more than an odor and yet less. It reminded her of the cry of a dying bird or the sound of a badly tuned *khur*, the two-stringed bowed viol used at Gathering dances . . . or the sky before the first crack of thunder, the taste of ashes and bile.

She had to get her son out of this place. She had to do it soon, before she succumbed again to the smoke. There wasn't much time. Thirst and weariness had left her more vulnerable than before.

"Please," she said to the priest, keeping her eyes low and her voice timid, praying he understood trade-dialect. "He's frightened. Let me take him outside. Let me care for him."

"Go! This why I made you brought here!" The priest's impatience showed through his atrocious trade-dialect. He followed up with orders in Gelone to the soldier.

Shannivar found herself unbound and placed under guard against the foot of the rock face, on the far side of the camp from the horse and the onager. The ground was hard, littered with sharp-edged stones, but at least she and Chinggis were in the open air.

The guard, a different one than before, brought a skin of water. As Shannivar drank, he took up a watchful stance. When she'd had enough, she settled on her side and curled her body around her son's. The chill of the rapidly falling night settled over them.

After Chinggis fell asleep, Shannivar studied the guard, assessing his vigilance and measuring the distance between them. Even if she were able to wrest away his knife and then reach the grulla mare, Chinggis was at the end of his strength. He needed rest if they were to have any chance of escape. Perhaps tomorrow, she thought drowsily, once she had lulled the Gelon into thinking she had given up.

*　　*　　*

The next day, they traveled on, continuing westward through the hills. The priest rode the onager and everyone else walked. The grulla mare served as a pack animal, but the captain, who clearly had some experience with Azkhantians, would not allow Shannivar anywhere near the horse. She held her son's hand for as long as he was able to walk, and then she carried him on her back. Although she was no longer tied up, she was constantly under watch. None of her guards spoke with her beyond the few necessary communications, mostly by gesture.

When they had halted and made camp on the first night, the priest came over and took Chinggis by the hands. Chinggis dug his feet into the ground, tensed his body, and refused to budge. When the priest picked him up, the boy shrieked and kicked. He pummeled the priest with his fists. Shannivar tried to intervene, but the guard forced her back, a knife to her throat.

"No, please!" she stammered, trying to sound pleading rather than enraged. "Don't take him away—let me go with him!"

The guard pressed the edge of his blade into her neck. She felt the wetness of her own blood. The priest, his face contorting, carried the boy into his tent.

Breathing hard, her skin stinging where she had been cut, Shannivar managed to hold still. The guard was taller and heavier than she, and much stronger. He had already demonstrated that he would not hesitate to use his knife on her. She would have no chance to take him by surprise.

The guard led her to a copse of wind-twisted trees. That night she was bound again, wrists and ankles looped to a rope around a stout tree. She did not have long to wait, however, before another Gelon, the one who'd guarded her on the first day, brought Chinggis to her.

Chinggis stopped fighting as soon as he saw his mother. His face was red and damp with tears, but he appeared to be unharmed. He curled up next to her.

"Rest now, little warrior," she whispered. "Save your strength."

"Want to go home."

What could she say? She would not make promises she could not keep.

"We are together and we are alive," she told him. "The Mother of Horses and her consort Onjhol of the Silver Bow and all the Sky People that have ever been are watching over us. Can you feel them?"

After a long moment, she felt him nod.

The next night, the priest did not try to take Chinggis away. Shannivar overheard one of the soldiers saying that the boy had bitten the priest and the bite was infected, that all savages were filthy and diseased. The other man scoffed at him.

The following day, the soldiers' talk shifted. A lookout had been dispatched to the top of the nearest hill at first light, and had returned with news of a body of horsemen approaching from the east, traveling fast. A second reported that no, the plume of dust was gone. It had been natural, a product of the accursed winds of the steppe.

The Gelon began the day's trek in their usual order, except for an increased rear guard. Shannivar and Chinggis walked. Laden with the tents and the priest's furnishings, the grulla mare trudged along, her head sagging. She had not been allowed to forage and her ribs stood out from her dull coat. At least the Gelon had not captured Eriu. Most likely, he'd made his way back to camp. She imagined her riders waking to find her gone, along with her son and Rhuzenjin. They would be searching for her, but she had left without telling others where she was going, a mistake she bitterly regretted now. If she'd had her wits about her, she would never have let Rhuzenjin rush her away from the camp, just the two of them.

By midmorning, the party neared the pass. Although he made no complaint, Chinggis drooped. Shannivar reached down to pick him up. The nearest Gelon scowled at her, hand going to his sword, but his expression lightened when he saw she meant only to carry the boy.

As she straightened up, settling his weight, she glanced back the way they had come. The height of the pass and the angle between the hills gave her a glimpse of the flatter land below. Squinting, she made out the darker shadows of oases and wondered which was the one where Rhuzenjin had died to protect her.

Across the drier terrain, the wind whipped up funnels of dust. The lookout must have spied one of these and thought it a party of riders. As she watched, the swirls dissipated. At the last moment, she caught a ripple of movement, faint against the line of haze that obscured the horizon. She clamped her teeth together to mask the rush of surprise and hope. Riders, running fast, had spread out to minimize a large cloud of dust. It made their numbers harder to guess. Even so, she did not think they amounted to more than a handful.

A handful of Azkhantian warriors were a force to be reckoned with.

By the end of the afternoon, the Gelon knew they were being pursued. The captain and the priest got into an argument so heated that everyone in the party overheard. The captain wanted to set up an ambush while they were still in the hills and could use the terrain to their advantage. The priest refused to stop. He insisted their primary objective was to make the best possible speed to Gelon. There was no need to worry. If the nomads caught up with the party, he would take care of them. The captain retorted that the safety of the expedition was his responsibility and therefore the decision was also his.

The priest made a gesture, and the two were wrapped in silence. Every sinew of Shannivar's body rebelled against the growing Qr magic. She wanted to run as fast and far as she could. It was all she could do to hold on to Chinggis. Whimpering, he buried his face against her neck.

The silence broke. The sorcerous taint lifted, blown away by the clean steppe winds. The captain bowed to the priest and then gestured his men to continue.

They made camp far enough from the base of the hills that anyone following them would not have any advantage in the angle of attack. The sun was still well above the horizon, for the priest, apparently taking the captain's arguments into consideration, had ordered an early halt and rest. They would have time to prepare for an attack, whereas the horsemen would just have finished a brutal climb and descent over the hills.

The Gelon set about laying out their camp in a defensive pattern. The captain moved about, supervising the placement of his men. They had set up near a patch of dead trees, which the Gelon cut and used as digging implements to erect earthworks. They arranged the rest of the wood as barriers and piles to be ignited. Shannivar watched their preparations with grudging respect. She saw no signs of fear.

A shout went out from one of the lookouts. The horsemen had come through the pass and begun making their way down. The captain watched, his forehead furrowed. His mouth was grim. The priest came to stand beside him and said something, too low for Shannivar to overhear. Then Chinggis stirred and she bent to let him slip off her back. When she straightened up, one of the Gelon who'd guarded her this day pointed to the priest and indicated she should go to him.

Shannivar took her son's hand. No matter what she felt, she must show no fear for the boy's sake. He must see how a child of the Golden Eagle faced evil.

The priest waited in the center of the fortified camp. His tent had not been set up, but someone had unpacked his folding chair and brazier. He sat on the chair as if he were a chieftain giving judgment. Although trail dust coated his robes, he had put on a fresh headband. The black outlines of the scorpion stood out in harsh relief against the whiteness of the cloth.

"Kneel," he said in Gelone. His gaze flickered to the ground.

Behind Shannivar, one of the soldiers shouted something. She sensed the rising tension in the camp. In her mind, she heard riders shout their war cries. The wind of their passing lifted her spirit. Her blood sang with theirs. Chinggis clung to her and the touch of his hands strengthened her courage.

"You cannot threaten my people with my death or my

son's," she told the priest in trade-dialect. "Gladly will we go to the Pastures of the Sky, if it will speed your death."

"*Kneel.*"

Shannivar's joints turned to jelly. Her legs folded. Black eyes fixed on hers. She tried to look away and failed. Those gleaming orbs, like openings into utter darkness, transfixed her. Her vision warped so that she could not tell if the eyes belonged to the priest or to the scorpion on his brow. A question shivered at the edges of her consciousness— *why?*

Why put his spell on me? I am his prisoner.

The riders were halfway down the hill. Nimble as goats, their horses scrambled and leaped over the rough terrain. She could not see them clearly, but she felt them. Her bones vibrated with the pounding of their hooves. Her spirit rode with them. She had been touched by Tabilit, Mother of Horses, and now she was bound to all the peoples of the steppe.

The world faded as a shadowy form took shape. At first it wavered before her, but as the sounds and sights of the camp dimmed, it took on definition: a body that tapered to an upturned tail, a hooked stinger gleaming with venom, and impossibly thin, articulated legs. And eyes, lightless with intelligence and hunger . . . hunger not only for her, but for the prey it sought to control *through* her.

As it gained solidity, the scorpion stretched out its pincers. Shannivar's ears filled with the rattle of pebbles on sand, of chitin over slate. The sound poisoned the air. She floundered, reeling.

Near the base of the hill, the lead rider faltered. He swayed in the saddle. His horse, a gray the color of tarnished silver, stumbled. The rider lost his balance, barely hanging on. Behind him, another rider cried out in confusion.

Color seeped from rock and sky and grass. A horseman fell.

Shannivar could no longer feel her own body. Everything seemed to be happening to other people and far away. Somewhere, someone was shouting orders in Gelon. Somewhere, a child sobbed in terror. Somewhere, a bowstring slipped from nerveless hands. A horse slowed and, driven past training and temper, arched its back to buck.

Somewhere, a shadow stirred behind the distorted form of a Gelonian god. *Olash-giyn-Olash. The Shadow of Shadows.* And behind it . . .

A sickening miasma rolled over her, compounded of cinders and sleet. Whiteness, cold and bitterly dry, pelted her. In its swirling chaos, she glimpsed something yet unformed, a power far more hideous than anything she had encountered beyond the mist, a monstrosity whose door into the living world was even now being prepared.

Chapter Twenty-nine

THE legs of the ghostly scorpion dug into Shannivar's body. They pierced her like a quiver's worth of arrows. She envisioned her hands grasping the legs, the chitin so hard and cold it might have been ice. Barbed ridges sliced through her skin. Her palms turned slick with blood, but she held on. She pressed hard against the barbs, driving them deep between the bones of her hands to keep her fingers from slipping. The scorpion thrashed its tail, hurling droplets of venom from its stinger. Some flew wild, but others splashed on Shannivar's skin, smoking and corrosive. She seized the pain and turned it into fire, fire to fuel her resolve and clear her mind.

Bracing herself, she yanked the arrow-legs with all her might. The barbed ridges ripped through the flesh of her belly. The harder she pulled, the deeper they sank, until they caught and held. She felt them anchor in her bowels, in muscle and artery and spine.

Unexpectedly, the pain eased. Her first thought was that she was slipping into shock. Perhaps the venom had seeped through her skin and was taking effect. She felt no numbness, no chill, no disorientation.

Another moment passed with no renewal of pain. Now she could feel a hard surface beneath her knees.

Voices broke through the clash and roar of the storm. She heard hooves battering hard ground and the neighing of horses.

The legs of the scorpion softened in her grip. Throbbing pain no longer radiated from each serration. She glanced down. The chitinous limbs were no longer solid and hard-edged. Before her eyes, they dissolved, fading into mist.

Shannivar fell forward and caught herself on her hands, her *empty* hands. The last wispy residue of the phantom scorpion dissipated. The aching in her belly eased. She raised her head. Chinggis was no longer beside her.

The priest rose to his feet. As she watched, he lifted his hands and began chanting. The sleeves of his robe fell back, revealing his forearms. Tattoos of scorpions and many-headed serpents twined around his arms, disappearing beneath his folded sleeves. They were not blue, like those of the Xians, but rusty brown, as if made with dried blood. As the priest's muscles flexed beneath his skin, the tattooed images seemed to swell. Any moment now, they would leap from his skin, crawling and slithering as they grew in size.

The priest took no notice of Shannivar, on her hands and knees before him. His eyes were half-closed, crescents of white. His concentration did not waver as she brought one foot under her.

The chanting grew louder. The syllables slurred together, jangled beyond any semblance of human speech. The sounds echoed, building into impossible reverberations.

Shannivar clapped her hands to either side of her head. Her skull buzzed as if a nest of serpents were coiled inside. They sank dagger fangs into the back of her eyes. Her heart yammered in her ears. The discordant rhythms brought a trickle of blood from her ears. She could hear nothing except the thunder of her pulse and the riotous jangle of the priest's spell.

Grimly, she held her position. She lowered her hands and dug her fingers into the dry earth—Tabilit's earth.

"You will know what to do." The words rested like honey

on her heart. The Mother of Horses had not forgotten her, would never forsake her. *Save my people.*

Shannivar crouched in front of the priest, her hands braced on the solid ground, her weight on one knee and one foot. The priest apparently had no further use for her. His attention was focused on the imminent battle. He had already set his trap, keyed to the minds of the horsemen. The air vibrated with his power.

Shannivar had no weapon, nor did she see any within reach. She was not helpless, however. As a child, she had run and raced and wrestled with her cousins. Until Alsanobal got his man's strength, she had bested him as often as not.

She dug the toes of her kneeling foot into the ground for traction. Shoving hard with all the power of her legs, she hurled herself forward. She tackled the priest low, around his shins. Yelping, he fell sideways. A loud *pop!* came from one of his knees. Instantly the deafening hiss ceased.

The scorpion-man screamed and lashed out with his good leg. He was thick around the belly, soft-muscled, but he fought with surprising strength. Shannivar scrambled backward, not an instant too soon. His foot grazed her shoulder.

The priest's mouth stretched wide and his eyes bulged. His fingers tightened like claws. His nails elongated to points like the stingers of his totem animal. Raising his upper body off the ground, he swiped at Shannivar with his talon fingers. She scuttled away, landing on the foot of his injured leg.

Shannivar grabbed his heel in one hand and his toes in the other. With all the power of her own legs, she twisted his foot. She shoved hard, pushing the leverage to its fullest. The priest's body jerked and flipped over. He landed flat on his belly. Shannivar held on to his foot, pressing into his bent knee. Thrashing and shrieking, the priest tried to claw her. She shifted the angle of her hold. His back arched in reaction. Keeping hold of his foot, she planted one knee between his shoulder blades. She jammed her weight into his back, praying it would be enough to hold him. He twisted, trying to reach back with his hands. Shannivar seized one of his arms, wrist in one hand, elbow in the other. With a hard jerk, she bent his elbow, bringing his hand up behind his back. His fingers went limp.

Bellowing in rage, the priest threw his body from side to side. The force of his thrashing took Shannivar by surprise. She couldn't keep him pinned. His movements were too wild, too frenzied. He no longer responded to the joint lock. It was as if a demonic whirlwind ruled him, immune to pain or injury. She fought for balance, trying to ride the prone priest the way she would a bucking horse. Her hold on his arm slipped. His free arm churned the air. The poison-barb nails slashed wildly, perilously close to her skin. Yellow droplets sprayed from their tips.

She couldn't find more leverage, and she dared not let go. Her only hope was to hold on as best she could until the spasm of unnatural energy passed. With a ferocious lurch, the body under her bowed upward. She felt herself sliding toward his searching claws. In desperation, she released his arm and flung herself to the other side. He flailed about like a maddened beast, lashing out with fists and feet, pummeling the ground and the air.

In a horrifying instant, she looked up to see him on top of her. His face was a hand's breadth from her own, his breath hot on her skin. Nothing human stared out of those fixed, unblinking eyes. Fingers like forge-heated arrowheads grabbed her by the shoulders. Her vest cushioned the worst, but two talons pierced the quilting. Fire exploded from each puncture.

Shannivar's vision blurred under a haze of yellow. Panic-stricken, she thrust at his chest, his arms, his face, anything she could reach.

In the tangle of arms and legs, one of her hands skidded across the side of his skull. His scalp was slick with sweat. Her fingers caught on the cloth. The folded fabric felt hot, feverish. It gave under her touch as if it were alive. She clutched at it. The headband came away in her grasp. Under it, the priest's forehead was not bare. He still bore the blackened image of a scorpion. The edges were curled and ragged, as if the insignia had been branded into his flesh.

The black was the color of emptiness. It seemed to penetrate the priest's body, bone and blood and brain, a
scorpion-shaped window into a lightless void. A frigid mist
wafted from it.

The priest went suddenly inert, smothering Shannivar
with his weight. She tried to push him away. Her right arm,
the side where she'd been stabbed, went numb. Her muscles
turned heavy and sluggish, barely responsive to her will.
She could not get any leverage on his body, which remained
still. Its bulk pressed the air from her lungs.

The hiss and rattle of the priest's incantation had
stopped the moment she'd tackled him. No serpents coiled
within her skull. Yet a muted buzzing hovered at the edge
of her hearing, a whirring as from an immense swarm of
locusts.

Moaning, she drew up one knee, braced herself, and
pushed. The priest flopped on to his back.

Spasms shook Shannivar's body. Her breath chilled her
from the inside. The wounds in her shoulder throbbed. The
locust horde bore down on her, drowning out the sounds of
men fighting, of horses neighing.

The sky faded into gray. Something wet trickled from the
corners of her eyes. She was cold, so cold. She wished she
could hold Chinggis. She wished she could see Zevaron, her
Zevaron and not the monster he had become . . . just one
more time.

The neighing came again, closer. It was no longer frantic
but belligerent, a stallion squealing in challenge. With it
came more shouting. Through her fading consciousness,
Shannivar recognized the words as Azkhantian, but their
meaning slipped away from her. Her thoughts blew away
like grains of dust.

She saw, as if through a veil of silver light, a woman on a
proud white mare. The woman's body was so bright, Shannivar could not make out her features, only the grace and
strength of her bearing. One hand lifted in greeting.

Shannivar tried to raise her own hand, but her body
would not respond. She felt herself sinking into the earth.
Her poisoned shoulder no longer burned. She could not
feel it at all. Her breath came slow and shallow. The pauses

between each faltering inhalation lengthened. The silver-white image dimmed.

Mother of Horses! Do not forsake me!

Daughter of the Golden Eagle, your task is not yet completed. My people still need you.

Then Shannivar felt her body once more, as weak as if she had lain abed in fever or been jerked out of a half-frozen lake.

She blinked. The day seemed too bright, the colors too vivid. The priest lay in a misshapen heap beside her. An arrow protruded from his back, still quivering. Shannivar recognized it as steppe-fashioned, although she was too befuddled to identify the clan.

Milling horsemen filled the camp. *Azkhantian* horsemen. A few Gelon were still on their feet and fighting, but bodies littered the trampled earth. The tang of dust and blood laced the air.

"Mami!" Chinggis bolted toward Shannivar. She struggled to her feet and caught him in her arms.

A riderless horse broke from the melee and galloped toward Shannivar. His ears were pinned back to his neck and his black hide gleamed like obsidian. White hairs shimmered like strands of silver in his mane.

Eriu!

A Gelonian soldier stepped between the horse and Shannivar. Eriu pivoted and lashed out with his hind hooves. With a crack of splintered bone, the soldier went flying.

The black slowed, prancing until he was almost trotting in place. His small, inwardly-curved ears swiveled forward. He halted before Shannivar and stretched out his head. His nostrils flared as he inhaled her scent. Stiff and weary, she stepped into the shelter of his shoulder, Chinggis still in her arms, and touched her cheek to Eriu's neck, resting into his solidness. He smelled of dust and horse sweat and excitement. He nickered, low in his throat.

My wings.

"Shannivar! Shannivar daughter of Ardellis!"

A rider came toward her. His big silver roan jigged sideways, snorting and throwing its head in excitement. Blood streaked the muscled forequarters, but Shannivar did not think it belonged to the horse. She knew that horse . . .

"Onjhol's own luck! You're still alive!" The rider swung down and stood before her. He looked as if he wanted to embrace her in the manner of warrior-kin but thought better of it. Instead, he offered her a formal salute, his right fist over his heart.

"May your days be long and your horse never stumble. I feared"—the rider hesitated—"I might have come too late."

"May all your arrows fly true, Kharemikhar son of Paza-rekh." Shannivar shook her head. "What are you doing here?"

Kharemikhar had been a friend to Shannivar's cousin Alsanobal but not Shannivar herself. They had ridden against each other in the Long Ride at the last *khural*. In the final stretch, just as Eriu was about to pass the silver roan, Kharemikhar had slashed the black across the face with his whip. It had been a cowardly act, a dishonorable act, but he had won, nevertheless. She had not seen him since, for his clan had not joined the others in fighting the mist.

"I came looking for you, for you were not at the encampment with the others." He looked awkward. "No one knew where you'd gone. The sentries had been drugged, so they saw nothing."

His gaze shifted to Chinggis, whose sobs were lessening. Shannivar whispered comfort to the child. She did not want to reveal Rhuzenjin's betrayal. In the end, Rhuzenjin had died as a true warrior of the steppe.

Kharemikhar went on, "Your party could not agree on whether to search for you or continue on with the mission. Some said they were too few to break into two groups, and others felt that because you were not the only rider who was missing, they must trust that you would rejoin them when you could. Then that crazy black horse of yours came racing into camp. A Badger clan woman managed to catch him. She's got a rare touch with horses. Anyone else . . ."

With a grimace, he rubbed one upper arm. Shannivar had no doubt that beneath his sleeve lay a bruise in the shape of a horse's bite. "In the end, your people went on with the original plan, and mine tracked you to a place where stone-dwellers had camped. It was deserted, but bore the markings of a fight. We found bodies. Five Gelon and one Azkhantian."

"Yes," Shannivar murmured into her son's downy hair. "Rhuzenjin son of Semador, once of the Rabbit clan but taken into the Golden Eagle."

"I remembered Rhuzenjin from the *khural*. We gave him an arrow burial."

Shannivar nodded. Such was the way in battle. The creatures of the wild, servants of Tabilit and Onjhol, would free the spirits of the dead in the ancient way of things.

"But why?" she said. "Why would *you* come looking for me?"

Before Kharemikhar could answer, one of his riders called out to him. A short distance away, the fighting was still going on. Shannivar loosened her son's arms around her neck and shifted him to one hip. He did not resist, although he kept his face against her.

Those few Gelon who were still alive stood in a circle, facing outward, backs together. Blood and dust tarnished their swords. The captain and Shannivar's first guard, the one she'd liked for his bluntness, were among them. The guard had taken a slash across his belly. His skin had turned so ashen that Shannivar thought that only the need to die fighting kept him on his feet.

Shannivar walked toward the circle. At her command, the Azkhantians broke off their attack. When the captain saw her approach, he settled deeper into his stance, clearly preparing for one last clash, one final burst of glory.

If he'd had his way, she thought, she and Chinggis would have been killed when they were first captured. Rhuzenjin had fallen to the Scorpion priest's schemes, not the captain's. This man did not deal in kidnapping and poison.

"Captain," she said, speaking in trade-dialect. "Will you bargain with me?"

He shook his head. "If you know anything of honor, do not toy with us, but make a speedy end to it!"

"What purpose would your death serve?" Shannivar countered. "Are we not both warriors, you and I? Do we not understand the proper use of power?"

He stared at her, but did not lower his sword.

"Your loyalty is to Gelon, as mine is to the steppe. I do not hold you responsible for the deeds of the Scorpion priest. If you will swear by the Protector of Soldiers to never again make war against my people, I will grant you leave to return home. You may keep your swords."

For the first time, the captain looked uncertain. "How do you know of our gods and our honor?"

"We are not the savages you think us."

The captain glanced at the injured guard, who was wavering on his feet. Shannivar watched him measure who would die regardless of what he chose and who might live. Slowly he lowered his sword.

"We must not linger," Kharemikhar said.

"As war-leader I have made a truce with these men. They are not to be molested. I have promised they may retain their weapons and be allowed to care for their dead according to their own customs."

"It shall be as you wish. However . . . the sorcerer still lives." Kharemikhar was asking her permission to finish off the priest.

The news startled Shannivar. She had thought the priest's injuries, both magical and physical, must surely be fatal. Her first thought was that she wanted to be the one to kill him. *She* had the right of justice, of revenge. None other had suffered at his hands as she had.

I will kill him for this. That was her promise. And yet . . . Could Tabilit have spared him for a purpose? What was more important, a moment's satisfaction or a key to the weakness of Qr?

In her mind, she saw the steppe beset from the west by Gelon and its Scorpion god, and from the east by the armies of the mist. The priest might well die anyway. He might refuse to talk to her, but Azkhantia had its own breed of magic.

"Keep him alive if you can," she told Kharemikhar. "We will see what the *enarees* can learn from him."

With a wolfish grimace, Kharemikhar complied. Shannivar did not think the priest would be gently handled, but if it were at all possible, he would live.

One of Kharemikhar's riders slung the priest belly-down over the back of Rhuzenjin's grulla mare. The arrow wound oozed, a sign he still lived. The mare flared her nostrils at the scent of the blood, but accepted the burden. She had no spirit left for fighting.

At the captain's command, the Gelonian survivors began tending the wounded and laying out the bodies of the dead.

Shannivar badly wanted to be away from this place. She felt sick and dizzy, but less so than before. She could ride. She was Azkhantian.

Kharemikhar untied a bridle from his saddle and handed it to Shannivar. "Your saddle's on the sorrel mare, along with the other remounts back behind that last ridge of hills. Zaraya daughter of Deranel has charge of them."

"Your help has been most welcome, but you still have not told me why you followed me."

"I came with news. A party of Gelon have passed the borderlands into the steppe. My people have seen but not yet challenged them." He held Chinggis while Shannivar slipped the bridle on Eriu's head, grabbed a handful of mane, and swung up on the horse's back, then he handed her the child. "They come not from the east, but the south. And they are not a small party like this, but an army."

Frowning, Shannivar gathered up the reins. *South? From Meklavar?*

Kharemikhar was waiting for her response. Whatever he had done in the past, these things no longer mattered. She would need every warrior for the battles to come, and she had no doubt of Kharemikhar's prowess.

"I cannot tell why these Gelon enter our lands," she said. "If it is Tabilit's will that we engage them, then she will place them in our path. We still face a deadly enemy, one we cannot hope to conquer without magical help. For this, we need the *enarees*." She paused, gauging Kharemikhar's response. He had never been one of those who placed great store in the pronouncements of the clan shamans.

"You are war-leader," he conceded. "It is for you to say where and when we ride. You summoned my clan to war, you warned us of the danger, and we did not come. We will not challenge your leadership now."

"Then we ride to the *dharlak* of the Golden Eagle clan."

Shannivar tightened her arm around Chinggis, shifted her weight, and lifted the reins. Eriu surged forward like a creature of molten silk and fire.

Chapter Thirty

THEY headed south, pausing only long enough for Shannivar to switch her saddle from the sorrel mare to Eriu. Unexpected rescue, a glimpse of Tabilit, her son in her arms, and the joy of having Eriu once more gave Shannivar a burst of energy, but it did not last long. The pace was easy compared to the gallop-and-trot of a war-party under pressure, but she felt as limp as one of the bags used in a Gathering game, flung about and trodden underfoot until it was little more than a rag. Her shoulder had gone beyond hurting. She tucked her fingers on that side into her sash to minimize jarring. That left only one hand with which to hold Chinggis and the reins. She had rarely been so glad for Eriu's responsiveness. He seemed to sense her desire even before she shifted her weight.

This was no time for weakness, she told herself. Saramark would keep going. So would she.

Chinggis no longer protested the tightness of Shannivar's hold. She felt as if he were keeping her in the saddle, not the other way around. Eventually, when they caught up with Shannivar's party and Zaraya took the boy on her own horse, Shannivar was shivering continually as one wave of feverishness after another swept her.

By the time the sun kissed the western hills, the last of

Shannivar's strength was failing along with the light. Fatigue and fever blurred her senses. Her bones craved rest, but she could not summon the clarity to find a suitable campsite and signal a halt. It was easier to just keep going, her body rocking with Eriu's strides.

By slow degrees, Kharemikhar assumed leadership of the party. He issued no orders, he simply reined his silver roan to a halt. Eriu slowed, one ear cocked back at Shannivar. Around her, the other riders dismounted and began tending their horses. She sat, too sick and weary to move, as Eriu rubbed his sweat-crusted head against his knees.

Someone, it might have been Kharemikhar, eased her down from Eriu's back. She felt hands guiding her into the dimness of a tent, lowering her onto something soft, folding back her sleeve, and then bathing her shoulder. Voices murmured in concern. She should know them. Her eyes would not work properly. When she tried to speak, only a sigh passed her chapped lips.

She was cold, so cold . . .

Someone lifted her head and pressed the rim of a cup against her mouth. An astringent tang stung her nose. "Here, this will help." The voice was a woman's, one she ought to know, one who meant her kindness and not harm.

Her throat was too swollen for speech. She turned her face away.

"Shannivar, you must drink." This time, a man spoke. By his tone, he would tolerate no opposition. When he lifted the cup to her lips, she accepted a sip and managed to swallow it. The liquid soothed her gullet and warmed her belly.

Hands touched her shoulder, pressing something wet and warm against the poisoned cuts. The pain eased, as did her shivering. Darkness rose up around her, cushioned her, lulled her. Her muscles went slack.

"Let her sleep," the man said.

Shannivar opened her eyes to find herself lying on a pile of blankets in a trail tent. Chinggis sat cross-legged beside her, watching her with a solemn expression. For a long moment, all she could do was to stare at him and he at her. Then he threw himself on top of her, hands twisting in her vest. For some reason, she was no longer wearing a shirt.

When she raised her arms to hold him tight, the movement sent jolts of pain through her injured shoulder. A gasp escaped her. Brow furrowed, Chinggis drew back.

"Mami?"

"It's all right, little eagle." Mustering a smile, she cradled him with her good arm.

She remembered the arrival of Kharemikhar and his riders . . . Eriu trotting up to her . . . the bargain with the Gelonian captain . . . riding through the hills . . . Now the memories came clearer. When they halted last night, she had been feverish with the scorpion-man's venom. Zaraya had offered her a medicinal tisane and someone had poulticed her shoulder.

"Auntie Zaru!" Chinggis sat up. "Mami's awake!"

Zaraya crept into the tent and squatted beside Shannivar. "You're better."

Gritting her teeth against the rush of pain, Shannivar sat up. A wad of moistened herbs slid off her shoulder. It must have been there some time, for it was cold.

"Why did you let me sleep so long?" Shannivar grumbled. "It's well past time we should be on our way."

"Indeed. You have slept for two days and two nights, as well you should, for you looked half-dead when Kharemikhar brought you to us."

Shannivar opened her mouth to say that was not possible for her to have slept so long, but her lassitude was proof enough. Craning her neck, she inspected the wounds on her bare shoulder. They had not yet closed and the edges were inflamed, but the surrounding skin looked clear. The infection had not spread.

"Are you well enough to ride?" Zaraya asked. "That is, after you've had something to eat? Kharemikhar went hunting, so there's meat."

Shannivar's stomach roused with an audible growl. Laughing, Zaraya backed out of the tent and returned a short while later with a cup brimming with shredded, braised gazelle meat in a gravy thickened with pounded barley. Shannivar had never tasted anything so wonderful.

"Slowly now," Zaraya cautioned.

Shannivar forced herself to pause between mouthfuls, lest she make herself ill. Chinggis sat on her lap. When she had finished, Zaraya wrapped her shoulder before helping her put on her shirt.

"May Tabilit look upon you with favor for your kind ness," Shannivar murmured.

"Chinggis is an easy child. He listens carefully. I have loved him since the first time you placed him in my care. I do not know what he endured during his captivity, but his spirit is resilient. He is a true son of the steppe."

Shannivar remembered that Zaraya was unmarried and had no children of her own. "No," she said, touching the bandage, "I meant this."

"Oh! That was none of my doing. I know only camp medicine and tending horses. Kharemikhar prepared the herbs."

Kharemikhar? "I did not know men of the Ptarmigan clan were learned in such things."

"I do not believe they are, in general. Kharu's brother trained as an *enaree* and I suppose that is how he learned it. The brother died when their *kishlak* was overrun. Did you not know?"

Shannivar felt ashamed that she had measured Kharemikhar's character only as he had first appeared to her, a braggart and a bully.

Zaraya paused at the tent entrance. "Don't say anything. He would not want you to know."

Shannivar followed the Badger clan woman into the camp. Riders were breaking down tents, loading packs and saddling their horses. Several of them wished her a bright day, and she heard their relief at having her return to them. They had wasted enough time between her foolish adventure and her illness.

Shannivar drew Eriu to a halt at the top of the last hill look-ing down on the summering-place of the Golden Eagle clan. She rubbed her shoulder, wincing at the tenderness. The last day's ride had opened up the punctures.

The *dharlak* occupied a teardrop-shaped valley, a broad northwestern expanse that narrowed as it angled southeast. The land itself had not changed since those long summers when she was a child. Everything was as she remembered it, the lake, the sloping pastures, the crumbling piles of stone so ancient that not even the *enarees* knew their purpose or who had built them. Where once herds had grazed on summer's bounty or drunk at the lake's edge, now she saw only scattered goats and camels, and a few horses too old to be ridden. The circle of *jorts* was also much reduced in size.

At the base of the hill, a mounted sentry lifted his bow in greeting. Shannivar recognized Jingutzhen's father, Timurlenk, who did not yet know of his son's death. The brightness of the day dimmed.

Behind her, Kharemikhar's roan shook its head, jingling the bridle rings. Shannivar gave him an encouraging smile.

"Surely Saramark herself must have laid her hand on this place, it is so fair," he said.

"It is not what it was," she replied, "as must be true of the *dharlak* of your own clan." Still, it was good to look upon this place, to remember what it had been and what it might yet be, to be reminded of what she fought for and not merely what she fought against.

She nudged Eriu forward. He pricked his ears, scenting familiar pastures, and began the descent. Kharemikhar followed, then Zaraya leading the sorrel mare with Chinggis on her back, and the rest of Kharemikhar's riders.

Timurlenk booted his horse, a rusty brown mare, toward them. "Shannivar daughter of Ardellis! You are most welcome!"

"May your arrows never miss." Shannivar introduced Kharemikhar before politely asking, "How fares my uncle?"

"Bitterness sits upon my tongue, for Esdarash son of Akhisarak took a lung fever and passed into the Pastures of the Sky in the dark of the Moon of Birds. Bennorakh performed the needful rites. But where is Alsanobal, who must now take his father's place? Where is my son and the others who rode with you?"

"Friend of my uncle, father of my friend, we will speak more of these matters when all are gathered," Shannivar replied formally.

Timurlenk went motionless on his horse. For a moment, it seemed as if he did not breathe, as if his heart had stilled. Shannivar had no words, no possible comfort. It was a hard thing to lose a parent or grandparent. Everything died in the fullness of Tabilit's time. But to lose a child, a son, a son as strong and brave as Jingutzhen, a son on whom the entire clan had relied . . . Shannivar closed her eyes to shut out the old man's anguish, but it seemed that everywhere her mind looked, she saw only death. Death after death after death. Grandmother and Mirrimal, Rhuzenjin and Jingutzhen. And now her uncle and clan chief Esdarash.

The news of her uncle's passing had caught Shannivar unprepared. She had seen so many of her own people die in battle, so the natural death of one old man shouldn't have affected her so. Esdarash, like Grandmother, had seemed as lasting as the sky, as the earth. She had never known a time without him. She could barely remember her own father, killed in one of the perennial clashes with the Gelon.

They followed Timurlenk down to the *dharlak*, where he left the others and went quietly to his wife's *jort*. No explanations were needed; every member of the Golden Eagle clan knew immediately what had happened once they saw the old man's blank features and the absence of his son. The rest of the community welcomed Shannivar and her party, although in a subdued mood. In Alsanobal's absence, the clan had elected old Taraghay, Timurlenk's brother, to act as chieftain for those matters that could not wait. Yvanne, chief Esdarash's widow, who had never been friendly to Shannivar, exclaimed over Chinggis as if he were her own grandson.

Bennorakh stood aside from the others, in the manner of *enarees*. When Shannivar looked in his direction, he raised his dream stick in greeting. The strings of sacred stones and amulets of carved horn rattled. Like all his kind, he wore a long deerskin robe over his loose trousers. Faded symbols of power covered the yoke and shoulders of the robe. His cheeks, once moon-round, looked gaunt. He must have spent long days in fasting as he wandered through dreamsmoke visions.

Shannivar studied him, remembering how intimidating he had once seemed. Now she saw his loneliness, his apartness, and the warmth in his eyes as he nodded to her. They might never be friends, but their journey to the territory of the Snow Bear had given them the understanding of shared experience. He too had seen the rending of Tabilit's Veil. He too had known Zevaron.

Leaving Chinggis in the care of Yvanne, Shannivar walked up to Bennorakh and bowed respectfully, her good hand tapping her chest over her heart. "May your sight be ever keen."

"Come with me." Bennorakh led the way to his *jort*. He lifted the door flap and indicated that she should enter. Moving carefully to avoid stepping on the threshold, Shannivar ducked inside. The familiar smells of the camel's hair felt, sandalwood, and the lingering pong of dreamsmoke greeted her.

The *enaree's jort* was very much like any other with its felt-covered lattice walls. Layers of worn carpet covered the earth. Set against the far wall, beside chests with intricate drawers and piles of cushions, was Grandmother's wooden bed, which had come to the shaman after the old woman's death. Coals glowed under a coating of ash in the three-legged brazier. A bronze bowl and an incense burner sat atop a low table, along with other utensils Shannivar could not identify.

She sat where Bennorakh pointed, on a pillow covered with embroidered felt, its designs so worn they could not be deciphered. He poured out a cup of tea from a pot set on the brazier, offered it to her, and lowered himself to a second cushion.

"Shannivar daughter of Ardellis, may your dreams bring good omens. My heart delights to see you once more."

Shannivar almost dropped the cup. In all their dealings, Bennorakh had never expressed affection for anyone. She recovered herself enough to reply, "May Tabilit and Onjhol guide you safely between the two worlds," meaning those of men and of women.

He waited while she sipped the tea, flavored with salt and slightly rancid butter. It slid down her throat.

"Bennorakh," she began, "we have been comrades and friends as well, I hope. What have you seen? What is to come?"

"We will speak of these things in their proper time," he said. "First, I must treat your wound."

Shannivar's good hand went unthinkingly to her shoulder. Beneath her shirt, the skin felt cold and swollen. "Leave it. It's not getting worse and there is much else to be done."

"You cannot lead your riders against the forces of *Olash-giyn-Olash* with the seeds of treachery in your own body. Yes, the outer injury gives the semblance of healing, but do not be deceived. This poison is not only physical but spiritual."

Fear swept through her. She was too weary and sick at heart to struggle against it. How could mere human strength prevail against what even now came freezing and burning from the north?

"Give it nothing!" Bennorakh cried, his voice piercing her lassitude. "This thing feeds on despair! Do you truly believe that Tabilit would abandon her chosen people?"

"I—I don't know."

To her surprise, Bennorakh smiled. "Then for a time, my faith must carry us both."

At the *enaree*'s instruction, Shannivar lowered herself to the worn rug. Her joints ached and a sonorous hum vibrated through her bones. She tried to relax, to open herself to the healing. The swelling in her shoulder throbbed in time with her pulse.

Bennorakh placed a bronze bowl containing herbs and incense chips on the bed of coals in his brazier. When she tried to draw the smoke into her lungs, it set off a spasm of

coughing. Her eyes watered. Her head felt so light, she was
sure Bennorakh had added more ingredients to the brazier,
perhaps the dried roots or resins that produced visions. He
began chanting, and she drifted on the rise and fall of his
voice. Even though she could not understand the words,
they soothed her as much as the utterances of the Qr priest
had terrified her.

Shannivar felt the warmth of Bennorakh's hand through
the fabric of her sleeve, as if his physical fingers skimmed
her skin while his magical fingers gently probed through
layer after etheric layer. Beneath that touch lay a gnarl of
putrefaction. She felt it as an icy fever, a swirl of sleet and
embers.

With her inner sight, she watched a spectral image, more
like the roots of a living plant than the fingers of a hand,
reach inside her. Thread-like tendrils followed the path of
the poison from where it had entered her skin. They penetrated muscle and nerve and blood. Sap, glowing gold and
green, pulsed along them.

Her eyes no longer stung from the incense-laden smoke.
Breath whispered, easy as silk, through her lungs. The chill
in her flesh thawed. Vitality and a sense of well-being suffused her.

From outside the *jort* came the normal sounds of the
dharlak, women singing, children playing, the distant
whinny of a horse, the *ting! ting!* of the smiths at their work,
and the rhythmic sounds of women beating wool for felt.
She wanted to be outside, under Tabilit's wide sky, with a
bow in her hands and Eriu beneath her. But one did not
rush from the presence of an *enaree* while there were still
matters of importance to discuss.

The air in the *jort* was laden with the residue of dreamsmoke and incense. She sat up and waited for Bennorakh to
speak first.

"I have done what I can for you, Shannivar daughter of
Ardellis. When you left us many moons ago, it was to summon the riders of the steppe to war. Why have you now
returned?"

Shannivar told the tale briefly. "We cannot prevail by
prowess and skill, as we have against the Gelon. This is no

mortal army. We need your help." When she described her plan for a council of *enarees*, he understood immediately.

"It is a thing of wisdom, this council," he said in a thoughtful tone. "Even without the prophecy, this matter is our rightful concern. Too long have we *enarees* held ourselves apart from the affairs of ordinary people. The time has come when we must fight together or else perish together."

Shannivar was more than a little relieved to have his support, for if he said a thing was to be done, then no one, not even the clan chieftain, would oppose it.

"We will do what we can," Bennorakh continued, "although we are few and scattered. Oh yes, we have seen the ancient evil arise beyond the Broken Mountains. Well do I recall the things you and I witnessed in the land of the Snow Bear clan. The smoke of dreams has shown much more, the past as well as what is and what is to come."

The *enaree's* voice went vague, as if he were speaking across a vastness of time as well as distance. "Not all the bows have been drawn, nor all the arrows flown. *Olash-giyn-Olash* threatens more than the steppe. Thus, more than our own riders must oppose it."

Shannivar nodded. "We must also decide the fate of the captured Or priest. Kharemikhar would have finished him," she said, "but I hope the *enaree* council can make use of him."

"I will see this man."

The scorpion-man had survived the journey, weak and silent. Upon their arrival at the *dharlak*, he had been laid out under a screen of woven reeds, for no one was willing to take him into their *jort*. From time to time, one or another of the older women would bring him barley gruel.

Bennorakh squatted on his haunches beside the priest, calmly studying him. The blackened skin on the injured man's forehead, the charred shape of a scorpion, still oozed. Shannivar stood beside the *enaree*, half-expecting him to be angry, to bid her not meddle in what was not her affair. To her surprise, he glanced up at her and asked, "Tell me what you see."

"He does not seem so fearsome as when the Scorpion god acted through him."

"I agree." Bennorakh resumed his scrutiny of the priest. "Whatever demon once possessed this man has departed."

"Perhaps it had no further use for him." Shannivar made no effort to hide her disgust.

"Are we not all servants of the gods?" Bennorakh asked with unexpected mildness. "Look at his face and tell me if he was always evil."

Shannivar did not want to examine the scorpion-man too closely. She did not know what she might see in those slack features, those sunken eyes. If what Bennorakh said was true, she must stop thinking of him as the *scorpion-man* and recognize his humanity. Or try to.

Until that moment, the Qr priest had not responded to his visitors. As Shannivar gazed into his face, he roused. Intelligence sparked in his eyes, but nothing of the power that had once inhabited him. Fresh blood dripped from his ears and nose.

The priest's lips moved. Shannivar thought he was struggling to speak. If he were Azkhantian, he would beg to have his life ended, rather than live on like this. She had killed Gelon, but always in battle, never as they lay helpless and destitute in spirit.

What hope did this poor wretch have? No Sky Pastures waited for him. If the dwellers in stone had their own heavenly cities, they were far away. None of his own people would perform the funeral rites for him, according to their own customs. What would happen to his spirit, then? Would he wander until the last star had fallen from the sky, or would his god punish him for his failures with an eternity of despair?

Shannivar got to her feet. Once things had been so simple. The enemies of the steppe had been predictable. The Gelon came in waves, more frequently since Ar-Cinath-Gelon had ascended the Lion Throne, but even then, their motives had been clear, their tactics unchanging. They marched or rode in their onager-drawn chariots; they fought with sword and spear. No gods, scorpion or otherwise, haunted them.

Now it seemed the world boiled over with supernatural adversaries. Things walked the earth that were not human, or not entirely so. A man she once loved—and still did—led an army of creatures that should not exist outside of nightmares. By comparison, what was the fate of one dying priest?

Chapter Thirty-one

AFTER a time of preparation, Bennorakh performed the prayers for the spirits of Jingutzhen and the other slain, entreating Tabilit to guide them safely to the Pastures of the Sky. Then life resumed a more normal character. Mourning might be intense, but it was always brief, even in times of peace.

Shannivar made room in her *jort* not only for her son and Zaraya, but some of the unmarried women riders. She had left the *jort* with Yvanne, as the Golden Eagle matriarch, in order to travel faster and lighter. Now Alsanobal's wife, Kendira, helped her to secure the lattices, unroll the layers of felt, and place the threshold with the traditional blessings.

The *dharlak* had more than enough room for Kharemikhar and his riders, as well as good pasture for their horses. Normally, clans did not share their summering-places, so the community took on the air of a *khural*. Chinggis had children of his own age to play with and Shannivar took him riding on the sorrel mare. From a distance, she often observed two riders, Zaraya on her favorite leggy bay and Kharemikhar on his silver roan.

As the days passed, the Moon of Mares swung through the fullness of its season. Shannivar left Chinggis with Yvanne, much to the older woman's delight, and went hunting. Riding back through the richly scented feathergrass, Eriu danced sideways and snorted at the dead gazelle slung over the front of the saddle. The rich summer grazing had put weight back on him, energy reserves he might well need. Shannivar cuffed him lightly on the crest of his neck and told him to be sensible.

She signaled Eriu to halt on the top of the last hill and studied the *dharlak* below for anything amiss. The long summer afternoon was drifting to a close. Ribbons of brightness spread across the western horizon. The grass shimmered in the lengthening shadows.

The black lifted his head, ears alert, nostrils flaring. A company of horsemen was moving along the valley floor toward the encampment, leading a string of laden pack horses. From their measured pace and the arrangement of the riders, this was no war party. A handful of riders from the *dharlak* had mounted up and were headed to meet the arrivals.

Slipping her bow from its case by her left knee, Shannivar urged Eriu downslope. Wind rushed by her face and sent the white-laced mane flying. The gazelle flopped across her thighs as she strung her bow and held an arrow ready.

As they reached the bottom of the hill, a cry went up from the foremost rider. He raised his hand, drawing the party to a halt. Shannivar slowed Eriu moments before the party from the *dharlak* arrived.

"Alsanobal! Tabilit's blessing!" she called out.

"Cousin! May all your days be lucky!" Alsanobal was grinning, laughing, whirling his horse, a thick-boned chestnut that was not much of an improvement over the big red that had almost gotten him killed. As usual, he was showing off. "Are we the first to arrive?"

"Yes, yes! I had not thought to see you so soon! Your horse has wings!"

He turned to the rider at his right side and let out a whoop. "I win!"

"What, you bet on being first?" Shannivar teased.

"Safer than wagering against that black demon of yours!"

Shannivar knew her cousin well enough to hear the strain in his voice, the effort of making such a show. "Alsu, be serious!"

He sobered. "I'm getting that way."

"Do not act pompous, or Kharemikhar will not recognize his old friend."

"Kharemikhar!" Delight lightened the tension on Alsanobal's face. "He is here? His clan was scattered and I could not find him. It lightens my eyes that he is safe."

Shannivar inclined her head. "And a more intrepid ally we could not wish for."

He regarded her for a long moment, clearly remembering the old animosity from the Long Ride.

"We all ride under the same sky," she said, and he smiled.

The riders milled around, offering each other wishes of luck and welcome. Alsanobal introduced Shannivar to Idantharis, *enaree* of the Black Marmot clan. He was younger than she expected, no more than her own years. She did not remember him from the *khural* three years ago and thought he might have still been an apprentice then, although it would be inexcusably rude to ask. It would be cruel as well to bring up the question of his teacher. *Enarees* died like other men.

There was little need for further conversation as everyone proceeded to the *dharlak* together, with Alsanobal and Shannivar leading the way. He joked that she had provided his favorite dinner in honor of his success, at which everyone who knew them laughed. She retorted that if he wanted roasted meat, he was going to have to cook it himself, at which even those not of the Golden Eagle clan laughed as well. Looking even younger than before, Idantharis flushed and kept his eyes on the mane of his horse.

Yvanne rushed forward and practically dragged her son from his horse. The rueful grimace he gave Shannivar was not feigned. Alsanobal managed to extricate himself to tend his horse while his wife Kendira waited. Bennorakh took the young Idantharis into his *jort,* and the rest of the camp welcomed Alsanobal's riders, leading their mounts to the best water and pasturage.

That evening, the entire camp gathered for as much of a feast as could be provided in these times. The new arrivals were not expected to contribute food, for they had clearly ridden a long distance. In addition to Shannivar's gazelle and a stew of smoked goat meat, Yvanne produced an astonishing array of delicacies, marrow dumplings, spiced meat cakes, *bha*, and summer berries in powdered honey. Skins of *k'th* passed around the fire, until even Timurlenk looked cheerful. Behind him, her face glowing, sat his wife, Scarface. She had been servant to Shannivar's grandmother, the deceased clan matriarch, and had no family connections of her own. To everyone's surprise, the old man had married her. From the look of Scarface's bright eyes and softly rounded belly, that act of kindness had blessed them both.

Not far away, Kharemikhar took the place next to Zaraya. Shannivar watched them, her arms wrapped around Chinggis on her lap. She bent her head to brush her lips against her son's hair. It was rapidly losing its baby softness, as the roundness was melting from his body, but he still smelled like a young child.

The songs shifted to tales of great horses and heroes of the past, winners of the Long Ride and of the wrestling contests at the *khural*.

They long for the past, when glory meant winning a horse race, Shannivar thought. Once that would have been more than enough for her. Now the steppe itself was at stake. Kharemikhar met her gaze and she saw the same grimness in his features. When one of his riders asked about his winning the Long Ride, he brushed the matter aside.

"Who cares about such a boring incident? Alsanobal son of Esdarash has a far greater story to tell!"

"Alsanobal! Alsanobal!" The cry went up around the circle. Shannivar joined in, thinking that the Golden Eagle clan could not do better for its next chieftain. Even if such an honor were possible for a woman, she would not want it.

With a somber expression, Alsanobal got to his feet and began his tale. He spoke of how he and his riders had ventured behind the path of the mist army. They had fought men under the enchantment of the power behind the mist. He told of skirmishes and ambushes, but always he named one or another of his own riders as the hero of the day. Two of his riders had fallen in a clash with a gigantic horned beast, something akin to an *ildu'amar*, that spat forth gouts of corrosive liquid. Whatever the droplets touched burst into flame, a fire that burned through skin and leather, bone and flesh. It would have seemed a tale to frighten naughty children, except for the flat, hard light in Alsanobal's eyes.

Shannivar listened to the murmurs of dismay. They had not seen the things within the mist, the winged serpents and stone-drakes, the ice-trolls and the giant beasts with their shovel-like horns. They did not know there might be even worse horrors.

After he finished, Alsanobal did not take his place again but wandered into the night. Careful not to wake Chinggis, Shannivar handed him to Yvanne. The older woman gave her a sharp look before cradling the child against her ample breasts.

It was not entirely dark, with the swathe of stars and the shimmering moon above. Shannivar followed Alsanobal where she least expected him to go, to the horse pasture. Eriu whickered softly at her approach. She found Alsanobal standing beside Kharemikhar's silver roan.

After a pause and a sigh, he said, "Shanu, it was bad."

Shannivar thought, *I need to know what we might face.* She ran one hand along the roan's spine, feeling the bony knobs sharpened by hard riding and hunger. The horse did not lift its head from grazing.

"The earth where those things had passed . . ." he said, "it was as if no blade of grass, no sprig of gentian, not even the lowliest moss had ever grown there. There was nothing for a locust to eat. I swear by Onjhol's bow, the soil itself had turned to dust, dust that bled and smoked. And the rot was spreading . . ."

In his silence, Shannivar sensed a soul-chill deeper than words. She wondered if they might look upon the Pastures of the Sky and see even that fair, eternal land laid waste.

The demons poison everything they touch. The malice of Qr receded, a paltry thing.

She was war-leader; she was Azkhantian. She was a daughter of the Golden Eagle. An enemy had dared to set foot upon the steppe. She had no time for despair.

* * *

Alsanobal quietly assumed the mantle of clan chieftain. He did so without posturing or challenge, only the natural leadership of one who has seen the enemy and knows what must be done to counter it. Kharemikhar would have made a natural second, for the two friends were in accord in most things, but the Ptarmigan rider refused any greater honor.

Shannivar and Zaraya, as well as the others who had ridden with her, took their turns drilling the youngsters in archery. The horse games continued with a new seriousness. Agility and speed, as well as prowess with weapons, were fighting skills. Those too young or too old to fight could still cut and fletch arrows. The encampment changed from *khural* to war camp.

The Moon of Golden Grass waned. The days were hot and long as the sun crisped the grasses. Another party returned, bringing a third *enaree*. A company of riders from the Skylark clan arrived the following day, all that could be gathered. Many were too old to fight and had traveled slowly to spare their aged horses. They brought flocks of goats and a few camels laden with their *jorts*. The *dharlak* filled until it held as many active warriors as when the clan was at the height of its numbers, yet the mood remained somber. No more feasts marked the evenings, although there were plenty of songs and stories around the fires.

Summer neared its end with the Moon of Gathering, also called the Moon of Stallions. Two more *enarees* set up their *jorts* near Bennorakh's. They held themselves apart from the rest of the community, although everyone heard their nightly chanting. Women and children, as well as older people, went out across the hills to reap what grain they could. The numbers of riders increased, as did the sense of expectancy.

One afternoon, just after Shannivar and Alsanobal returned from their daily circuit of the horse pastures, one of the older children who had been assigned sentry duty galloped into camp. A small crowd gathered around her within moments. The scene reminded Shannivar poignantly of how another child, one of her young cousins, had brought the news of the arrival of the Isarran ambassador to this very *dharlak*. How simple those times had been, how innocent.

Kharemikhar waved the onlookers aside while Zaraya took charge of the pony. The girl stood in a circle of clansmen, her face flushed with emotion.

"Shannivar—" The girl was breathing so hard with excitement and terror, she could barely speak. She pointed in the direction of the ridge where she had been set to watch. "Just—just as you said—a cloud, low on the ground, coming from the north."

It has come. The waiting is over.

"Zaraya, saddle Eriu for me!" Shannivar turned and raced for the *enaree*'s *jort*, adding over her shoulder, "And a horse for Bennorakh!"

Chapter Thirty-two

SHANNIVAR sprinted toward the *enaree*'s *jort*, Kharemikhar at her heels. "Not you!" she yelled over her shoulder at him.

He caught up with her two paces later. "Yes, me. Zaraya will kill me if anything happens to you, and if she doesn't, Alsanobal will. Besides," he added with the grin he once used to charm the eligible young women, "you might need help."

Shannivar bit back a reply. She didn't have time to argue with him. At least that silver roan of his could keep up with Eriu. She hoped Zaraya found a fast horse for the *enaree*.

Just as she reached the *jort*, Bennorakh flung open the door flap. His hair looked wilder than usual and his cheeks were pale. As Shannivar drew breath to explain, he held up one hand. "I have seen," he said.

Zaraya galloped up on her leggy bay, leading Eriu and Kharemikhar's roan. She jumped down and shoved the reins into the *enaree*'s hands. Shannivar grabbed a handful of frost-laced ebony mane and vaulted into the saddle. Bennorakh took longer. Like all children of the steppe, he could ride, but he spent his days afoot more often than not. Zaraya's bay stood quietly while he clambered onto her back. The silver roan pranced and blew through its nostrils with excitement.

Kharemikhar stood holding Zaraya's hands, gazing into her eyes. Her cheeks were flushed, her lips parted.

"Come *on*!" Shannivar turned Eriu into a neat pivot on his hindquarters. The black lifted into a low rear, then leaped forward. Kharemikhar tore himself away from Zaraya and vaulted onto the back of his running horse.

They pelted up the sentry's hill, chosen because it afforded the best view of the steppe to the north and east. Shannivar leaned forward, balancing her weight over the black's forequarters. The roan lowered its head, settling to run in earnest. A glance behind showed Bennorakh gripping the bay mare's saddle.

The horses were blowing by the time they crested the hill, so fast was their pace. Trampled grass and horse droppings marked where the girl had waited and watched. Shannivar shaded her eyes with one hand and peered toward the east.

Where the land stretched into a long slope, a blanket of gray blurred the line of the horizon. It could easily fill the *dharlak* valley, and Shannivar could not see the end of it. At least, it did not seem to be moving with any great speed. It did not need to, any more than night or winter or death itself. The top line was not smooth but, as best as she could make out, had its own peaks and valleys, as if it masked objects within.

More ice-trolls? she wondered. *Or the monsters named arsinoths in the ancient lore?*

Dropping the reins, Bennorakh raised his hands as if he held an invisible dream stick. His lips moved soundlessly. His eyes were blank, his pupils hugely dilated. Under him, the bay stood like a rock.

Shannivar turned her attention back to the mist and the shape of the hills. If it followed the obvious, easy path, it would swing south where the land flattened out. That would take it away from the *dharlak*. Unless, she corrected herself, the monsters or their general—*Zevaron*—became aware of the encampment and meant to destroy those he could not enslave.

The wind keened in her ears. She touched her face with one hand and felt streaks of wetness, quickly drying. Kharemikhar met her eyes and quickly looked away. Her heart felt like a lump of rust. From above came the cry of a bird of prey. Stark against the vast white sky, a golden eagle hovered on the air currents. Its grace and power lifted her. *I am a daughter of the Golden Eagle,* Shannivar repeated to herself, *born of earth, but also of the heavens.*

Shannivar reined Eriu beside the bay. "Now you have seen the mist for yourself, *enaree.* Can you and the others fight what lies within it?"

Bennorakh straightened up. His eyes cleared, but remained grave. "Ours is the magic of the steppe, of our own lands and our own gods. We draw wisdom from the unseen, not the unnatural. Our strength lies not in physical might but in our dreams."

"So you cannot help." Shannivar could not mask her disappointment. Had it all been for nothing, sending out her riders, searching out the scattered *enarees*, clinging to a hope that turned out to be worthless? "If you cannot be of any other use, have you had a vision of what is to come? You've been shut up with your dreamsmoke night after night. What is your advice? Is it better to wait, chancing that thing will pass us by? Or should we ride out to meet it, as we would the Gelon?"

Shannivar had not expected Bennorakh to respond with anything of value, so she was surprised when he said, "I did not say we could not help, only that we do not fight by force of arms." He jabbed one finger toward the east. "That army shrouds itself in mist. Do you know why?"

"To disguise its numbers," Kharemikhar said, as if the answer were obvious.

That was how the riders of the steppe would reason. The Gelon would never do such a thing. They would try to be as visible as possible, in order to intimidate their enemies.

"They hide in the mist," Shannivar said.

"What?" Kharemikhar asked. "Do they shrivel up and die in the sun, like maggots?"

"That I cannot say," Bennorakh answered. "That mist may have been created and maintained by sorcerous means, but it is no different from any natural fog. It is water and dust, nothing more."

"Water and dust . . ." Shannivar repeated. "Like a ground fog?"

"Just so."

"Fog . . . clouds . . . And clouds produce rain . . ."

Bennorakh shrugged. "I cannot say what good it might be to change cloud into rain but yes, this we can do. If Kharemikhar is correct, these creatures might then lose their strength in the sun."

The mist was enormous. If what Bennorakh said was true, it would produce a torrent of rain. If that were added to a lake that was already present, could those creatures drown?

The entire *dharlak* would have to be moved immediately to higher ground, and the children and herds taken deeper into hilly country. By Tabilit's blessing, a *jort* could be taken down in an hour. However, it would take longer to arrange the household goods and load them on the pack animals.

Again Shannivar peered at the mist between the hills. It had advanced, but only a little, and it seemed to be veering south. She reckoned they would have enough time for the evacuation. The biggest question was whether she and her riders could lure the mist into the valley, taking it through the gap formed by the two steep-sided hills at the southern end.

Atop that same crest the next day, Shannivar, Alsanobal, and Kharemikhar watched the last of the goat herds disappear between hills to the west and north. The clans had loaded up everything they possessed, even scraps of leather and old reed mats. No one knew when or if they would ever return, but such was the way of the steppe. Some clans had no fixed places in which to pass summers and winters, following their herds in all seasons. Shannivar grieved the loss of this place. Whatever happened today, the *dharlak* would never be the same. Here Grandmother had died and Shannivar had cut the felt for her own *jort*. It was a place of beginnings and endings and beginnings again.

While they evacuated the valley, the mist had traveled even further south. During the night, it had passed beyond the cleft between the hills. A ways distant, on the slope leading up from the summering-place, the wing-leaders waited. Bennorakh and the other *enarees* were already positioned on the summit at the far side of the *dharlak* valley. Last night they had slept out under the stars, praying and preparing.

Signaling for the others to follow, Shannivar sent Eriu down the far slope. Fields of summer-crisped grasses sped past in a blur. To the south, the land opened, broad and flat. The wall of mist covered most of it.

"Do not engage the monsters," Shannivar called out loudly, so that the leaders could hear her. Those who had ridden with her into the mist knew what she meant, and the others would learn soon enough. She meant to not lose a single one of them through recklessness. "These are not Gelon, to be slain by arrow or sword. There is no glory in a wasted death! You will all be needed afterward." She hoped there would indeed be an afterward. "Draw them into the trap! Leave them to the *enarees*! Now ride, ride!"

Alsanobal's whoop followed her. "Ride! Golden Eagle, ride!"

"Ptarmigan, ride!"

Other voices shouted out their clan cries. The wind blended the separate names as their voices echoed from the hillsides.

"Ghost Wolf! Ghost Wolf!"

"Silver Fox, ride!"

The war cries and the rushing wind and the racket of the galloping hooves blended together in Shannivar's mind. Fire shot through her veins. She and Eriu were one creature, bound by a single driving need.

"Antelope, ride!"

"Ride!"

Shannivar's bow sang to her from its case beside her left leg. Her arrows wailed to be set loose. Between her knees, Eriu skimmed the earth, a thing of darkness and wind. His mane, scarred by frost, whipped her vest.

"Falcon, ride!"

"Ride! Ride!"

The rush of war swept through her. She drew it in with

every quickening breath. The pounding of hooves became a roar. She was no longer a woman of bone and flesh. Onjhol, Father of Battles, raged in her blood. The madness of the charge flayed away all thought.

At a flat gallop, the massed riders burst out onto the last open stretch before the wall of mist. Shannivar dropped the reins, trusting Eriu to hold a steady course. She strung her bow. The bow, smooth and resilient, was a gift from Tabilit herself.

Do not forsake your people, Mother of Horses! Ride, ride with me now!

Shannivar set an arrow to the string. She did not expect to hit anything. The mist was too thick and dense, too uncertain in its swirling currents. No solid target presented itself. She meant instead to provoke the creatures into a chase. As the Gelon had discovered over the generations of attempted conquest, the riders of the steppe were not easily caught. Azkhantians fought when and where they willed, using familiar terrain and the swiftness of their horses to best advantage.

They were almost upon the mist. Currents of gray and white loomed over them.

Shannivar gave a high-pitched whistle, a signal to the leaders. At a shift in her weight and a tap with one heel, Eriu switched leads in midstride and turned, racing along the front edge of the mist.

"Azkhantia! Azkhantia!" Screaming at the top of her lungs, Shannivar loosed her arrow into the mist. The vapors swallowed it without a trace. She wheeled Eriu and galloped away, drawing another arrow.

Behind her, the body of riders split according to plan. Roughly a third peeled off to each side, while the center third slowed, holding their course. The two wings shot a barrage of arrows. Some aimed high, on wide sweeping arcs, while others shot directly into the mist.

The mist continued on its path, relentless. The riders turned and sped back toward one another. Their war cries turned to taunts. No one expected the monster army to understand human insults, but it was common practice when facing a force of Gelon, teasing the enemy into a rash move, drawing him deeper into the steppe, and then picking off those who outstripped their comrades.

The wing riders made a second pass, turned, and came around again. Still the mist continued to creep stubbornly southward. Shannivar brought Eriu to a prancing halt, facing the central group.

"This isn't working." Alsanobal growled. "We must attack!" He meant to ride directly into the mist.

"No!" Shannivar shouted. "I am war leader and I say no. No one takes that risk." *No one except me.*

"Keep shooting until you've run out of arrows!" she ordered. "Then yell at it, piss on it, I don't care! But stay outside!"

"Shannivar—" Alsanobal's voice took on a shading of horror. "You can't—"

"Stay clear, I said!" Shannivar spun Eriu around and booted him toward the mist.

The black shot over the level ground. His ears were pinned against his neck, but he did not hesitate. With a burst of added speed, he carried Shannivar through the outer margin of the mist. Within a single stride, the mist changed. It was like entering a cloud of lightning. Energy, sharp and tingling, sizzled over her skin. Eriu's back tensed. Without conscious thought, acting by reflex, Shannivar shifted her weight, deepening her seat. The black sat down on his hindquarters, dug his feet into the frost-rimed ground, and slid to halt.

The mist swirled around them, its droplets like slivers of ice. Shannivar could see no further than Eriu's flattened ears. For an unspeakable moment, she could not move, not even to draw breath. She felt as if she were encased in glacial ice, except for her heart, hammering against the inside of her chest.

Streamers of gray and white danced through the sullen gray. Something was coming, something enormous. Something that whipped the supernatural fog into a frenzy.

Moisture collected in the inner corners of Shannivar's eye sockets. Her hands gripped her bow. Any moment now, the weapon would fall from her paralyzed fingers. The thing—*ice troll? arsinoth? something even worse?*—was coming closer. She felt its looming bulk. Its malevolence pressed against her like a weight.

The bow hummed in her hands. Warmth spread along her sinews. Air rushed into her lungs, sweet and vital. Her throat ached in relief. Astonished, she lifted the bow. It glowed. Rainbow lights shimmered along its curved length. Its wood took on a pearly opalescence, so smooth and supple that it felt alive.

. *Tabilit's gift.*

Resolve ignited like a resin-soaked torch bursting into flame. She bent the bow.

"Zevaron!" She had no time for tenderness. His name was a weapon, a barb to hurl into the mist. *"Zevaron!"*

The bow grew brighter, streaming multihued brilliance. Eriu recovered his footing, head up, weight balanced, once more a warrior's steed. Strength flowed into Shannivar. Her shoulder muscles flexed, steadying her grip on the bow. The tip of the arrow did not waver.

The mist receded, revealing a diffuse, granite-dark shadow, easily twice the size of the largest camel.

"Zevaron!" For a moment, she thought the shadow responded. It shifted, drawing itself up.

She loosed the arrow. It sped away, piercing light and mist. The bowstring shrilled in her ear. Her arms reverberated with the release.

Tremors shook the gray figure. Its edges blurred. The mist surged as if lashed by a thousand whips. The ground beneath Eriu's feet rumbled, a deep, rolling boom.

Eriu startled, rearing. Shannivar reined him back the way they had come. The horse pivoted and accelerated into a full-out gallop. She leaned over his neck, balanced on his forequarters, letting him run unhindered.

Shannivar glanced over her shoulder as they broke through into normal day. The mist was shifting its course. White and gray clashed and shredded, dissolving into wildly agitated patterns. The ground cracked under its sudden, crushing weight.

Eriu raced toward the central group of riders. Shannivar raised her bow. It caught the sunlight, blazing like a torch.

"Go!"

Alsanobal took up the cry, louder with each repetition. "Go! Go! *Go!*"

Already the riders were urging their mounts back the way they had come. Eriu streaked to the forefront. The riders thundered behind them. The mist followed, faster than it had ever moved before. Even so, it could not match the speed of the Azkhantian horses.

She twisted in the saddle, gauging the distance to the fog. If the riders got too far ahead, then Zevaron—or whatever had reacted to her shot—might decide the effort wasn't worth it and swing back to the previous course.

"Ho! Easy!" Shannivar settled her weight and increased the tension on the reins. Eriu wasn't hardmouthed like many steppe horses. She did not need to savage him with the bit. He dipped his nose, collecting his hind legs under him, and slowed from his breakneck pace.

They rounded the base of a hill, halfway to the *dharlak*. Shannivar slackened one rein and Eriu turned away from it, running easily now. His ears were still cocked backward but no longer pinned to his neck.

The other riders rushed through the gap, Alsanobal in the lead. Tarabey called out to Shannivar as he rode by. She nudged Eriu back down the slope and brought him to a prancing halt in front of the mist.

"Coward! Dweller-in-stone!" she yelled at the mist. "Defiler of rivers! Catch me if you dare!" The mist rushed forward, vapors churning in renewed agitation. Laughing and shouting more insults, Shannivar turned Eriu. She kept him to a canter, though he tossed his head at being restrained.

The *dharlak* came into view, the sweep of scooped-out land, lake and pastures and thickets, the groves of willow and birch, the packed earth where ring upon ring of *jorts* had stood, the forge and crumbling piles of stones.

Shannivar glanced at the southwestern rim, just beyond the entrance, to see the dreamsmoke fire set by the *enarees* and beyond it, a shelter of a reed windscreen. Smoke drifted skyward. She heard the shamanic chanting, sonorous and hypnotic.

By the time Eriu had reached the far end, the mist filled the valley. It lapped at the surrounding hills, as if ascertaining the shape of the landscape. Shannivar's plan depended on the nature of natural fog. Seasonal low-lying clouds clung to sinks and gullies, drifting through the lowest passes between hills. Only the fiercest winds drove them higher. She had wagered that this mist had the same constraints. Indeed, as she watched, it faltered on the slopes, then ebbed.

She tapped Eriu's sides with her heels. He scaled the southern hill in a series of gazelle-like leaps. She grabbed his mane with one hand, holding her weight forward. As they neared the summit, he began to slow. His barrel heaved, his lungs working like bellows.

Below, the mist now covered the valley floor and trailed off into the far end. Shannivar strained to see where the mist had passed. The summer-golden grass and the rich ochre hues of the soil were gone, the ground bleached and charred-gray. Steam rose from heaps of yellow-tinged mud. Eriu whickered uneasily, urging her to be gone from this place.

The *enarees* chanted on. Shannivar imagined the pungent smell of dreamsmoke, of the herbs and resins that were the catalysts of magical power.

The surface of the mist took on an eerie sheen, no longer vaporous. Sun glinted on wetness. The currents whirled, but more slowly now. Then, gradually at first but gaining in speed, the mist condensed into rain.

Chapter Thirty-three

THE upper boundary of the mist darkened, although it did not appear significantly thinner than before. This fog was not entirely natural; the power that had created it might provide it some degree of protection. Shannivar sent a silent prayer to Tabilit that the spell of the *enarees* would prevail. She dared not believe otherwise. The shamans were in their own place, under their own sky. They wielded their own magic, woven like the threads of an immense tapestry into land and sun and grass.

Discordant roaring shook the valley floor and traceries of brightness flashed in the depths of the mist. A whiff of ozone stung Shannivar's nose. Meanwhile, more and more of the mist poured into the valley, piling into enormous billows. Cloudy tendrils spurted up the shallower slopes, as if attempting to escape. They splashed against an invisible wall, only to fall back. The *enarees* had blocked the clefts between the hills, sealing the valley like a gigantic bowl. The mist and everything in it was trapped, contained. Soon rain would drown the monstrous army.

Shannivar made her way along the eastern rim of the valley, heading south. Alsanobal met her, for he had remained behind to witness the flooding of his clan's *dharlak*.

Kharemikhar accompanied him so that he would not be alone, and Zaraya came because Kharemikhar did.

In silence they watched the lake of clouds that now covered the valley floor in uneasy waves. Alsanobal gazed down at the turbulence with an unreadable expression. In the mist Shannivar saw an eerie beauty, terrible in its mockery of the natural clouds that often cloaked the lower ground during the Moon of Melting Snow.

More lights glinted in the murky depths. Again Shannivar received the impression that the mist was struggling for its very life, even as she had struggled against the sorcery of the Qr priest. She thought, too, of the creatures below, the ones she had encountered in her foray through the mist wall and those she had not yet seen. Did they fear the sun and its bright warmth? For all she knew, they had no awareness, no spirit, no gods of their own. No merit, no valor, no dreams of glory.

But the man who rode in their midst, whose will drove them, he was no amalgam of stone and frozen mud. He had lived and breathed and loved . . . If only there had been a way to reach him . . . to save him.

No, do not think of him now!

Waves wracked the cloud lake. Sunlight gleamed on sheets of water that formed on the surface and then disappeared, absorbed from below. Again and again, the mist rose, peaked, and fell away. Each time, the resulting troughs were deeper than before, as the condensing moisture eroded the cloud layer.

A wordless ululation rose from the mist. Soon other cries echoed it. The sound built, reverberating through the valley, but the chanting of the *enarees* grew louder in response.

The surface of the mist sank even lower. Almost all the white streaks had vanished, revealing shades of water-laden gray. With each moment, it looked less like fog and more like the underbelly of a storm cloud. The cries of the monsters seemed to be getting weaker. A shape pushed up through the currents like an enormous creature surfacing from the bottom of the lake. The cloud-waters swelled, sheeting off its emergent form. Its raucous cry sounded more like a challenge than a bellow of pain.

Blue-tinged smoke shot skyward from the *enarees'* fire. A quaver interrupted the rhythm of the shamanic chanting.

Shannivar tensed, sending Eriu into a sideways jig. The bay mare snorted and flicked her ears back in disapproval. Shannivar stroked the black's neck. The next moment, the *enarees* resumed their spell. The creature in the mist raised massive forelimbs, visible through the thinning layers of moisture, and then plunged back down.

She wondered how long Bennorakh and the others could maintain their efforts, but she dared not voice her doubts, even though her companions must surely be asking themselves the same thing.

The clouds were breaking up with astonishing speed. No solid earth showed through the widening gaps. Water now covered the floor of the valley. Rain pelted down, adding to the flood.

Struggling bodies whipped the brown water into froth. Wolf-shaped beasts thrashed about, lunging and scrambling on top of one another. A flurry of yelps rose above the sounds of splashing. Swirls of mud marked where flying serpents, their wings drenched and sodden, had fallen. A stone-drake reared up on its hind legs, forelimbs stretched skyward as if in supplication, and then toppled. It hit the water with a splash and did not resurface.

Waves laced with filthy gray foam crashed against the sides of the valley. When they receded, they left whitened ulcers. The earth looked as if it had been cauterized.

The steady rhythm of the *enarees'* chanting faltered again, but the last of the clouds were almost spent. The water was no longer rising. The smaller monsters disappeared beneath its surface, although many still remained.

It was almost over. Yet ... Shannivar had not seen Zevaron, whether mounted on another ice-troll, some other creature, or on his own feet. He must have drowned while the clouds still concealed the water. It was better this way, to not have watched him die.

A patch of mist still lingered in the center of the valley. It hovered low over the water, small but dense. Although the *enarees* no longer chanted as vigorously as before, their spell would soon overcome this last remnant. Whatever creatures sheltered there would succumb as surely as all the others had.

"Go, make sure the *enarees* lack for nothing," Shannivar told the others, "and that all is well with our riders. Alsu, you, too," she countered her cousin's objection. "I will remain here until you return, for someone should keep watch through the night while the others rest in camp." To forestall any discussion, she slipped from her saddle and set about loosening the girth and taking off the bridle so that Eriu might graze.

They left her, Kharemikhar and Zaraya toward the watchfire of the *enarees*, and Alsanobal in the direction of the camp hidden in a narrow dell among the eastern slopes. Shannivar found a chunk of smooth rock with a good view of the valley and settled into her vigil. Eventually the *enarees* fell silent and no more smoke arose from their fire. The spells that contained the mist seemed to be holding. Only a few wisps of fog remained at the southern end.

She had fought the army of *Olash-giyn-Olash*, and she had destroyed it, yet she found no joy in her victory. She thought of the riders enslaved by the Shadow of Shadows, clan after clan gone, whole territories deserted, and her spirit ached.

Shannivar pulled her knees to her chest and rocked, keening softly. Those riders would never return to their families. No clan *enaree* would chant the way to the Pastures of the Sky. There would be no ceremony to protect them from becoming lost or taken by demons, no sharing of grief and *k'th*. No mourners to pray,

> "*Let them return to you, O Tabilit,*
> *Let their pure spirits rise up to the your Sky Kingdom.*
> *Let them take their place with the chosen ones.*
> *Let them sit at Onjhol's strong right hand.*"

Tears blurring her sight, Shannivar whispered the words. She did not know the names of the dead or their clan totem animals. She knew only the grief in her heart.

Tabilit had commanded her to save her people. *"One by one, the horse clans will fall,"* the goddess had warned. *"Like a swarm of locusts, the enemy will sweep across the steppe."* And now it was over, that fate averted. The barren land might recover in time and if not, the steppe was wide and its clans resourceful.

Why then did she feel no triumph, no relief? She wanted only to lose herself among her horses and weep.

A war-leader does not weep.

The sun swung toward the west. The waters lapped the shores, leaving borders of whitened rock. The waves looked pale, as if all color had been leached away from the water as well. Here and there, something thrashed, breaking the surface. The clot of clouds in the center remained.

As dusk neared, an eerie luminescence appeared on the borders of the lake, flickering blue-white. Lightning flashed briefly in the central cloud.

Alsanobal joined Shannivar on the hilltop. All was well in camp, he said. Kharemikhar and Zaraya had reported that the *enarees* were weary, although determined to finish their task. There was nothing ordinary warriors could do at this point to aid them.

The pallid rim was visibly wider now, extending well into the lake. Nothing disturbed it, as if the water were frozen solid, although ice was impossible at this season. Whatever had condensed from the mist was clearly not ordinary water but a poisonous solution. Every child knew that some springs were deadly, indicated by a ring of crystallized salts. That put an end to any hope that the *dharlak* might be reclaimed after the lake had drained.

Shannivar tightened Eriu's girths in preparation for her descent to the encampment. The horse needed rest and better forage than the hilltop provided, and she felt drained in spirit as well as body. Yet she lingered for a time, watching the lake with her cousin, as if they were mourners for the death of their summering-place.

At the encampment in the dell, Shannivar stripped Eriu of his tack and hobbled him to graze with the other horses. She made a circuit of the camp, speaking briefly to everyone there. Zaraya had set up a tent and prepared a trail

meal for Shannivar, *bha* and porridge from parched barley.
Chinggis was asleep when Shannivar crawled into the tent.
He stirred when she pulled him close and wrapped him in
her arms.

"Mami?"

"Yes, little eagle, I'm here."

The sounds of the camp comforted her, and yet she
could not sleep. In her mind, the souls of the dead-eyed
horsemen wailed silently, unable to rest. She kept seeing the
monsters struggling as the waters rose, the stone-drakes and
winged serpents, the horned behemoths and the ice-troll . . .
and Zevaron drowning with them.

She had failed Tabilit once, when she'd held her bowshot.
This time, she had not failed. Why then was her heart so
heavy, her spirit so restless? She tried to pray, and the words
sounded as false as any promise made under *k'th*.

A war-leader does not weep.

Chapter Thirty-four

SHANNIVAR woke to the sounds of hushed voices outside the tent. A horse whinnied, close by. Despite her broken sleep, she came instantly alert. Chinggis was still in her arms, soft and heavy with sleep. Careful not to disturb either her son or Zaraya, she disentangled herself, pulled on her boots, and crept outside. It was not yet dawn, barely light enough to see by. Alsanobal had just ridden into camp.

"What's happened?" Shannivar asked, just as Zaraya emerged from the tent.

"The lake—it's changing," Alsanobal said. "Something's going on—"

"The *enarees*?" Shannivar asked.

"When I left, it was still too dark to see much," Alsanobal replied. "Their fires are lit again. That much I know. If they have resumed their chanting, I could not hear it above the wind. I sent Tarabey to check on them." Tarabey, on sentry duty, would have been the first rider Alsanobal encountered.

The rest of the camp was rousing, passing Alsanobal's news from one to the other in murmurs. Everyone looked to Shannivar. She did not know what weapons they might bring to bear against a new threat from the cloud lake. All hope—and all explanations—must come from the shamans.

She directed the best of her riders to come with her, except for Zaraya and a few others. When Zaraya protested, Shannivar pointed out that there was no one else she trusted to care for Chinggis. Zaraya cast an anguished glance at Kharemikhar but agreed to remain behind.

Before they had finished saddling their horses, Tarabey galloped into camp. "Shannivar! I bring dire news! The Rabbit clan *enaree* is dead, and two others are too weak to stand. That leaves only Bennorakh and the Black Marmot boy to deal with what's moving under the ice."

"What did he say?" one of the riders cried. "Something's *coming through* the ice?"

"No, under it," someone else answered. "But all the creatures were drowned. How could anything have survived?"

"Come quickly!" Tarabey exclaimed. "Bennorakh is asking for you!"

They pushed their mounts hard, arriving at the southwestern hilltop before the sun had cleared the eastern ridge. Two bodies wrapped in blankets lay in the shelter of a reed windscreen. Beside it, a smoldering fire gave off pungent, choking smoke.

Shannivar's heart ached at the sight of the bodies. She had not known these men personally; they had not been part of her clan the way Bennorakh was. Their courage and their sacrifice had been no less than that of any warrior going into battle, even if their weapons were of the spirit instead of the body. She sent a silent prayer that Tabilit would welcome them with the honor they deserved.

"Bennorakh!" she called above the fitful wind blowing from the lake.

"I am here." Leaning heavily on a younger *enaree*, Bennorakh emerged from behind the windscreen. He seemed to have aged a score of years overnight. His eyes were red, his cheeks haggard.

"What's happened?"

"See for yourself, Golden Eagle Daughter."

Dismounting, Shannivar and the others approached the edge of the hill, where a rocky outcropping formed a ledge. In the valley below, she saw that the cloud was gone and the whitened rim had expanded to cover the lake. The surface was not uniform, but rumpled in places like dirty ice. Other areas looked translucent, revealing darker shades beneath. In places, the sun gleamed on ice-slick hardness.

A rumbling, like thunder passing through solid rock, issued from the ice. A horse squealed and pranced, its hooves drumming the ground. Its rider tried to soothe it but it remained restive.

"I don't understand." Shannivar turned to Bennorakh. "Tarabey said something was coming through the ice, but I don't see anything. I thought the mist creatures were drowned, that we had seen the end of their foulness."

"Look . . . beneath the surface," Bennorakh wheezed. The skin around his mouth went pasty gray and he swayed on his feet.

Shannivar drew herself up and gave her best imitation of Grandmother's glare. When she was certain she held Bennorakh's attention, she said, "*I* will look. *You* will lie down. We have already lost two of your kind. We cannot lose you, too."

Without a syllable of protest, the *enaree* shuffled back to the reed mat shelter. Shannivar watched him, astonished at her victory. Then she turned her attention to the frozen lake, studying the broad gray ribbon, like a winter river swollen in flood, that cut obliquely across lighter areas. A flash like lightning was quickly followed by a darker shape, a shape that moved beneath the ice.

More flashes brightened the underside of the ice. Some bursts were so short and faint that unless Shannivar was looking directly at the place they arose, she could not be sure she'd seen them. Others were stronger, jagging over greater distances. More tremors rumbled underground.

Something had sheltered beneath the last remnant of cloud. It had hidden there while the *enarees* turned mist into rain and rain into an inland sea. It had gathered its strength, changing the water to solid ice. Now it hid beneath a frozen shield and the *enarees* were drained, their spells fading.

Toward dusk, the lights under the ice took on a ghostly luminescence. Occasionally, crackling broke the muted thunder. Something was happening in the murk of the lake, and she could do nothing about it.

She was so frustrated, she was ready to lead a charge into the valley. And do what? Shoot arrows at a lake of ice? Of all the torments of war, waiting was the worst. At least the two most weakened *enarees* had regained a measure of strength, or at any rate gotten no worse. They had gone down to the encampment, where they were being cared for. Bennorakh and the Black Marmot boy remained on their hilltop and continued to work their spells as best as they were able. As yet, nothing had emerged from the ice, but whether that was due to the confining power of the shamans, she did not know.

When a party of riders arrived to relieve those who had been on watch, Alsanobal advised Shannivar to go back to the camp with the others. "Eat," he urged her. "Get some sleep."

She set her chin. "No, I'll watch."

"Shannivar, you will drive yourself and everyone else mad. I'll send word if the *enarees* say there is anything to be done."

"If you stay, cousin, then so will I."

Alsanobal looked and sounded very much like his father, Esdarash, as he said, "We are indeed cousins, and you are war-leader. But *I* am chieftain, and *I* say you will be in no fit state to lead us if you go on like this." He lifted one eyebrow as if to say, *What goes for the* enaree *goes for the war-leader as well.*

Shannivar opened her mouth to protest, and then closed it again. He was right. She wasn't as tired as if she'd been riding hard and fighting all day. But anxious as she was, she would not make good decisions. "You'll send word?"

"I have said so," he replied, but more gently, because he had already won.

Chapter Thirty-five

THE next morning, the ice had crept over the lower slopes of the hills surrounding the lake. Shannivar could not make out its full extent, for haze cloaked the distant shoreline. Accompanied by Kharemikhar and Zaraya, she and Alsanobal climbed the *enaree*'s hilltop as soon as it was light. They dismounted for a closer look, leaving their horses a short way behind. Behind them, Bennorakh and the Black Marmot boy kept up a low chanting.

As best as Shannivar could determine in the pastel dawn, whatever grass remained on the base of the hills had been bleached white. It looked as if—but surely that was not possible—the ice had worn away the bedrock, undercutting the slope and forming a chain of cavernous pits. The shadows were too deep.

The sea of ice had changed. Ripples marred the surface, and yellow-tinged vapors drifted upward from crevasses. In the center, where the cloud had cast its shadow, the ice buckled upward, as if an underground mountain were pushing its way through. Something had arisen under the ice or perhaps in the bedrock beneath it. Or something in the mist itself had burrowed into the earth and was now inching its way upward, like an enormous, bloated larva about to burst forth from the carcass it had fed upon.

Rumbling shivered through the ground, louder and more insistent than before. The edge of the rock on which Shannivar and Alsanobal stood fractured and broke off. They both jumped backward as it went tumbling down the slope in a shower of pebbles.

"The lake's gotten bigger, hasn't it?" Alsanobal said.

Shannivar pointed to the southern rim. "You're right. It's risen. We thought we had it contained, that it was in our power." She glanced in the direction of the *enaree* and his assistant. "I don't think Bennorakh's spell is holding it any longer."

"You think it *wants* to be kept here?"

Shannivar nodded. "Think of water. In itself, it has no form. Spill it and it is lost. But pour it into a cup," she gestured with her hands, "or dam it into a lake—"

"Water doesn't do *that*."

"This isn't water, not the water we know."

"Then what is it?"

Shannivar turned her attention back to the shoreline. She had not been mistaken. The ice—if it were ice—had eaten into the hillside. Below its surface, it might also be corroding the valley floor, gouging into unguessable depths.

Alsanobal looked toward the distant hills where the women and old people, the children and those who could not fight had fled.

Another crack split the ice. Vents sent up jets that looked like filth-laden steam. Lights flashed beneath the surface. As Shannivar and Alsanobal watched, the central peak soared higher. Its frozen slopes shuddered and then, against all reason, it *bulged*.

Layers of brittle gray-white ice broke off in a thunderous clatter. The sound echoed off the surrounding hills, rising to an unbearable pitch. Shannivar bent over, clapping her hands over the sides of her head. Her skull rattled, and the noise built pressure in her head until she felt her eyeballs would swell and her eardrums would burst.

I am a daughter of the Golden Eagle! I will not be intimidated by mere noise!

Alsanobal was struggling to stay on his feet, his body bent under the curtains of sound. His mouth stretched wide, but Shannivar could hear nothing, not the cries of the other riders behind them, not the frantic neighing of the horses. Even Eriu was gripped by panic. White rimmed his eyes. He threw his head up, ears pinned back, muscles rigid.

Only Bennorakh seemed unaffected. With his assistant at his side, he continued to circle his watchfire. The riotous din from below smothered his chanting, but he kept moving. One measured step after another, lifting his dream stick, gesturing with his hands, he held fast to the pattern of his magic.

Rivers of darkness spread through the white opacity of the ice. In the crash and snarl of thunder, the cracks spread wide and wider. The peak of the central mass fell in on itself with a rumble, leaving an open cone like the mouth of a volcano. Cinder-laced fumes spurted from the rifts and gathered overhead, obscuring the sun. Shannivar smelled brimstone and the faintly metallic reek of lightning. Blue-white glare throbbed beneath the icy crust, lingering like ghostly branches.

Another thunderclap roared, before dying into angry muttering. The earth quivered, but less violently than before. Steam continued to pour from the vents, but for the moment, no new cracks appeared.

Shannivar straightened up. Her ears buzzed, but her hearing was returning. She caught muted booming and the sound of ice scraping over ice, but saw no new movement below. Behind her, riders were calming the horses and looking to her for orders.

"War-leader." Alsanobal's formal tone made her turn to face him directly. "What is to be done? The time of watching is done. Are we to flee or to fight?"

And, he was clearly asking, *how can we do battle against earth and air and water?*

Tabilit had given her no sign, no direction, and yet she had to think of something. They could not wait.

Bennorakh's chanting drew her attention. *He* was not giving up, not while he still drew breath.

We cannot fight this battle alone.

From the time before stories, the riders of the steppe had held themselves apart from the doings of other people.

They had neither sought nor accepted any outside alliance. Leanthos of Isarre had ventured into the steppe in search of help against Gelon. The Council of Chieftains had rejected the Isarran's proposals, even when Danar had promised not only truce but friendship.

Danar ...

She could not imagine the Gelonian youth without Zevaron at his side, a panther to Danar's red-gold lion. No, she must not think of Zevaron now, except as a creature of frost and flame, a tool of the Shadow of Shadows.

If only the chieftains had made a pact with Danar, if only Gelon, with its thousands of soldiers and hundreds of gods, now fought with Azkhantia.

Hundreds of gods ... Shannivar shivered at the memory of the Scorpion priest's enchantments. *There* was power, twisted into vile purposes, but power nonetheless.

"The Qr priest. Bring him here!"

Alsanobal looked puzzled but he said, "I'll go for him myself."

Shannivar turned to the riders waiting a short distance away. "Kharemikhar, go back to the camp. Make sure it's cleared and everyone is ready to ride. Zaraya, bring Chinggis to me. Please."

The Badger clan woman had been holding the reins of Eriu and her own bay mare, doing her best to keep them calm. She handed the black over to Shannivar and vaulted up on the bay.

A short time later, Alsanobal's horse scaled the last stretch on the incline and halted, breathing hard. The Qr priest rode behind him, his bound hands clutched to his chest. Shannivar barely recognized the man. Dust caked the robe that had once been white. Scabbed, half-healed scrapes covered his bare legs and feet. A ring of ashen skin encircled his mouth. His lips were chapped and split.

Alsanobal hurled the priest to the ground. Gasping, the priest wiped his mouth with the back of his joined hands, smearing blood.

Shannivar nudged Eriu closer, so that she looked directly down at the man who had tormented her. The scorpion brand on his forehead was no longer black, but an angry red, peeling around the margins. She studied his face and found none of the ruthless mania of before, only resignation.

"Do you know who I am?" She spoke in trade-dialect to test his understanding of that language. If she had to communicate in a smattering of Gelone and gestures, she would, but it would be better if they understood one another directly.

He rose to his knees. From his bearing, he expected to be executed.

"I asked you a question, man who speaks for scorpions!"

He nodded, leaving his head bowed. "I you hear, horse master woman."

Like his expression, his voice had changed. In it she heard a weary acceptance of whatever punishment might come.

"Look at me." When he complied, she saw that her suspicions had been correct. The Scorpion no longer peered out through his human eyes. That might end any hope of his being of use, if he no longer had access to his god.

"Get up. Go there," she said, pointing to the overlook. "Tell me what you see."

He walked to the edge of the rock. The wind had thinned the sulfur-tainted vapors, rendering stretches of the far shoreline visible. No trace of vegetation remained, and the underlying rock was now the color of old bones.

The priest's shoulders rose and fell, but he made no sound. Shannivar waited. When he looked up at her, tears streaked his cheeks. She was startled, for she had expected confusion or horror or even vengeful gloating. But not this. Not from a man who had made himself into a cesspool of malevolence.

"I did not know," he said in Gelone, more to himself than to her. "I did not know the world had such evil in it."

How could you not know? After what you did and what you served? Shannivar wanted to grab the priest by his filthy robe and scream in his face. That, or else knee Eriu into a rear, propelling the priest off the cliff.

With an effort, she controlled herself. Gladly would she cut him down in battle, but not as he was, helpless, his hands tied and his body wracked with sobs.

During their conversation, the soot-dark fog had crept up the denuded hillside. Like a hungry beast, it lapped at rock and soil. Then, as if gripped by a rip current, it retreated.

Shannivar's breath froze in her lungs. Alsanobal cursed softly.

Gouges, like wounds left by an immense, iron-clawed beast, ran diagonally across the naked earth. Thick, blood-dark liquid oozed from them. Some of the cavities looked big enough to hold a half-dozen *jorts*. A rider on camelback could not reach their upper edges. Other areas were masses of bubbles, crowded together so densely that their stone walls must be as thin as eggshells.

The ground shook once more. This time, a splintering sound cracked the air. The overlook edge broke into shards. Without thinking, Shannivar reached down, grasped the back of the priest's robe, and spun Eriu around. The weight of the priest wrenched Shannivar's shoulder, but she did not let go. With astonishing agility, the black pivoted and scrambled back onto solid land.

When Shannivar released the priest, he lay panting, curled on one side. She glanced over her shoulder as the opposite hill began to collapse in on itself, too. A keening arose in Shannivar's bones, in her heart, in her tearless eyes. Men and women died, and horses died, as did all creatures in their season. But never had she imagined such an unmaking of the very fabric of the steppe.

The Qr priest clambered to his feet. Blood seeped from the new abrasions on his legs and one corner of the festering scorpion image. He shuffled up to her. With painful stiffness, he bowed until his forehead touched the toe of her boot. When he spoke, his voice quavered.

"Power little have I. Qr not answer. Qr *gone*." The priest gestured to his scarred brow. He paused, searching for words. "Qr promise all power. Gelon call to power, power serve Gelon. Call Qr into world." He pointed to fracturing, fog-lapped hills. "Qr serve *that*. Gelon become . . . But I say, no. Service of me is yours."

She had been right: without his god, the priest was no more than a man like any other, feeble and ordinary. Then it came to her that this must be the case with all men and all women, that they were both weak and resourceful, wise and gullible. This priest—if priest he could still be called—had loved Gelon as she loved Azkhantia. He had thought he was acting for the best in his devotion to the Scorpion god. It was now up to Bennorakh to put whatever remained of the priest's knowledge and skill, not to mention his regrets, to good use.

Shannivar pointed to where Bennorakh stood beside his watchfire. "Go to the *enaree*, the shaman. Do what he says. Alsanobal, untie his hands."

The priest bowed again, once to Shannivar and then to Bennorakh. Shannivar spared a glance as the *enaree* led the priest to the fire and showed him the dream stick. Would the priest understand Bennorakh's magic? Could Bennorakh use Gelonian spells? The matter was out of her hands.

The hill was still collapsing, although at a slower rate than before. The fog thickened, obscuring long stretches of the north end of the valley. Glimpsed through the dust and fog, the ice seemed to be melting, or else evaporating into mist. Blackened areas lined the shore. Shannivar noted other signs of impending landslides. Curiously, neither the fog nor the sea itself spilled out along the gaps. An invisible wall kept it penned within the valley.

Zaraya returned, leading Chinggis on the sorrel mare. He pelted the mare with his heels, but his hands were quiet on the reins. His grin faltered when he reached the top of the hill and spotted the Qr priest.

"Come here, little warrior," Shannivar said in the calmest voice she could manage. She took the sorrel's lead line from Zaraya. "That man can't hurt you now. See, Bennorakh is looking after him, and Bennorakh has powerful magic."

Somberly, the child regarded the *enaree*. Then he turned his gaze toward the ruined valley.

"I don't know everything that's going on," she said, as much to herself as to her son. "But this I know—they will sing songs of what happens today. Perhaps you will be in one of them. Would you like that?"

Chinggis did not respond. The ground shuddered and the sorrel threw her head up, nostrils flaring. She pulled on the lead rope, but Shannivar held her firmly. Eriu stood like a rock, although he was sweating.

The hilltop was no longer safe. Shannivar shouted out commands for everyone, including the two *enarees* and the priest, to head back toward the camp and lower ground.

With a *whomp!* that was more vibration than sound, the ground fell away beneath them. Rock shrieked, splintering. The drop was only a foot or two, but it was enough to stampede horses and blind men with terror. A moment later, the ground steadied.

"Go! Go!" Shannivar shouted.

Hauling on the sorrel's lead rope to draw her close, Shannivar reached out to her son. It was a precarious stretch, taking her half out of the saddle. Chinggis came to her, grabbing her arms, and scrambled into place in front of her. She pulled him against her, flipped the lead line over the sorrel's neck so it wouldn't drag on the ground, and released the reins.

The other riders were already racing for the slopes. Only Alsanobal lingered, guarding their rear. Eriu wheeled to follow them, the sorrel in his wake. Before the black had gone more than a stride or two, however, the hilltop bucked and heaved. A fissure split the ground in front of him, too wide for any horse to jump from a standstill.

Shannivar clutched Chinggis, bracing herself in the saddle. The black sat down on his hindquarters and slid, sending a rain of dirt and pebbles into the gap. He came to a stop inches from the edge.

On the far side, Alsanobal hauled his horse to a halt. His mouth opened, but if he cried out, Shannivar could not hear him above the renewed din.

"Go!" she shouted, although in all likelihood he could not hear her, either.

Eriu recovered, snorting in the billowing dust. The sorrel mare crowded up behind him. The ground juddered again, almost knocking the horses off their feet. Alsanobal's roan scrambled down the far side of the hill.

As she turned her attention to her own route of escape,

Shannivar gazed back over the valley. In that moment, the miasma of dust and fog cleared, revealing the floor. Everything she had known was gone, even the contours of the land itself. Unnaturally smooth, white-bleached stone formed a broad cup from one blackened shore to the other, except for a trough running down the center. A cleft, straight and wide, ran down the lowest part of the trough. On the stony floor to either side, the creatures of the mist were rising to their feet. There seemed to be even more of them than before, rank after rank of stone-drakes and ice-trolls. One behemoth, gray as granite and boasting a rack of rocky daggers protruding from its elongated bony neck frill, was lifting its feet free, one by one.

For a terrifying instant, Shannivar felt herself being drawn into that lightless rift. Shadows, not all of them natural, cloaked its sides. Bedrock groaned, as if the cleft itself were sinking deeper and deeper into the earth.

Go!

A touch of one knee, a shift in her weight, and Eriu launched himself down the southern slope. The earth crumbled under his feet. Chinggis shrieked as the black dropped precipitously. Somehow, the horse managed to gain enough traction to leap to surer footing. Dirt gave way and gravel sprayed in all directions as he landed, gathered himself, and bounded on.

Nimble despite the added burden, Eriu scrambled down the hill, away from the waking monsters. Shannivar lengthened the reins, trusting to his instincts. Holding Chinggis tightly, she did her best to not upset the horse's balance. He'd escaped injury so far, but if he put a foot wrong and went down, the fall might break not only his neck but hers and her son's.

She risked a backward glance. The hill had not entirely fallen in on itself. Jagged ridges of stone still stood, like splintered, weathered bones. Underground thunder rumbled, muted now. Shannivar saw no sign of the others, horses and riders, and *enarees* and the Qr priest. She sent a silent prayer to Tabilit that they had reached safety.

A piteous whinny sounded above her. A moment later, the sorrel mare, her coat choked with dust and sweat, clattered out from behind a saw-edged ridge of rock. She raced toward them at a breakneck pace, by some miracle not stepping on the dragging lead rope. Shannivar halted Eriu just as the mare pushed up against him. Both horses were breathing hard, their muscles trembling from their frenzied run.

"Horsie!" Chinggis cried, waving one hand toward the sorrel. "My horsie!"

My Eriu . . . my wings. Shannivar patted the hot, damp neck. *You never fail me.*

The nearness of another horse calmed the mare. She stood still long enough for Shannivar to grab the lead line.

The ground had stopped shaking, and in their present location, there wasn't much danger from falling rock. Shannivar took a moment to assess her surroundings, to determine the best route to rejoin her riders. Framed by the surrounding hills, the land rose gently to the south. Haze blurred into the distance.

No, not haze.

Dust.

Dust from an approaching body of men, for neither steppe riders nor wild herds traveled in such a massed formation or in such numbers. Only Gelonian soldiers would create that elongated column of dust.

Gelon. Here. Now.

Chapter Thirty-six

SHANNIVAR made out the shapes of men on foot, wagons, and pack animals, as well as mounted onagers. Once she would have ridden out to battle the Ar-King's men with joy in her heart. If the invaders had any eyes in their skulls, they had already spotted her. Eriu's black coat would stand out against the pale, bare rock. How could she fight an entire Gelonian army by herself?

As Eriu shifted under her, Shannivar assessed her own situation. Tabilit had preserved her life and that of her son. Although she had neither water nor food, she still had her bow and arrows. She had two tired and shaken but reasonably sound horses. Chinggis had wet himself, but she had no dry clothing for him.

A war-leader does not weep.

The *dharlak* valley was a wasteland of stone and mud, inhabited by creatures of frost and fire, and even worse, whatever was pushing its way up from the depths of the rift. She should leave the Gelon to them, but her pride bristled at such a notion. She told herself it was not cowardice but duty. Tabilit had called her to defend the steppe and its people.

A war-leader thinks. Plans. Fights.

Then she remembered Kharemikhar's rumor of a strange

party passing the southern boundaries of Azkhantia. *Gelon and Meklavaran*, he'd said. Between dealing with the Qr priest, her own poisoning, and the struggle to contain the mist army in the *dharlak*, she'd scarcely had a moment to consider why two such enemies might combine forces. And whether that boded well or ill for her own people.

A small party detached itself from the rest of the force. She counted four riders, two on horseback, the others on onagers. The horses surprised her because Gelon never used them, but she supposed that if Meklavarans numbered among them, it was possible. Zevaron had known how to ride, and he had spoken of the horses in his father's stables.

Chinggis whimpered and twisted around, searching for comfort. The shock of their flight was wearing off. Shanni-var held him where he was. "See there? Those men are out-landers, dwellers-in-stone. We must show them how brave we Golden Eagle riders are." Chinggis subsided with a snif-fle.

The party halted, with the two horsemen in front. There was something familiar about one of them . . . *Danar?*

A smile rose unbidden to her lips. Of all the old friends she might encounter, he was the least likely. The last she'd seen of him, he and the Isarran ambassador were headed for Durinthe. Before leaving the Gathering, he had sworn friendship with the peoples of the steppe, witnessed by the council of chieftains. She believed in the sincerity of his promise. Relief swept through her as she realized this army might not be here to invade the steppe, although she could not guess their purpose. If it were possible to make a truce—or better yet, an alliance—with any Gelon, it would be with Danar. For the moment, it was enough to hope that she would not have to battle a Gelonian invasion force while trying to defend her own people from the monsters emerging from the valley ice.

Shannivar let Eriu set his own pace down the rest of the slope and halted him a horse's length from the newcomers. "Danar son of Jaxar, may your wisdom never fail and may your words always be true," she said in trade-dialect.

"Shannivar daughter of Ardellis! I can't imagine anyone I am happier to see!" Grinning, Danar replied in the same language. Outlanders were not good at masking their feelings, and he had always been frank and unguarded. "May your day be lucky! Is that the right thing to say?"

"My day is already lucky to greet an old friend."

Shannivar glanced at Danar's companions. The other horseman was an older man, with a frosting of gray in his beard and unbound, shoulder-length hair. By his dark eyes and honey-gold skin, he was clearly not Gelon. A sword hung at his belt, undrawn. He watched her with a gaze as keen as a hawk's. The other two men, on the other hand, had the pale skins, red-tinted hair, and armor of Gelon. They kept their expressions carefully neutral, but she read the wariness in their posture, the tension of their hands on the reins of their onagers.

What are you doing here? she wanted to demand, full of anxiety and hope. *Are you indeed here as my friend?*

Danar's eyes lit on Chinggis, and his eyes grew wide. "Is that—could it be—"

"This is my son, Chinggis son of Zevaron."

"God of Forgotten Hopes! *Zevaron's* child?" Danar exchanged astonished glances with the other horseman, then turned back to Shannivar. "I will explain our presence here, but for now, will you take my personal word that we are not here to conquer your people?"

"You have never spoken falsely," Shannivar admitted.

"I've got a long story to tell," Danar said, his gaze flickering toward the shattered hills, "and it looks like you do, too."

"Indeed, but there is a time for telling tales around a campfire and a time for action." Shannivar turned her head, indicating the ruined hillsides behind her. "You come at a time of great peril, for what was once a green and fertile summering-place is now a jumble of rock and ash. The lake where our herds used to water has turned to ice and fumes, and from them arise monsters out of legend."

Although the horseman and the Gelon soldiers masked their reactions well, she read astonishment and dismay in their eyes. Danar paled, frankly aghast. "We saw the collapse of the ridge," he said in a low voice, "but we did not know the cause."

"A rift has opened in the center of the valley, a portal for something even greater and more terrible than those we have already battled—ice-trolls and frost-wolves, stone-drakes like the one from the Gathering, and worse things. These creatures will not wait while we exchange news over skins of *k'th*. I do not know how much time we have, but your people must withdraw to a place of safety, and I must go in search of mine, for we were separated during the avalanche."

Danar shook his head. "We have not come all this distance to turn back now, not when our task is still unfinished. If we have limited time before what lies beyond those hills emerges, we must use it to best advantage. You will understand when we explain why we're here. As for your people"—his gaze flickered to the collapsed slopes—"may the Protector of Soldiers keep them safe."

The two Gelon murmured what Shannivar assumed was their own prayers. She was surprised they would beseech their god to protect the steppe riders, against whom they had fought since time beyond memory.

"A search under such conditions may take some time," Danar said, urgency plain in his voice, "and our discussion—our plans—cannot wait. Would you entrust one of my men to carry a message?"

Shannivar kept her face immobile, although Eriu caught her reaction and tossed his head. Danar could not seriously mean to send a lone Gelon. If the roughness of the broken hills did not block the path, and the emissary managed to find survivors, then her riders would most likely shoot him on sight.

"War-lady, if I might carry your message," said the other horseman, the one with the same honey-dark skin as Zevaron. To her surprise, he spoke Azkhantian, not trade-dialect, although his accent was not good. "I have some skill in finding people, as well as negotiating difficult terrain."

As he inclined his head to Shannivar, she saw that he was not as old as she had first thought. A deep vitality ran through him. Of the four, she judged him the most dangerous.

"Shannivar, this is Sandaron of Meklavar," said Danar,

turning to the gray-haired man. "He has my confidence, and he does not boast when he says he can find your people. He's also not likely to be taken for a Gelon."

"No," she said, "but we Azkhantians do not accept strangers on our lands."

"Yet Denariyan traders have traveled here by your leave," Sandaron said. "Have you a token I might carry? Or words that your people will recognize as coming only from you?"

So Sandaron was not entirely ignorant of the ways of the steppe. She had no trade token, but she gave him an arrow with its distinctive Golden Eagle clan markings. "If that is not enough proof, then tell whoever you meet the color of my bow," and she took it from its case and held it aloft. Sunlight gleamed softly on the opalescent wood, bringing forth inner fire. The Gelon murmured, their eyes dazzled at the sight, but Sandaron regarded the glowing bow calmly.

Shannivar put the bow away and gave Sandaron directions to the dell beyond the eastern ridge. Survivors from the landslides might be combing the broken hills, looking for her, but the encampment was still the best place to meet up with them. Sandaron inclined his head to her again and nudged his horse into an easy canter toward the eastern edge of the valley.

Danar led the way back to the main body of the army, finishing his introduction as they rode. The two Gelon were army captains, Irvan and Haslar, clearly trusted by Danar. "There's someone else you have to meet," Danar added.

The main body of Gelon had started erecting tents, settling up picket lines for the onagers, and digging latrine ditches. Shannivar repeated her warning to Danar that the army might have to move quickly and with little warning. Anywhere might be safer than camping right outside the mouth of the valley. He assured her that they would set watch. Perhaps he thought his number sufficient to defend themselves. She told herself that although he was utterly mistaken, a little rest would benefit them all. Eriu was in no condition to fight and needed to be walked cool. He'd likely be stiff tomorrow, even with careful tending. The sorrel would need time to rebuild her confidence or she'd be ru-

ined for anything that called for steady nerves. Perhaps
someone in the camp could spare an old shirt that she could
wrap around Chinggis while his own pants dried.

"Irvan, tell General Manir we'll meet with him shortly."
Danar rattled off a series of orders in Gelone. Grooms
came forward to take away their mounts. Shannivar looked
doubtfully at the one who stared, clearly terrified, at Eriu.
Perhaps he had heard tales of the savagery of Azkhantian
horses.

"Go with this man and do not bite him," she whispered
in Eriu's ear. "I will come to you soon." The black sighed,
blowing through loose lips, and went quietly. Head hanging,
the sorrel mare plodded behind him.

"This way." Danar gestured toward the smaller of the
tents. It was far more than a minimal shelter for the trail,
being tall enough to stand up in. A fly of gauzy fabric
shielded the open roof from the sun. Shannivar took her
son's hand as Danar pushed the door flap aside for them to
enter.

Light filled the interior of the tent and a carpet of deep
blue covered the ground. Three women, none of them Gelon, sat on cushions, setting out food on a low folding table
and preparing tea on a brazier.

Shannivar paused, struck by the domesticity of the scene.
Suddenly shy, Chinggis clung to her side. In all the years she
had fought the Gelon, she had never imagined them as doing something as ordinary as serving tea.

The youngest of the women rose with a dancer's grace.
Shannivar saw the tenderness in the fleeting smile she gave
Danar. One woman wore a flowing wrap of crimson silk,
clearly Denariyan, and the other, a long, closely fitting
sleeveless vest of blue-and-white patterned cotton over full
gathered pants and riding boots. Shannivar knew little of
outlander women, but there was nothing weak or silly about
any of them.

Danar went to the woman in the vest. "This is the Az-
khantian woman I told you about—Shannivar daughter of
Ardellis," he said, still speaking trade-dialect. "And her son.
Zevaron's son."

The woman in the vest put out a hand to steady herself

on her cushion. When she smiled, a radiance transformed her features. Weariness fell away, leaving astonishment and joy, a joy Shannivar had never before seen so clearly on a human face. With immense dignity, she got to her feet, went to Shannivar, and bowed.

"Be welcome to my tent, Shannivar daughter of Ardellis." Her trade-dialect, although accented, was clearly articulated. "I am Tsorreh san-Khored, daughter of Xianthe of Isarre. Zevaron is my son."

Shannivar felt as if the world had suddenly turned itself inside out, day changed for night, earth for sky. "You're ... you're dead."

"I assure you," Tsorreh replied gravely, "I am very much alive."

"But Zevaron said—he thought—"

"*Te-ravah*, clearly you should either have never died at all or else you should have remained decently dead," the Denariyan woman said.

"You are right, as usual, Jenezhebre-*dir*. Alas, it seems I have nothing to say about the matter. I am sorry to have brought so much grief to the people I love."

"All this fuss."

Shannivar stared at Zevaron's mother. "How can this be? Zevaron saw your body with his own eyes."

As she studied Tsorreh's features, Shannivar's doubts faded. In this woman's image, she saw the roundness of Zevaron's eyes, the strong arch of his cheek and brow, the length of his nose. More than that, she sensed the same stubborn pride, the same resolve, the same traces of pain and sadness. She would do well to not underestimate this woman. There were other ways of being formidable besides strength and skill at arms.

"He thought you were dead," Shannivar repeated, struggling to gather her words. "It all but destroyed him! He swore revenge on the Gelon, all who had done this to you. He went to the north, seeking the power to bring down the Golden Land—for your sake." Her temper flared at the unfairness of it all. "And it was all a lie! You have brought the world to the brink of ruin—all of us, not just the Gelon—for a *lie*!"

Shannivar whirled, pointed north, back toward the devastation that had once been a rich and fair valley. "Do you have any idea what he's done? What he's summoned up? *Do you?*"

For a terrible moment, no one spoke or moved or breathed. Shannivar's furious words hung in the air.

"Yes," Tsorreh said in a voice resonant with truth, "I do."

Shannivar's anger receded. She had thought that no one else could understand what she had faced—not just the army shrouded by the mist and the devastation of the valley, but most of all, the certainty that if Zevaron were not still leading that army, he was dead.

"Please sit down." Tsorreh's voice was velvet-clad adamant. If Shannivar had any doubts as to who was war-leader here, those few words settled it. "We have much to discuss and very little time in which to prepare."

"At last, someone agrees with me that you must not linger here!"

Tsorreh gave her a quick nod before continuing. "We are allies, unlikely as that seems, representing Gelon and Meklavar and Denariya. Now you speak for Azkhantia. I hope you will be able to set aside past differences, as each of us has. We face the same enemy, although in the past it has come in different guises."

Shannivar lowered herself to the cushion that the young woman deftly slipped behind her. Still clinging to her leg, Chinggis looked about curiously. Tsorreh smiled at him in a friendly manner, but when he did not respond, she turned back to Shannivar.

"I see that you understand me," Tsorreh said. "There is but one enemy of life, known by many names. It casts its shadow over every land."

"*Olash-giyn-Olash*," Shannivar murmured. "The Shadow of Shadows."

The woman in Denariyan red, the one Tsorreh had called Jenezhebre, added, "And the Eater of Souls."

"And the *Takryn-armara*, that lurks in the dark seas beyond the Mearas," the younger woman added. She handed Shannivar a white porcelain cup containing tea without the usual butter and salt. It was light, almost golden in color, and smelled faintly of flowers.

"And Qr in Gelon," Danar said in a voice edged in bitterness.

"Now we must face the original, the source of the many shadows," Tsorreh said, setting her own cup aside to cool. "Do you know of the ancient writings of Meklavar, of the *Te-Ketav*?"

"Zevaron spoke of it," Shannivar said. "I know of your great chieftain, Khored, and how he stood against this evil."

"As we must now."

Shannivar held her words with an effort. *Do you know what waits for you in the* dharlak?

Yes. Yes, Tsorreh did. And if that were true, she also knew what was taking shape in the rift, gathering substance and strength to emerge into the living world.

"We have Gelonian troops now," Danar said, "and your riders, if you agree."

"I have led mine against what lies in the valley," Shannivar said. "I have penetrated the wall of mist. I tell you, ordinary weapons cannot prevail against those creatures."

"We do not mean to win by physical force," Tsorreh looked grim. "Six of us bear the very *alvara* wielded by Khored's brothers in that battle."

Khored's Shield—the combination of colored gems Shannivar had seen in visions of the Meklavaran chieftain. The visions had come from Zevaron, shared during the trials of dreamsmoke. Shannivar had not the slightest doubt these things were real. She had seen and spoken with the Mother of Horses more than once. Tabilit guided her, as the spirit working through the great king had guided Zevaron.

In wonder, she searched the faces of the others. She found no trace of deception, but she did sense something else, like a thread of rainbow light running from one to the other, all except Tsorreh. A magical weapon to counter a supernatural foe! No wonder Danar had resisted her advice to leave. These people would not run from what was coming through the rift. If anything, they wanted it contained, so that it could not escape from them. They meant to engage it in battle, even as their legendary king had done with Fire and Ice. Their confidence—or perhaps their desperation— astonished Shannivar.

A chill brushed the back of Shannivar's neck. Zevaron had borne the seventh gem. "Six, you say? Not seven. Will six be enough?"

For a moment, no one spoke. The young girl went to Danar and slipped one arm around his waist. The Denariyan woman stared at her tea. Tsorreh lifted her chin, reminding Shannivar of Grandmother at her most determined.

"It must be enough," Tsorreh said. "In a moment, you will meet the others and we will confer with General Manir. For now, though, I would like to meet my grandson properly. How is he called?"

"Chinggis. The name is ancient and much-honored among us."

Tsorreh smiled at Chinggis, held out her hand to him, and said in Azkhantian, "Sweet one, I am your grand-mami. Will you come to me?"

Shannivar thought the child would refuse. He had been through so much in the past moons, more than most hardened warriors ever endured. Now this strange woman was speaking to him in his own language. He let go of Shannivar's leg, walked over to Tsorreh, and touched the fingers of her outstretched hand. Then, with a shriek and a giggle, he ran back to Shannivar. To Shannivar's surprise, Tsorreh laughed aloud.

"It's a good beginning," the Denariyan woman observed.

"Jenezhebre-*dir*, would you see to clean clothing for him until his own can be washed," Tsorreh said. "Offer him food or whatever else he needs. Shannivar will tell you."

One slender eyebrow arched upward in the Denariyan woman's dark face. "While I appreciate the compliment to my competence as quartermaster, I must ask if this is a ruse to exclude me from strategic planning."

Tsorreh turned to Shannivar with a conspiratorial grin. "Jenezhebre and our general, Manir, have almost come to blows on more than one occasion. He does not readily accept advice from women."

"Especially from me, it seems," the Denariyan woman

replied dryly. "I take that as a *no* and so will expect to participate fully when I return."

Jenezhebre provided breeches and a vest of brilliant green silk, too large for Chinggis but manageable with a belt, as well as a basin for washing and a cube of lemon-scented soap. Shannivar suspected that the clothing belonged to Jenezhebre herself. The others departed, leaving Shannivar to tend to her son. Chinggis curled his nose at the soap, but allowed himself to be cleaned and dressed.

By the time Shannivar emerged from the tent, the war council was waiting for her. Sandaron had not yet returned, nor did she expect that he might have made his way to the dell and back in so short a time.

The Gelonian general, Manir, was much as Shannivar expected, a tough-minded man accustomed to having his orders obeyed without question, no matter how harsh. She had already met the young woman attached to Danar, whose name was Marisse, and Jenezhebre. She assumed another of the magical tokens was carried by the quietly dangerous Sandaron. Two Meklavaran men, neither of them warriors, completed the six of whom Tsorreh had spoken. The one named Iskarnon looked as if he had been ill recently. Had he been a clansman, he would surely have become an *enaree*. The other, a middle-aged man, was soft in body but spoke well, and was called Ganneron.

After introductions, the *alvar*-bearers went off by themselves, apart from the Gelonian officers. Shannivar sensed an unspoken bond between them, as if they were listening to a conversation none of the others could hear. Tsorreh was not one of them, which surprised Shannivar, since they deferred to her.

Manir's aides set out folding chairs under a canopy of sorts, ringed with guards. Shannivar and Tsorreh appeared to be the principals, along with the general. A handful of his senior officers, including Irvan and Haslar, sat down with them. One seat was left empty.

As they were getting settled, Tsorreh said to Shannivar, "To avoid misunderstanding, it would be best to conduct the discussion in Gelone as well as Meklavaran. Will you trust me to translate into trade-dialect or would you prefer to have someone else do it?"

Shannivar sensed the respect underlying the question. "That will not be necessary on my account. I understand Gelone well enough."

General Manir began by relating how he had come to leave Meklavar, to serve Danar as claimant to the Lion Throne. He told the story in spare, concise terms, betraying nothing of his own sentiments. No god commanded him, only logic and law and an unswerving loyalty to Gelon. He did not admit to any failing on the part of either Cinath or his reckless sons, nor that he believed Danar to be more fit to rule than Chion. If he had any scruples about participating in what might be deemed a rebellion, he gave no sign. But who could say with stone-dwellers and outlanders?

Tsorreh's motivations were less opaque to Shannivar. The Meklavaran *te-ravah* cared for her city and its people, but their welfare was not her primary concern. The enemy, Tsorreh repeated, lay behind the vanguard of stone-drakes and ice-trolls. So the two were allies for the time being. Manir served Danar, and Danar was of one mind with Tsorreh.

Manir listened with quiet intentness to Shannivar's tale of her forays behind the mist wall and the monsters she encountered there. He asked for detailed descriptions of those fighting tactics that produced success. Privately, she thought the Gelon had little chance of replicating them while mounted on slower, less agile onagers, but Manir was clearly a man of intelligence and ingenuity. He might find a way to adapt his own resources to exploit the weaknesses of the mist creatures.

When the *alvar*-bearers reached the end of their almost-silent deliberations, Danar joined the general's circle and took the empty chair. "We have agreed. The incarnation is not yet complete, but it will be soon."

"How soon, Highness?" Manir asked.

"It is difficult to say. Something obscures our perception. It is as if"—he paused, brow tightening—"as if we see it through a pane of glass that is sometimes clear, sometimes mirrored."

Shannivar caught the flash of emotion on Tsorreh's face and knew they were thinking the same thing: *It is the* te-alvar. *Our greatest strength now shields our enemy.* "I do not know that Zevaron still lives. He was inside the valley when it flooded, although I did not see him die."

Tsorreh lifted her chin. "When Fire and Ice enters completely into this world, we will know. We will be ready."

"Until then, the rest of us must wait?" Manir scowled.

Danar countered, "This thing, this incarnation, is not an enemy that can be fought with steel and cunning."

Shannivar sat forward, restless. In this, she and the general were alike. She'd had all the *waiting* she could stomach.

Outlander fools! The creatures in the valley aren't going to wait! They'll come pouring through the gap right into your laps! You *can be killed, even if the stone-drakes cannot!*

"If you can sense the thing in the rift, it must be able to sense you as well," she said, looking at Danar but speaking to Tsorreh as well. "If I were not yet ready to fight, I would send out my servants to clear my path. You must move from this place."

Manir saw instantly what she meant. His bearing straightened and his eyes gleamed. Now he had a task and a purpose. "Then we ordinary soldiers must keep them penned in the valley. It goes without saying that you, Highness, should move your group to a more protected place, the heights perhaps."

Danar nodded. "It would be advantageous to use our eyes as well as the senses of the *alvara*. We could observe until the time came for us to act. Shannivar, what would you suggest? Where would it be best for us to set up our watch?"

She thought of the hills, weakened and undercut by the corrosive foam. The remains of the southern hill from which her own people had watched and where the *enarees* had gathered might be the best. With any luck, Sandaron would have met with her riders by then. If not, she would go in search of them after she had guided the *alvar*-bearers to the heights, for she doubted she would play a part in supernatural battle.

Shannivar waited until the meeting was breaking up to speak to Manir. She did not know how he would react to what she had to say, and she did not want to humiliate him or provoke a conflict when they needed to work together. He looked up when Shannivar approached.

"Lady rider," he said, inclining his head.

"You cannot hope to hold the entrance to the valley," she said in a low voice. "If you try, the result will be defeat." *Slaughter* would be a more apt description.

Manir's jaw muscles stood out briefly, clenching and releasing. The light in his eyes turned flat. He expected to die.

"We will do what we must, as Gelon always have," he said.

She eyed him warily. He would not ask for help and might not accept it if she offered. For her entire life, men like this one had been her enemy. Her father had died on their spears. They dwelled in stone. She had already given him a significant edge by providing knowledge of tactics against the mist army; she did not need to do more.

If they could not hold fast, more than the steppe might be lost.

"Your sacrifice will not achieve anything of value," she pointed out. "My people have stood against the might of your Empire as have none other," she told him. "Will you not listen to my advice?"

"You have no reason to help me."

I have reason to kick you in the balls for your imbecility!

She forced herself to breathe. Once, twice. "You have spent your life doing the bidding of your Ar-King. I myself have fought your kind since I could shoot an arrow over the rump of my horse. Once that was all the glory I sought. But I have seen stranger things, beasts out of legend, impossible happenings. The goddess herself—our Tabilit, Mother of Horses—has spoken to me." She shook her head, listening to her own words. "There is far more at stake here than either of our lands."

"So Prince Danar believes," Manir admitted.

"And you? Do *you* believe that the thing in the rift—the *incarnation*—threatens us all?"

"Does it matter what I believe, so long as I do my utmost?"

Shannivar's jaw dropped. No Azkhantian would say such a thing.

She closed her mouth. The Gelon was being honest with her. He truly did not think his own opinion mattered, at least not in this respect. He would do as Danar commanded, to the best of his ability.

He would see and then he would believe. Or if he did not, he was right—what did it matter?

"Listen to me, soldier of Gelon," she said, but in a less confrontational tone. "Your onagers are too slow and your archers are not accurate enough. But you have other strengths, the discipline and coordination of your men, their skill with sword and spear. My riders can supply what you lack."

For an instant, she saw genuine surprise in his eyes. She went on, "I must guide the *alvar*-bearers to the safest of the heights. From there, I will go in search of my warriors. We were cut off when the hilltop collapsed, but those that survived will not go far. Sandaron is looking for them, so they may already know I am here with you. If you can slow the monsters, not engage them but impede their progress, we will join you as soon as we can."

"I will not throw away the lives of my men. We will do what we must to give Prince Danar and his people the best chance."

It was as good as she could hope for. She went to explain things as well as she could to Chinggis. Although her heart ached at being separated from him again, she saw no other realistic choice. It was the best chance for her son's survival as well.

PART FOUR:

Zevaron's Peace

Chapter Thirty-seven

STEAM and dust churned the sky like the waves of a wind-tossed sea. Where the currents thinned before spiraling together, the sun hurled down lances of jagged brightness. Squinting, Zevaron pushed himself up from where he had fallen and silently commanded the light to free itself from that single, harsh spectrum. It resisted him. His lips tightened into a mirthless rictus. The unmaking of the physical world would come soon enough. It had already begun.

He took a moment to study his surroundings. The countermeasures of the primitive aboriginals had been their own doom. Pathetic savages! Had they thought to drown his servants, who neither breathed nor slept? Water was easily transformed into ice, and ice to steam, and steam to sheltering cloud, and then back to ice again.

Under the protective shroud, the layers of filth and desiccated corpses of plants had been scoured away. The valley floor was now sterile stone. Around him, creatures of the many races that comprised his army lifted their heads. The flood had scattered them and drained their vitality, but they would soon recover. And if they did not, they were as individually insignificant and impermanent as the steppe riders who had once formed his advance guard.

Echoes rippled through his mind, the riotous din of hillsides collapsing on their rotten foundations. Below the tumult thrummed a vibration too low for hearing, the slow corrosion of the bedrock beneath the valley.

Zevaron opened himself to the molten song. From a place beyond light, beyond void, beyond heat and form, the Essence took shape.

In a place unimaginably deep, the solidity of the world weakened and gave way. A fissure appeared, an infinitesimal discontinuity in the strata of rock. Slowly it enlarged, spreading upward. The pressure that moved *beneath* and *through* and *inside* all matter widened the crack. It pierced the surface, long and impossibly twisted, its edges jagged.

Zevaron's pulse throbbed like muted thunder. For some time now, his heart had seemed distant, the needs of his body irrelevant. He no longer slept but drifted through the hours like an unmoored ship. He turned for solace to the memory of when the world burned with the glory of frost, the incandescence of fire. Only then did his vision come clear, liberated from brutish distractions. Only then did he feel himself ice and cinders, at one with the fire of the heavens and the gelid core of earth, a single heart aimed at a single purpose, with all the world his to command.

He got to his feet and picked up his halberd, a long staff of steel-pale wood fitted with a razor-edged axe, from where it had fallen during the torrential rain. Spurs clicking on stone, he strode over to an ice-troll, his preferred mount. It lay on one side, slime dripping from its overshot jaw. In the watery overcast light, its hide looked lusterless. The stench of ashes clung to it. When the troll saw him approach, its eyes glowed, red and sullen. It heaved itself into a kneeling posture. Zevaron climbed nimbly to his perch atop its shoulders. With a shudder of its ice-slick hide, the beast moved off and began a slow circuit of the valley.

Beyond the pristine rock, the land sloped upward, growing more foul and green in the distance. The sight of it sickened Zevaron. Ice-trolls and arsinoths, frost-dragons and stone-drakes, they would see to its cleansing. His own task was to lead, not to purify.

The holy scriptures had not described a fraction of the

changes to come. What did they know, the scribblers? Their secret knowledge had not availed them. Their city had still fallen. His mother had still died in a Gelonian prison.

The army that he now led was another matter. What human weakness could not accomplish, the power of Fire and Ice surely would.

Without the prodding of Zevaron's diamond-chip spurs, the ice-troll shambled to a halt. He jabbed it impatiently with his halberd. It reared on its hind legs, moaning a protest. Pale blue ichor spurted from the wound. The ichor thickened and steamed as it oozed down the cragged skin. When Zevaron sank his spurs again, it trudged forward obediently.

The creatures stirred at his approach. So far from the White Kingdom, they went torpid without his will to drive them. He lashed them awake. Stone-drakes hissed, exhaling acid-laden steam. Winged serpents slithered and then took flight, while the thick-bodied, six-legged arsinoths shambled to their feet, swinging their horned heads. Sky-toppers, granite-dark behemoths massing twice as much as the arsinoths, moved ponderously forward, crushing stone to powder. Other creatures crawled in their midst, part-beast, part-mineral, some of them so unstable in size or shape, they had no names. The largest of the arsinoths, ill-tempered from struggling free from the mud, ripped up chunks of rock and hurled them into the air, where the winged serpents exhaled their frozen breath. When the shards crashed, they splintered into billows of powdered ice.

The cloud cover thickened. No sun would cast its poisonous rays on the battle to come. The smell of unspent lightning and sodden embers wafted down like perfume.

The rift widened ever farther, exuding a chill like the void between the stars. The stone on either side groaned as darkness spread outward from the margins. Obsidian fire smoldered in its depths.

Soon . . . Soon . . . The syllables echoed in Zevaron's mind. He could not tell if the thoughts were his own or the sympathetic resonance of something far greater.

Birth was an uncertain time. Transition carried with it vulnerability. Sparks were easily extinguished. Snowflakes melted. Human menace lurked in the world beyond.

Vigilance would prevail. Vigilance, and ruthless singularity of purpose.

Zevaron continued his reconnoiter. As he neared the southern mouth of the valley, movement drew his attention. A steep-sided mound of rubble marked one side of the gap. On the heights, he spotted a woman on a horse, silhouetted against the sky. The horse pranced, tail bannered in the wind. Sun flashed on the curve of the woman's bow. The next moment, she was gone.

He knew her. He recognized the way she carried herself, the sureness of her hands, the grace and strength of her body, her perfect balance in the saddle.

Zevaron frowned. The woman was a danger, a distraction. She stirred up disquieting sensations. From the time he had led his army from the White Mountains, she had placed herself in his path. Only once had he permitted her to approach. At first, she had not seemed so extraordinary. She had the same sallow skin and slanting eyes of the other steppe people. Like them, she wore riding clothes and a quilted vest, only hers bore the stylized image of a great bird of prey.

She had cried out for him to *remember*.

Remember what? What could he have had to do with her? The only use he had for any of the nag-riders was to clear the path to Gelon.

He had intended to make alliance with the Azkhantian riders, the fiercest fighters in the known world. They should have leapt at the chance to press the battle home to their traditional enemies, in razing the City of Scorpions. But they had proven recalcitrant, insular, caring only for their own petty concerns. They fought him as fiercely as they fought the Gelon.

Damn them! Damn them all! Damn her*!* His fingers tightened so hard, the knuckles of the hand holding the halberd cracked.

"Send her away," he had told his blank-eyed slaves. "I will not see her."

Zevaron had now reached the southern end of the valley. The clouds thickened, a blanket of cinder-gray vapors. In the profound lightlessness of the rift, an icy flame flared in unseen alarm.

Danger . . . danger on the heights . . .

Zevaron searched the piles of rock that had once been hills, golden and green in the venom of the sun. Now they were nothing more than ravaged dirt and stone.

Shadows coiled around his gut. Sorcery shimmered in the air, just beyond his mortal sight. Drums throbbed, or perhaps he felt only the sudden leap of his own pulse. Voices rode the wind, rising and falling, the words unrecognizable and yet fraught with secret meaning.

Nag-riders and witch-men! Things of straw and mud! And yet . . . yet . . .

Power raged like fever beneath the chanting. Something in him *woke*.

Zevaron rubbed his chest. It was an old habit, its purpose long forgotten. Irrelevant. Under his fingers something pulsed, distant. In a flash of half-memory, half-longing, he saw his skin not icy pale but sunlit amber . . . and the scintillation of pure gold just beneath the surface. He should know . . . he should know . . . *what?*

Almost, he knew. Almost, he remembered.

Damn the woman! Damn them all!

Bile filled Zevaron's mouth. He spat, watching with satisfaction as the liquid froze and shattered into steaming shards on the ground. He would crush the earth these nag-riders held so dear. He would obliterate this woman and anyone who stood with her. The wind would scatter the dust of her bones. She would never trouble his thoughts again.

As for the rest, he would throw them on the pyre of Aidon. Gelon would pay. Gelon would burn.

Incandescence flashed, exultant, in the rift.

Burn . . . Freeze . . .

Zevaron raked his spurs across the flanks of the ice-troll. The monster heaved itself over the lip of stone that marked the end of the valley. From here, the steppe opened up into flatter terrain. The land beyond the ruined hills was no longer empty. A war-party had assembled, some on horseback, others mounted on Gelonian onagers, still more on foot.

A glow ignited in Zevaron's heart as he surveyed the Gelon arrayed before him. They seemed to be waiting for him, these men with their puny shields and swords, their undependable beasts, these men whose bodies broke and burned so easily. From the ranks before him, an onager squealed. It must have caught the reek of the ice-troll. He drank in its terror. The men were afraid, too, even though they did not cry out.

Zevaron prodded the ice-troll with his halberd. It bellowed loud enough to strike paralysis in any mortal foe.

Now let them taste the poison of fear, of pain, of their own deaths.

With a thought, he launched the winged serpents. They hurled themselves into the air, green and silver and ice-white. Their bodies undulated with the strokes of their wings. Caustic steam spurted from their gullets. Here and there, a droplet fell and where it landed, the earth blackened.

Zevaron peered through the fumes. Against all sense and reason, however, the men held their ground. Swords remained high, a sea of blades. He had seen swords like that before, standing on a high place . . .

The heights . . . Look to the heights! There lies the true threat.

Threat? The nag-riders were cowards all, and the shamans stayed in hiding.

Over the drumming of his heart, Zevaron heard shouts from the waiting soldiers. The first winged serpent was closing fast. He sensed its hunger.

At the last moment, the Gelon raised their shields. They moved as a unit, each shield precisely overlapping its neighbor. Not a hair-thin gap remained.

Most of the snakes swerved and pulled up, wings beating frantically, but the foremost reacted too late and smashed into the barrier. Yellow-tinted steam shot up from its mangled carcass. Its blood glowed dully on the polished metal. The Gelon dropped his smoking shield. Immediately, his comrades shifted their positions to cover him.

Stone-drakes and frost-wolves yammered in frustration. Behind them, one of the sky-toppers rumbled. It was difficult for the massive creatures to stop, once they had begun moving. Their nature urged them to keep on, slow and inexorable, crushing everything in their path.

Zevaron released a gaggle of wolves. Eyes blazing, they heaved themselves forward in great lurching strides over the rutted earth. Their claws rattled on the bare rock of the valley.

The Gelon lowered their shields, overlapping them in front. In unison, without the slightest disruption of their formation, they shuffled forward a step. Sun glinted on their helmets, crescents of brightness above their shields. As one, they took another step, tightening their ranks still further.

The wolves increased their speed. Patches of crazed, whitened clay marked their footsteps. Their yowling, harshly metallic, filled the air.

The Gelon did not retreat.

The leading wolf hesitated. The inferno glow in its eyes wavered. In all the time its kind had run with Zevaron's mist army, it had never encountered a prey that stood firm against a charge.

"Steady!" shouted one of the Gelonian officers.

The frost-wolf gathered itself again, arching the sinuous length of its spine, and leaped. The others followed an instant later. Their bodies hurled through the air, high enough to clear the wall of shields.

"*Now!*" came a shout from the Gelonian line. The front row of men dropped to their knees. Behind them rose a palisade of spears, braced hard against the ground and angled outward.

The wolves twisted in midair, but it was too late to change course. A moment later, they impaled themselves on the spears. The sharpened steel slipped through their unnatural flesh and jutted out their backs. One or two writhed, emitting cries like metal snapping. Others went instantly still. Ocher liquid, stinking of sulfur, oozed from their wounds.

In the silence that followed, the soldiers inched forward. As before, they hunkered down behind their shields. Were they going to stand there all day, enduring one salvo after another? Why didn't they counterattack? The Gelon might be many things—rapacious and cruel, yes—deceitful, always—but they were not stupid. Such men had set fire to the gates of Meklavar and brought the city to its knees.

At the thought of those walls and towers, those soaring mountains, Zevaron felt a rush of warmth behind his breastbone. Part of him still stood on those ramparts or in the Great Hall, bathed in the light pouring through the stained-glass windows. Magic thrummed from on high, voices rising in wordless descant. Colors shifted, danced . . .

Gold and crimson sang to him, and the deep green of summer, and pale rose and purple and yellow and blue, achingly clear blue that stretched on forever. They called to him. They summoned him.

The heights . . . rasped through his mind.

The colors winked out, smothered in a whiteness of frozen ash.

Zevaron turned the ice-troll as the inner voice urged. The avalanches had left the inner hillside so jagged and steep that not even the nimblest of his creatures could scale it. He could have sent the winged serpents, but he dared not risk them.

So the Gelon thought they could stand against his army? Their maneuvers might prevail for a moment, an hour, against the smaller creatures, the snake-dragons and frost-wolves. But no human troops could withstand the arsinoths and sky-toppers, or the form-shifting mineral beasts. Against the terrible power that even now coalesced within the abyss, there was no defense.

Zevaron felt rather than heard a sound like the earth itself splitting apart. Dark fire pulsed through his veins. Frozen tendrils clutched his heart. Pain, hot and metallic, lanced through his chest. His lungs struggled for breath.

Behind his breastbone, a tiny sunburst flared, no greater than a pinpoint of brilliance. For an instant, it softened the glacial brittleness of his flesh. Air flowed into his lungs, bearing the faint smells of moist earth, of green shoots, of sun on running water, of heated copper.

Ash-pale light shot through the overhead clouds. Magic shimmered on the heights, a tapestry of human song and celestial hues. The pallor directly above the hill thinned to the color of a clear autumn sky. Sun filled the gap and poured down over Zevaron and his forward troops. The shields and armor of the Gelon gleamed. The stone-drakes scuttled back, mewling.

The thing in the rift flinched. Tectonic shudders shocked through earth and air.

The ice-troll barely managed to keep its feet. It threw back its head and wailed. The cry was taken up by other creatures.

"Enough!" With voice and will, Zevaron silenced them.

The witch-men were the cause of this, but their puny spells would not avail them for long. Hills could be scaled and leveled, mountains could be ground into deserts, and plains flooded and frozen. If the Gelon thought to impede him, they would discover their error soon enough.

The sky-toppers and mineral beasts were too far behind to be of immediate use. Impatient, Zevaron summoned the nearest pair of arsinoths. They responded, trudging forward. As they left the valley floor, they dug their horns into the still-living earth. With powerful wrenches, they hurled gigantic clods aloft. The gouges smoked, oozing slush that reeked of phosphorus and cinders. Where the chunks of earth rained down on the Gelon, they smashed into acrid dust.

Let the Gelon choke on *that!*

Several of the onagers panicked, throwing their riders. Bolting, they trampled the nearest soldiers, but still the front line held fast.

The stone-drakes and one of the frost-wolves sidled forward. Slavering in anticipation, the wolf sprinted ahead. An arsinoth put on a burst of speed, building up momentum for a charge. It lowered its head, leveling its horn.

Soon, the Gelonian line would break, and the slaughter would begin.

Chapter Thirty-eight

AN Azkhantian rider bounded out from behind a jumble of rock at the base of the hill. It was the same woman who had so disturbed Zevaron's thoughts. Her black horse flew across the earth. On her heels raced mounted men. Their horses leaped and scrambled over the broken ground.

The arsinoth swung its massive head toward the riders, but too slowly. The lead rider—the woman—galloped across its path. She twisted in the saddle and loosed an arrow over her horse's rump. The arrow struck the flint-hard arch of the arsinoth's brow. The metal tip plowed through the tough hide and into the eye socket, drawing a rush of blue-green blood. Trumpeting, the arsinoth tossed its head. Blood sprayed from its injured eye. The other riders galloped between Zevaron's army and the Gelon. They split into two groups, whooping as they set off a volley of arrows. Their horses wheeled without missing a stride.

Zevaron could not understand what he saw. The steppe riders were *protecting* the Gelon? That made no sense.

Still bawling in pain and fury, the arsinoth turned and lumbered after the woman archer.

"No!" Zevaron shouted.

It swung around just as a handful of stone-drakes

charged the Gelon. About half of them collided with the
arsinoth's forequarters. Others tripped and went sprawling.
One huge, splay-toed foot came down on a fallen drake.
Stone-brittle bones snapped and the mineral-laced hide
split apart. Enraged, one of the drakes sank its fangs into
the arsinoth's unprotected flank. The behemoth wrenched
its head around, trying to rid itself of its attacker. Dust
spewed up in great clotted billows.

Zevaron sent a silent command to the half-blind arsinoth, which was now lunging in a circle. Its six feet pummeled the packed earth. The stone-drake went limp,
dangling from where its teeth still anchored it to the arsinoth's hide.

The arsinoth did not respond to Zevaron's orders. The
node of awareness that animated it had gone blank, washed
in madness. It kept circling and bellowing, snapping at the
carcass of the stone-drake. Careening, it trampled yet more
stone-drakes that were not quick enough to scamper out of
its way.

The Azkhantian riders sped past, raining arrows at the
frantic beast. This time, they were shooting for its remaining
eye. Through the pandemonium, the Gelonian line held
firm. Their only movement was a slow approach of the middle and rear ranks, as if they meant to shore up their comrades at the fore.

If he could regain control of the arsinoth and direct its
frenzy, it would smash through the line of riders as if they
were straw. Their horses wouldn't stand a chance against its
massive bulk. Then he could drive it into the midst of the
Gelon.

The ice-troll lurched forward, drawn by the stench of the
arsinoth's blood. Zevaron made no effort to stop it. He
needed to be closer to the commotion. Before the troll had
taken more than a few lumbering steps, however, it faltered.
It turned its nose to one side, slit-nostrils flaring, neck and
shoulders rigid.

Through the haze of dust, the woman on the black horse
pelted back toward them. Her bow shone, iridescent, in the
sun.

Rainbow-hued light poured down across the forefront of

Zevaron's army. Slate-dull hides glittered in a dozen fleeting shades of color. The wind carried the scent of water cascading over mountain stone, of wildflowers in the rain, of ripening barley.

Heat crested in Zevaron's breast, a wave of scintillating brilliance that threatened to set ablaze the lump of ice that was his heart.

Incandescent frost roiled up in the depths of the rift, and in response, pain shot along Zevaron's nerves. His chest muscles locked. His vision went white. Then it cleared so that once again, he saw the world through a film like rime-pale cinders.

"Zevaron!" The woman rider was almost upon him. The horse ran with head outstretched, tail a banner of ebony silk stitched with white. Against all sense, the woman threaded a path behind the arsinoth, through the milling drakes and straight toward Zevaron.

The woman shot another arrow from her opal-hued bow. For a fraction of a heartbeat, he saw it speed toward him, toward the quiescent echoes of gold in his chest. It landed instead in the throat of the ice-troll.

She could not have missed, not at this range. She was a warrior of the steppe, a daughter of the Golden Eagle.

The troll gave a strangled cry and reared on its stumpy hind legs. When it wrenched its neck from side to side, Zevaron saw that the arrow had lodged in its windpipe. Only a short length of shaft and feathering protruded from the wound.

The troll pawed at the arrow, tearing its own flesh. Ichor spurted from the wound. Twisting, it lost its balance. Zevaron had only a moment to jump free. He landed hard. The impact jarred every joint in his body. Somehow he managed, by luck or instinct, to roll away from the spot where, a split instant later, the troll slammed into the earth.

"Zevaron!" A voice pierced the ruckus.

Zevaron pushed himself to sitting. Inhaling against a jab of pain, he gathered his feet under him. By all the powers of Fire and Ice, by the Most Holy, he would meet his death standing.

The woman did not slow the horse as she neared him. In

a single fluid movement, she slipped her bow into a case behind her left knee and reached down toward him. Her hand was empty, her fingers outstretched. Battle-grime masked her cheeks, which were the color of sun-touched honey, but her eyes gleamed.

Zevaron. Beloved. Come with me!

Colors danced, blue and rose, yellow and green of valley grass, purple and crimson . . . and the gold within him answered.

Though his entire body quivered with the effort, he lifted his hand. Touched her fingers. *Remembered . . .*

Lying with a woman—*this* woman—beneath a shared blanket, while outside the felt walls of the *jort*, the night sky rippled with color. They had made love with stormy passion and aching sweetness. His body retained no imprint of it, only of what happened after . . .

His back was to her, as if he could shut her out, along with all the pain of the world. Then he felt her lips like sun-warmed petals against the ridged scars. He had never in his life imagined such tenderness. Over and over, she had traced the pattern of his suffering, his humiliation, his despair. She left a trail of tears as well as kisses.

As if a stronghold had been unlocked, as if his heart had burst its armor, he told her then. Of the flogging that almost killed him. Of the slave-master who had laughed when he said Tsorreh was dead. Of discovering his mother alive. Of seeing her lifeless body in Cinath's prison.

"And there was nothing left . . ." he had said, "except—" *except to bring down those who ripped her from me not once, but twice.*

He had kissed her then, this woman who now reached out to him, kissed her brow, her lips, her breasts, her belly.

Through it all, he had thought, *I have always been alone. Until you. Until now.*

Zevaron's awareness returned to the battle. Horses whinnied, desperate. Men screamed, and bodies thudded into the ground. The arsinoth's maddened bawling smothered the other sounds. The reek of the troll's ichor drenched the air.

At the last moment, before Shannivar's fingers could

close around his, a chill so cold it burned blasted through Zevaron's flesh. Reflexively he jerked his hand back. The skin on his hand went numb, even as white-hot pain jagged along every nerve. His mouth filled with charred acid.

The black horse raced past.

Zevaron found himself on his feet. He held the halberd, although he had no memory of having picked it up. Its solidity reminded him of his purpose.

The world appeared red, as if he now viewed it through a mist of blood. With a sense beyond hearing, he felt a howling in the abyss. Its reverberations shivered along his bones, blanketing all other sound.

Like the clamor of a distant bell, gold chimed.

His thoughts shredded like bits of blizzard-driven snow. A whirlwind, ice and flame, scoured away his doubts. He had been wrong about so many things. That night with the woman and all the nights that followed had been beguilement, distraction. A cheat, an illusion sent to snare him. The only thing that mattered was opening the way for Fire and Ice to come into the world. Even now, it was gathering form, coalescing, emerging in all its might and glory. Ice howled through the chambers of his heart.

Like the sun breaking through storm clouds, yellow light glimmered overhead. In that moment, it seemed aware, alive. Intelligent. It thought to summon him. To rule him.

In answer, he lifted the halberd in both hands above his head. It was time to return to the battle. The stone-drakes and mineral beasts of the front line were slinking back toward the valley. The Gelon, under the cover of the riders, had advanced even farther and now guarded the base of the broken hill.

Two riders wheeled their mounts away from the fallen ice-troll. The great beast lay still. The arsinoth was down, too, pierced by a dozen arrows. Many of them had hit vulnerable points, eyes and throat, and the thinner hide behind its shoulder.

The nearest arsinoth was some distance back. It must have retreated at the sight of its fallen comrade. Zevaron reached out with his mind and tightened a noose around its dull-witted thoughts. He sensed fear and a simmering desire to rend, to dig, to mutilate. Deftly he shaped that need. Bawling, it broke into a shambling run in his direction. Frost-wolves and mineral beasts scattered before it. The riders fled.

Zevaron waited until the arsinoth was almost upon him. Stepping to one side, he hooked the back-curved talon of the halberd blade into the hollow above the eye ridge. The point caught and held. The arsinoth reacted to the pricking by swinging its head away. Zevaron kept hold on the halberd staff as momentum pulled him up. He braced one foot on the creature's heavy shoulder, then scrambled onto its withers. The ridge of bone and ligament was not as solid a seat as the ice-troll's shoulders, but he held on.

He touched his spurs to the arsinoth's sides. It flinched, for it had never been ridden, never commanded by a man on its back. It was not made to serve in this way as the ice-trolls were. Nonetheless, another jab sent the arsinoth lumbering forward. It set off in the direction of the Gelon, so Zevaron needed only a little goading for control. Emboldened, his army followed.

He did not mean to attack the Gelon themselves. The true enemy lurked on the hilltop above—the glint of gold, the iridescence of color and thrumming song. The Gelon were simply in the way. Before he reached the first rank of shields, the riders came racing toward him from two directions. A man on a gray roan led one group, while the rest followed the woman on the black.

Wind-slashed ice streamed through Zevaron. The colors of the world faded into lustrous white. No longer were the oncoming riders garbed in indigo and madder red, nor were they mounted on horses of chestnut and bay, dun and ebony. No longer did rainbow hues radiate from the hilltop. All washed to shades of gray in the true light of the world.

The power of glaciers, of mountains, of comets, of the dark between the stars, froze his blood and seared his bones. Ice nudged him, slow as flowing rock and as inexorable. A sense of imminence radiated from the rift. He felt it behind his heart, in the beating dark and the chill. *Let her come— let them all come!*

A few paces from Zevaron's arsinoth, the roan horse

slowed. Its head went up, eyes rolling, nostrils flaring wide. It dug in its hooves and slid stiff-legged to a halt. Only the rider's skill kept him in the saddle as the horse scrambled backward, trying to bolt.

Zevaron urged the arsinoth to go faster. It tensed, for a moment rebellious, and jabbed its horn into the earth. Bracing itself on its hindmost four legs, it shoved. The earth split apart into a ragged trench. With a resonant cry, the arsinoth jerked its head up. Lumps of dirt and grass went hurling through the air.

Over the valley, clouds darkened, pouring out cinder-dark streamers. They wafted over the battle, bringing a sultry chill. Zevaron laughed, and a rumble of thunder vibrated through the ground. Lightning flashed behind the clouds.

Even though the steppe horses were trained for battle, the rain of foulness soon broke their nerve. Panic-stricken, they scattered until only a few remained. The black horse never faltered. It sped past as the woman drew her bow and shot over the horse's retreating rump. The arrow flew low, skittering across the arsinoth's beak-sharp nose.

Startled, the arsinoth reared up on its hind legs. It crashed back to earth, its forelegs rigid. Zevaron slid forward and almost tumbled over its head.

The woman turned her horse for another pass. She did not mean to kill, only to bar the way, to keep him and his army away from the hill. A handful of riders, perhaps heartened by her boldness, forced their horses closer.

Zevaron glared at the woman rider. She had readied her bow, the bow that glinted like the inside of a precious shell, like sea and sky. He drew on the power that flowed into him from the rift. Vitriol laced his veins, numbing as it burned. He gathered it in his hands, but before he could send it forth, the black horse plunged into the midst of the frost-wolves and stone-drakes, the slithering shadows, even the mineral beasts. Scrambling over the rough ground, the horse circled behind the arsinoth and leaped over the trench like an ebony eagle.

Zevaron cursed aloud, because he could not blast them without inflicting massive damage on his own creatures. This woman had no such limitation. With every step, it seemed, she fired another arrow. The moment one was loosed, her hand whipped another from the case beside her left knee. The opal-sheened bow sang out with each shot. The other riders fired in volleys, no longer just two riders— five, six, eight!—how could so many be willing to go up against the arsinoth?

One of the shadow beasts belched flame, igniting the arrow that sped toward it. The others were not so fortunate. A handful went down, shot through the eyes or behind the shoulder, or hamstrung and immobilized.

How could stone and fire, ice and ichor, fall to mere arrows? Human weapons should not have touched them. When Zevaron had conquered the northern clans, none of their resistance had made such an impact. But none of them had such a bow, a bow that sang of magic. None of them rode haloed in rainbow glory.

Zevaron aimed a spout of burning lye at the black horse. He did not care who or what else he hit. The only thing that mattered was to have that beast and its infuriating rider wiped from existence.

The caustic acid shot through space, as searing bright. The woman's eyes widened. The black horse seemed to pause in midstride, all four feet off the ground.

A clangor rocked the world, reverberations of a colossal gong. Zevaron's senses spun. His vision fractured and his hearing was split into a thousand jarring sounds. His muscles jerked, arms and legs thrashing so hard that he had to throw himself forward on the arsinoth's shoulders to keep from falling off.

The ball of vitriol exploded, disgorging clumps of snow-pale ash in every direction. The black horse landed, slowed, and turned, hooves dancing over the broken ground. The woman still held her bow, another arrow nocked to the string.

From the abyss came a temblor of rage. The rainbow light flickered and Zevaron thought it might fail entirely, but then it steadied.

The arsinoth clambered to its feet, stiff and unbalanced. Shuddering shook its frame. Somehow, Zevaron had no memory of how, it had scaled the lower part of the hill.

Ahead of Zevaron, the line of the Gelon had broken. To

either side, soldiers and their animals milled around, some in mindless retreat, others struggling to reform their ranks. The officers shouted out commands, trying to rally their men. Their efforts would be of no use. Already, a cadre of mineral beasts and stone-drakes swarmed into the breach. They fell upon the unshielded men.

The arsinoth raised its snout, scenting blood. Dipping its horn, it swung its head toward the nearest fighting. Zevaron held it back, refusing to be diverted.

Up! He touched the arsinoth with his spur-clad heels. It tensed, balking. Zevaron set his jaw and repeated the mental command, this time reinforcing it with another jab. With a rumble of resentment, the arsinoth moved forward. One step and then the next, testing its footing before shifting its weight, it heaved itself aloft. Other creatures followed, but reluctantly. They didn't like the naked dirt, still redolent of living things, any more than the arsinoth did.

Just as Zevaron expected, the riders retreated up the hill. Their horses snorted and jigged sideways as the arsinoth advanced. Soon they would scatter and flee, and this time there would be no regrouping, no second chance. The man on the silver roan shouted and pointed back toward the valley.

The rift now extended for many miles, even wider than before. A fleet of Denariyan pirate ships could have fit inside. The surrounding terrain bulged upward, taking on the appearance of an elongated volcanic cone. Cracks laced the sides. As Zevaron watched, the layers of stone tilted until they were almost vertical. It was difficult to tell at this distance, but he judged the topmost ridges to be half the height of the surrounding hills, and rising fast.

Molten rivers cast ruddy shadows over the inner sides of the rift. Shadows moved in the blood-tinged darkness. No, not shadows . . . *a* shadow. One shadow. The shadow from the beginning of time.

Fire and Ice . . . The whispered thought echoed in his mind, sweet-toned like a bell. Fire and Ice and a name, a name he almost remembered. *Remember* . . .

He imagined the coalescing form, the heart of shadows, spun of dark and cold and searing flame, of crushing im-

mensity and utter void. It craved release, and lusted for the
world that now lay almost within its grasp.

Storm clouds piled high and thick overhead. Lightning
jagged down, harsh and bright. Where it touched the slopes,
it shattered stone. A peal of thunder followed, then roll after deafening roll with hardly a moment between. Blue-
white branches shot earthward. Shock waves, higher and
harder than those of any sea storm, racked the ground.
Fumes stinking of brimstone and phosphorus, of magma
and rime, spurted from the newly formed vents.

Blood seeped from Zevaron's ears. His teeth ached and
his lungs labored to draw in the ozone-laden air, but a fierce,
inhuman joy seized his heart. *It is coming. Soon, soon.*

Oceans would turn to dust and mountains to barren desolation. The very earth would be unmade. Not only Gelon,
but all the nations of the living world—Denariya with its
stinking incense, its chants and dances. The frigid wastes, the
Fever Lands, the sea-rat ports of Isarre and the island nations. And Meklavar.

Ah, Meklavar.

Ice-trolls and arsinoths would batter down the walls,
winged serpents would rain down brimstone and frost from
above . . .

. . . and the great incarnation of Fire and Ice would tear
down every tower, to the last brick and stone and morsel of
mortar . . .

. . . not a single living thing, not a page of one of those
accursed books, not a shard of painted glass would remain,
not a particle of that vile sorcery. For all eternity, it would
be as if the upstart king and all his descendants had never
existed.

Movement within the rift drew Zevaron's attention.
Shapes crept from the fire-licked depths—not Fire and Ice
itself nor any of its creatures that had yet walked or crawled
or flown beneath the sun. He could not be sure what they
were. Darkness cloaked them, so that he caught only fleeting glimpses, yet even those were enough to make his guts
writhe—oozing, hump-backed things—skeletal things with
too many appendages, with hooked stingers the size of
horses—things that trailed tentacles that bulged and

twitched—things with grotesquely distorted bat wings and the eyes and jaws of wasps.

A thought came to him, unbidden, that he was one of them, perhaps the most hideous monster of all.

Gold pulsed behind his breastbone, warm like summer sun and fragrant as lilies. Gold echoed on the heights, falling away into a veil of pale rose and blue, of green and butter-yellow, of scarlet and twilight purple.

A clap of sound, like a hundred thunderbolts at once, burst from the rift. The shock of its passage shuddered through the hillside. The arsinoth staggered but somehow kept its feet. Horses screamed, scrambling for footing as the ground shifted and slid beneath their feet.

The black horse reared and neighed, a brassy challenge. With a sharp glance at Zevaron, the woman spun her mount and galloped away.

Let the she-rider run! In the end, flight would not save her.

Chapter Thirty-nine

THE volcanic cone was visibly taller now. Its slopes extended from one side of the valley almost to the other. The stone was buckled and torn. Vents burst through the crust, giving off gray and yellow steam. In the shadow of the thickening clouds, the fumes took on the hues of clotted venom. Within minutes, they obscured the far hills, which were now collapsing, their foundations eroded and undercut. The din of a dozen landslides blotted out all other sound, except for the rolls of thunder.

More of the monstrous creatures emerged from the rift, crawling and slithering or taking to the turbulent air. A bevy of winged serpents circled upward. They were larger and more numerous than the ones Zevaron had previously commanded. Many of them had multiple heads, and some flew on insectile wings.

Zevaron reached out with his thoughts. He sensed nothing, no traces of individual consciousness, only the smoldering anger of their progenitor. Beside it, his own hatred paled to the merest whisper, a straw in a hurricane. Until this moment, he had thought only of how that primordial, brooding menace might help him achieve his own goal. Now he sensed more than the poison-bitter frustration born of ages of captivity. Fire and Ice had dominated the Scorpion cult of Qr, had harnessed the energy of the massed devotion of its followers, had brought down the comet. Its earthly prison of rock and ice lay in shattered ruins. The shadows of its will, stone-drake and arsinoth and ice-troll, had prepared the way. Even now, it had more substance, more material reality, than it had enjoyed in millennia.

Even now, a power blocked its full embodiment. Even now, though the bonds were gossamer, though the jailors were weak and fleshly frail, it was still imprisoned.

Gold throbbed in counterpoint to the beating of Zevaron's heart. Longing shot through him, so intense and sudden it took his breath away. He could not think what he yearned for, except for an end to all yearning. A hot wind brushed his face, and he realized his cheeks were wet.

He sensed Fire and Ice battering against invisible walls, and felt the walls quiver. In his mind, the colors bleached momentarily, cinder-gray and white.

Zevaron...

Someone was crying out, calling his name. It could not be the nag-rider woman. She was gone, saving her own worthless skin. No, this was many voices. One voice.

It did not matter who tried to lure him from his path, to seduce him from his purpose. The human world held nothing for him, except the satisfaction of seeing it burn. The magic on the heights was of men's making, and men would fail. Their will was weak and their memories faithless. Fire and Ice did not forget, did not surrender. It was not in its nature to submit.

He saw the rift clearly now, widening with each moment. It cut so deeply into the sides of the cone that it seemed to have no end. The ruddy shadows that flickered on its inner walls were the color of glowing iron or fresh arterial blood. Lava appeared on the jagged edges of the rift. Sluggish and inexorable, it crept down the outer slopes and in the direction of the hillside on which Zevaron stood. Ash dusted the thick, glowing liquid.

There was something eerie about the flow, as if it possessed a mind and purpose of its own. It neither slowed nor increased its speed with the inclination of the terrain. The irregularities of the rocky slopes had no effect on its direction.

Zevaron glanced at the heights where the sorcerers huddled. *It's coming for them.*

The smell of heated metal added to the stench of brimstone. The arsinoth flung its head from side to side. It whirled, almost unseating Zevaron. He dug his spurs into its sides and held on.

Horsemen reappeared from behind the curve of hillside. The party broke into two, the greater number heading for the embattled Gelon. The man on the silver roan cut a path between the remaining stone-drakes and the soldiers. The Azkhantian riders were taking the Gelon on their own horses, urging the rest to flee on foot or on those few onagers that remained. They might once have been adversaries, but they were human. All of them now faced a common danger. The flaming rock would make no distinction between them.

The middle and rear ranks of the Gelon had already turned, retreating with astonishing discipline. In the fore, the soldiers dropped their shields and scrambled up behind the riders. The horses had slowed, but did not halt. One Gelon tripped. The rider went on to grab another, but a man on a spotted horse wheeled and came back. Without a break in his horse's stride, he reached down, grasped the arm of the fallen man, and used the horse's momentum to swing him over the animal's rump. Something in the skill of the rider and the refusal to leave the fallen Gelon behind left Zevaron with a feeling of inexpressible sadness. Danar too had risked his own life to keep him alive during their breakneck flight from Aidon. It had been so long since he had spoken in kindness to another person.

The lava reached the bottom of Zevaron's hill. Lightning flashed and thunder crashed. Jagged bolts blasted the molten surface.

Zevaron could still feel the colorful nodes of brilliance and power, weakened but not quenched. They were, against all odds and reason, still holding. Just as the shimmer of gold within him held.

The ground dropped away and the rock underfoot turned to powder. The arsinoth plunged downward, body twisting, legs churning, stump-like feet fighting in vain for purchase. Acting by blind instinct, Zevaron rolled free as the beast slid into a gaping pit. Luck was with him, for his shoulder slammed into a ledge of stone. The shock laid him flat, distributing his weight. The ledge was pocked with holes. It shuddered under the impact but did not break. The arsinoth was not so fortunate. An instant later, its body disappeared into the red-tinged crater.

Panting, Zevaron clung to the ledge. He could not see what was happening to the rest of his army or the Gelon and their rescuers. His ears went numb, so that he felt rather than heard the crash of rock and peal upon roaring peal of thunder. Heat washed his face. He inhaled the tang of molten rock, of sulfur and ashes and sleet.

He had to move, and soon. He had been the servant, the emissary, the chosen one of a force so powerful, so ageless, than mortality had no meaning. Now he sprawled here, a heartbeat away from plummeting into the lava pit. Through the patter of his frantic pulse, he sensed his own death only moments away.

His only regret was that he had failed in his most crucial task. Fire and Ice, which had offered him the sweetness of vengeance, was poised on the brink of incarnation. Out of all the servants at its command, *he* had been entrusted with eliminating the rainbow light, the subtle web of human magic.

Rage squeezed his heart like fingers of charred steel. His will was strong, but his human flesh was imperfect, all too easily charred or severed or crushed. But he was not entirely without power. He reached within himself and seized the resonant glory of the gold. It flared as he tightened his grip. Knowing it might be the last thing he ever did, he pressed the node of brightness with all his strength.

I am the master, not the slave! You will do as I wish, even if we both go up like flaming straw.

For a sickening moment, the world staggered. The red of the gaping maw smeared across his vision, mixed with another red, pure and crimson, and faded into pale rose like the first intimation of dawn. Green, yellow, blue, and violet flecked the gray of the rock under him.

The gold yielded. Power flooded through him. It sustained him as the ledge disintegrated, shards tumbling into the pit. He hovered, buoyed by the air itself.

Turning, he gazed into the pit of the mountain. It continued to enlarge, splitting apart, opening up. A form surfaced from the abyssal rift. It was not solid, not yet, but limned in cinder-gray. As it emerged, it grew.

Roughly the shape of a man, it stood upon two thick legs. Its feet were still buried in the roots of the mountain. A tail stretched away into shadow. Its shoulders were massive, its back curved and ridged, bulging as if wings lay just beneath the skin.

Its head . . . Zevaron could barely bring himself to look at its head. Roughly triangular, the top part of the skull dwarfed the shoulders. Each of the upper corners terminated in a horn that split into three parts. Two curved forward, the upper pair almost meeting over the wide brow, and the third faced down. Lightning crackled between the forward-curving horns. The third pair ended in stingers, and their tips gleamed wetly.

There were no eyes or nose, only three pairs of slits that almost touched in the center. Orange light flickered behind the slits. Below, the entire face was featureless and black. Then the jaw swung open to reveal a cavernous mouth filled with flames, yellow and white and dusky red. They reflected off the saber-curved teeth, fangs of ice that dripped and reformed as they melted.

The great head turned. The gaze of those sixfold eyes enveloped Zevaron. For a moment, he thought he had summoned the form himself, using the power of the gold. In that moment, with that thought, whatever had sustained Zevaron disappeared. He fell.

Fire and Ice opened its mouth still wider. Flames rushed forth, an eruption of heat and hail.

The fall would not kill him, nor the lava beneath. He would die frozen and incinerated, his life the penalty for his failure.

The blast engulfed him, rending him between the heat of

the volcano and the frigid pith of a glacier. Shadows cracked and twisted, rock to magma to blowing dust.

He had no breath to scream. In that moment, he was neither body nor senses nor mind . . .

He was fire. He was frost. He was chaos unchained.

Chapter Forty

AN inferno surged through his veins. Like caustic lye, it scalded away all traces of human blood. His bones ignited, melted, bent. Elongated. Splintered. Re-formed. His spine flexed, vertebrae mineralizing like coal, like onyx. From his shoulder blades came a wrenching, a drawing-out. The bones of his hands, what he could feel of them, contracted, then thrust out to impossible length. Nerves smoked and charred until he thought surely they must have burned out. Skin softened, elastic and coriaceous, as it stretched over those too-slender bones. Talons longer than a man's forearm sprouted from what had been his fingers. Wings unfurled to catch the heated air rising from the pit.

A volcano rumbled in his belly. Lungs like leather bellows sucked in air. He opened his throat, his jaw hinging wide. Flame poured out. His body quivered with the fierce, wild pleasure of it. He drew in the fumes rising from vent and lava flow. They curdled in his gut, fueling yet more flame.

He tightened the muscles across his chest and extended his tail. Thermal currents lifted him. His wings beat strongly, stroke after stroke. His tail acted like a rudder to stabilize him in the shifting winds. There seemed to be no end to his strength or his mastery of the air.

Below him, the divided mountain dominated what was left of the valley. Most of the surrounding hills had either toppled in on themselves or been completely obliterated by the uplifting peak. To the south, the remaining Gelon struggled for order as they retreated. The cadre of new monsters from the abyss reached the stragglers and engaged them. Bodies, mostly Gelon but some horses and a few rift creatures, littered the stony ground.

The arc of his flight took him back toward the rift. Even from this height he could not discern its depth, but perhaps his vision was not made to work in that way. The form of Fire and Ice wavered, one moment almost solid, the next moment phantasmal. It tilted its head back to glare at him. Spiderwebs of pain shot through him as if a metallic net tightened around his torso.

The Shield! Destroy it!

Zevaron's back arched reflexively, faltering in his flight, but only for a moment. Extending wings and tail, he steadied himself, dipped one clawed wing tip, and circled back. There, to the east, beyond the tumbled remains of the southern hills, he spotted horses galloping, a flowing wave of brown and gray and black. Human eyes could not have made them out at this distance, but his eyes were no longer human. The riders came from two directions, some bearing Gelonian soldiers, others racing to meet them. In the middle, a small group, mostly on foot, had formed a circle.

Gold stirred in his breast, restless in its bondage.

The circle. The guardians of the Shield. The rainbow of color and song and power.

He belched out fire, but was too high for the blast to reach the circle. His flames dissipated into rust and sulfur.

Men, riders and soldiers alike, set up a defensive perimeter around the circle. With the disciplined order of the Gelon and the speed and agility of the Azkhantian archers, they might hold off the monsters for a time. And while they did, Fire and Ice would be trapped in its present half-existence. How long it could remain so, he did not know. The urgency of its command still echoed through him.

Destroy the Shield!

A challenge rose up in his throat, hoarfrost and brass.

Haze shaded his vision in burnt carmine, in umber and slag-gray. He wheeled through the colorless sky. Men wailed in his shadow. Horses reared. Their screams pierced his flight. But the heart of the enemy magic remained. They stood together, hand in hand, that knot of men and women. Red-gold glinted in the hair of one of the men.

Gelon!

Zevaron dipped, thrashing the air with his wings. The wind whipped a woman's garment, turning it into a crimson pennant.

All but the man with red-gold hair and the woman in red were honey-skinned and black-haired, with strong facial features that marked a common heritage. They were so focused on their work that none flinched as he glided even lower. All except the man with the red hair, who glanced up.

Zevaron missed a beat. He *knew* that man, those distinctive pale-green eyes, that expression. The man's mouth moved, lips forming syllables and syllables a name. Almost, he remembered. Then he darted away, wings punishing the air. Dragonfire blasted through the chambers of his heart, cauterizing his instant of weakness.

Memory carried only bitterness, and bitterness meant frailty, and frailty lead inevitably to failure. He had no past, no kisses beneath a rapture of many-colored night-veils, no enfeebling friendships, nothing but revenge, hoarded and nurtured over ages.

No great king of men stood upon the hilltop. No armies answered his call. They were dust and less than dust, their deeds obliterated, their names erased. Compared to the men of that bygone time, what were these few puny humans, this mongrel assembly? One was no more than a mewling girl-child, and another doddered on the brink of his grave.

At the back of his mind, he felt the pulse and leap of color, the gossamer web that linked each to each. It would unravel when put to the test. Human will alone could not hold it together without a center. *A center . . .*

Gold echoed like the far, far, farthest tolling of a bell.

Blistering ice roared through him, filling his gullet. It pressed hard against his throat, demanding release, but he swallowed it down. He had already seen how the flames dissipated with distance. This time, there would be no diminution, no hope of survival. No room to escape. Heat and pressure built inside him, scaling the walls of his throat. He welcomed the pain as a promise of the eruption to come.

Soon now, very soon . . .

He arced toward the circle. The ground seemed to rise up to meet him. Dust shot into the air, churned by his wings. And still they did not break and run. Still they made no attempt to save their pitiful lives. He heard their voices above the wind. The words might once have been familiar — chants, prayers, incantations, he did not care.

Above the human voices came the sound of galloping hooves and the high, clear whinny of a horse. He faltered and his control of his internal fire stuttered. Ice-flecked flames burst from his mouth, but too soon, unfocused and poorly aimed. It caught the circle obliquely, not dead on.

Driving hard with his wings, he shot toward the sky. No screams reached his ears. Perhaps they had died instantly. He slowed his ascent and bent to look. Ashes, pale as snow, pale as hope, drifted to the ground around the untouched circle. A few pinpoint embers sparked where they fell on grass, but quickly died. A sphere so thin and pellucid it might have been glass surrounded the humans. For an instant, its iridescent sheen reflected sky and mountain, grass and ocean.

Fury seized him, but it was not his own, just as the power fueling his jets of fire did not belong to him. He was its channel, its instrument, and he had failed. Now Fire and Ice directed its rage and frustration at him. Ice raked spurs across his flesh, sharper than the diamond chips he had used on the troll. A blizzard scorched the inside of his skull. His mind went white as soundless howls wracked his frame before dying into shivers.

Attack again! Quickly—before they recover!

Reeling, he struggled to obey. His marrow felt like powdered glass. Blood-tinged acid laced his wings. His heart hammered, bruised and frantic, against the prison of his ribs. He wondered if it were possible for him to die.

When he neared the circle again, the black horse reappeared and swerved toward him. The rider drew her bow. Sun flashed on the opal-hued wood. He glimpsed her expression, set and unreadable. A second woman rode pillion behind her. This one wore a sleeveless vest and loose gathered pants instead of the quilted jacket of the steppe people. Seven dark braids rippled down her back.

The steppe woman fired a shot over her horse's rump as they raced past. Too late, he recognized the danger. He veered away, but the air resisted him. The arrow pierced the membrane of one wing. It was a minor injury, a puncture rather than a disabling tear. Although it produced little pain, the wound was enough to unbalance him.

Damn her!

The black horse circled and came at him again. The woman had already set another arrow to her bow. If she should damage the other wing . . .

He struggled for height.

Her second shot tore through his good wing. The arrow head snagged on one of the long supporting bones. The bone cracked and splintered. The arrow kept going, slashing through vein and membrane.

His body canted sideways in the air. He extended both wings, thrusting hard. Too hard, for the next instant, the damaged bone snapped. The edges grated together, the pain enough to stop his breath in his throat. Blood sprayed from the ragged cut.

Downward he plunged. Sky and earth whirled sickeningly. An upward gust of hot wind battered his good wing. Air whistled through the hole left by the arrow, but the membrane held. It stretched, belling. He could not fly, but that momentary lift allowed him to right himself and slow his fall.

His feet touched the ground, knees bending to break his fall. He stumbled, barely catching himself. The drag of his mangled wing rendered him clumsy. He could not fold it out of the way. When he tried, the pain almost blinded him, so he let the wing drag. He would not be able to fly again, and in a few moments, that would not matter. The black horse was already poised for another run.

He pulled himself as upright as he could manage. Let her

come. Already, the fire in his belly had renewed itself. He would save it, waiting until the steam and ice built into a hurricane. Horse and riders would burn and freeze. Then, wing-crippled or not, he would turn his attention to the circle. In another moment, he would incinerate them.

"Shannivar, stop!" A woman's voice rose above the sound of the galloping hooves.

"He doesn't know us!" the archer shouted.

"Enough! You've brought him down, now let me—"

The black horse switched leads, beginning to turn. The second woman, the one riding pillion, jumped from the horse's back. She hit the ground and rolled.

"Tsorreh, no!" the archer screamed, wrestling the horse down to a canter.

Tsorreh?

The world convulsed around him.

No.

But she was getting to her feet with the awkward grace of someone for whom even such a rough landing meant nothing. Abrasions stood out, dark red, across one bare arm. There was no hesitation in her step, nor in her gaze. She looked up at him, for in his winged form he had grown beyond human dimensions.

He fell to his knees. Fire and Ice howled through his mind and flesh, blood and nerve and sinew. Its warning hammered through his bones. She was an illusion . . . a trick, a cheat. She was not possible. The circle had summoned her up, spun her out of remembered grief.

The cruelty of such a deception—the cheat of hope— most surely and inevitably—only to open him to a *third* loss—he could not conceive of it.

One blast, and she would be dust. Dust and less than dust, less than a memory of dust. Then the ones who dared such perfidy would be next.

Flame and ice gathered. His gut roiled with its power.

Someone cried out, a man's hoarse, desperate tones. The voice bore a treacherous familiarity, carried the weight of past friendship. It stirred up vile longings in his breast. He flung away the sound.

His skin glowed, molten. He seized the pain from his

mutilated wing and breathed it out as glacial vapors. And still the woman did not flinch. She did not vanish like an evil spell.

The circle had broken. He sensed it in his core. Exultation flashed along nerve and sinew. The last resistance to Fire and Ice had fallen.

"Danar—stay away!" This time it was a strange woman.

"Tsorreh!" the man shouted, and again, memory ricocheted at the sound of the name.

The firestorm within him had reached critical pressure. He should release it now. He should transform his body, throat and gut and heart, into a conduit. He should open himself so that all the rage and power, the eons of simmering hatred, came roaring out. Already, he could see in his mind how the roots of the mountain would spread, sending out a thousand, a million, lightning-jagged fissures in all directions. His nostrils flared, anticipating the reek of magma and sleet, of acid geysers and torrential hail. The steppe would go up like a torch. The oceans would freeze and sink.

Gelon. Gelon would burn.

"Zevaron," she said, and laid her hand on his smoldering skin.

The pressure of her fingers, no heavier than a butterfly's kiss, shattered him. He knew that touch, knew it in the stillness between one beat of his heart and the next. Behind his breastbone, as twisted and deformed as it was to support his demon's wings, gold woke. Gold called, and the memory of gold answered.

The world dissolved. *He* dissolved.

He was no longer flesh, no longer fire, no longer raging blizzard.

He was tears.

Chapter Forty-one

HOW is this possible? he wondered. *You're dead. I saw your body. Your flesh was cold. Your heart did not beat.*

Her lips curved with a trace of sorrow. He saw then the new lines around her eyes, the roughness of her skin, as from many days in wind and sun. She lifted her hand from his arm and placed her palm flat on his chest. His heart fluttered like a bird against the fused-glass cage that had been his human chest.

How could she stand to touch him? How could she look on what he had become?

This is what saved me. Her words shimmered in the air, each syllable a musical chime. *Let it save you as well.*

He would have torn himself away, but her touch, light as breath, as dream, as hope, held him fast.

It was too late. He had become a monster, worse than anything spawned by Fire and Ice. Those creatures had never chosen their half-living condition. He had given himself freely. Now nothing remained of the man he might have been, the son of this woman.

Before, he had been smoke and flame, brass and vitriol. He had been ice. As ice he had emerged from the White Mountains astride the troll, and as ice he had subdued the Azkhantian clansmen. Now that ice was melting, weeping as he himself could not. His ruined eyes were as dry as the summer-parched steppe. The pain from his broken bones had changed from lancing jabs to a rhythmic pulse. The wing itself no longer trailed on the ground. He realized, almost startled, than his body had shrunk. His wings were changing back into human limbs. Still on his knees, he now looked up at his mother.

If she were dead, he thought in a daze, then so was he. He could make no sense of it. He did not feel dead, not anchored to such corporal suffering. So if he were alive . . .

Her words echoed in his mind, *Let it save you.*

Until that moment, he had not known he needed saving, or that it was even possible. He could not change the past. What was done could not be undone.

Am I what happened to me? Or am I what I decide to be?

He lifted his good hand, the fingers still elongated but no longer trailing leathery membranes, and placed it flat on his chest. His palm touched shreds of fabric. The arch of his ribcage was smooth, his breastbone no longer a thickened keel for the attachment of wing muscles but a shallow indentation. He remembered rubbing his chest in just such a way, focusing on the pulse of gold within, the scintillation of light just below his skin, and the vision of the great king on the hilltop.

Zevaron folded over, as if his joints could not support his weight. His muscles had gone watery and inert. He felt the ground rise to meet him, or perhaps he fell so gently, his body so light a burden, that there was no shock at all.

"Help me." Tsorreh slipped her hands under his back.

A second woman knelt beside him. She smelled of cedar and horse and honey-ripe grain. When he looked into her face, his eyes stung. She was strong, levering him to sitting, pulling one hand across her shoulders.

"Let me help." The young man with the red-gold hair took Tsorreh's place. Together with the Azkhantian woman—*Shannivar?*—

Shannivar!

—he hauled Zevaron to his feet.

Zevaron wavered, trying to support himself on his own legs.

"Into the circle!" Danar cried. "Quickly . . ."

And then they were half-carrying him, half-dragging, running and stumbling, the sun-crisped grasses a blur, the clods of bare earth an intricate pattern, and the sky whirling overhead. Through it all, beneath and above it all, came the raging ferocity of Fire and Ice. Zevaron felt its fury, its frustration, its implacable enmity. It reached out ephemeral claws, hooked like scorpion stingers and razor-edged. His bones quivered in response.

Feet pattered on the earth. More hands reached out, caught him. Held him.

"Wait." Stillness pooled around Tsorreh's words.

Zevaron's sight sharpened. He stood between Danar and Shannivar. Before him waited the five other members of the circle. He knew none of them, only the stamp of their features. Most were Meklavaran, except for one Denariyan woman. His transformation into winged demon and back to human had left his vision altered, for he saw each one haloed in a different color.

The Denariyan woman, who was older than he thought at first glance, shimmered like a cloudless sky. Even the red fabric of her wrap-dress had an undertone of cerulean. She touched her fingertips together and said in Denariyan, "I greet the soul within you."

"The light greets us both," he responded, as Chalil had taught him, and saw her eyes widen in surprise. Zevaron felt buoyed by the golden light growing within him, and by the colors surrounding him.

The stout man who looked like he came from one of the old ruling families wore a mantle of crimson, and the thin one with the haunted look in his eyes shone like sun on daystar lilies.

"I am Ganneron of the house of Cassarod, *ravot*," said the stout man. "I remember your father, and your brother Shorrenon as well. They were good men."

A peculiar feeling rose in Zevaron at the mention of his family, at being called *prince*. He turned to the other, who bore the stone of Dovereth. "I do not know your lineage."

The frail-looking man was overcome with emotion. "It is

just as I foresaw...the visions were true. The heir of Khored has returned to us."

Ganneron slipped a hand through the other man's elbow, steadying him. "This is our prophet, Iskarnon. He is not mad, only touched with a different sight."

If he is mad, Zevaron thought, *then I am even more so.* As he took the Prophet's hand, Iskarnon's trembling ceased and an expression of wonder spread over his face.

A woman with traces of a child's softness in her face lifted her chin and regarded Zevaron, indomitable purple in her gaze. "I am Marisse, keeper of Shebu'od's strength."

"I did not know...it is not written...that any of Khored's brothers passed down the inheritance to their daughters."

"Then it is past time such things changed," said Tsorreh. "I was not meant to carry the *te-alvar* that is now yours, but I dare anyone to say I did not keep it safe. Perhaps our best hope now is in *not* following tradition."

Bathed in ethereal light, Danar moved to Marisse's side. They did not touch, but Zevaron read much in their nearness. He saw his friend's face in a series of images. Here was Danar as Zevaron had first seen him, an untried youth after the attempted abduction from a backstreet alley in Aidon ... and here, Danar bending over him as he lay wracked by the fever of an infected wound and, as he now know, the tumultuous awakening of the *te-alvar* ... and now Danar at the Azkhantian Gathering, facing the Isarran ambassador, refusing to fight ... and now this man of healing and compassion, a man come fully into his own power.

Tsorreh's attention flickered to the last of the group, a strongly built man who carried an aura of quiet wisdom shaded in palest rose.

"This," she said, "is Sandaron, who brought me safely from Gelon." Her voice carried an undercurrent of singing.

Zevaron said, "Then I owe you a great debt."

Sandaron shook his head, so small a movement Zevaron could not be sure he'd seen it, only felt the negation. "You owe me nothing."

It was not an insult. Behind the steady eyes, Zevaron

heard the other man's unspoken thought, *The debt and the service belong to Meklavar, not to any one man.* He was a great man, this Sandaron, a great leader. But he could not lead now.

Only I can do this.

"It must be your own choice," Tsorreh said.

Zevaron pulled away to stand unaided. He did it gently, for he did not want to rebuff those who loved him.

They loved him. How could he have not seen it? How could he have not realized that underneath his hatred lay pain and loss, but under that, what else but love?

His legs were steadier than they had been only a minute ago. He drew in a breath and felt the air sweet and easy in his lungs. One step followed another until he stood in the center of the circle.

Chapter Forty-two

THE circle closed around Zevaron. He stood in the center, as it must be, as it had always been. As much as he was able, he surrendered himself to the *te-alvar*. The pain from his arm, from uncounted bruises and abrasions, dimmed. Light suffused him, lifted him, cradled him.

Swords shimmered in the dawnlight, horses neighed, and men shouted, *"Khored! Khored!"*

He stood on a hilltop as the wind tore at his hair and his skin burned with inner fire. He lifted his bare arms against the gathering storm. The world brightened in his sight. He recognized what he held, each petal glowing with its distinctive radiance, the center more brilliant than any flame. Words flowed from his mouth, as they had from the great king so many ages ago, words shouted, whispered, prayed. Words became light, and light flowed through spirit, and spirit shaped itself back into words.

BY GRACE, ALL THINGS ARE MADE.

As if in response, the ground rumbled again. The cleft mountain must be pushing even higher, devouring more of the surrounding terrain. In his mind's eye, in the part of him that was still bound to the forces of Fire and Ice, Zevaron saw it swell until it blotted out the sky.

BY JUDGMENT, ALL THINGS ARE UNMADE.

The great form raged, a shadow upon shadows. It battered against the last invisible barrier. Part corporeal, part spirit, it could not yet emerge completely into the living world. The six *alvara* had been able to accomplish that much, but no more, and the guardians were human. They would need to replenish the strength they had poured out. But Fire and Ice would never tire, never grow old, never need to sleep or eat.

I will end it here.

Zevaron reached within himself, peeling away the layers of willful blindness with which he had kept the *te-alvar* confined. Time fell away like the husk of a giant seed, along with his confusion, his disbelief, and every moment in which he had turned away from its guidance. Finally he came to the pivotal instant, the moment of betrayal. He was not Khored, could never be. He was not worthy. He had broken faith. From the first awakening of the *te-alvar* to when he entered the White Mountains, he had pretended he could remain true to the teachings of his people and pursue vengeance against Gelon. He had convinced himself, but he had not convinced Fire and Ice. By slow degrees, the subtle and ancient enemy had enticed him and lured him, diverted his purpose . . . and deadened him to the truth within himself.

Now the *te-alvar* blazed up like a sun. In its searing brightness, he could see nothing and everything. One by one, the lesser petal gems came into focus, each in its proper place, glowing with its distinctive color and adding its unique virtue. He knew them all, from the earliest teachings of his childhood to the present rhythms of his heart.

"May the light of Khored . . ." began the blessing, and the *alvara* answered.

Eriseth. Blue held fast, endured, kept faith in the long years of exile in a foreign land.

"Ever shine ever upon you."

Benerod. Green brought healing of the wounds of war and injustice, and engendered compassion and kindness and fellowship.

"May his wisdom guide you . . ."

Cassarod. Red heartened with courage, not the absence of fear but the determination to act rightly despite it.

"Through every tribulation."

Dovereth. Yellow saw through lies and madness and terror into the heart of truth.

"May his Shield protect you . . ."

Teharod. Pale rose, subtle as dawn and as powerful, touched vision with wisdom.

"When all else fails."

Shebu'od. Purple, as intense as a butterfly's wing, as amethyot, as wine, spun out oceans of strength.

The power and depth and vividness, the very life of the *alvara* filled him and yet he felt something lacking.

"At the end of time, O Holy One,
Deliver us into the hands of peace."

Like the first breath, like the last, the clear center of the Shield became one with the others. There was no sense of domination, only the quiet acknowledgment that there was no essential division between the aspects of the Shield.

It is one as we are one.

Khored had stood upon his hilltop, looking down at the battle, but Zevaron had no need for physical sight. Having been ensorcelled by Fire and Ice, he perceived it and its creatures far more accurately with his mind than with his eyes. He sensed the cleft mountain, the fuming vents, the barren rock, the great lumbering arsinoths, the combinations of mineral and beast, brimstone and hoarfrost. Most of all, he was aware of Fire and Ice.

Quick as thought, the monstrous form reacted. As Zevaron was still linked to it, it was even more acutely sensitive to him. It recognized the magic that had defeated it ages ago. It howled out its frustration and pent-up fury. A blast exploded on top of the *alvara* circle with gale-strength winds, blizzards of flaming cinders, and razored shards of hail. The attack was only partially physical. The greater force tore and ripped at the Shield, which glowed under the assault. The earth flinched as if it were a living thing in agony. Horses and men screamed in terror. The creatures of Fire and Ice wailed, their cries barely distinguishable.

I am the center, Zevaron thought, and it came to him that the function of the *te-alvar* was not to anchor but to aim, not only to unite but also to give purpose. He stood in

Khored's place and wielded Khored's stone. But what was his purpose? To repeat Khored's victory? To exile Fire and Ice to the north from where, an age later, it would surely find another way out of its prison?

The *dharlak* of the Golden Eagle people lay in smoking, twisted ruin. He would not trust to mountains, to stone and snow. He would trust to fire. It might not prove more secure, but choose he must. Indecision would have far worse consequences than choosing wrongly.

Down, he sent the silent command through the bond forged by obsession and beguilement. In his mind, he saw the Form falling through streams of molten rock, down through the heart of volcanoes to the glowing fundament beneath. Ice sizzled and steam churned with magma. In that infernal heat, no trace of chill survived.

Down!

He hurled the command like an arrow, like a spear, with all the power of the Shield behind it. His aim was true. His will pierced the chaotic heart of the Form. The *te-alvar* channeled its power through him. In a moment, it would all be over, the danger passed, the threat vanquished.

Nothing happened.

Silence blanketed the steppe. Through his connection with Fire and Ice and the senses of the Shield, Zevaron knew that every mist creature and abyssal monster had obeyed his command. Frost-wolf and ice-troll, winged serpent and stone-drake and all the things that had no names, all plummeted through the rift. Fire and Ice alone remained, and it was untouched. It loomed above the shattered peaks like a monarch on a throne looking down on the least of his slaves. Laughter like bile, like sulfurous ichor, like frozen blood, rolled down the mountain slopes.

Did you think to compel me, man of dung and earth? Your words have no power over me! Never before had the voice of Fire and Ice been so clear, its meaning so unambiguous. *I will recreate my army from your night terrors. This time, I shall not fail.*

Zevaron recoiled. Dismay crept like smoke through his mind. He had been so certain. The power of the Shield had been flawless.

Through his shock, he sensed Fire and Ice becoming even stronger with each moment. The ancient adversary was feeding on the failed attempt. In the abyss, shadows condensed anew into solid form.

What had gone wrong? Had his own certainty—his arrogance—betrayed him? Had all the harm he had done left an indelible stain that warped even his best efforts?

The unity of the Shield began to dissolve. Individual colors appeared within the sphere of light. He thought of all the gifts he had received in his life, the sacrifices made on his behalf, the friendships freely given, the love and fellowship ... and how he had set it all aside. He had thought only of his own petty hatred, had sought only to inflict even greater pain on those who had wronged him.

All your fault ... murmured the seductive mental voice.

The sphere of power generated by the Shield diminished further. Through the thinning brightness, the lineaments of surrounding objects emerged—people, horses, the bloated outline of the mountain.

Voices reached him, muted. "Zevaron, what's wrong?"

"Try—you must try again!"

What was there to try? His words had no power over Fire and Ice.

His own words, perhaps, but not those of Khored of Blessed Memory. If he had commanded Fire and Ice to the northern mountains, would that have worked? Might it still work?

A flicker of intuition nudged Zevaron away from the thought. It did not matter *where* he sent Fire and Ice, only *how*.

Something whispered through the back of his mind, a sound like a hissing serpent, and then a long exhalation. Not *Fire and Ice*, the common appellation, but syllables of conjuration ...

O Most Holy One, help me!

There was no answer. But "The Holy One" was not the name of God, any more than Fire and Ice was the true name of the remnants of Creation.

Its true name. He must command it by its true name.

There was very little time left. Moment by moment, Fire
and Ice grew stronger and more solid.

*Khored! Father, ancestor—speak through me! Save our
people—save all the earth's peoples as you once did!*

His chest thrummed, his pulse accelerating and growing
in intensity like thunder. The *te-alvar* reflected and gathered
power from the lesser gems, and also from sky and steppe,
from the heartbeats of men and beasts.

The thrumming built into an avalanche of sounds, the
clash of steel against steel, the crack of breaking ice, the driz-
zle of rain, a woman singing, winds on the heights, the roll
and ebb of ocean waves . . .

> *"In the desert, my soul cries out in thirst,*
> *On the heights, my heart is filled with longing,*
> *In the temple, I find no rest.*
> *All is dust between my hands;*
> *My fire gives no warmth, my bread no savor.*
> *Come to me, O Holy One of Old;*
> *Speak to me as you spoke to my fathers!"*

Fire and Ice, he had named it, speaking contemporary
Meklavaran. But in the ancient holy language . . . He remembered sitting beside his mother's knee, her lamp filling
the room with amber-soft light. Her voice rose and fell, half-
singing as she read to him from the *Te-Ketav*.

Fire . . . *sar*, and ice . . . *korak*. Zevaron racked his memory. There would be a linking modifier, barely a breath.
Sar-h korak. No, the letter *reth* reversed the order—*sahr*.

Sahr-Korak.

He lifted his arms, drawing power to him. Colors inten-
sified as each virtue heightened. Courage and strength
flared again like a sunburst, anchored by truth and wisdom,
tempered by compassion, deepened by endurance.

Zevaron sensed the enemy's ages of yearning, of bitterness, of implacable hatred. More rapacious than any
wildfire, it hungered without end. In it, he also saw what he
had nearly become.

In that moment, *Sahr-Korak* was no longer an enemy to
be conquered, but a part of Creation to be restored. Not, as

he had first thought, to the infernal regions of the earth, but to the limitless heavens. There nothing and everything remained constant, the stars fixed in their places, the moon fluid in its phases, meteors and comets, veils of undulating iridescence, pools of emptiness.

There, he thought, *there is your place. May it bring you the peace you never knew on Earth.*

In that instant, he felt a lightening of the awful presence, a ripple of surprise. A pulse of weariness, of relief. Almost, he could imagine, willingness. Assent.

"*Sahr-Korak,*" he whispered.

And it was gone.

Chapter Forty-three

AIR and breath, sky and earth, flesh and stone, all shimmered as the power of the Shield faded. Stillness woke to movement, to hearts beating, chests lifting, voices murmuring.

Then so many things happened at once, Zevaron could not spare more than an instant for any one of them. The mountain folded in on itself. The force that had lifted it so far, pushing up layer upon layer, had vanished. Now the weight of stone and cooling magma crushed the lower levels.

"Zev!" Danar caught Zevaron, knocking him off balance and then holding him firm in a brother's embrace. He pounded Zevaron's back. Pain throbbed in Zevaron's arm, but it was a distant soreness, not the acute misery of a new fracture. "You did it! I knew you would!"

Danar turned as Zevaron did, to watch Sandaron pick Tsorreh up around the waist and swing her in the air as in a dance. She threw her head back. Her laughter was half-delirium, half-rapture. When Sandaron set Tsorreh down, she stood on tiptoe, grasped his shoulders, and kissed him. Zevaron was astonished by the passion with which Sandaron returned the kiss. Danar apparently was not, for he exclaimed in Gelone, "It's about time!"

Marisse, the young woman of Shebu'od's strength, darted up to Danar and threw her arms around him. The two Meklavaran men, the old aristocrat and the Prophet, stood looking at one another in amazement before the Denariyan woman let out an ululating cry, joyous for all its shrill pitch, and took up their hands in a dance. Beyond them, Gelonian soldiers and steppe riders were helping the wounded and quieting their frenzied beasts.

Tsorreh approached Zevaron and gently took his good hand. She gazed into his eyes, tears in her own. There was so much he wanted to say, his heart overflowed. He did not know where to start. If he made a sound, he would surely break.

Her eyes moved from his, looking past him. He followed her gaze to see an Azkhantian woman sitting on a black horse. Sweat slicked the horse's hide, but the head was carried proudly. In one hand, the rider carried a bow that glinted with a faint opalescent sheen. Her other arm cradled a small, solemn-eyed boy in front of her.

Shannivar . . . His lips framed her name. And a child.

"Go to her," Tsorreh said, and released his hand.

The steppe woman watched him come, her posture wary. As the agent of Fire and Ice, he had rebuffed her and sought her death. He had laid waste to the steppe and enslaved her countrymen. As the wielder of Khored's gem, he had placed himself beyond human desires. Now he must come to her as a man, not an avatar.

The black horse laid his ears back and danced sideways as Zevaron approached. Zevaron halted, remembering yet another betrayal. He didn't know how to proceed, how to ask forgiveness of a horse.

"Eriu is the finest horse I have ever known," Shannivar had said when she had handed him the reins on that first journey into the mists. *"A horse to carry you through frost and fire, a horse to bring you back from the very gates of death."*

A horse to bring you back to me.

He wondered if he would be trying to make amends for the rest of his life.

Shannivar's expression changed, quicksilver. She slipped

the bow into its case, dropped lightly to the ground, and set the boy on his feet. The child looked up at her gravely as he slipped his hand into hers. Walking slowly and with great dignity, they came to stand in front of Zevaron. A hint of wariness still hardened the edges of her mouth. She touched his cheek, as if to reassure herself of his solidity. Perhaps she doubted his humanity as well. Her fingertips were rough and amazingly warm.

He captured her hand with his good one, turned it over, and kissed her palm. She tasted of salt and dust and herself. He felt her whole body respond. When he looked up, she was smiling. For what seemed like a long time, they stood, hand in hand, gazing at one another.

"You have truly returned," she said at last. "I was not sure."

"Nor I."

She nodded, a quick dip of her chin, and then glanced down at the child. "This is our son. I named him Chinggis."

Our son.

Zevaron's knees threatened to buckle under him. He wanted to touch the boy, to make sure Chinggis was not an illusion, a waking dream, a figment of his own disordered yearnings.

Shannivar was speaking again, this time to Chinggis. Her Azkhantian was simple enough for Zevaron to follow, even in his dazed state. She explained that Zevaron's mami was grand-mami Tsorreh, and Zevaron was his papi. She told Chinggis that Zevaron spoke a different language so he might not understand all the words, and that Zevaron had been far away, fighting monsters just as Onjhol did. The boy's dark eyes widened.

"Papi?" Chinggis gave an awestruck bow.

Zevaron recovered himself enough to bow in return. He knew nothing of children, let alone those as watchful and self-possessed as this one. He had not thought anything so wonderful, so startling, so new, so tender, could arise from his tortured life. How did one speak to such a miraculous being? Where could he begin? If he knelt, so that he was no longer towering above the child, he might never get up again.

Chinggis solved the problem by moving to Zevaron's

side, placing his hand in Zevaron's and saying, "My day is very lucky, papi."

For a long moment, Zevaron could not breathe. Then he said, in fumbling Azkhantian, "Mine is, too."

Shannivar left them, Zevaron grinning and Chinggis smiling his shy smile, to fetch Eriu. The horse eyed Zevaron nervously but did not resist. With Chinggis happily in the saddle, they walked back to where the circle had stood, going slowly because with each step, Zevaron felt an increasing lassitude, a diminution of senses as well as strength. Shannivar adjusted her pace to his.

Zevaron realized that some time must have passed since he went running to Shannivar, because a small crowd had gathered. An older man, a Gelon wearing a general's armor, seemed to be organizing a formal caravan. Zevaron couldn't understand everything he saw, only the orderliness with which the soldiers went about their tasks. Steppe riders moved between the lines of Gelon and the onager-drawn carts. The other members of the circle were already mounted, most of them riding double on Azkhantian horses.

Someone—Tsorreh, he thought—cried, "He's back!"

A rider on a silver roan trotted toward them. Zevaron thought, *I know this man*, and then a name came to him. *Kharemikhar*. He remembered the man from the wrestling games and dances around the bonfires at the Gathering.

The rider touched one fist over his heart and said to Shannivar, "War-lady, may your arrows fly true."

"And may your words find favor with the Mother of Horses," Shannivar replied, switching to trade-dialect. "How fares it with our people?"

"We must move from this place. The land is too unstable. Zevaron Outlander, may your day be lucky."

"It is already so, beyond my wildest hopes. I am happy to see you once again, Kharemikhar son of Pazarekh."

"Zevaron Outlander, the chieftain of the stone-dwellers respectfully awaits your decision." He paused, looking unsure. "About which direction to go."

Zevaron's thoughts were still clouded, but he suspected that the Gelonian general had said no such thing. Why ask *him*?

"Let's join the others," Shannivar suggested. "You can talk it over then."

At Shannivar's insistence and with some difficulty, Zevaron managed to haul himself on Eriu's back. She lifted Chinggis on the saddle in front of him. Chinggis clearly thought this a grand adventure, to ride with his father on his mother's warhorse.

The crowd parted to let them through. At the center, Danar stood talking with the Gelonian general. Marisse was beside him, eyes alight, mouth serious. She placed one slender hand on Danar's arm in a posture so delicate and so affectionate that Zevaron felt deeply moved at the sight.

"There you are!" Danar turned away, cutting the general off in midsentence. Marisse moved with him, as if they were coupled in a dance. "I see Shannivar's taken good care of you. We need to get some distance between us and that great hulking mountain." He sounded entirely too cheerful and energetic.

"The only question is which direction to take," Danar went on. "Manir wants to continue west toward Gelon, but Shannivar's kinsmen need to find what's left of her clan and I agree that must come first. That is, until the wounded have recovered and we've all had some rest. We can decide how to proceed from there. I'll have to go on to Aidon eventually, but we hope that in the interim, the Qr cultists will have lost the nastier aspects of their practice. They were tied to that thing"—meaning Fire and Ice—"or so Tsorreh tells me. Is this a good plan, do you think?" He paused for breath.

Zevaron started to answer that his own opinion was of no importance. He could barely stay upright and he didn't understand half the things Danar was talking about. Surely, it should be the general—Manir?—giving the orders. But the older man was looking expectantly toward Danar, having taken no offense at being interrupted. The only explanation he could think of was that Danar was acting advisor to the Gelonian war-leader.

Danar noticed the confusion on Zevaron's face. "We've much to catch up with, you and I. I am now Prince of Gelon, even as you are Prince of Meklavar. You see, we are brothers after all."

Zevaron shook his head. "There is no Meklavar, only a Gelonian province."

"Meklavar is free once more." Tsorreh and Sandaron approached, riding double on a dun horse. Tsorreh was smiling. "Danar has given it back to us."

Zevaron felt as if his skull were about to explode with impossibilities.

"We have many stories to tell," Sandaron said, "but this is not the place or the time."

Danar looked up at Zevaron. Zevaron felt how still Shannivar stood, as if she were waiting for his answer. He remembered her lips like sun-warmed petals on his back, the soft intoxication of her touch.

"Shannivar," he murmured, and whether he meant it as the decision Danar was waiting for or simply the choice of his heart, he did not know.

The sun was lowering behind the jagged western horizon three days later when they met up with the remnants of the Golden Eagle clan at the encampment they had set up at a safe distance from the ruined valley. The reunion was joyous and tearful, with many questions and stories. Zevaron could not keep track of Shannivar's kinsmen, although he recognized a few by name. He felt utterly incapable of dealing with the onslaught of strangers. At the same time, he wanted desperately to stay close to his own friends and family, as if they might vanish the moment he let them out of his sight. Shannivar seemed to understand. With quiet tact, she brought one or another of them to ride beside him, then steered them away when the talk wearied him.

The journey had taken its toll. The carts moved slowly and many of the fighters, Gelon and Azkhantian alike, were weary or injured. A few more soldiers had died while traveling, and Zevaron, with the strange, lingering awareness from the *te-alvar*, sensed each passing like the reopening of a poorly healed wound. He felt the wariness of the Gelon, a combination of exhaustion, not only of the flesh but of the spirit, and generations of hostility. Yet they had fought well together, he reminded himself. Danar was clearly on friendly terms with both parties, and General Manir followed Danar's lead. Perhaps there was hope after all.

Shannivar had taken Zevaron under her care. Where she'd gotten the easy-gaited sorrel mare for him to ride, he didn't know. He wondered if it was one of Radu's foals, for there was hardly any jarring of his splinted arm.

The clan had set up tents and a few *jorts*, corrals for horses and goats, cooking fires and latrines, even an area where children were playing a game involving snatching colored scarves from one another's hats. Shannivar's cousin Alsanobal and a frighteningly competent older woman, who Zevaron gathered was his mother, set about organizing the newcomers. The wounded were taken to shelter and the animals tended. Manir wanted to place his men separately, but Danar would not hear of it. As many as possible would be housed with the clansmen and the rest distributed throughout the camp.

In the midst of the spasm of activity, two men emerged from a *jort* set apart, one supporting the other. Shannivar had been coaxing Chinggis to go with his nani Zaraya, and the boy was not having any of it, clinging to Zevaron's leg. She turned around as the men approached.

"Bennorakh!" From her tone, she had not expected to see him again. "And"—to the other man, a Gelon who looked out of place with his stubble-covered scalp and a blotchy red scar across his forehead—"Tabilit's crimson tits! *You?* You're still alive!"

Zevaron recognized the Golden Eagle *enaree*, although he had never seen Bennorakh so cheerful. He had difficulty believing Shannivar when she explained that the second man had been a Qr priest, but had changed sides and worked alongside the shamans.

Bennorakh added a number of details, including how the former priest, whose name had been taken from him at the time of his vows so that he now had none, had pulled him from the debris and carried him down the jagged ruin of the southern hill. The whole tale was so improbable that Zevaron thought it must be true.

"We will have a naming ceremony in your honor," Shan-

nivar said to the former priest. Zevaron noticed that she
kept her distance from him, nonetheless.

Some things, like trust, would take time. The old divi-
sions were changing, some gone forever and new ones yet
to be discovered. Zevaron found himself wanting to think
well of this odd, scarred man who had saved the shaman.

It was almost dark before the most urgent tasks were
finished. The women of the camp stoked up the fires and
brought out platters of food. In the festive atmosphere, the
children overcame their shyness of strangers. They spoke no
Gelone and most of the soldiers had only a smattering of
trade-dialect and no Azkhantian, but that seemed to pose
no difficulty.

Zevaron sat at the fire reserved for the *alvar*-bearers and
other dignitaries. He didn't know most of the Azkhantians,
but he surmised they represented other clans that had
joined with Golden Eagle riders. Manir had joined the circle only on Danar's command and clearly would rather
have been with his own men. Bennorakh was still too fa-
tigued from his injuries and had retreated to his own *jort* to
be cared for by his Gelonian friend.

Resourceful and inventive, the steppe folk had put together a remarkable feast, considering the circumstances.
The vegetation for miles around was dead or dying, as were
many of the animals that had not fled, but there was an array of dishes, including a savory stew. Zevaron ate a little
grain simmered with herbs, but his gorge rose at the smell
of the meat—rabbit, he thought, although it did not matter.
A skin of *k'th* was brought to the fire. He refused with as
much grace as he could, but Danar took a swig and urged
Manir to try it. After a cautious taste, the general drank his
share. The conversation flowed more easily after that.

After everyone had eaten, clansmen brought out their
lap drums, reed flutes, and a few bowed viols. Zevaron
feared this meant a night of dancing. Even without *k'th*, he
did not think he could manage a single step. He remembered enough of the ways of the Gathering to be certain
that to refuse to dance would be to dishonor the hospitality
of the clan. However, it turned out that the music was a
prelude to storytelling.

Shannivar, as war-leader, began. She recited in a formal, cadenced style, clearly following a traditional formula. From the intent expressions of the Azkhantians, Zevaron had no doubt that the exact same rendering would be repeated many times over the years.

Alsanobal spoke next, an abbreviated version that overlapped Shannivar's tale. By the time he finished, everyone in the circle was more relaxed, so that when it was Danar's turn and then Tsorreh's, they entered into the telling with zest. Tsorreh's trade-dialect was stronger than Danar's, but the Azkhantians remained politely appreciative, even when Danar made humorous mistakes.

As the evening wore on, Zevaron felt the nostalgic echoes of the Gathering. A knot of tension loosened inside him. He drifted on the rhythms of conversation, not following the words but letting them carry him, even as the waves had carried him in Chalil's pirate ship.

No one asked Zevaron to tell his own story, and for this he was grateful. He suspected Shannivar's hand in it. Even if he had been willing, he found himself drained to the point of incoherence. The food and the storytelling had revived him briefly, but his bone-deep weariness returned a thousandfold stronger.

There came a pause, a sense of deep listening. Shannivar got to her feet and began to sing.

"May the strong bones of my body rest in the earth.
May the black hair on my head turn to meadow-grass."

A ripple of response arose from the circle, from Azkhantian and outlander alike. The fire seemed too bright, and Zevaron's heart too full. Her words, clearly known to the clansmen, were at once a lament, a dirge, a prayer, a blessing.

"May the bright eyes of my forehead become springs that never fail."

"Ayay," murmured the women, repeated by the men's deeper voices, *"ayay."* The low ridge of hills, the summer-

browned grass, the animals in their pens, the milky swathe of stars, gently echoed, *"Ayay, ayay."*

> *"May the hungry camels come and eat."*
> *"Ayay, ayay!"*
> *"May the thirsty horses come and drink."*
> *"Ayay, ayay!"*

Words came to him at last and he found himself standing alone with all eyes turned toward him and a hush like night-fall rising from the earth. The glimmering radiance of the stars poured down as if they too strained to hear, and for a moment, it seemed that Fire and Ice listened as well.

A river of light coursed through him, arising deep in the past, flowing through his flesh and his dreams and his child into some unimaginable future. Currents washed away the ashes of pain, of longing, of weariness, leaving only a still pool, a wellspring without end.

In the battle with Fire and Ice, he had shouted out lines from the *Te-Ketav*, but only the beginning of the verse.

> *"By grace, all things are made,*
> *By judgment, all things are unmade.*
> *At the end of time, deliver us, O Holy One,*
> *Into the hands of peace."*

Chapter Forty-four

·

OVER the following weeks, the decay of the *dharlak* valley spread over so wide an area that it was no longer safe to remain in the encampment. Riders reported sheets of fractured and twisted rock, deep crevasses, and ponds of gray-blue mud. They found antelope and marmots near the ponds, their muzzles covered with charcoal-tinted froth. No flies buzzed around the carcasses, nor did any vulture circle overhead.

Zevaron heard the shock in the voices of the scouts as they related what they had found. He wished he could offer them a measure of comfort, beyond his certainty that Fire and Ice had indeed departed. The poisons now emanating from the mountain might spread, for the rift was deep, but eventually they would run their course. The *Te-Ketav* told of similar devastation following the battle with Khored of Blessed Memory. Then a fertile valley had been transformed into a waste and then a sea so lifeless and foul that it had been called Desolation. Yet Danar and Tsorreh had sailed across that very sea and its waters were no longer poisonous. Perhaps in the fullness of time, this part of the steppe would live again.

Meanwhile, it was not prudent to linger. In an astonishingly short time, the Azkhantians had folded their *jorts* and trail tents, packed up their belongings, found mounts for everyone who could not walk, clansman and Gelon alike, and set out.

They traveled until the Moon of Fire Leaves, when they reached the near-empty lands of the Spirit Horse clan. Here they formally honored those who had died. Bennorakh delivered an elegy, part mournful lament, part celebration of the valor and deeds of the dead. Zevaron could follow only a little of it, something about purified spirits rising up to the Kingdom of the Sky, and prayers to the Mother of Horses.

A member of each family stood to recite the names of their loved ones, mostly names Zevaron did not recognize, but a few that he did. Rhuzenjin son of Semador of the Rabbit clan was one, Tarabey son of Vandanakh of the Ghost Wolf clan, and Ythrae daughter of Lisarre of the Golden Eagle were among them. He remembered the pair from the Gathering, how young and ardent the couple had been in the first stirrings of love. No relative was present to speak for others, so Bennorakh himself performed that office. No one was forgotten, and no daughter or son, brother or sister, cousin or parent, went unlamented.

Days melted into one another for Zevaron, often spent riding through the waving grasses with Chinggis in the saddle before him, Shannivar on Eriu at his side, days of sitting quietly with Tsorreh and Sandaron, with Danar and the other *alvar*-bearers. He could not bear the thought of being parted from his son, so newly discovered, but at some time, Chinggis would have to study the ancient Meklavaran texts and languages in order to properly understand his other heritage, the gem of Khored. For that, Zevaron must take him to Meklavar. But not yet.

After his arm healed, Zevaron practiced horsemanship with the other men, pounded barley and milked goats with the women, and learned to make *k'th*, the only form of food preparation traditionally permitted men, but he would not touch a weapon. Then came nights of stories and dance and looking up at the changing moon. Zevaron had never felt such contentment. Perhaps the time felt so precious because he knew it must come to an end.

Already the company of the Shield was breaking up. He

saw it in the recovery of the Gelonian soldiers and the eagerness of Manir to be off. "Soon," Danar would say. Zevaron heard Tsorreh speak of returning to Meklavar, but only when she thought he could not overhear. Jenezhebre, the Denariyan woman, mentioned finding her family's trading clan as they traveled the steppe. Only Shannivar said nothing.

Meklavar needed the stability of Tsorreh's presence. The situation in Aidon must be resolved. None of them belonged on the steppe. The Shield was a product of one kind of magic, a scriptural tradition, a faithfulness to word and memory. It belonged to its city, not here beneath the endless sky, the uncounted stars, the vast plains, and the people who knew no fixed place. As the moon changed its name, so too would the clans move on. None would remain in this place.

It was his responsibility, as the bearer of the *te-alvar*, to ensure the continuation of the Shield. For this age and this day, Sahr-Korak had been defeated. The elements of chaos, the remnants of Creation, could never be destroyed, only imprisoned. Even if it remained in the heavens, other supernatural powers bent on destroying the living world might arise. These might be the lingering shadows that Tsorreh had spoken of, Qr in Gelon or the Denariyan Eater of Souls, for example, or they might be entirely new. The guardians must be ready. But how to preserve that memory over generations and across nations?

In this mood, Zevaron summoned the *alvar*-keepers to a council. He asked Shannivar and Bennorakh to attend as well. The roles they had played earned them both a place. Besides, it was becoming ever more apparent to him that this burden could not be borne by only one people. The Azkhantians, who had suffered more than any other in the destruction of their lands, must have a voice. At the last moment, when they were assembling in Bennorakh's *jort*, the *enaree* asked with uncharacteristic humbleness if his friend and colleague, Desert Runner, might be included. Desert Runner was the name given to the former Qr priest, chosen by Bennorakh in a smoke vision.

They settled in a circle in the *enaree's jort*. Bennorakh

rolled up the door flap and tied it out of the way. The sounds of meal preparation, the giggles of children at play, and the occasional nicker of a horse, drifted in with a breeze. A soft light drifted down through the smoke hole in the roof. Kendira, Alsanobal's young wife, brought cups of buttered tea, then departed. Zevaron did not know another place where such a council would be inviolable, its privacy universally respected.

He sipped the tea, hot and salty, with a familiar greasy richness. The others waited, studying their own cups. As the silence deepened, the *te-alvar* radiated a gentle warmth.

Zevaron closed his eyes and turned his vision inward. He felt as if he were filled with light, gold and blue, green and red, yellow and pale rose and purple. With each shimmering color, he sensed another presence enter the unity. This might well be the last time the Shield — *this* Shield, for *this* time — would be together. The realization filled him with joy and grief.

"We will always be together." A woman spoke in a silken whisper. He knew without having to open his eyes that it was Marisse, the young woman with whom Danar was so clearly in love. The one who embodied Shebu'od's strength.

"We are spirit, not flesh," added Sandaron, the pale rose of wisdom.

"We are a thing that has never been before." Ganneron burned with the scarlet courage of Cassarod.

Jenezhebre encompassed them with Eriseth's steadfast blue. "We will keep faith, no matter how far apart we are."

"We will ease the sorrows of our peoples, for do we not all weep and laugh and sing under the same sky?" murmured Danar, his voice echoing the compassion of green Benerod.

After a pause, Iskarnon the Prophet of Meklavar intoned, "All this is true," and Dovereth's sun-bright blessing filled the air.

With each phrase, a vision and a certainty built in Zevaron's mind. In Khored's time, one man and one land had stood against Fire and Ice. Those days were long past. No one people should bear that responsibility or keep that knowledge to itself.

*Here we are, Meklavaran and Gelon and Denariyan, met
on the steppe of Azkhantia. I am not of pure Meklavaran
descent, for my grandmother was Isarran. Danar has reached
out to that people in friendship, so in a sense they are here as
well.*

We will share the burden and the glory, all of us.

The light melted as sunrise, as dew, as honey on the
tongue. When Zevaron opened his eyes, the first thing he
saw was his mother's face. Her cheeks were wet and her
eyes shone.

Bennorakh lifted his dream stick. The shells and tiny
bones rattled like once-living gems. "What has been done
here is good."

Zevaron nodded, knowing this was true. Also true was
the sorrow he felt at the approaching farewells. No matter
which path he chose, he would have to part with at least one
of the people he loved best in the world.

He did not know the three Meklavaran men and the woman
from Denariya except through the Shield. The conversa-
tions he'd had with them had been pleasant but distant,
none of them knowing quite what to say to him. Ordinary
talk seemed inconsequential after what they had shared.
Marisse he knew a little better, mostly through Danar. He
had never expected that his life and Danar's would follow
the same path again, but now he regretted its brevity.

He found Danar standing with Marisse in a grove of oil-
brush. Danar's head was bent toward hers, hers down and
turned slightly away, so that Zevaron could not read her
expression. Zevaron paused, struck by the intimacy of the
pose.

Danar took Marisse's hand. ". . . too precious to risk . . . I
will send for you . . ."

She would not be going with him, then. Her posture
changed, a barely perceptible shift. In understanding, Zevaron thought with a pang, and in acceptance of the peril
awaiting Danar at Aidon.

They had noticed him, perhaps sensed his nearness
through the sympathy of the petal gems and the resonance

with the *te-alvar*. Marisse slipped her hand free and hurried toward the tents. Danar waited while Zevaron approached.

"You will be off soon," Zevaron said.

"Yes." Danar collected himself. "It is time. Manir is correct—we dare not wait much longer, nor is there any reason to delay. The weather will soon be our enemy, and his men have recovered enough to travel."

Zevaron wanted to ask how Danar felt about returning to a home without his father, a city ruled by his cruel and thoughtless cousin. The phrases that came to mind were insensitive at best. Danar deserved better of him.

"I do not think of this as good-bye," Danar went on, gesturing their way back to the camp. "Desert Runner will be coming with us—to deal with his former brethren, so he says, or to advise *us* how to do it. I don't think the Qr cult will pose a serious problem, and at any rate, Chion was never popular."

Zevaron did not ask what would happen if Danar failed in his bid for the Lion Throne. Danar would only shrug as if to say that after what they had faced, one demented cousin and a cult of Scorpion worshippers were a paltry obstacle.

"We will see one another again, you know," Danar said, "as one prince to another. Meklavar is now free and I mean for it to remain so, a free and equal ally. I wanted to tell you back at the Gathering, but you were so angry, there was no chance."

Zevaron had no words to thank Danar for a gift of this magnitude. He held out his hands and they clasped forearms in Gelonian fashion. The physical touch, skin on bare skin, catalyzed the bond between the *alvara*. Danar's gem pulsed gently in rhythm with Zevaron's heartbeat. Soothing, green-kissed warmth radiated through Zevaron. The *te-alvar* caught the verdant light, deepened it, and enhanced its grace.

Compassion, Zevaron thought, *and kindness. An open heart. Healing for Gelon as well as Meklavar.* Benerod's stone had chosen its guardian well.

He found his voice. "I will always be your friend, but I will not be returning to Mcklavar." Until the words were said, he had not been certain.

Danar looked startled, then concerned. "Have you told Tsorreh?"

Zevaron continued walking. A group of children were riding near the camp, playing a game that developed horsemanship and fighting skills. Shannivar on Eriu and her friend Zaraya on her bay shouted encouragement as they watched. Zevaron recognized Chinggis on the sorrel mare. The boy had shot up in height during their brief sojourn, and was now as gangly and awkward as his young steed.

"Don't say anything. I'll tell her myself," Zevaron assured his friend. "It will be difficult, but I can't go back to who I might have been, the Prince of my city. I'm . . . broken."

Danar frowned, concerned. "Is Fire and Ice still inside you?"

"No. That much is over. Danar, I've done things, terrible things, thought them, *felt* them—things that cannot be easily undone. If I am to find my way to—to making them right, it must be here"—he gestured, encompassing the immensity of the steppe—"where the harm has been greatest."

"Where Shannivar is."

Zevaron smiled gently. "I am in as great a need of healing as this land. Where else can I be only myself and not Maharrad's son, Khored's Heir, the mate of the Denariyan pirate ship . . . the agent of Fire and Ice?"

"I think," Danar said slowly, "that some things we cannot change. You will always be Khored's Heir."

Zevaron would bear the *te-alvar* until the imminence of his death. Certainly, it would be possible to pass it on before then, to rid himself of its burden. Again the vision came to him of the Shield stretching across lands and peoples. Where better to place its heart than here, under Tabilit's sky? Who better to guard it and heed its wisdom than himself? He might not be the most able and was far from the most worthy, but he was the most in need.

He nodded, as much to himself as to Danar. "I think you are right."

They returned to the camp in companionable silence. Now that he had spoken aloud of his intention to remain on the steppe, Zevaron could not delay speaking with his mother. He found her before the threshold of Yvanne's *jort*, where she frequently sat with Jenezhebre and Alsanobal.

Tsorreh emanated a subtle but unmistakable aura of authority, *te-ravah* despite her worn Meklavaran attire and lack of jewels. Although Sandaron was not present, Zevaron observed the older man's influence in Tsorreh's rose-touched cheeks and the laughter that never left her voice.

The Denariyan woman was talking, gesturing animatedly, and as Zevaron drew near, he understood that she had devised a plan to send messages between the steppe clans, Meklavar, and her own people, by way of her family's trade routes. The topic might provide an opening into the difficult announcement ahead of him.

Jenezhebre's expression shifted as Zevaron approached. She rose and excused herself with such tact that neither of her companions took offense. Tsorreh preceded Zevaron into the *jort* and then lowered the door flap behind them.

Zevaron felt a sense of homecoming upon entering the *jort*. It seemed now, as it had before, that the outward world, with all its deceptions and dangers, fell away, leaving only a circle of comfort.

Tsorreh lowered herself to the folding wooden chair. It had been Yvanne's honor to take the outlander queen into her own home. Tsorreh did not choose her seat out of privilege, but as a simple acceptance of her rank. She would hear him not as mother but as monarch.

He bowed formally to her, Meklavaran-style, and looked up to see her smiling. She held out her hand and drew him to sit by her knee. No, he thought, not monarch, but as one who has borne the heart of the Shield to one who now carries it.

She knows.

He laid his head on her knee as he had when he was small. A shudder passed through his body, neither sigh nor sob. There was so much he wanted to say, and none of it in words.

She sang to him in a low, sweet voice, verses from her favorite book, *Shirah Kohav*, the music of the stars:

" 'What seek you, O my sister,
    So far from the mountains of your birth?'
    'When I left the tent of my fathers, O my brother,
    I yearned for fame and treasure,
    I found sand and empty skies.' "

" 'Then seek no more, but abide with me,
    And I will pour cool water for your thirst,
    And fill all heaven with songs of rejoicing.' "

And then nothing more needed to be said, and it did not matter whether his eyes would ever see her again. His heart would see her always.

Whether in the way of her people or through her own intuition, Shannivar set about making a home for Zevaron, Chinggis, and herself, when she was not called upon to speak in council. Representatives of the various Azkhantian clans met regularly to hear the reports of the spreading waste, now called The Great *Chor'tar*, which he gathered meant "poisoned land." They had no written maps but a keen, instinctive sense of the shape, range, and relationships of traditional clan territories. Now those old boundaries were breaking down, partly because of the loss of so much Golden Eagle land, but also because so many other populations had been decimated or displaced. From Shannivar's description of the talks, Zevaron inferred an unspoken competition of hospitality. Every clan that was represented, and undoubtedly those that were not, as well, wanted the honor of welcoming the war-leader who had defeated the Shadow of Shadows.

Soon after their conversation, Danar departed with General Manir and a grim but refreshed army. Tsorreh and the others stayed long enough to dance at the wedding of Zaraya daughter of Deranel and Kharemikhar son of Pazarekh. On the morrow, she and the other Meklavarans would depart for their city.

Not finding Shannivar among the other merrymakers, Zevaron wandered to the horse pastures. The earth still held the last autumnal heat, but a chill breeze blew from the north. The lingering twilight turned the backs of the grazing horses to velvet. A few of the younger animals had lain down, waking from their doze as he passed.

She was waiting for him beside Eriu, as he knew she would be. The black raised his head and blew gently through his nostrils, but did not threaten to bite. He stood, one ear cocked warily, as Zevaron stroked his neck.

Shannivar moved closer, so that Zevaron could feel the warmth from her face on his lips and smell the mixture of cedar paste, wool, and her own scent. He drowned in longing. She took his hand and led him beyond the pasture, past a line of low, tangled brush, and over a rise.

The last western light dimmed. He could feel the earth underfoot, rock and root, burrow and ridge. It was as if the land had forgiven him and now welcomed him into its loving embrace. A moist, green smell wafted upward and Zevaron realized that they were standing on perhaps the only patch of still-green grass. The ground was so dark that the stars glowed like a river of light. The moon glimmered like a drawn bow.

They made love, slowly and with infinite tenderness, beneath those stars, lying on that grass. As they lay in each other's arms, their clothes partly folded under them and partly draped over their bodies, Shannivar said, "I have been thinking about the prophecy."

There had been more than one, for the sea-king had uttered one during the time Zevaron sailed with Chalil. She meant the one received by the council of *enarees* at the Gathering. "And has it come true?"

"Oh yes. Much of it has been clear to me for some time. All but the last part, and now I understand that, too.

> *"When the woman finds what is lost,"* she recited,
> *"She gives it to the stranger.*
> *Thus the gods have spoken to us."*

"I thought I was the woman who had found your mother and brought her to you," Shannivar said. "But you wouldn't have been a stranger to her, would you?"

Yes, I was, Zevaron thought. *I had made myself a stranger to everyone I loved.* "What did the prophecy mean, then?"

She lifted herself to one elbow and laid her hand flat on his chest. The stars were now so bright, she seemed to be made of silver. "You were a stranger . . . here. And what was lost was not Tsorreh. It was you yourself. It was hope for us all."

She bent close to him, and in her shining eyes he saw, for a fleeting moment, a woman proud and tall, mounted on a silver-white mare, a warrior's bow beside her left knee. Her arms were raised in blessing, her face radiant with love. Then she was gone, and only Shannivar remained. Her eyes held that same love and he knew that she saw the same love reflected in his own eyes, and all his doubts died away into peace.

Appendix: Quotations

MEKLAVARAN QUOTATIONS

Blessing:

> May the light of Khored shine ever upon you;
> May his wisdom guide you through every tribulation;
> May his Shield protect you when all else fails.

From the *Te-Ketav*:

> By grace, all things are made,
> By judgment, all things are unmade.
> At the end of time, deliver us, O Holy One,
> Into the hands of peace.

* * *

> In the desert, my soul cries out in thirst,
> On the heights, my heart is filled with longing,
> In the temple, I find no rest.
> All is dust between my hands;
> My fire gives no warmth, my bread no savor.
> Come to me, O Holy One of Old;
> Speak to me as you spoke to my fathers!

Let me not perish alone.
Reach out your hand, lift up my soul,
Be with me now, be with me now.

My soul longs for thee,
As a gazelle in the wilderness,
as an eagle in the heights,
as a willow in the snow.
O Beloved, forget not the promise of our fathers,
Do not forsake the one who loves Thee.

* * *

At the beginning of time, the world was formed in Fire
and Ice, in darkness and light, in sadness and joy. The Source
of All Things, the Holy One, caused the elements to become
separate, and thus did Earth and Heaven come into being,
along with all that lies between, above, and below. For a
time, the world existed in perfect order, but as the sun set
on the first day, twilight opened the gates to evil. Fire once
more embraced Ice, and that which the Holy One had made
separate now joined in an unholy union. Defying the Holy
One, it gave itself a secret name.

And men walked upon the earth, some shining with
goodness, others nursing greed and envy in their hearts. In
the hidden places of the world, the union of Fire and Ice
conceived a terrible hatred for all who dwelt beneath the
sun. Slowly, it gathered an army unto itself, dragons of frost
and flame, stone-drakes, ice trolls, and, most dreadful of all,
the invisible shadows that cast themselves upon the souls of
men.

And as the minions of Fire and Ice swept across the land,
men fought against their domination. From them emerged
a *te-ravot* both powerful and wise, Khored of the Blessed
Memory, and his six warrior brothers. Khored forged a magical Shield: six perfect *alvara* crystals like the petals of a
flower surrounding a single luminous center. Each *alvar*
was a gem of utmost clarity, a vessel of light, but none was
more pure or more powerful that Khored's own gem, the
te-alvar, the soul of the Shield.

With the power of the Shield, Khored learned the secret

name of the incarnation of Fire and Ice. He conjured forth the ancient enemy and bade it submit to judgment.

And Khored and his brothers, united through the Shield, fought the might of Fire and Ice. Rivers boiled; mountains crumbled into sand and then melted into glass; green fields became peaks of hardened ash, the Var Mountains, the Mountains of Guard. Waters flooded the battlefield, leaving in their wake the Sea of Desolation, whose water is death.

And it came to pass that Khored and his brothers defeated Fire and Ice and exiled it to the far regions of the world, to the ring of glacier mountains of the north, and then beyond the veil between the worlds. He set a citadel in the heights of the Var Mountains, overlooking the battlefield, and called that city Mekla-Var. Men lay down their swords and embraced one another. For a time, the world knew peace and joy.

But Khored in his wisdom knew the enemy was vanquished but not destroyed. Long he pondered, thinking of the ages to come, when the will of men might weaken, and evil arise once more.

And Khored took the Seven-Petaled Shield, and gave each brother one of the *alvara* crystals, reserving the central stone, the *te-alvar*, the heart of the Shield, for his own. With all his arts, he worked upon the stones, so that each *alvar* might be placed in the heart of a living man, hidden from profane sight. Each brother undertook the stewardship, and they swore eternal fidelity to one another.

And ages passed, and descendants of Khored and his brothers kept faith with the pledge their fathers had made. The seven petals and their guardians are the hope and refuge of the living world, for as long as the Shield of Khored endures, the ancient enemy will remain imprisoned and righteousness will reign.

May it be forever so.

— *Book of Khored,* I:1-10

From the *Shirah Kohav:*

> "What seek you, O my sister,
> So far from the mountains of your birth?"

"When I left the tent of my fathers, O my brother,
I yearned for fame and treasure,
I found sand and empty skies."
"Then seek no more, but abide with me,
And I will pour cool water for your thirst,
And fill all heaven with songs of rejoicing."

* * *

Exiled from Thy sight,
my soul is a realm forsaken,
filled with lamentations,
strange portents and darkness.
By day, I long for Thee,
I thirst for Thee at night.
The shadowed avenues of my soul
wait in hope for Thy light.

GELONIAN QUOTATIONS

From the *Odes* of Cilician:

I hear the song of the flute,
The flower blooms, although it is not spring.
The sky roars and lightning flashes.
Rain falls.
Waves arise in my heart.
Hidden banners flutter in the air.
My soul is dying, yet I live.

Oh that I might see that country once again!
There, wisdom fills her pitcher from the well,
Yet needs no rope to draw the water.
There, no clouds cover the sky,
Yet rain falls in gentle waves.
Let us not sit on the doorstep,
Let us bathe in the holy rain!

* * *

Across the frozen plain of my heart,
I tremble with the warmth of your breath
I feel the blood thawing, flowing.
You are near.

Now the mists of time draw apart,
Now I awaken with yearning long denied.
Now is the triumph of love.
You are near.

From *A History Of The Gelon Empire* by an unknown scholar of Borrenth Springs:

In the twelfth year of the reign of Ar-Cinath-Gelon, the Scourge of Isarre and Protector of the One True Land, word reached the capital city of Aidon, Crossroads of the World, of prophecy and unrest in the ancient city of Meklavar, of plots against the Sacred Land of Gelon in alliance with the treacherous sand rat brood of Isarre. The Ar-King, desiring to extend the grace of his brilliance, like unto the midsummer sun, and bring peace and prosperity to all realms of men, determined to crush the vile insurrection. Meklavar, in its pride, refused to bow to his supremacy, but clung to delusions of sovereignty.

Therefore, he sent forth two armies under the command of his most loyal general, Executor of the Divine Will, Ner-Margus-Aulith, and his own son, Ar-Thessar-Gelon. Ner-Margus-Aulith advanced upon treacherous Isarre, where he burned three cities to the ground, and what did not burn, he ordered torn down and the fields sown with salt. Those who surrendered were taken as slaves and brought back to Gelon, but some fled into the desert, where they perished miserably of thirst. The next season, the Ar-King in his munificent grace sent northern slaves to re-populate the cities. Two cities failed by drought, but the third prospered and was renamed Valoni-Erreth.

The second army, commanded by Ar-Thessar-Gelon, was sent to degenerate Meklavar.

*   *   *

Qr temple chant:

> O Spirit from between the worlds,
> Wonder of wonders,
> Beyond life, beyond death!
> Come speedily into the world
> Across flame, across ice,
> Come to us! Come to us!"

AZKHANTIAN QUOTATIONS

Saramark's Lament:

> May the strong bones of my body rest in the earth.
> May the black hair on my head turn to meadow-grass.
> May the bright eyes of my forehead become springs
>   that never fail.
> May the hungry camels come and eat.
> May the thirsty horses come and drink.

The Azkhantian Prophecy

> The city lies in shadow.
> A fire burns in the snow.
> Blood flows across the steppe.
> The horse gallops on the edge of a knife.
> When the heir to gold is drowned,
> He returns with treasure.
> When the heir to light goes to the mountain,
> He will not return.
> The woman finds what is lost,
> And gives it to the stranger.

The Sea God's Prophecy:

> When the shadow of the scorpion
> Dims the Golden Land
> And heaven's spear to the mountain falls,
> One shall come from the sand, from the sea,

Heir to the ancient shield,
Son of a mother twice reborn,
Servant of the Frozen Fire.
Then shall the prophet weep,
And the lion lie down with the deer,
Gladness will lighten every heart,
And peace will return to the land.

Deborah J. Ross
The Seven-Petaled Shield

An all-new high fantasy trilogy of magic, myth, and war—from a co-author of the Darkover novels!

THE SEVEN-PETALED SHIELD
978-0-7564-0621-9

SHANNIVAR
978-0-7564-0920-3

THE HEIR OF KHORED
978-0-7564-0921-0

To Order Call: 1-800-788-6262
www.dawbooks.com

DAW 166

New novels of DARKOVER®
by Marion Zimmer Bradley & Deborah J. Ross

"[*The Alton Gift*] is a must for fans of the series, and reads as if Deborah has been channeling Marion's spirit."
—*Center City Weekly Press*

The Clingfire Trilogy

The Fall of Neskaya	*978-0-7564-0053-8*
Zandru's Forge	*978-0-7564-0184-9*
A Flame in Hali	*978-0-7564-0267-9*

and

The Alton Gift	*978-0-7564-0480-2*
Hastur Lord	*978-0-7564-0649-3*
The Children of Kings	*978-0-7564-0854-1*

"Ross has fleshed out Bradley's encyclopedic vision of the Darkovian Dark Ages..."
—*Publishers Weekly* for *The Fall of Neskaya*

To Order Call: 1-800-788-6262
www.dawbooks.com

DAW 165

DARKOVER®

Marion Zimmer Bradley's Classic Series

Now Collected in New Omnibus Editions!

Heritage and Exile 978-0-7564-0065-1
The Heritage of Hastur & Sharra's Exile

The Ages of Chaos 978-0-7564-0072-9
Stormqueen! & Hawkmistress!

Saga of the Renunciates 978-0-7564-0092-9
The Shattered Chain, Thendara House
& City of Sorcery

The Forbidden Circle 978-0-7564-0094-1
The Spell Sword & The Forbidden Tower

A World Divided 978-0-7564-0167-2
The Bloody Sun, The Winds of Darkover
& Star of Danger

Darkover: First Contact 978-0-7564-0224-2
Darkover Landfall & Two to Conquer

To Save a World 978-0-7564-0250-1
The World Wreckers & The Planet Savers

To Order Call: 1-800-788-6262
www.dawbooks.com

Sherwood Smith
Inda

"A powerful beginning to a very promising series by a writer who is making her bid to be a major fantasist. By the time I finished, I was so captured by this book that it lingered for days afterward. I had lived inside these characters, inside this world, and I was unwilling to let go of it. That, I think, is the mark of a major work of fiction…you owe it to yourself to read *Inda*." —Orson Scott Card

INDA
978-0-7564-0422-2

THE FOX
978-0-7564-0483-3

KING'S SHIELD
978-0-7564-0500-7

TREASON'S SHORE
978-0-7564-0634-9

To Order Call: 1-800-788-6262
www.dawbooks.com